THE MONGOL OBJECTIVE

A MORPHEUS INITIATIVE THRILLER

DAVID SAKMYSTER

VARIANCE

Published by Variance LLC (USA).
www.variancepublishing.com

ISBN-13: 978-1-935142-43-0
ISBN-10: 1-935142-43-7
e-ISBN: 978-1-935142-44-7

Cover Design and book layout: Stanley J. Tremblay

Visit David Sakmyster on the web at: www.sakmyster.com.

10 9 8 7 6 5 4 3 2 1

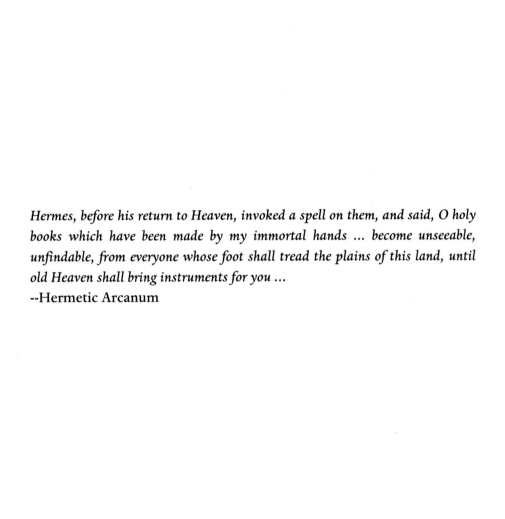

Hermes, before his return to Heaven, invoked a spell on them, and said, O holy books which have been made by my immortal hands ... become unseeable, unfindable, from everyone whose foot shall tread the plains of this land, until old Heaven shall bring instruments for you ...
--Hermetic Arcanum

PROLOGUE
NEW ORLEANS
1985

The pencil, wielded like a wooden stake gripped in his little fist, speeds over the page, creating details here, shading in areas there, stabbing at the heart of his horrific vision. And as the drawing takes form, emerging from the sharply detailed chrysalis of his young mind, sweat beads down the boy's face. He shakes his head to clear a thick lock of matted red hair from his eyes, awash in robin's-egg blue innocence, as they lose focus, crack, then tremble with inescapable dread.

The pencil point breaks and he absently reaches into a box of sharpened pencils on the rug beside him. He ignores the sounds from the babysitter, the fifty-year-old neighbor with her fingers to her lips, watching over him in astonishment that slowly turns to horror as the lines on his page darken and the images take clarity.

Finally, the boy sets down the pencil, blinks and looks up at the sitter with tears spilling from his eyes, cascading down his puffy red cheeks. He lifts the page, tears it from the pad and holds it up for her to see.

"Help them?" he whispers, but the sitter only bites the knuckles on the back of her hand. She crosses herself and steps away, dropping the page. It descends, drifting side to side like a pendulum, before gently landing in front of the boy. He tries to look away, but can't.

He stares at it again, at the profile sketch of two people in an overturned car; a man clutching his chest, the woman next to him with her mouth open in a desperate scream, even as flames explode through the shattered windows, melt their flesh and char their bones... .

Minutes pass, seconds dragging on with both the sitter and the boy silent, staring at each other, without a word. The phone rings.

The boy slowly turns his head, and as the sitter goes to answer the call, he gets up, shuffles to the stairs and climbs. He struggles to ascend, every step an anguished effort. At the top, he enters his bedroom and closes the door before he can hear the cries from downstairs.

He sits on a small wooden chair in the middle of his room, and desperately looks over the walls, trying to find just one bare inch—any small space that could serve as a refuge. But the walls are completely covered. A haphazard assortment of pages, all rendered with his mad sketches, more than a hundred sheets of paper taped over the superhero wallpaper, attached crookedly, without aesthetics in mind. Scribbled drawings from a dozen sketchpads, some pages clearly torn out in haste, many overlapping each other and forming larger collages.

On each sheet are images no six-year-old should ever see, much less contemplate putting on paper. Drawings of men drowning, men burning, falling into deep pits crammed with long spikes, crushed under huge stones. Fires incinerating entire rooms. Acid chewing away at flesh. Severed limbs floating under water, heads bobbing along the surface. Amidst all this grotesque butchery, almost as background stage art, he's drawn enormous structures: colossal pyramids, crumbling ancient temples, a huge statue, an underground city. And in several frames an enormous tower with a blazing light at its peak, lording over a turbulent harbor. On each of these pages it's as if the wondrous architectural structures are merely a backdrop for death and dismemberment, scenes of extreme, punishing violence.

The boy blinks and his eyes lose focus again. He reaches down and picks up a sketchpad and a pencil lying on the floor. And he starts drawing, even as the footsteps approach up the stairs. Slow, heavy steps.

And what sounds like crying.

He keeps drawing, sketching, shading, using light and shadow, creating ...

... *a crude rendition of what looks like the top half of an enormous head crowned with spikes, peeking out from a landscape of either sand or possibly ice. Tiny human forms are gathered around it, using shovels and pulleys.*

And then the door creaks open.

"Honey, I have to tell you something. There's been an accident. Your father and mother were on their way home, and ..."

The boy lowers his head, and his eyes focus momentarily, filling with uncontrolled emotion. Then he blinks the swelling tears away. He looks up to the window, the pale light suffusing around his pupils, and again the room loses focus as if he's staring at something a long, long way off.

"Xavier? Do you hear me?"

He directs his attention again at his latest drawing, then glances at the wall in front of him, focusing on one sheet in particular, puzzled as to why this one should pull at his attention. Another depicts a huge seal—an eagle over a star. And there's a drawing done in colored crayons. A drawing of a woman strapped to a bed while two men are crumpled on the ground around her, crimson splatters on their chests. A third man—a man with red hair—.

"Xavier?"

The boy blinks again and smooths back his hair.

"Xavier honey, did you hear what I said?"

He turns his head and manages a smile. "Yes, but I'm sorry, I still have work to do."

Turning away from her, Xavier Montross picks up his pencil and flips to a blank page.

BOOK ONE:
THEFT

1.

Phoebe Crowe spoke softly into the microphone as she watched the action on three separate laptop screens. "Okay, big brother, we've got the link working. We see what you see. Let's get this show on the road."

Itching from the heavy cotton sweater worn under her ski coat, she still battled the chill from the two-hour Sno-Cat ride from Fort Erickson. It was the longest two hours in her life, with the exception of that time spent writhing on the tomb floor in Belize. And this was the last leg of a journey that earlier featured a white-knuckle helicopter ride from the *Starboard Ulysses,* was currently trawling a mile out beyond the ice shelf.

While Phoebe and Orlando Natch, her lone teammate, still shivered, the six other people in the room seemed used to the forty-degree temperature. Point Nelson's commander, Colonel Eric Hiltmeyer, stood nearly seven feet tall. Bald, with a chiseled jaw and a scar on his left cheek as if he had taken one swipe too many from a sharp razor in a prison fight, he lurked over Phoebe's shoulder as his staff—two scientists, a geologist, an environmental engineer and a lab assistant—spaced themselves around the table, observing as Phoebe and Orlando tracked the progress of their other team members.

Phoebe moved the microphone to her left, in front of the man—the boy really—who had made all this possible. At age nineteen, Orlando Natch was the youngest member of their psychic research group known as The Morpheus Initiative. was their technological whiz kid who, ironically, had never been to Florida, much less Orlando. Jet black hair, curly and ragged, wild blue eyes, and a narrow elfish face, with his 150-pound frame covered with baggy jeans and a black *World of Warcraft* sweatshirt. Orlando had been recruited directly by Phoebe while she was a graduate assistant at the University of Rochester. Not only did he excel at applying cutting-edge technology to the study of ancient relics, but he displayed exactly the type of intuition that indicated he might be a candidate for the Morpheus Initiative.

Orlando *saw* things. Before they happened mostly, but sometimes, given just a little prodding with a picture or an object (or the right question), he'd drift into a trance and then wake up and rush to his iPad, wielding it like an artist, where he'd set about crafting a computer-generated rendition of his vision on one of its graphics applications.

This technique was miles ahead of the old pencil-and-sketchpad method used for years by the other remote viewers, and Phoebe was only too grateful to have him on board—as was her brother Caleb, who had leveraged the value of the group's scanned drawings, uploading them and then interfacing with image-recognition software to find matches with photos on web-based public databases or in photo-share servers like Flikr.com.

"Lookin' good," Orlando said, rubbing his hands together, then directing a joystick, which now controlled the camera on Caleb's helmet. "Just focusing ... there. I see it. Holy shit, do I see it!"

Phoebe leaned in, looking from screen to screen, from the cameras mounted on their three members at the dig site a mile away. In addition to Caleb, two other Morpheus Initiative members, Andy Bellows and Ben Tillman, had volunteered for this mission. An hour ago, all three had suited up and left in a Sno-Cat with Colonel Hiltmeyer's other newly-arrived guest, an anthropologist named Henrik Tarn.

"So you're getting this?" Caleb's voice crackled from the speakers. His name was on the third screen in front of Orlando. The shaking screen.

Phoebe whistled. "Yeah, but stop moving so much. You shivering or something?"

"It's freakin' cold, in case you didn't know. Minus twenty and—"

"And no wind chill," she said, aware of the hypocrisy as she snuggled in her coat. "You're in a cave, so stop whining and stay still so we can get some clear images of that thing."

Orlando glanced at the other screens. "Bellows and Tillman, please move around and space yourselves equally apart from Caleb. Let's get this from all angles."

On the screens, within the frozen cavern, emerging from the ice-shelf, were several views of something dark and huge, with sharp protrusions spiking from a rounded edge. Phoebe leaned over. "Hey Orlando, can you pull up our sketches for comparison?"

"No problem." Orlando quickly tapped some keys and another window on the middle screen appeared, displaying a succession of scanned drawings, most of them crude and awkward, but unmistakably the same general structure as the object on the live image feed. He moved the pictures into different orientations to match the unearthed artifact.

"I still can't believe this," Colonel Hiltmeyer said, edging past the other group members and peering over Phoebe's shoulder.

"What?" Phoebe asked. "That you guys found this thing in the ice at a depth equating to a geologic period of more than fifteen thousand years ago? Or that we separately drew the same thing four years before your team even set up shop here?"

He blinked at her, his dull gray eyes impassive. "Both, I guess."

Phoebe stretched her legs, still relishing the ability to do just that. For ten years, during all of her teens, she had been in a wheelchair, her legs useless, her hip and lower vertebrae shattered after rushing into a booby-trapped tomb in Belize. But then the cure—the miraculous technique discovered in the original *Hippocratus Manuscript*, one of thousands of lost scrolls she and Caleb had discovered under the remains of the ancient Pharos Lighthouse in Alexandria, one of the Seven Wonders of the ancient world. The miracle she'd never thought she would experience: to be able to walk again. To run. It still made her giddy, humble and grateful beyond words.

She clicked the microphone. "Okay Caleb, what do you have for us? You guys want to try to remote view it now that you're within actual sight of the thing? Get some glimpses into its past and let us in on the big mystery?"

Colonel Hiltmeyer licked his lips. "Like how big it is."

Orlando tapped some keys and called up a smaller window which began running a graphical projection based on the tip of the head, then extrapolated a body, arms simply at its side. "It's about 130 feet tall, if the curvature of the head's to scale." He looked up, grinning. "Any other easy questions, or should we hold out for the big one?"

Her voice dropping a notch, Phoebe said, "You mean, like how the hell did it get here?"

Caleb Crowe pulled back his hood and adjusted his earpiece before resealing the polypropylene fleece hat. He was still freezing, despite the layers of a pile fiber sweater and a North Face Parka, with 550-fill down content and a two-layer HyVent waterproof/windproof fabric. His fingers were tingly and getting number by the minute, notwithstanding the thick goose-down mittens. But as Phoebe said, at least he was out of the wind.

He gave a quick thought to his nine-year-old son, Alexander, in their nice warm house on Sodus Bay in upstate New York. Hopefully he was doing his homework, or at least some light reading, which to him was something like *Herodotus*. But more likely the kid was just playing around the old lighthouse on the hill. Caleb's wife, Lydia, was there with him, taking a much-needed break from her duties at the Alexandrian Library. She and her brother Robert were co-leaders of a two thousand-year-old organization called the Keepers, who just recently, with Caleb's help, had rediscovered a secret vault below the remains of the great Pharos Lighthouse—a vault which had protected the most important writings the world had ever produced, secreted away before the original Alexandrian Library's destruction in 391 CE. During the past five years, the Keepers, Caleb himself one of them now, had been slowly reintroducing certain manuscripts to the world, those which could benefit mankind the most, while keeping a lid on others with more explosive content until their impact could be controlled.

He envied his wife and son right now. Lydia and Alexander—warm, surrounded by familiar books, those timeless friends. And here he was, in one of the most inhospitable places in the world. And in a cave of all places. But if this find proved to be what he thought it was, everything would change. The archaeological equivalent of a meteor impact, finding evidence of an advanced civilization existing in Antarctica during prehistoric times would rock the academic world and shake the pillars of all major institutions. A civilization that could build such an immense statue, a guardian standing upon the field of an ancient city, with other monuments perhaps still preserved, frozen. And its libraries! Dare he even begin to hope? To dream that they could discover books containing all that lost knowledge?

"This could be Atlantis," Ben Tillman said, reaching out a gloved hand to the closest thorny spike of the head's crown. Free of ice, it was a greenish-blue color, oddly metallic. Tillman was dressed in a heavy parka and a woolen hood that all but concealed his face. Icicles hung from his mustache.

"Could be," Andy Bellows said excitedly, rubbing his mittened hands together in the steam from his breath.

"Impossible," Henrik Tarn said. The anthropologist who had been brought in two days ago was the tallest of the group. Almost comically tall, Caleb had thought when he first met the bony, long-armed man with a narrow face and dark, button-like eyes. "Plato was very specific about his location of the legendary submerged island: 'beyond the pillars of Gibraltar, past the Aegean.'"

"But," Caleb countered, gazing now in wonder at the hint of curvature, a giant eye protruding from the ice, "Plato could have been right and that's where it *was*, but during a cataclysmic event, the earth's axis flipped, the crustal plates shifted, entire continents shook free and—"

"—and Atlantis could have shifted to the South Pole," Tarn supplied. "Yes, yes, I've heard that hokey theory about how the Earth's crust is like the skin of an orange and can shift over the core. But it's nonsense."

"Then how do you explain this?"

Tarn shrugged, hugging his shoulders. "I'm not yet convinced. We need to dig, expose more of the structure."

"What about sonar readings? Would they do it for you?" Caleb asked. Then louder into the microphone, "Orlando, when can we get that imaging equipment out here?"

The speaker crackled. "In the morning, I think. The colonel here said he'll contact Fort Erickson and have them haul out the sensor equipment once the storm clears."

Tarn grunted. "We'll see."

Caleb knelt closer to the head, reaching out to tentatively touch one of the spiked protrusions. "Definitely sun-worshippers. This is similar to the prevalent Greek depictions of Helios, the sun god. I'm dying to see the rest of this statue. Maybe ... maybe just a touch ..." He started peeling off his right mitten.

"Don't be an idiot!" Phoebe shouted over his earpiece. "At those temperatures, your skin will fuse to it and burn right off."

Reluctantly, feeling like he had just been scolded by a grade-school hall monitor, Caleb pulled his hand away and slipped his mitten back on.

Phoebe's voice admonished, "You weren't seriously about to touch it, were you?"

"Sorry, got caught up in the excitement. Thinking back to my dive under the Alexandrian harbor, where I had that psychic vision after touching one of the statue heads."

"Well, try it without physical contact, dummy. Or else wait."

"But we've already tried it," Tillman said. "A couple trance sessions on the plane, and another in the station. Didn't see squat."

Tarn made a scoffing sound. "Self-induced daydreams and fanciful imaginations are no substitute for sound fieldwork."

"Say what you'd like," Caleb said, "but we saw this thing, exactly in this position. Orlando can tell you; he was one of the first to draw it when we started actively looking for the remnants of a past civilization." He had to cut himself off before saying too much, indicating the real subject of their search, being the origin of the Emerald Tablet, the powerful but inscrutable tome that was once safeguarded under the Pharos. The tablet was the one artifact Caleb had kept for himself, believing its power so great that he needed to hide its existence even from his wife and the other Keepers.

Caleb thought for a moment. The questions they had asked on the plane had been broad, maybe too general. The very existence of the Emerald Tablet, hidden now in a vault under his own light-house back at Sodus Point, indicated that its creator, the legendary Hermes-Thoth, was a member of some pre-Egyptian, pre-Sumerian civilization, a race that not only pre-dated them, but may have actually given birth to those cultures—to their language, their myths, their very existence. One that had left no records other than those shrouded in legend.

So the latest Morpheus Initiative effort focused on just this problem: if there was an advanced civilization, one that had been eradicated in some tragic cataclysm, where could they find evidence of its existence? *Where was the Emerald Tablet created? And what, really, did it do?*

A number of hits popped up through the intervening years of searching through the Morpheus Initiative's efforts, through hundreds of trances and thousands of drawings. But the most consistent and similar image perceived among its members was this vision of an enormous half-concealed statue head, lying in this very position.

And then, almost coincidentally, came the call from Nelson Point in the South Pole. A two-time veteran, Colonel Hiltmeyer had known of the CIA's Stargate Program, which utilized remote-viewing psychics during the Cold War (and secretly beyond). But while unaware of its previous leader's extracurricular activities, Hiltmeyer had known enough about the Morpheus Initiative to seek its services when his research team stumbled across this potentially ancient discovery.

Now, Caleb knelt in the ice and crossed his legs.

"What are you doing?" Tarn asked. He had a shovel out and was carefully digging around the eye area.

"Just give me a minute," Caleb said. "Bellows and Tillman, if you want to give it a try too, maybe just by being in the vicinity, we'll get clearer visions." He held out his hands, palms outward toward the statue, then closed his eyes.

Phoebe's voice came through his speaker. "Orlando and I will try to RV it too. Just keep still so I can focus on the statue."

"This is nuts," said Tarn.

"Tell that guy to zip it," Orlando said over the earpiece. "He's getting annoying."

"Hang on," Caleb whispered, feeling suddenly dizzy. "I'm getting something. I'm in …

… a warehouse. Leaded windows. Dusty floor. Scaffolding around a partial spherical construction, still with lattice-grillwork on half of it, while heavy metal plates are fitted into position.

Looking down from the ceiling, then descending and circling around the structure, seeing teams of workers toiling with the frame, hoisting the sheets and hollowing out the eyes. Workers wearing blue jumpsuits, dust-masks and goggles. A rumbling sound and suddenly a forklift drives forward, preparing to lift the partial head onto a waiting flatbed truck.

Caleb staggered to his feet, scrambling and slipping on the ice. He tried to back up, then toppled forward, clutching one of the protruding sun-ray spikes to break his fall.

"It's—"

... a partial head, the exterior sealed now, set in the back of a truck as the door slams shut, and the vision wheels around to see the back of a tall, lanky man in a black silk suit, nodding and talking on a cell phone.

"It's ready. Just as you specified. We'll ship it to the research station tomorrow and have it transported to the cave by Thursday night. Hiltmeyer's team is ready for it?"

The man listens, nods, then turns. His face—his too familiar face—pulls from the shadows ...

"—a FAKE!" Pushing away from the statue with disgust, Caleb turned to the anthropologist.

But it was already too late.

"Damn psychics," Henrik Tarn spat, as he pulled off a mitten and with a thin glove underneath fished out a gun from inside his coat. Aiming at Caleb, Tarn tugged at his collar and spoke into his own microphone. "We've got to move up the timetable."

"What!" Caleb began, but then there came a shriek from Phoebe in his earpiece before the microphone shorted out, just as Tarn, sensing Ben Tillman foolishly rushing him, swiveled and shot him point-blank in the chest.

2.

Phoebe screamed as Colonel Hiltmeyer and another one of his staff pulled out strange-looking guns, and as soon as Tarn finished speaking, they fired.

"You've got to be kidding me" was all Orlando could say before the red dart thunked into his chest, the toxin spread, and he immediately slumped over. Phoebe ducked below one shot from the colonel, then dodged around a desk. No point in hiding, she rose and raced for the back room when the dart struck her leg and she hit the floor.

The red dart, embedded in her thigh, would have brought her down, if not for her artificial hip, thigh and a portion of her calf—all fitted and retro-purposed with a prosthesis after that tragic fall during the Belize expedition.

A quick thought, a plan forming: *Fake it!*

She let her body go limp, flicked her eyelids, then closed them. She willed Hiltmeyer and his men to accept that she was now tranquilized like Orlando.

But why did they turn on us? Who was behind this? Something so elaborately staged to bring them to this frozen pit of the world? And for what—not to kill them, or they would have done it already. Her thoughts raced as she heard the scrambling activity. Laptops unplugged and packed up. Coats zippered. The thudding of heavy boots.

A door whisked open, bringing with it a blast of frigid air and a new voice, somehow familiar but not enough for Phoebe to place it.

A woman's voice. Controlled, confident. In charge, and with a note of satisfaction.

"Set the charges for ten minutes, then head back to the chopper. Leave that laptop. I need to see what's going on down there."

Colonel Hiltmeyer cleared his throat. "Tarn has it in hand."

"I heard a shot."

"Tillman, I think—dead."

"Fine. But still, Tarn blew it. He was to keep them from remote viewing until I was ready."

"Caleb didn't even touch the thing, not from what I could see."

"Doesn't matter. He's too good."

Phoebe bit her lip and peeked with one eye but could only see the newcomer's lean legs and chiseled calves, clad in tight white thermals, with shiny boots. *Who are you?*

"Just go," the woman snapped. "The chopper's waiting. I'll finish up here."

"Fine. So, the tranquilizer ... it'll keep them knocked out for about an hour."

"Your point?"

"Well, the detonators ... You're really just going to leave these two here?"

Silence.

Phoebe could almost feel Hiltmeyer shrinking away from whatever look the woman was giving him. "You know our orders. If you have a problem with them, you can stay here as well."

"No problem, I just—"

"Then go."

The door opened. The colonel followed his team out, and over the wind Phoebe could now hear the thrumming of the helicopter engine.

The woman turned and leaned over the desk. Phoebe inched around the leg of the table so she could get a better view, but could only see a head of short dark hair over the woman's face as she spoke into the microphone.

Caleb stared at the red puddle steaming on the ice under Ben Tillman—Ben, the man Caleb had recruited directly from a seminar in Virginia. He had shown great promise, scoring high marks on the remote-visualization card tests, and once during a linked video conference call from over two hundred miles away he had drawn the exact sequence of symbols that Caleb had placed in a sealed envelope.

"Tarn! What are you doing?" He spread his arms, holding one hand out to Andy Bellows, warning him back. Andy was a hot-head, always impatient and full of Hollywood-like visions of tomb raiding and treasure hunting, never quite appreciating the hard work and finer points of the Morpheus Initiative's process.

"This whole time, you and Hiltmeyer buried this thing to get us down here... ." Caleb fumed. He closed his eyes, cursing his stupidity. *I wasn't asking the right questions.* "You've got someone in our group. Or you've hacked our servers. Found what we were drawing, the exact image and specifications of the colossal head, and then you built it and buried it where you knew it would send us running in a hurry."

"Sorry," said Andy Bellows, shrugging and then lowering his hands. He slid closer to Tarn, and in a forced Italian accent said, "But they made me an offer I couldn't refuse."

Caleb stared weakly at Andy, then shook his head. "Damn it, kid. You don't know what you've done. You don't know who these people are."

Then his earpiece crackled. "Hello down there, and hello Caleb. It's been a long time, but I wonder, did you miss me?"

Under all his layers, Caleb broke out in a feverish sweat. He recalled a steamy night in Alexandria, entwined around a woman with olive skin and burning green eyes. "Nina?"

"Hi, honey."

The air chilled, as if the wind and the cold had found a crack in the ice and rushed through to find him.

"Caleb, Caleb. How is it that you never tried to RV me after the disaster under the Pharos Lighthouse? Not even a glimpse, after all we meant to each other? Surely, with your vast abilities you would have seen me in a coma suffering the worst dreams you could possibly imagine. All the while, a part of me hoping, praying, believing that maybe you'd be my prince, that you'd come to my rescue and wake me with love's true kiss."

Caleb clenched his eyes shut, shaking his head. "You were in league with him, with George Waxman, all along. You killed so many of the Keepers."

"Bygones, Caleb. Besides, I've watched you since then, you don't trust your new friends either. None of the other Keepers. Even your wife."

That point chilled his blood. His eyes snapped open. *Does she know about the tablet?*She had to have RV'd him, and would have seen the vault where he'd hid it away.

She knows, damn it, she knows!

"I tried to see you." He had to stall her, think of a way out of this. "But—"

"You didn't try, lover. Admit it. You forgot all about little old me. Let your gift languish, too wrapped up in guilt over the things it kept showing you. You let it wither until that Keeper tramp Lydia came along and fired you up again. Tell me, who was better at freeing your powers? Me, or the little missus?"

Caleb tried not to look at the gun pointed at his heart. His mind reeled. *How did she survive?* first trap under the Pharos Lighthouse had released a torrential wave of water that had smashed her against a pillar, and she fell and was sucked out into the Alexandrian harbor, her body never found.

A sudden flash appeared in Caleb's head, like the lifting of a veil, and he saw ...

... a recompression chamber, a familiar one, the same he had once spent a day in. On board Waxman's boat, only in this vision Nina was inside, motionless.

And then he was back in the icy cave with Tarn pointing the gun at him and Andy Bellows grinning. "Fine," Caleb said. "You got me, Nina. Got us. The Morpheus Initiative. Played us, but for what? We're here."

"That's it, Caleb. That's all there is. I just wanted you to know who it was, wanted you to know that back then you shouldn't have dropped me."

"Nina," he said, slumping over, "I couldn't—"

"Goodbye, Caleb. Mr. Tarn, Mr. Bellows, thank you for your service."

Andy looked up. "What?"

Tarn lowered the gun, said, "NO!" and in a burst of surprising speed, ran for the cave's exit just as an enormous explosion rocked the tunnel—followed by a series of detonations above them.

Caleb looked up and didn't even have time to cry out as the ceiling collapsed.

Phoebe held her breath. *What just happened?* heard the name and remembered. Nina Osseni. A beautiful European, one of George Waxman's first recruits for the Morpheus Initiative. She was exotic and cat-like, always seemed a little dark and mysterious around Phoebe, but she had never had much contact with the woman, especially since Phoebe was confined to that relic of a wheelchair and couldn't go on any more globe-trotting expeditions with the team.

But then the tragedy under the Pharos. Nina and Waxman going in too strong, believing they had decoded the symbols on the door, but having them all wrong, releasing the first trap, which killed everyone in their group except for Caleb, Waxman and their mother.

And apparently, Nina.

Somehow she had survived, and then what? She had tracked Caleb ever since, hoping for some misguided revenge? Maybe revenge for Waxman, or for Caleb's inability to save her?

After taunting Caleb and the others, Nina shut the laptop, unplugged the microphone, and pressed a button on a small device.

A distant rumbling vibrated the station, overpowering even the chopper blades. Phoebe felt the trembling under her body and she realized what Nina had done.

Nina turned and left through the door without so much as a look behind her.

Then Phoebe sprang up and looked around frantically for the explosive charges. In another moment, she heard the chopper ascending and then it was quiet outside, except for the screeching wind.

Thoughts of Caleb blown to bits—

No, can't think that yet.

She continued looking around the room, then stuck her head under the desk. There was something there, a round device like a hockey puck, with a blinking red light. She took hold of it, but it was stuck. She was about to kick it free when she thought better of that idea.

Could she move the whole table out? No, not without disassembling it. And there had to be at least one more of these things.

Damn!

She went back, judged Orlando's weight, and then bent down. She lifted him, grunting. "Gotta get to the gym more often." She dragged him toward the door, then stopped to grab two heavy parkas, and, from the table, the keys to the remaining Sno-Cat.

At least we won't freeze.

Outside, assaulted at once by the icy wind, she hauled Orlando by the ankles, the job a little easier on the slick surface. She tugged him toward the isolated garage that was only ten yards away but seemed like a mile, fell, got up and stared into the stinging blizzard, into the night's black swirling face, to see the flickering lights of the chopper angling toward a distant red light beyond the ice barrier on the sea.

"Come on, Orlando!" She lugged his body over the threshold into the outbuilding. "Got to get—"

Just then, the station exploded into a roaring fireball. The force of the blast tore Phoebe free of Orlando's inert form and knocked her sprawling awkwardly to the floor.

3.

THE LIGHTHOUSE ...

Caleb could see it as if his mind circled the hill from a great height, focusing on the small tower rising out of the morning fog, glinting in the sunrise.

My lighthouse, he thought. Sodus Point, looking out over the bay, the waves battering the rocky shore in the cold autumn wind. A narrow, rectangular-shaped tower, the 150-year-old lighthouse was anchored to the attached house, his house, where Alexander should be just waking up, Lydia in the kitchen in her terrycloth robe, making Armenian coffee and blueberry flapjacks.

But why am I seeing this?

As if in answer ...

... a black Hummer arrives, slowly pulling up the long drive. At once, the front doors open and two black-clad men burst out. Men with guns. Then the back doors open and two other men emerge.

One, a shorter, lanky man with a full head of blond hair, wearing a long gray trench coat. The other, meticulously dressed in a blue silk suit with a power tie—crimson—matching the color of his hair, shining like fire in the sun.

Caleb shuddered with recognition.

... The red-haired man nods after the other man points to the lighthouse.

He knew the other man too.

Robert. Lydia's brother. *What is he—?*

Caleb's eyes flew open and a scream tried to explode through his nearly crushed lungs. *The Emerald Tablet!*

He struggled, tried to kick free, to move his arms, even an inch, in this suffocating, dark and frozen tomb. He had seen the tunnel implode just as Henrik Tarn and Andy Bellows were racing for it, still shocked at being betrayed. They disappeared, gruesomely crushed under a massive slab of the collapsing ice shelf, and then Caleb jumped for the only bit of cover—beneath the statue's head, where the protruding crown offered some degree of protection.

But it wasn't enough. He was still sealed up, buried alive. He couldn't tell, with all the weight and pressure and numbness in his extremities, if anything was broken, but it seemed the statue had deflected the direct impact and left a small air pocket to save him from serious injury.

So that he could die slowly of exposure.

In spite of his predicament and the prospect of an unimaginably horrible death, all he could think of was Alexander and Lydia.

Men are coming for the tablet.

Was it a vision of the future or something happening right now? Was there anything he could do other than try to go back into the vision and see for himself?

Robert's presence there terrified him, even more than that somehow familiar red-haired man. Robert Gregory, Caleb's brother-in-law, had been frustrated that the Emerald Tablet, the prize the Keepers had sought in the Alexandrian Library's collection, had been missing when Caleb beat the Pharos's defenses and found the way inside.

Robert had never stopped looking for it, and Caleb was sure that his brother-in-law suspected the truth—that Caleb had stolen the tablet and lied about its absence. And lied again and again when Robert and Lydia had asked him and the Morpheus Initiative to remote view it, find where it might have been taken before the Pharos vault had been sealed up.

Caleb hadn't told Lydia, knowing her convictions belonged with her brother in this case, and while she spent the better part of each year back in the new Library at Alexandria, cataloguing and studying the collection of recovered scrolls, Caleb had fashioned his own secret vault below the Sodus lighthouse, modeled after the original architect's design, the Pharos's creator, Sostratus of Knidos. Caleb designed a similar set of traps that he hoped someday only his son Alexander could bypass. When he was ready to be a Keeper himself. When he had learned what he needed to know. Even Caleb hadn't spent much time with it, afraid of its power, its ability to enhance his visions and stimulate other powers. Powers he didn't need, or want, just yet.

Until then, the tablet would wait inside.

And of course, there was the problem of its translation. What exactly was recorded? Instructions for incomparable power or eternal youth? Or a recipe for something much worse?

Caleb struggled against the ice, but it was no use. The cold was penetrating, painfully seeping through his layers, and as the darkness pressed in, he had no choice but to stop fighting.

He tried to relax, pull away from the cold and pain, from the stiffness and pressure. To draw his mind away, set it free. He had done this once before, in an Alexandrian jail where his body had all but deteriorated and wasted away until his spirit had been released, exposed to a new realm of sight, revealing what he needed to see.

So now he let go, released his hold on the flesh, and hoped that once set free, his mind—and his abilities—would discover something worth seeing.

Leaping from the chopper onto the deck of the ice-rigger, Nina Osseni pulled back her hood and lifted the satellite phone to her ear. She paused for a moment to watch the station burn along the ridge. And she smiled.

Goodbye, Phoebe.

Colonel Hiltmeyer and his team left the helicopter as the blades slowed, and they rushed past her into the cabin. Nina could feel the engines revving up, the rigger turning, heading north. She waited, feeling the snowflakes slowing, the wind then blasting them away along with the clouds. The night sky, revealed in its sparkling glory, turned the ice shoals below a crystalline blue.

She pressed the redial button on her satellite phone. After one ring, a man's voice answered. "Is it done?"

"Yes, they're dead. Phoebe and Caleb and the other members of the Morpheus Initiative."

"I somehow doubt that," returned the voice.

"What do you mean?"

"It doesn't matter. Just a vision I had a short time ago."

"I had no such vision."

"Maybe, as your old boyfriend liked to point out repeatedly, you weren't asking the right questions. In any case, they'll be delayed long enough for me to get what we came for."

Nina frowned, still scanning the ice cliffs and plateaus. "Any resistance?"

"None so far, but I wasn't expecting any. Not until we approach the vault."

"You've got your drawings?"

"I do, but I don't need them."

Nina eyed the flickering wreckage on the shore, then glanced back to the helicopter. "If there's a chance Caleb survived, I could go back and wait for him to show."

Silence for a moment. "No, I don't think it would do any good. I've had other visions—stronger ones—of meeting him again. It was worth a shot, but in this case I don't think we can change fate. Go back to the rendezvous point, meet me at Saint Peter's Castle, and I'll join you once I have the prize."

"Very well." She shut off the phone, still gazing at the shore, considering her options.

How did they survive? she wondered.

But another part of her secretly tingled at the thought of another encounter, far more personal and direct, with Caleb.

Revenge just might be better the second time.

The visions flew at him like a desperate flock of ravens, plucking at his mind's eye, showing him ...

... the lighthouse on the cliff, and the main home, where Robert and the red-haired man approached the front entrance ... the icy landscape above, sprinkled with stardust on the fresh snow, where the research station burned, churning fiery smoke into the sky ... a Sno-Cat, racing from the wreckage on huge rolling treads ... *Phoebe's face, behind the Plexiglass. Orlando Natch, unconscious in the back....* .

In the dark, using the only muscles he could still control, he smiled. *Come on sis, don't be too long.* He saw her ...

... on the CB, making a distress call to Fort Erickson ... a research installation bursting with activity, men racing to Sno-Cats and snowmobiles, hooking up digging equipment and ice-breakers... .

And then, as if satisfied with what they had shown him so far, the visionary black birds pecked away with renewed vigor, excited at having undivided access to his exposed senses. *Look this way,* they cried, and he saw his son, Alexander ...

... standing outside the silver vault door, hands pressed against the reflective surface, while in the square window that mane of curly red hair, those familiar blue eyes, trapped inside, yet exuding triumph... .

Caleb pushed his memory, recalling a hotel room years ago, in Alexandria, and those eyes peering at him from a crack in the door. *Who ...?*

And then he saw new visions of ...

... sprawling scenes of an arid landscape, with ruined pillars over an archaeological dig site on a hill; and then a scene of a medieval castle basking in the sun, before ... again, the view of a giant green-hued metal head, a crown of spiked rays, those regal eyes ... a huge underground cavern lit by sickly yellow light, and a host of cold, dead eye sockets set below helmets ... an army waiting patiently in the darkness, brandishing spears, swords, bows, protecting something beyond immeasurable walls ...

Caleb moaned—a sound he barely heard, his spirit soaring now, glimpsing simultaneously ...

... Phoebe's Sno-Cat, followed by the armada of rescue vehicles, arriving at the collapsed site ... the Sodus Lighthouse, hurtling now down the basement stairs, through the underground passage to the vault door, over Alexander's shoulder, through the door, inside, where that man, that familiar man kneels cross-legged, holding the artifact, the greenish-blue aura dancing from the Emerald Tablet.

His face is bathed in its kaleidoscopic hues, and he suddenly looks up, cocks his head, and his eyes lock on, staring straight into the vision's point of view. He smiles ...

... and Caleb rocked back into his body, screaming. That face! It was the person he had seen through the door in Alexandria. The Morpheus Initiative member who'd had a premonition of disaster under the Pharos and had stayed behind, had warned Caleb.

"Xavier!" he shouted, his lungs burning. "Xavier Montross!"

4.

Lydia Gregory-Crowe didn't see them coming.

One minute she had been sipping her cup of steaming Armenian coffee, the next, two armed men in black ski masks had guns to her head. She tried to call out to warn Alexander, but remembered he was back at the lighthouse, most likely prowling in its basement, playing make-believe or whatever he did down there.

Seconds later, she was led out onto the front lawn to meet the last two people coming out of a black jeep. A red-haired man with brilliant blue eyes stood first, glanced at her, smiled, then looked down to the lighthouse. Lydia started to pull herself free, struggling until she saw the next person emerge from the passenger side of the jeep, a cigarette dangling from his lips.

"Hello, Lydia. Sorry to drop in like this."

Her expression went from anger and fright to outright shock.

"Robert!"

"Can we not point guns at her?"

The man beside him sighed. "In a minute. Lydia, where's Alexander? Where's your son?"

"I'm not telling you—you, who the hell are you? What do you people want? Robert, did they abduct you?"

"Settle down, Lydia. I know this might look a bit like overkill, but Xavier didn't want to take any chances. Not with something of this magnitude." He sighed. "We've come for the tablet."

Lydia's bright green eyes sparkled. "The Emerald Tablet? What—? Wait, you think it's here?"

Xavier Montross brushed past her, heading to the lighthouse entrance as the rising sun glinted off the mist-shrouded bay. He turned his attention to the tower. "Oh, it's definitely here. Your husband, it appears, never quite trusted you." He gave her a sympathetic look. "Maybe it had something to do with your not being entirely honest with him from the beginning about who you were."

"The fact that I was a Keeper had nothing to do with my feelings for Caleb." She held up fists, wrists still cuffed. "And you. I remember you. Skipped out on the team in Alexandria."

"Saved myself, more like it, from their stupidity. Saved myself for more important things."

Lydia released a long breath. "Well, I don't believe you. Caleb didn't take the Emerald Tablet. He couldn't."

"He could," Montross said, heading to the entrance, "and he did. It's been right under your nose, all these years."

Robert followed, helping Lydia along after dropping his cigarette in the snow. "Your son knows too."

"Impossible. I would know if Alex were keeping such a secret."

Robert smiled. "A mother doesn't know everything, not in this case, Lydia. He's more his father's son."

"How can you be sure?"

Robert pointed. "Ask him. He drew it."

Montross grinned, moving quickly now to the steel door, blazing in the rising sun. "I'll show you my sketches later. Over a hundred of them, some drawn during the past decade, but most over twenty years ago, when I was a boy." He blinked at her, then reached for the door. "Even then, my destiny was clear. Even then, this day was in my sights."

Lydia shot out her bound hands, caught her brother's collar with both hands. "Robert, you can't allow this! If the tablet is down there, you can't let this man—anyone other than a Keeper—get his hands on something so powerful!"

Robert held his sister's cuffed wrists, and looked into her eyes. "Don't worry, he's going to give it to us. And then it will finally be where it belongs. He only needs to read a portion of it, something his visions have shown him. Don't ask me to explain it all."

"If you don't know his true motivations, why would you take this risk? Our father taught us better than that."

"Don't bring him into this. The Emerald Tablet, and all its ancient knowledge, is our birthright. Bad enough our ancestors had to wait over two thousand years for its release, keeping the damn secret, but then to have an outsider steal it away?"

"Caleb's not an outsider."

"Not anymore, true, but—"

"He *was* a Keeper, truer to the cause than we ever were."

"You're softening, Lydia. Too much in his shadow, I think."

Lydia glared at him. "You should have just come to me, I would have talked to Caleb." She pounded his chest.

"Enough," Montross said, then turned to his men. "You two stay up here. Keep an eye on them."

Robert's head snapped around. "'Them?' But—"

"Don't worry, Robert. I will still give you what you want, but first, I must do this alone." He reached into his suit coat pocket and pulled out a sheaf of pages. Unfolding them, he looked at the first page of a schematic-type drawing of the steps below the ground floor of the lighthouse, to the basement sub-cellar and storage area that decades ago had been used to store fuel for the lighthouse.

He flipped through the pages, nodded, opened the door, then closed it behind him.

At the top of the stairs, Xavier cocked his head. He glanced through his drawings again. Nothing on the pictures, except the last one—one showing his own face looking through a glass-like porthole—and what looked like the reflection of a boy's face in the glass. He held the pages and looked down the granite staircase, the steeply withering descent, thirty-six stairs to the first bend, then around another thirty-six to the sub-cellar itself. Two lamps burning dimly, set on the walls.

He walked calmly, descending with his eyes closed as if he'd walked these stairs a thousand times before, if only in his mind. To the bend, and then around and down. On the second stairwell he stopped and flipped through the pages again, twenty of them now, and he paused at each page. He stopped at one showing a room with a door and three ledge-like shelves on either wall. Above the door were three large, emboldened Greek letters, and on the six shelves were round peg-like objects. On the shining metal door itself was a single porthole-like window.

Montross continued. At the bottom, the air was dank, musty, the floor cobbled and uneven. Reaching out along the wall, he found the light switch he knew to be there. Flicked it and said, "Hello, Alexander."

In the light that blasted through the darkness like a sunburst, the small boy with curly dark hair kneeling before the door shielded his eyes, and then stood up.

In a cracking voice, he said, "You're not getting inside."

Eight thousand miles away, Caleb was being airlifted to the Fort Erickson research station to a waiting team of medics. In the helicopter, Phoebe and Orlando were by his side, Phoebe holding his weak hand while Caleb muttered about the visions still roiling in his head.

"Montross is in the vault, our vault ... with Alexander."

Alexander balled his fists, squinting, getting used to the light again after running below and then shutting off the lights, hoping to hide. *Bad idea*, he thought. Obviously a group of armed men showing up could only be after one thing—the artifact in the vault behind him.

Trying to sound as brave and confident as his favorite hero Dash, the boy with super speed from his favorite movie *The Incredibles*, he said again, "You're not getting inside."

Alexander's focus cleared as the well-dressed red-haired man stepped into the light. The man had dazzling blue eyes, shamefully blue—so much that they seemed the color of a newborn's eyes, brilliant and desperately *hungry*. Alexander saw something of himself reflected in them.

"Hello, Alexander. My name is Xavier Montross. I was a friend of your father's years ago. I've seen this vault chamber"—he raised a sketchpad and waved it around the room—"saw it and saw you long before you were even born."

Alexander swallowed and stepped away, his back now against the wall. *Uh oh.* "Great, so you're psychic too."

"One of the founding members of the Morpheus Initiative."

Alexander shrugged. "Everyone else is dead. Being psychic makes people act stupid."

Montross stifled a laugh. "But not you, right? You're too humble."

"I'm only nine."

"Well, anyway, my very astute youngster, you're definitely your father's son. Probably reading at college levels already, right?"

He thought of his books, all those precious books lining the shelves in his room, and all those he could reach in his father's study.

"Of course you do. Well, you should know this: I was the only one with enough sense not to go under the Pharos on that fateful trip. Because I knew." Again he raised the sketchpad. "I saw what was going to happen."

"Why didn't you tell anybody?"

"I warned your dad. Might just have saved his ass so he could live long enough to father a son. Ask him about that, if he comes back."

Alexander shivered, his eyes closed and suddenly, just for a moment, he had a jolting vision of crushing ice, of an enormous head with sad, regal eyes looking on protectively. He heard helicopter blades, and what sounded like his Aunt Phoebe's voice.

"I saw this too." Montross gazed at the walls to his left and right, nodding to himself as if in vindication of his drawings. Then he looked above Alexander's head, over the door.

Blinking away the vision, and the certainty that his father and the others were in big trouble, Alexander stood up straight, spreading his feet to cover something on the ground, hoping—

"Don't bother," Montross said. "I know what's there. Oh, your dad's a clever guy, I give him that. Taking elements of the Pharos's vault design and incorporating them here. Thinking he's following in Sostratus's footsteps, right? But I wonder, Alexander, have you figured it out yet?"

"I don't know what you mean."

"Sure you do, kid. You're the sole child, the son of two Keepers. No choice really, you're their chosen replacement. You're being groomed, just as Keepers have done for over two thousand years. But your dad, being such an admirer of Sostratus and a stickler for the Egyptian mystery school's technique of learning by experience, he would have you discover the truth first-hand. To prove yourself worthy and to fully understand the concepts, you must solve the puzzle and find the treasure on your own." Montross stepped closer, carefully. "So, have you done it?"

Alexander slowly shook his head.

"Not lying to me, are you, boy? Worried that I'd threaten you, or your mom, to force you to let me in?"

"Not lying. I don't know the way in, not yet."

"I believe you." Montross closed the sketchpad, tossed it aside casually, then pointed to the door. "Move aside, please."

"No."

"Just a step to your left, that's all. I'm not stupid enough to try to open the door yet, but I need to confirm what letters lie under your feet."

Alexander glared at him for another long moment, then shuffled sideways to let Montross lean in and look.

"Ah, as I thought."

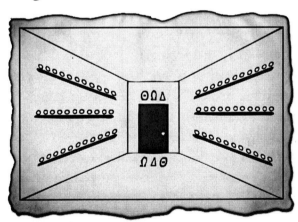

He studied the letters on the floor, and then again over the door. "So, in the Above we have the Greek letters: Theta, Omega, and Delta. And Below by your feet, reading again left to right, we have Omega, Delta, Theta."

"You won't figure it out," Alexander said.

Montross only smiled, then walked to the shelves running the whole twenty-foot length of the left side of the room. He glanced over his shoulder at the opposite wall, and the three identical shelves. "I've already figured it out, kid."

He touched the mahogany tracks, more like frames around a series of peg holes bored into the wall. "Three to a side. Each one with eleven peg holes. And there's a rounded wooden pin inserted, randomly it appears, in one of the holes on each shelf."

Alexander made a sound like a laugh.

"What?" Montross glared at him.

"Get it wrong and there are no second chances."

"Really? Your dad would be that ruthless? Kill his own son if he made the wrong choice?"

Alexander shivered again. "He said I would know when I figured it out. And if I didn't know for sure, I should never try it. No hunches or guesses."

"I see. Well, then,"—Montross smiled—"I'd better get this right, for both our sakes." He touched the peg on the top row, grasped it, and pulled it out sharply. Alexander winced, then they both looked at each other and smiled.

"Nothing's going to happen yet, right?" Montross asked. "Not until I set everything in position. Put all the pegs where I want them, and then try the door. At that point, either it opens ..."

"Or," said Alexander, "we both get squished."

"Squished?" He looked up at the ceiling, then the cracks along the walls. He cocked his head. "What's he got up there? A trap ceiling? Something to crush the hapless intruders? Or do the walls close in like that garbage compactor in the first *Star Wars*?"

"It was actually *Episode Four*," Alexander corrected.

"First for me," Xavier said. "So, how do you know there aren't hidden blades that might come out and slice us to pieces?"

"I don't know."

"How about fire? A release of natural gas and a spark? And after the inferno your mom can come down here and sweep up our ashes?"

Alexander grimaced. "I don't know, but I've dreamed of stuff like that."

"Have you now?"

"Traps just like that taking care of people like you."

"And what kind of person am I, Alexander?"

Without pause he said, "A thief."

Montross smiled. "You know, your Uncle Robert came here with me. Is he a thief, too?"

"I don't believe he's really with you, but I guess he is if he came to take something that doesn't belong to him."

"He did, and let this be an early life lesson for you, kid. Some people will do anything for power. Anything. And the kind of power promised by that artifact in there, it can make friends turn against friends, family against family. You just can't trust anyone. Can't trust your mom and dad, can't trust them even to come home and see you again after a night out. Can't trust the world, can't trust God or Fate or anything. The only thing you can trust are your visions, and sometimes not even those, not until you're really sure your head's not fu—" He smiled, catching himself. "Your head's not playing games with you."

"What are you talking about?" He looked to the stairs at the other end of the room, and thought he might be able to make it if he burst into a run, sprinting with Dash-like speed, but then he was struck with the thought that if he left, the treasure would be defenseless.

He was its protector. While it was true he hadn't quite figured it all out, he had spent more time down here in his short life than anyone else had. He was closest to it, and sometimes he felt that just by being outside of the entrance, in this testing room, he could feel its power. Feel it calling to him, feel it changing him. Making him stronger. And he could be more patient, since he knew it was there, his birthright.

"Never mind, kid. We're going in. Sorry to cut short your lesson and interfere with your dad's teaching plan, but I'm going to cheat and give you the answer." He started pulling out pegs and resetting them. Alexander tried to look around his broad shoulders to see where he was inserting the pegs, to see if it made any sense.

"What have you figured out so far, my boy?" Montross said after placing the third peg in a new position on the lower shelf.

"I learned that I'm not to share what I've learned with thieves."

"Very good," Montross said, shaking his head. "But I'm guessing you at least understand the basic concepts of alchemy, one of the key tenets which is 'As Above—'"

"'—so Below," Alexander whispered, completing the mantra he had learned years ago.

"Correct. All that mumbo-jumbo about recreating the heavenly aspects down on earth, in architecture as well as literature, reflecting the orientation and movements of the heavens onto the earth, but also doing the same thing spiritually. Becoming more than mortal, achieving the immortality promised by heaven."

Alexander swallowed. "So is that what you're here to steal? Immortality?"

Montross began work on the middle shelf. "You wouldn't understand my motives, Alexander. Not until you're a little—no, a lot older." He took one peg from the middle and moved it two holes to the right, then he stood back, nodding.

"My dad," Alexander whispered, "did you hurt him?"

Montross turned, regarding the boy quietly. "Did you see something?"

His eyes filling with emotion, Alexander nodded. "Under the ice."

Montross turned away, lowering his head. "I think he'll be okay. Sorry, but I needed the Morpheus Initiative out of the way, preoccupied. Needed their focus elsewhere, so they wouldn't be tipped off about this."

"There was a woman," Alexander said. "She's scary."

"God, kid, you're good. Maybe you're more like me than I thought."

Alexander withered under the man's gaze. He felt like he was being analyzed by a crocodile looking for a hint of fear, or just the juiciest area to bite first.

Montross said, "I saw my parents killed before it even happened. It did wonders for me, let me tell you. That kind of freedom, at such a young age. I spent so many years believing that what I saw, what I drew, could have the power to kill. That it was my fault."

"But that's not what it does. You're just seeing the future."

"I know. But when I was your age, I saw the world a little differently. Thought I was so much more." Montross looked down at his empty hands, and Alexander wondered if the thief imagined himself holding some scepter of kingship or a torch of knowledge. Whatever it was, Alexander didn't care.

"Are you going to kill me and Mom?"

Montross turned to him and sighed. "Listen, I'm not a killer, not normally. That's why for those times where it's necessary, I use someone like that woman you saw, like Nina. But no, you can help me. You and your mom will be having pie and ice cream in no time, waiting for your daddy to come home. Just a nice happy family again"—he bent to the lowest shelf, took out a peg and moved it all the way to the left— "minus one Emerald Tablet, of course."

Up at the farmhouse, Lydia sat at the kitchen table, the two mercenary types standing at the door, hands on their guns, while Robert made another pot of coffee.

"Robert," she whispered. "It's not too late. Call this off. Send these men out of here before someone gets hurt."

"I've searched too long for that tablet, given up so much. We both have."

"I know, but if Caleb does have it, he only has our best interests at heart. And, knowing him, he's probably rigged the lighthouse basement with some god-awful traps, and heaven help you if Alexander is down there when they go off."

"Montross has it figured out. Don't worry, I trust him."

"Like I trusted my husband?" Lydia shook her head. "Robert, this artifact is too powerful. It makes liars out of everyone. How do you know he won't just turn around and kill us all once he's found it?"

"He won't."

"He could be just like Waxman. Have you thought of that?"

"I have, and he won't. Besides," Robert patted his side where Lydia could see the outline a gun strapped under his heavy sweater in a shoulder harness. His face darkened and his eyes tinted with a heady sense of power she had never seen in him before. "We Keepers have our defenses."

Lydia shook her head, eyeing the two guards. "This is insane. And my son—your nephew—might be down there."

Robert smiled. "Something tells me Alexander can take care of himself just fine."

"I don't understand," said Alexander, a little braver now that he didn't feel like his life was in immediate danger. "I felt like I was close, but couldn't figure it out. How do the shelves relate to the 'As Above, So Below' thing?"

"You'll see."

"I could get it if there were just two shelves—a top and bottom, above and below, but the middle one messes everything up."

"Because you're not seeing the full picture."

"But the above and below puzzle at the door, it doesn't make sense.

The letters don't match. They're not mirror images, and it's not even like the lower one is the reverse of the top. The letters don't move, they're not on blocks, you can't—"

"Just settle down, kid." Montross worked faster now, rearranging pegs, moving from top to bottom, then to the middle, setting them into different holes. Occasionally glancing back to the other side.

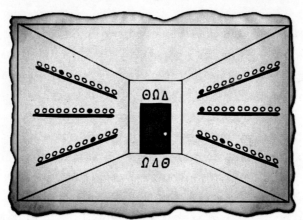

"Why are you—Oh! Wait." Alexander looked at the left wall, then back to the right. Then back to the door, pointing to the letters. He blinked, the room's colors shifted, and for a moment, he saw it. In his mind he saw lines of light stretching from the letters to the shelves: the above left letter, Theta, with a line angled down, concurrently with the bottom shelf on the right wall; the above right letter, Delta, highlighting a trail to the bottom shelf on the left wall. Then the lower letters doing the reverse.

"But what about the ones in the center?"

Montross turned to him, smiling. "Ah, welcome aboard. You're close now. So close. See, isn't it great figuring things out intuitively?" He set the last peg in place. "Course, it helps if you can cheat. Although, eight years of trying to remote view this thing I'd hardly call an easy cheat."

"But the middle ones!" Forgetting all about the danger, Alexander ran to Montross. "I get it. Above and Below *are*maintained, but in the whole system, the whole room, not just the letters at the door. The Delta letter, top right, lines up with the bottom left shelf, so that's why you put the peg in the ... Hold on! The seventh hole?"

"Egyptian, boy. Think like an Egyptian. They wrote—"

"Right to left!" Alexander smacked his own head. "I would've gotten myself killed."

"You can thank me later."

"It's the fourth letter in the Greek alphabet, so the peg goes in the fourth hole from the right." Alexander moved closer, looking in the dim light. "And the top shelf on the left, matches up with the letter Theta on the right-most letter on the floor. The eighth letter in the alphabet, so you've got it." He counted off the peg holes. "Eight holes from the right."

"Yeah, okay, you've got it, kid. And I did the same on the right wall. Omega for the first hole and Theta again for the eighth." Montross approached the door, smoothing his sweaty hands on his pants as he reached for the great bronze handle.

"But the center ones, I don't understand those. Omega on the top ... Why'd you match that up to the right wall, and Delta went to the left? I don't see any signs, anything that could—

Montross stopped, hand inches from the door.

"Oh no," Alexander said, looking at the back of Montross's head. "You don't know, do you?"

"You should go back up the stairs, Alexander. In case I'm wrong."

"You guessed?"

Montross gave him a steady look. "I guessed." He turned his head slightly just as his hand settled on the handle. "I spent months trying to view which way was correct, but I never saw it, never asked the right questions, maybe. But what I do know is that I saw myself—visions of myself—after this moment. So I know, I just know whatever I choose, it won't get me killed."

Alexander frowned, taking a step back. "That's a little sketchy. Thought you said not to trust Fate, or your visions."

"Touché. Call it a hunch, then. I trust those. But as I said, get on upstairs if you don't believe me and don't want to risk being squished flat or sliced into cubes. But I'm going in or dying a horrible death, with or without you."

Alexander frowned, looking again at the letters above the door, then at the position of the pegs. He sighed, then stepped closer, right behind Montross.

"So you believe me?"

"It was a good hunch," Alexander said, pointing. "The only one where you wind up with both Deltas on one side and both Omegas on the other. So if you orient the room on its side instead, you'd have the same arrangement. One Theta on top and bottom, and then two like symbols. It's the only way that works."

Montross smiled and rubbed his hands together. "See, you figured it out after all. Now, let's go. Do you want to do the honors, or shall I?"

5.

"No broken bones, just two sprained ribs and some nasty bruises. And some frostbite on your neck and fingers." The medic, a middle-aged woman whose skin seemed far too tan to be in this climate, looked him over again, shaking her head. "Lucky."

"Yeah," Caleb said, holding his side. "What do they say, better to be lucky than smart? I should have seen this, should have known it was a trap."

"How could you?" the medic asked, and Phoebe, standing beside her brother, coughed into her hand. "Just trust us, he should have seen it."

"We all should have," Orlando Natch said. "And I'm a bonehead for missing it. Got too damn excited about a match on the freakin' head. Rookie mistake that almost got us killed. Sorry boss."

"It's not your fault," Caleb said. "And I'm not your boss." Then, lower, "Nina. She's alive."

"I know," Phoebe said. "Seems like a nasty bitch. Had it in for you." She gave him a sly look. "What, did you sleep with her and not call her back?"

Orlando choked on a sip of hot chocolate. The medic raised her hands. "Sounds like a family moment. I've got a report to make, and my boss will want to debrief you before you leave, especially about Colonel Hiltmeyer's actions."

"Have you been able to contact him?" Phoebe asked.

"No, nothing." She looked down. "Apparently he's gone rogue. And again, I'm sorry."

"Got to get back home. Fast. And," Caleb added to the departing medic, "we need a phone. Please." He turned to meet Phoebe's look of concern. "Alexander and Lydia are in danger. This was all a diversion. They're going for the tablet."

Montross had a moment of fear as something hissed and huge metal bolts pulled backwards from holding the great silver vault door in place. The door opened. Reflexively, he held back an arm to shield Alexander in case something deadly came flying out of the darkness. *Shame*, he thought, *actually starting to like the kid.*

A moment later, the door opened all the way. Motionless now, Montross took a deep breath. "Inside," he whispered, nudging the boy forward into the darkness that glimmered as oil lamps around a circular room ignited, triggered by the door's opening.

"You first," Alexander said, trying to twist away but held fast. He stumbled forward into the vault—at last! He was finally here, inside after all that time, wondering and dreaming about it. Reading, studying, listening to his father's stories.

He was here.

But then he froze, staring first at the beautiful zodiac images painted on the ceiling, and then at the lone pedestal basking in the glow of four lamps, and the single object resting at its apex:

The Emerald Tablet.

"There's a note beside it," Alexander said, his voice cracking.

"A note?" Montross took another step in, hesitantly still, as if expecting a rack of stainless steel, poisoned-tip spikes to come plunging down through the ceiling and skewer him at any moment. "I didn't see a note."

"Maybe," said Alexander, picking up the loose-leaf piece of white paper with a jagged left edge, "Dad only left it for me recently."

"What does it say?" He glanced at the paper, frowned, then checked out the ceiling. "Looks Greek to me."

"It is Greek." Alexander read the words and translated to himself: *Son, this is your legacy now, and that means it's yours to protect. If you've been forced here against your will, and if you have the chance, tap the pedestal twice, and then …*

He lowered the paper, dropped it, then inched his fingers toward the wooden outer frame. In another second, Montross had his back to him and Alexander seized the opportunity. He pressed the pedestal once, then again, and heard a *click*. And then he did just what the note told him to:

He ran.

Bolted straight for the door—

—just as another door, a door made of vertical steel bars, came grinding out of a slot in the ceiling, crashing down.

Alexander dropped and rolled under it into the sub-basement. The grate slammed onto the concrete floor with a force that echoed in his ears like a thunderclap.

He turned, about to try to push the outer vault door shut, when he saw Montross standing there, gripping the bars like a prisoner in a cell.

"Caught you," Alexander said triumphantly.

Montross released the bars and stepped back as the vault door drifted nearly shut. Breathing deeply, calming himself, he turned and scrutinized the room, seeing now the grate opening in the ceiling, the notches he should have noticed in his visions.

The boy continued talking through the gap in the outer door. "Guess you didn't see that coming, did you?"

Montross stopped, lowered his head and gave the kid a stare, considering all this. Then he pointed through the crack. "There's my sketch book. Look at the last page." He turned back and approached the Emerald Tablet, saw it shimmering, giving off a surprising bit of heat, its strange symbols appearing not only three-dimensional, but *multidimensional*. Layers upon layers, hundreds of levels deep.

His head spun and his stomach felt tingly, a little nauseous.

"Oh crap," he heard the boy say, the words so distant. "You did draw it—this exact scene." Then he looked through the window, gathered his courage and yelled, "But you're still trapped in there!"

Montross returned, pressed his face against the thick glass porthole, let his lips pull away into a smile; and before heading back for the tablet, he said, loud enough for Alexander to hear:

"Oh, I'm not trapped."

6.

The air transport left within the hour, Caleb, Phoebe and Orlando sitting in the back with fifteen empty seats, painfully aware of the loss of two of their members, including one traitor. *Wiped out again*, Caleb thought, holding his head as if he could still hear their screams.

"I was responsible," he said somberly, staring out the window at the dawn rising over the vast horizon of blue ahead of them. "We need to bring them back, their bodies. Notify Ben's family, tell them... I don't know."

"It's not your fault," Phoebe said as Orlando worked on his iPad.

"I feel as callous as Waxman," Caleb said as he crossed his arms over his bruised ribs, "and as selfish. But we need to get back."

"We've called the police; they're on their way to our house."

"It's probably already too late."

"Hopefully you were seeing the future," offered Orlando.

Caleb shook his head. "My visions are usually firmly rooted in the past. Can we connect with the police?"

"Trying," said Orlando, using the VOIP voice connection on the laptop. "But they keep putting me on hold." He looked up, and his voice trembled. "I think they've got a problem."

The first officer barely got out of the cruiser before he was shot through the heart. The round had punched through the driver's side window as he was opening the door, and he'd only had a moment to guess where the gunshot had come from before he fell back, sliding along the car and down. His partner, instead of ducking and radioing for backup, pushed his way out the passenger side, and drew his weapon.

He turned, stood up and opened fire at the front of the house, having seen movement in that direction. His bullets strafed the door, shattered four windows and exploded an outdoor light. For a brief second he allowed himself a measure of satisfaction. *That got those bastards.*

But then the door kicked open and a man in a ski mask, limping on his right leg, swung an HK MP5 submachine gun in his direction and let loose a hail of metallic death.

Lydia hit the deck as soon as the first man aimed out the window. "Robert, down!" she yelled as a barrage of gunfire burst through the house. Glass shattered, wood screamed, and one of the masked guards spun around, half his face a bloody mess.

Cavalry's here, she thought, as Robert dropped beside her. Then she saw the other guard kick open the door and return fire.

"Robert." She shook her brother. "Come on, now's our chance. We can turn them in, and I promise, I'll confront Caleb, get him to release the tablet, we'll—"

Robert turned with her touch, rolled onto his back. Mouth open, blood bubbling up from his lips. A red stain spreading on his right breast.

"No ..." Lydia grabbed his tie, and not knowing what else to do, fit the edge in the bullet hole, trying to stop the blood flow. "No, no, no."

"Cops are dead," came the voice at the door. "But we have to move, we—"

Lydia looked up and saw the man staring at his dead partner. The MP5 wavered. And then Lydia saw the outline of the gun holstered against her brother's side. Before she knew what she was doing, she had the gun free and was standing, pointing it at the masked man.

He looked up from his partner, saw her and raised the gun, but she shot him first—a direct hit despite the recoil that knocked her back a yard. The man went down. His legs twitched once, twice, then lay still.

And Lydia gave her brother a parting glance before breaking her paralysis and rushing for the door. She had to get to Alexander.

It had been quiet for the better part of ten minutes, with Alexander waiting at the foot of the stairs. Keeping an eye on the vault door, ready to run if Montross had some explosives or something. *But what could he have? He didn't use anything to get in, and the only thing in there is the tablet!*

Alexander knew it had power, but thought it was merely something along the lines of knowledge, advanced stuff like the scrolls his mom and dad had found in the old Pharos vault. And surely it was nothing that a novice, someone who might not even know how to read that ancient language, could use to free himself.

A low mumbling sound came from *behind him*, on the stairs, and Alexander spun, expecting—hoping—to see his mom, or better yet, his father, triumphantly returning to save him and take care of this intruder, but instead he saw what at first he thought must be a ghost, a shimmering, flickering image of *him*, man trapped in the vault. But then the vision descended the stairs, into the glimmering light. The shadows peeled from his face, the fierce eyes almost glowing, making Alexander think of a movie he once saw part of on the Sci-Fi Channel, something about giant worms and desert nomads who all had spice-enhanced bright blue eyes.

Montross pointed to him and opened his mouth in a mock laugh.

"Impossible," Alexander whispered, and when he saw Montross reaching inside his coat pocket for a gun, he turned and raced back to the vault door, the only sanctuary. He cranked the knob, turned it and tugged back the door on its hydraulically fueled hinges. Behind him, Montross shuffled forward across the basement floor, eerily. Alexander paused for a moment, wondering why the effect seemed unreal, but then he saw that gun coming out, aiming at him, and he pushed forward through and under the bars, which were now rising. He had a glance only of the tablet, still in its resting place on the pedestal. That was enough and he ran for it.

He lunged for the pedestal, planning to slam his palm against it, knowing that would bring the bars crashing down again, stopping Montross before he could get in.

But an instant before his hand touched the surface it was caught, grabbed by Montross himself, who had been crouching behind the pedestal all along.

What!

Alexander jerked his head around to look back at the door, where no one stood. The bars were up, the door swung open, and the chamber beyond was empty.

"How ...?"

Montross smiled as he gripped Alexander's wrists, and then casually tossed him toward the corner farthest from the door. "A little trick I knew the Emerald Tablet could teach me. Ask your dad about it, about what your grandpa had learned to do."

"What are you talking about?"

Montross grabbed the tablet, hefted it as he lifted it off the pedestal. "Gotta run, sport. Thanks for your help, and hey, tell your dad if he makes it back—well, he'll know where to find me."

He took two steps, and suddenly, without the tablet's weight on it anymore, the pedestal began to drop.

"Uh oh," Alexander said, and Montross snapped his head around.

"Damn."

Lydia raced through the backyard, her bare feet pounding on the cold ground, then she burst through the lighthouse cellar toward the open door and the stairs. *Damn it, Caleb!* Why couldn't he have trusted her? And to present such a thing, a riddle for their son to solve? She had known about the vault door, but had never been inside because Caleb had told her it was just an old root cellar. It was the Keeper way, she thought grudgingly, but to leave her in the dark about what was really there, after all they'd been through, after what she'd proven to him?

Granted, things had never been the same after their reunion, after he'd learned she had faked her own death under the Pharos—partly to trigger Caleb's psychic powers, which often emerged only through psychological trauma, but also because she had become pregnant and couldn't let the impending birth of his son derail his mission. But even afterward, they had spent long months apart, raising Alexander like separated parents, and the rare times they were together, well, it was never like it had been before Alexandria.

She burst down the stairs, gun in hand, sure she would find the worst. And when she heard the tiny shrieks and felt the rumbling in the tower's foundation, she threw herself down five stairs at a time, stumbling finally upon the chamber floor, where she saw the vault door closing on Montross and her son.

"No!"

The chamber began to rumble, dust falling from the constellation-covered ceiling. The sconces flickered. And through two side vents on the ground, a light oily substance poured into the chamber.

Cursing the continued surprises, Montross lunged for the door, knowing it would be pointless. *At least the gate's not falling.*But the hydraulic door whirred and pulled shut as if some monstrous titan pushed on it from the other side. He was close enough to slide through, but hesitated, seeing the door accelerate and not wanting to be caught—and cut—in half. So he did the only thing he could think to do, the only thing that might save him.

Since he was closer to the door hinge than the aperture, he shoved the Emerald Tablet into the slot where the hinge was closing flush with the wall. The tablet's width fit perfectly, just sliding into place as the door ground into it.

Montross let go and backed up, almost slipping on the slick floor and the flood of oil. The door was still open a crack, large enough for the boy to get through, and maybe himself if he really sucked in his stomach, but he was hoping for something else.

Alexander whistled. He was at his side now, staring. "It's stopping the door."

"Unbreakable," Montross said, "whatever that substance is. I suggest we back up."

The hydraulics ground and hissed, the door sputtered and ground against the tablet. Then the upper hinges popped and the edge tore away from the frame. Steam burst from the twisted metal, then another series of bolts gave way and the whole wall shook.

The tablet, unsecured now, fell to the floor and plopped into the rising pool of oil.

Alexander lunged for it, but Montross was quicker and scooped it up with one hand. And then, watching his step, he trudged through the now knee-high flood. Out of the vault, he dragged Alexander behind him, both slipping as they stepped over pieces of the broken door.

Then, sensing movement outside, Montross stopped short.

Lydia was there, crouching, aiming a gun at him.

But from behind him, something sizzled and cracked. The sconces broke apart, and the flames dropped like leaves into the waiting pool of flammable oil.

Lydia was about to shout for Alexander to duck so she could get a clear shot at Montross, but she saw a river of some kind of liquid pooling out from behind the shattered door, rolling all the way to her feet. She saw the tablet in Montross's free hand, saw it shimmering hypnotically in that green-hued aura.

At last, I've seen it, actually seen it.

Then she smelled oil and saw flames spreading from the vault.

"Run!" she shouted as the next chamber exploded into a blinding fireball, which then burst out into the next, where Lydia stood. She had a glimpse of Montross scooping up her son and dodging to the side before the inferno roared straight into her.

She had a sudden flashback to another vault, standing before a far more ancient door ten years ago and deliberately setting off a trap that had turned the room into a storm of fire. A trap she had prepared for, a trap she had been able to avoid.

Then, she was ready.

Today, she was not.

"Mom!" she heard, and turned toward the sound before the fiery tsunami fell upon her. She tried to cry out to him, tried to say something meaningful in that moment. What could she possibly say in her final seconds to the son who would grow up, grow into a man and live his entire life without her?

Instead, she just clasped her burning hands together, lowered her head, and met her fate.

Caleb, now it's up to you.

Halfway across South America, cruising at top speed, Caleb woke with a scream that ripped Phoebe and Orlando from their trances. They stared at him wordlessly.

His mouth was dry as a desert, his lips cracked, splitting. "Did you see it?"

Phoebe reached for him. "No, I didn't get a clear view. The vault room, a fire ..."

"Yeah," Orlando said, "and some crazy red-haired dude, his clothes smoking, dragging a boy up the stairs."

"Lydia. I saw her consumed in the explosion. My trap." Caleb held his head. "What have I done?"

Phoebe was there, holding his hands. "Don't jump to any conclusions. Remember, this could be anything. A future glimpse, or maybe you were just seeing the past again. The Pharos trap and—"

Caleb met her gaze with pained and desperate eyes as he shook his head. "No, she's gone. I felt her reaching out to me. Begging for me to save Alexander."

"He's got him," Orlando said. "I was pretty sure about that."

"Alive?"

"I think so. But I had the sense that he was protected somehow, and maybe holding your boy, it saved him too?"

Caleb nodded slowly, and closed his eyes.

"He's got the tablet."

7.

Alexander watched from the prow of *Old Rusty* as Xavier Montross piloted the boat out into Sodus Bay and around the bend into Lake Ontario before the legion of police and fire engines descended upon his house. He watched as the dawn lifted out of the mist, the clouds swallowed up the roiling black smoke, and his lighthouse burned like a biblical pillar of flame.

Mom. He wanted to dive overboard, to brave the icy currents, to swim back to her, or to run over the water itself, back home, to join her in the cleansing fire. But then he thought of his father and his Aunt Phoebe.

They needed him.

He sensed footsteps behind him, a shadow over his shoulder. Silent, the winds stealing even his breath, Alexander wiped away tears that wouldn't stop flowing. He turned and tried to sound strong as he faced Montross. "What are you going to do with the tablet?"

A silhouette before the rising sun, Montross stood quietly a long time considering him. "The better question, I think, is what am I going to do with you?"

"Let me go?"

"That was my original plan, but now, I think you may be useful."

"Why? You gonna ransom me?"

"Not at all. I have plenty of money. But since I'm fairly certain your father survived, and since the regrettable incident in your lighthouse basement, I fear he will be after me with a vengeance now. So, it would be prudent to have some leverage."

"They're going to look for the boat," Alexander said. "My dad knows I know where the key is hidden, that you made me tell you how to start it. They'll come after us with helicopters, jets, satellite stuff. And of course they're psychic. There's nowhere to hide."

Montross walked back toward the cabin. "I'm not worried about that. I avoided their detection for years."

"How?"

He smiled to himself. "I've got something. Something I found after the Pharos incident. It's old. And it has the side benefit of blocking the user from certain prying eyes."

"I don't understand," Alexander said. "But—how old?"

"Never mind. In any case, we're not going to be on your precious boat much longer. Maybe this was my escape route all the time."

Montross cut the engines and they drifted into a choppy area of the lake. A moment of calm, and then suddenly Alexander had to hold on tight, feeling his stomach lurch. Just then, a big wave caught them and they rose higher than he could have imagined, then slammed back down.

Wiping spray from his face, Alexander looked over the side at the sleek black thing rising from the lake, the thing at first he took to be some fanciful lake monster. But then he saw the hump wasn't a hump at all, especially when a door in its base opened.

"Come on," Montross said. "Our sub is here."

Five hours after the rogue submarine and its small crew made its way into the Atlantic Ocean, Caleb, Phoebe and Orlando arrived at Sodus Point, jumped out of the car and passed through the crowd of neighbors, firemen and police. They walked to the edge of the caution tape, where they stared in silence at the smoldering wreckage of the house that had been in the Crowe family for four generations.

The lighthouse alone stood above the ruins, just its brick and concrete façade remaining, up to the scorched glass cupola. The intense heat had turned it black, and now it stood lording above the smoking ruins, like one of Sauron's towers.

"All gone," Caleb whispered, with Phoebe at his side as the police approached.

"Your books ..."

He held out his hand, seeing black body bags lying in one section of the lawn. "Wait, we need to be sure Alexander wasn't inside."

"He wasn't," she voiced hopefully.

"Mr. Crowe?" The first officer took off his hat. "I'm sorry to tell you this, but your wife ..."

The FBI agent arrived an hour later.

She found Caleb with a blackened book in his hands, the pages crumbling, the cover brittle. He held the book, and without a word remaining on its cover, he knew it was the first book he had written, *The Life and Times of the Alexandrian Library*. Not only that, it was the one he had signed for Lydia. The day they met, at his first book signing.

He trembled as the images rolled through his mind like a tender wave, picking up the shells and stones and sand with the flotsam of his memories. Not psychic visions, just clear, pure memories. *Their* memories, together. Like a kaleidoscopic light show, Lydia and her jade eyes, her scent of cinnamon perfume, cascaded through this vision.

"Caleb?"

At first, the word mingled with Lydia's voice, speaking close to his ear. *Caleb, goodbye.*

"Caleb Crowe?"

A tremor shook him and he let the book drop. He blinked, then glanced up into a woman's face. Short auburn hair, brown, not-unsympathetic eyes that were darting around a little too fast for him to follow. Grey suit. She held out a hand, helped him up, then pulled away. "Renée Wagner, FBI."

Caleb forced his eyes to focus. "FBI?"

She nodded curtly. "The police chief called us as soon as it was clear that in addition to arson and murder, this involves a kidnapping, with evidence that the perpetrators have fled to international waters. I'm so sorry for your loss, but time is of the essence. We really have to—"

"You know," Caleb said softly, looking at the brittle book at his feet, "there's a theory beloved by bibliophiles everywhere, one that suggests that the way to keep alive, to stave off death itself, is to constantly read. If you're reading many books at once, perpetually awaiting the resolution of cliffhanger moments, you'll be unable to rest until you know it all works out. All the mysteries, plot twists and turns, everything that keeps you guessing—and turning pages—all of that will keep you striving to live another day."

"That's interesting," Renée said, frowning. "But we really need to start a workup on who did this and what they want. We've got agents canvassing the vicinity, checking satellite photos, police logs, all concentrated on finding your son and his abductor."

Caleb looked away from her, toward the sea and the missing boat. "I'm pretty sure I know how we can find them."

Renée followed his line of sight. "Ah yes, the lightship. Sorry, but the Coast Guard found it deserted about thirty miles out. Seems they jumped ship. Any other ideas?"

Caleb shook his head. "No, I just need some time."

"Any idea who did this?" Renée looked around. "Or who the two other bodies we're still trying to identify are?"

He nodded. "Robert Gregory is one of them. My wife's brother."

She glanced at him suspiciously. "How do you know that?"

"I just do."

"I see. So, you're involved with parapsychology, research and remote viewing."

Caleb stared at her.

"Unusual line of work, Mr. Crowe, but I understand your group has had some successes. Located sunken wrecks. Salvage, treasure—"

"I know what you're getting at," he said. "Wondering if we had enemies."

"Or just jealous followers."

"Look, Agent Wagner—"

"Renée."

"—I'll help in any way I can, but please, give me and my sister some time. An hour maybe, at one of our neighbors' homes. We need to sort things out."

She looked at him steadily, and Caleb had the sense that red lights were lighting up inside her skeptical brain. Facts and figures, percentages. Wasn't the husband the perp in something like seventy percent of these cases? Right now she was probably running scenarios and creating a follow-up checklist: see how he and Lydia got along, whether he'd wanted full custody, what unsavory friends he might have contracted for arson and murder ...

"All right," she said at last. "I'll continue working the scene here, and I'll call on you in an hour."

"Thank you."

"But Mr. Crowe."

"Yeah?"

"Whatever you find out, promise you'll share with me."

"I'm not sure what you mean."

She smiled. "Let's just say, Caleb, that I'm open-minded about what you do here, and in what you're about to do."

He considered her for a long time. "I can't believe I'm going to say this, but would you like to watch?"

Phoebe and Orlando were off to the side, sitting on a bench overlooking the lake.

"I'm sorry about Lydia," Orlando said. His hand hovered around her shoulder uselessly, not sure whether to touch her or not. He had felt something close to a connection with Phoebe ever since interning for her class four years ago. Although only a few years older than he, she had a way of making him feel like an awkward teenager. "I know you were close."

She gave an attempt at a shrug, trying to appear stoic despite her tears. "Sometimes, she could be like a sister to me. When she wasn't being all Keeperly." Her voice cracked. "And Robert ... Are they sure it's him in there?"

"Two other men with Lydia. Everyone was so burned up, though. Still have to do the dental records."

"You really think he teamed up with Montross?"

"I gotta believe he never trusted Caleb, or me. Obsessed with the tablet twenty-four-seven."

Orlando scratched the back of his neck, then stood up. "So, the FBI. What's Caleb going to say to her?"

"Probably going to try to get rid of her," Phoebe said. "So we can track Alexander without all the dead weight. We should probably start. Come on, we can go to the Hurleys' house, use their basement. Kids down there have hundreds of pencils, markers and paper. We'll find him."

A minute later, when Caleb was alone again, they approached him. Phoebe gave him a hug, then backed away, searching his eyes. "You going to be all right? I can't believe she's gone."

"Not now," Caleb said, clenching his eyes shut, drawing Phoebe back into a crushing hug, not wanting to let go. "I've got to focus on Alexander. Nothing else until he's safe."

Sniffling, Phoebe nodded. "You told that agent about Xavier, didn't you?"

He nodded. "Thought I'd give them something to work on. Maybe they'll dig up a clue from another angle while we try it our way. She's got her people checking on Montross, but she wants to be in on our session."

"What!" Phoebe asked at once. "Are you nuts?"

"Well," Orlando said, "she is cute". He craned his neck to watch the agent as Phoebe glared at him.

Caleb cleared his throat. "We're going to need federal assistance with this. Travel arrangements, security, weapons. We're lucky we drew an agent with an open mind."

"Yeah," said Phoebe. "Lucky, or something else."

"We *are* talking about the government here," Orlando said in a suddenly refrained voice. "They screwed you over last time."

"We won't make the same mistake again," Caleb voiced.

"No we won't." Phoebe crossed her arms. "I'll RV her while you guys focus on Alexander."

"No," Orlando said. "You're closer to your nephew, you'll get a better hit. I'll spy on the FBI chick."

Phoebe glowered at him. "Perv."

"Anyway, I'm surprised that we haven't gotten a call."

"Oh crap." Caleb dug into his jacket pocket. "My phone battery was dying, so I turned it off."

"I'll call your voicemail," Orlando said, grabbing his phone before Phoebe got hers.

In a moment, Orlando handed over the phone and Caleb entered his code.

Caleb held up a hand, signaling to Agent Wagner. "It's him."

Renée walked over, and Caleb gave her the phone after he listened to the message. "You may want to have your people run that through their analytics. See if they can pinpoint a location."

"What did Xavier say?" Phoebe asked.

"He said I'd know where to meet him. But to come alone."

"Or he kills Alexander."

"Of course," said Orlando. "Got to be dramatic."

"Come where?" Renée asked.

"He said I'd remember, the place where he last told me I'd see him again."

"When was this?"

"In Alexandria. Twelve years ago. He backed out of a project we were working on. Then said he'd see me again." Caleb closed his eyes, remembering. "At the mausoleum."

"Mausoleum?" Renée asked. "In a cemetery somewhere?"

"I'm not sure," Caleb answered. "But I have a thought."

"Care to share?"

"After," he said, pointing to the neighbors' house. "Now we need to get to work."

The Hurleys brought coffee for Renée, green tea for Phoebe and Caleb, and located a can of Red Bull for Orlando. "Drink of champions and psychics everywhere," he proclaimed, grinning at Renée who just frowned and sipped at her coffee.

They were all seated around a ping pong table. The basement was furnished with a circular rug over the concrete floor, a dusty basketball game in the corner next to an equally dusty stair machine and a 20-inch TV.

"Now I'm not so sure about this," Renée said. She held up a pad of blank white paper and a pencil. "Really, I can just observe and check on my colleagues, see how the search is going for this Xavier Montross."

"They won't find him," Caleb said.

"We'll have a dossier on the guy in an hour, everything from his favorite TV shows to how often he wet the bed as a kid. We've got his picture at all the airports, borders, etc. Anything he does, down to the color of socks he wears, we'll know."

"That'll help," Orlando said, "if we ever get our laundry mixed up with this nut, but my guess is that if he doesn't want to be found, then the only chance of finding him is *ourway*."

"And," said Phoebe, "we tried to find him for years after he left our group. And sorry, but we had better tools than you, and we couldn't even get a glimpse. It's like he was a ghost."

"Or he had some help," said Caleb.

"What do you mean?" Renée asked.

"Never mind. It's just a thought. There may be things, or people, who are able to block what we can do, where we can see. I've heard anecdotal evidence about it, but I thought that it was more like an excuse for failure. But maybe there's something to it."

"Anyway," Phoebe cut in, "come on, Agent Wagner. Try it. You might have a knack for it. We've had successes with the most skeptical of volunteers."

Renée sipped her coffee. "I don't think I'll have any—"

"That's okay," Caleb said, his voice wracked with suffering and pain just below the surface. "It's fine if nothing happens. We normally work as a team, but our team, well, I'm sure you know all about what happened in Antarctica."

"I know what was on the report, but as far as exactly what the hell happened down there I have no idea. Forgive me for asking this bluntly, but what are you people caught up in?"

"Just research," Orlando said, hands raised defensively.

Caleb started to answer, but Renée was quicker. "And does 'just research' involve globe-trotting adventures into booby-trapped tombs, underwater shipwrecks and other Indiana-Jones-type shenanigans?"

Phoebe and Orlando grinned in spite of themselves and said at almost the same time: "Sometimes."

Twenty minutes later they were drawing. Caleb had given them instructions, what he felt were vague enough so as not to lead anybody, but also give enough direction to focus them on where he thought Xavier might be.

I hope I'm wrong, he thought, after having them visualize Alexander, where he was now, and where he was headed. To focus on the destination, a place with a tomb.

That was all. To say any more might influence the process too much. What he had given them was enough.

He trusted Orlando and Phoebe, the best of the Morpheus Initiative members, to come up with the right answer, to remote view their destination and confirm his thinking. But for himself, he would attempt a different visionary destination. If he could, if it was at all possible. He was going to focus on Xavier himself. On Montross, the man, the psychic. The FBI might have their methods, but Caleb needed something more direct.

He needed a first-hand experience, a psychic get-to-know-you of his adversary. His wife's murderer, his child's abductor.

He wanted to *see* the man he was going to kill.

Phoebe finished her sketch first, then stared at it before turning her attention to her brother. Caleb was in a meditative pose, hands on his knees, eyes closed, brow furrowed in frustration. Orlando was drawing on his iPad, shading in what looked like a pillared structure on a hill.

"I still get weirded out," she said, turning her sketch pad his way, "when we have the same damn visions."

"Copycat," Orlando said with a smirk.

Renée looked over from the other side of the table. "So, is this what it's like?"

"More or less," said Orlando. "Though usually we have a few more people here, and we can cross-reference details and see what elements get the most hits."

Renée turned her pad around. "See, I don't have any talent. I drew some kind of horse and buggy thing." On her pad was a crude sketch of two horses pulling a cart with two people inside. "Guess my mind was just wandering, but that's all I saw."

"Interesting," Phoebe noted. "You drew crowns on their heads."

"I knew it."

Phoebe looked up. Her brother's eyes were open, with failure written over his face. But he managed a smile as he looked over Renée's drawing. "She does have some talent."

Renée stood up, backing away, still looking at her horses. "What are you talking about? I—"

Suddenly her cell phone rang. "Hang on, just a second."

She put her ear to the iPhone. "Yeah, what do you got? Okay, I see. Hang on, I'll call you back, we may have something here that can confirm that."

She hung up. "NSA traced a coded satellite phone call from Antarctica shortly after the explosion at Fort Erickson. They couldn't get much after decoding the call, but they confirmed a man's voice—that of your very own Xavier Montross."

"Did they get anything else?" Phoebe asked.

"Only a name. He was telling someone where to meet." Renée looked at them steadily. "'St. Peter's' was all they got."

Caleb thought for a moment, nodding to himself. Then he pointed to Orlando. "We could do an online photo search match in various databases, comparing those drawings with other pictures, but it would take far too long. Adding the detail of the 'horse and cart' would help, but again, we don't have the time. Orlando, just go to good old *Wikipedia*."

"Cop-out," Orlando said as he opened the tablet and used the keyboard.

"Look up 'Mausoleum.'"

"Where is this going?" Renée asked, her face showing complete confusion.

Phoebe chuckled, shaking her head. "Don't worry, you get used to Caleb's roundabout way of getting us all to confirm what he already knows." She moved back, then whispered to Caleb, "What's wrong? Didn't you get anything?"

Keeping his voice low, he said, "I couldn't even bring about the start of anything. Something's wrong." His eyes were bloodshot, his face pale. Lowering his voice still further, he added, "I tried to see Xavier, went at it a couple different ways, with different questions, all focused. I should have seen something, but not a damn thing came up. Just a flickering green haze around a center of darkness."

Phoebe frowned. "Do you think you're being blocked? Maybe by the tablet?"

"Maybe, but I fear it's something worse."

"What's worse?"

"Remember when we were kids? Remember Dad? What happened after he was gone, after I thought maybe it was my fault we couldn't save him?"

"Yeah," Phoebe said. "Your visions, they didn't come again for years."

Caleb sighed. "I need to try again. With a different target, something besides Xavier. Something I should be able to see. If I can't,"—he met her stare, and she nearly cried seeing the loss, the guilt, so familiar, bubbling inside of his expression—"if I still can't, then it's her. It's Lydia. I killed her, and this is my penance."

"No, Caleb."

Orlando cleared his throat, interrupting and bringing them back to the moment. "Ah, this is what he's talking about." He turned the screen so the others could all crowd around and see it. "*Mausoleum*. The word derives from the tomb of King Mausolus, the Persian satrap of Caria, whose large tomb, completed in 350 BCE, was one of the Seven Wonders of the Ancient World. And there's a picture."

Renée bent forward to stare at it. "It's almost the same as what you've both drawn."

They looked at the photo Orlando just enlarged: a huge structure set on a hill overlooking a bayside city, with it had a pyramidal step structure on top of a larger base and two more tiers surrounded by immense white columns and statues.

"And," said Caleb, "check out the roof."

"A chariot," Renée whispered. "Four horses. Two people inside, wearing crowns."

"Mausolus and his queen, Artemesia," Caleb said. "He died early into his reign. And Artemesia, so in love and desperate to immortalize her husband, spared no expense for his tomb, bringing in the greatest architects and sculptors in all the world. It was a tourist attraction for centuries, but unfortunately, by the twelfth century, the tomb was destroyed, like the Pharos, in a series of earthquakes."

"Wonderfully tragic," said Phoebe. "So we've all drawn a tomb that no longer exists. Why? What does this have to do with some castle in Rome?"

"It's not in Italy," Caleb answered.

"Turkey," Orlando said, cutting him off, scrolling down the text. "Come on, let me do something useful here. It says here nothing's left of it except the foundation, in the town of Bodrum, Turkey, but—"

"—but there's a castle nearby," said Caleb, letting a smile form. "Built by the Knights Hospitaller in the fifteenth century."

"Construction started during the Crusades in 1402," Orlando clarified. "Knights from four different countries helped build this castle, using many of the blocks and pillars from our friend Mausolus's tomb. It wasn't finished until around 1480. And they called it the *Petroneum*." He looked up, eyes shining. "Or the Castle of St. Peter."

Caleb steeled his jaw, closed his eyes, and felt a tingle—a familiar stirring at the base of his spine, one that would often shoot upwards, triggering a flood of visions. But this time, it fizzled, leaving greenish sunspots in the corner of his eyes. He had to focus, had to keep trying, but not now. Now, he would have to rely on his sister and Orlando, and on the skills of the FBI. They had to find Alexander.

"That," he said, pointing to the castle on the screen, "is where he's taken my son."

8.

Alexander woke to a feeling of his ears popping. He sat up in his tiny bunk, the sole cot in a room no bigger than the old downstairs bathroom in his house. The dream had returned, smashing at the inside of his skull like a nightmare trying to get out. The smell of burnt hair and flesh, sulfur and death. *Mom...* He leapt out of bed, wobbled unsteadily on his feet, then went for the door.

Locked.

After a moment, he remembered the submarine. Being herded down the tight stairwell, his battered Nikes thumping along behind the shoes and boots of the other men ushering Xavier Montross down into the sub's metal belly. Two men had locked him in this room, after first giving him "something." Alexander didn't even consider that they might have drugged the glass of water they left for him, but within ten minutes of submerging, feeling queasy enough from the descent, he fell onto the cot and was fast asleep.

It felt like the craft was surfacing. He wished he had a porthole window, or access to the periscope, to see where he was. He got up, fought a dizzy spell, then tried the door. Still locked.

Again he thought of the *Incredibles.* If only he could be like Dash.

Just as he was thinking about creating a diversion to get the door open, like setting something on fire and tripping the alarms, then running out in a blaze of speed, something clicked and the door pulled outward.

A pretty, dark-skinned woman in a black suit stood there. She crossed her arms. Looked him up and down. "I guess you look like your father. Come on." She moved aside and motioned him out. "I've been sent to collect you."

Alexander blinked at her as if she were some kind of mirage. "Where are we?"

"Where we need to be. Now, move it."

Alexander stepped out into the night and immediately felt the difference: the humidity and the glare of the city streets, the boats twinkling in the bay, the lit-up stucco and red-tiled houses on the hills, and the blaring, techno-beat music from a nearby disco. But the imposing sight straight over his shoulder that made him turn and gasp was something out of a fairy tale book.

A castle.

Huge reinforced walls were lit with multi-colored lights that made it look like a model on a movie set. Three square towers were visible, equally bright, presiding over the rocky shore and the small armada of boats tethered to the piers.

Impressed with the sight of the medieval castle, Alexander almost didn't see Montross at the prow, a pack over his shoulder. He was dressed all in black, blending into the night, except for his exposed head of red hair.

"Ah," he said, "Nina and our little guest. How did you sleep, kid?"

Alexander felt his attention wavering back to the castle. "Bad dreams." Then he had a thought, a flicker of a memory that grew into something bigger. Something he remembered all of a sudden about his dreams. "A nightmare, about my mom dying. But you know all about what that's like, don't you?"

Montross flinched, and suddenly Nina's hand shot out and spun   Alexander around by the shoulder. She was kneeling now, her eyes swallowing his vision as if they were miniature black holes. "What did you see?"

Grimacing, trying to be strong and not cry out, Alexander wriggled in her grasp. *Bad idea*, he thought. *Should have kept that to myself.* "Just a wreck, a car crash." His eyes glazed over and suddenly he was there. "A woman ..."

... reaching for the man at the wheel, the man holding his chest and staring at her as if she had just wounded him.

"How did you keep this from me? You bitch. You little lying bitch."

And then he turns the wheel—hard—toward an oncoming truck, just as his eyes lose all emotion and the woman screams ...

Alexander rocked back to the moment, and now Xavier loomed over him. Scooped him up by the front of his shirt so he was dangling in the air.

"What did you see?" he screamed.

"Nothing." He cringed, biting his lip, withering under the intensity of Montross's stare.

Alexander dropped, fell back into Nina's grasp as Xavier lowered his hands, breathed deeply and continued staring. "Bring him."

"Are we going inside the castle?" Alexander asked, with a dose of hope.

Montross ignored him, turning to Nina. "Is everything set inside? Did you find what we need?"

She nodded, a smile curling at her lips.

Montross turned back to Alexander. "We've left a present in there for your father—that is, if he's heading here as I expect."

"We aren't going inside?" Alexander asked.

Montross straightened. "I'm sorry, we'll be going somewhere else. Somewhere far less hospitable."

9.

Inside the government jet, Phoebe, Caleb and Orlando sat with Renée and two other agents, both working their laptops. Orlando eyed them occasionally, with more than a hint of interest. Earlier, he had probed Renée's past and questioned her involvement here. The hits were vague, but the visions and impressions concrete enough. Definitely she was legit, but there was something else. Something murky at the corners of his sight. Something of interest and, perhaps, something she was hiding. He needed more time, and some peace and quiet.

Renée was analyzing the castle's layout on her laptop screen. "We can post agents at all the exits, and we've got four snipers covering all the angles and any blind spots they can't hit. Here, and on this chapel rooftop, on this hill, and at the minaret here." She looked up, took a breath. "So what do you think this guy wants? Money?"

Caleb shook his head. "Despite our treasure-hunting exploits, we really don't have that much in the way of money. No, the only true item of value I had Montross just stole. I can't imagine what else he wants from me. What did you turn up?"

She clicked a few keys, then read aloud: "Xavier Montross, Born in New Orleans, 1978. Parents killed in a car accident when he was six. Raised by a succession of foster parents." She looked up. "Seems he frequently wore out his welcome."

"Maybe," said Phoebe, "something he did, or drew, freaked them out."

"We can find out. Interview some of the foster parents. But it might take some time. Anyway, he joined the Marines in 1997. Served with

Special Ops, decorated in Iraq, then was discharged after refusing direct orders—orders which, ironically, got the rest of his unit killed in a helicopter training accident."

Caleb scratched his head. "So, he dodged another bullet there. He might have had a premonition of his death."

"Seems to be his specialty," Phoebe said.

"Then," continued Renée, "he was hand-picked to join *The Morpheus Initiative* in 2002 by—"

"George Waxman," Caleb said. "Who must have been alerted to his talents by his unusual behavior in the Corps. And then we know the rest, up until he disappeared in Alexandria."

Renée nodded. "That's all we've got. Except for his travel visas. Egypt, Lebanon, Turkey, Iran, Mexico. Don't know what he did or why he went to those places. And"—she shuffled some papers—"this is interesting. His image was just flagged as a possible match to an unresolved case of a break-in and murder at the Smithsonian Institute in Washington ten years ago."

Caleb perked up. "What did he get?"

Renée shook her head. "No details of a theft. At least, nothing the officials cared to elaborate on. Can you use your remote viewing, clairvoyance or whatever to find out?"

"Possibly, but it works best if we focus our efforts. We need to know what to look for, and it helps to ask ourselves the right questions."

"Then what are the right questions?"

"Well, let's think like Montross, get inside his head. What do we know?"

"That he swiped our tablet," Phoebe pointed out.

Killed my wife and kidnapped my son, Caleb thought. "Right, but why?"

"What is this tablet thing? What does it do?" Renée asked. Her voice cracked a little, and when Caleb's eyes darted to her she glanced away. *Hm.* Again, he wondered whether she was hiding something.

He shook away the thought. Too much paranoia lately, after the elaborate trick in the Antarctic. He was leaping at shadows, certain they all contained monsters. But still, his impotence at being able to RV her past was frustrating.

The others waited for Caleb to decide whether or not to tell her. "You won't believe it," he said finally, "but you'll have to trust me that mere rumors of its powers were enough to inspire great quests and conquests to seek it throughout the ages. And a dedicated brotherhood was created to hide it so it wouldn't fall into the wrong hands."

"What powers are we talking here?"

"Thoth, the Egyptian god, or enhanced man—the jury's still out on that one—was believed to have created the tablet, and inscribed on it certain spells. Ancient knowledge. We're not entirely sure what that knowledge was, but by simply reading it initiates could gain access to powers and abilities."

Orlando looked up, grinning. "Abilities that would make what we're doing here look like the difference between the Space Invaders and Halo 3."

Phoebe rolled her eyes.

"There are all kinds of stories," Caleb continued, "about how the early master magicians, people around the time of Noah and the great Pharaohs, had such powers. The ability to live for centuries, cure diseases, be in many places at once. And they could foretell the future, like the coming of the Great Flood."

"My Bible's a little rusty," Renée said, "but even my four-year-old niece knows that God warned Noah directly, before He wiped out everybody else on the planet."

Phoebe cleared her throat, eager to get in on the discussion. "Well, the theory here goes that the language used by Noah to speak to God was more *indirect*. Noah was using these kinds of powers, abilities like prophecy, clairvoyance. These were the same as 'talking to God.'"

Renée nodded. "So, Noah *saw* what was coming."

"And," said Caleb, "these learned men, people with abilities, wrote down their knowledge and stored it away in safe locations."

"But you found this tablet," Renée said, staring at Phoebe, Orlando and Caleb in turn, as if half-expecting them to pull off their outer garments to reveal superhero costumes underneath. "Have you used it?"

"Nope," said Phoebe, glancing first at her brother for approval. "But not from lack of effort. Actually, we haven't quite been able to read it."

"The language," Caleb admitted, "is a little mind-blowing. It's not like anything ever seen before. I've tried cross-referencing it for years, sent partial scripts to etymologists, but so far, nothing."

Phoebe smiled. "It also hurts to look at the letters. They're somehow multi-dimensional. It's the only word I can use. It's kind of like watching a 3D movie without the glasses, and in Chinese subtitles. After you've been drinking."

"Or smoking weed," Orlando said, then wiped the silly grim from his face, glancing at the agents.

Renée frowned at him. "So you can't translate it, but Montross believes he can?"

Caleb clasped his hands together, held them in front of his face. "There's a theory. Yes, I know, another one. One we've been pursuing during our RV sessions."

"The Books of Thoth," Phoebe said. "Other writings. We're not sure if they're scrolls or tablets, pillars, or what, but supposedly after Thoth created the Emerald Tablet, his followers deciphered it and wrote the translation of all that knowledge."

"Theoretically," Orlando said, "we only need to find one of those to get what we need."

"A Rosetta Stone," Caleb finished. "A translation of just a part of the Emerald Tablet, in any language, and we can use that as a cipher to decode the rest."

Renée rubbed her eyes. "So, these books or whatever, where are they supposed to be?"

"Lots of theories there too," said Caleb. "The most common being that they're kept together in a sealed, unbreakable box in the Hall of Records."

"In Washington?" Renée asked, hopeful.

"No, the Hall of Records referred to was a mythical storehouse of ancient wisdom, much like the library of Alexandria. Legends relate several possible locations, the most credible being that it's under the Giza Plateau, beneath the Great Pyramid or the Sphinx."

"Ah," said Renée, shaking her head. "Of course."

Caleb felt sorry for her, knowing the agent must be way out of her element now. "There have been studies of the ground in that area, sonar and satellite radar images showing potential pockets, caverns and tunnels under both the Sphinx and the Pyramid complex. The psychic Edgar Cayce predicted a chamber would be found below the Sphinx, and Herodotus relates tales about a staircase leading down between the paws, down to a great door that led into a labyrinth of serpentine passages and chambers. And somewhere down there is this lockbox containing the books. But," Caleb pointed out, "that's not what concerns us now. Because now, what I think Xavier Montross might be after, are the *keys*to that box."

"The keys?" Renée frowned. "Plural? How many are there?"

"Three, according to the legends. Spread out across the earth at ancient sites, or buried with the dead rulers who might have had the means to construct elaborately defended resting places. Hidden, some maintain, by men related to the ancient order of Thoth. Followers like Noah and Ziusudra and all the rest."

"Magicians and prophets?" Renée noted.

"Psychics," Phoebe whispered.

Renée stood and started pacing, gripping her cell phone like a pointer. The plane dipped and she reached for a chair to steady herself. "So Montross broke into your lighthouse, stole this Emerald Tablet which, if I hear you right, is likely an Egyptian archaeological artifact, and its theft is a serious breach of international law, but never mind that now. Montross then kidnapped your son and is now off seeking three legendary keys, all of which he'll need in order to gain access to a chamber under the Sphinx and open a box which contains a translation of the text?"

Caleb shrugged. "Sounds about right. I know it's less than convincing, but that's the only rationale I've got right now."

"So why St. Peter's?"

"The Mausoleum," Phoebe said. "He must've RV'd the keys, found that one might have been hidden there. Mausolus must have found one, recognized it as something special, and Artemesia had it entombed with him in his mausoleum."

"It fits," Caleb said, "with the tenet of alchemy which maintains that secrets are best hidden 'in plain sight.' The Mausoleum was a huge, ostentatious structure. Alexander the Great would have been well aware of it, as Mausolus was a contemporary, and Alexander went on to conquer Halicarnassus a decade later. My guess is wherever the key was, Alexander couldn't find it. But he posted guards to keep the mausoleum safe from trespassers before putting his best philosophers to work at analyzing its construction to find potential secret compartments."

Renée rubbed her eyes. "So what about the other locations?"

Caleb sighed. "I didn't know about Mausolus until now, but I believe one of the keys may have been at the tomb of another charismatic and powerful leader. Cyrus the Great, the first great conqueror. He was a Persian in the sixth century BCE who created the largest empire the world had ever seen, a feat unrivaled until Alexander came along. And what's more, we know that two centuries after Cyrus's death, Alexander invaded Persia, and in what is now modern-day Iran he found and entered Cyrus's tomb, looking for something in particular."

"Did he find it?" Renée asked.

"Well, we're not entirely sure what he found." Caleb took a sip of tea, blowing at the smoke first. "We tried to RV the event and got a lot of jumbled images, but nothing definitive came out of those sessions." He thought back to the candle-lit room at home, the ten people madly scribbling on their pads, day after day, trying to see. What had become of Cyrus's possessions? People had drawn things ranging from snow-capped peaks to marvelous palaces to a remote desert landscape and a cavern underground, but nothing consistent.

Phoebe leaned in. "We've been going on the theory that Alexander the Great found Cyrus's key, and that maybe he himself discovered, or was handed, another key in the desert at Sais, at the Egyptian oracle where he was heralded as king, given the mandate of Heaven, and promised a marvelous destiny."

Caleb continued. "So Alexander had two of the three keys, at least, and was likely searching for the third. We believe he died before finding it and achieving that destiny, although history still reveres him as one of the greatest rulers of the world, and responsible for the spread of democracy and knowledge. He was most likely buried with those two keys, and we may need to focus our efforts to find his body to verify that, but more likely we weren't asking the right questions to define our search. I'm starting to think that maybe someone took the keys from his tomb before it was hidden."

"But we doubt anyone has managed to collect all three," Phoebe said, "since we're pretty sure the lockbox is still unopened."

Caleb put down his cup. "It's more likely that someone else, someone very powerful, must have found and dug up Alexander. And now those keys are hidden somewhere else. But as for the third key, we've tried remote viewing it before, but only came up with vague, unreferenced and uncorrelated images—which made us go all the way back and try to view the creation of the Emerald Tablet again. Who actually created it and where."

"And what did you see at those sessions?" Renée asked.

"Not much."

"Except for the head," Orlando pointed out. "The damn head."

"The what?" Renée asked.

Caleb stretched out his legs. "It was just something else we'd been drawing a lot, the only consistent image our members came up with in connection to questions about the origin and meaning of the Emerald Tablet. Don't know what it means yet, but because of a spy in our group, Montross knew about it, and used it to get us as far away as possible so he could steal the Emerald Tablet."

"But now," said Renée, "you think one of these keys is at the Mausoleum, or this castle now in Bodrum?"

"Almost sure of it," Caleb said. "If for no other reason than that Montross is heading there."

The plane lurched, then started on a descent.

"Well," said Renée, "I guess we're about to find out."

10.

BODRUM, TURKEY, 8:12 AM.

Caleb and Renée entered Bodrum Castle through the museum's main entrance, pushing past a line of caution tape.

"Police and museum officials are cooperating," Renée said. "Giving us two hours. They're telling the tourists and workers that the site is undergoing a minor repair and will reopen shortly. So we've got to get in and out quickly."

Caleb considered the massive medieval architecture, the conglomeration of turrets and courtyards, crenellated walls, the statues and heraldry marking the approach.

He whistled, touching a few eroded birdlike figurines as they passed under the gate and into the main courtyard. Here and there he saw larger granite blocks, some tinted green, denoting their volcanic origin. "Stones from the Mausoleum," he whispered, then stopped before the main hallway. "Okay, I go in alone from here."

"But there's no one inside," Renée said. "Turkish police have searched the whole place, and we've got agents on boats in the harbor, snipers where we talked—"

"Alone," he said again. "I think you're right. He's not here, but he could still be watching. Seeing if I disobey orders. I don't want to risk anything happening to Alexander." It had occurred to him, of course, that this could be a trap, another chance to kill him after failing in Antarctica. Maybe that was all this was. Xavier and Nina wanted him dead the Morpheus Initiative gone.

But why? Just so they wouldn't stand in Xavier's way? See his plans, cut him off and recapture the tablet? Caleb held his head. It was too much, like trying to understand a time travel paradox. It was impossible to outsmart someone who could see the future, someone who could change the rules during the middle of the game.

"I'll see you soon," he said to Renée, patting his cell phone. "We're just a phone call away."

"Be careful," she said, touching his arm for just a moment before pulling back, and then he was gone, heading off into the darkness toward the first gallery.

The castle had been converted to a museum for maritime archaeology, showcasing some of the region's magnificent relics recovered from a number of major shipwrecks and dredged from the sea floor. Byzantine artifacts, earthen jars, jewelry, and in one room-sized glass case, a reconstructed merchant ship from the twelfth century BCE. Caleb lingered in the first dimly lit gallery, marveling at the treasures plucked from Neptune's grasp and stored here for years, at a site partially built from the stones of the greatest tomb in the ancient world.

He wished he still had his ability so he could RV some of these pieces to get a glimpse into the ancient past and see what sort of tragedies had left these relics at the bottom of the sea. But he pressed on, heading toward the section of reliefs that the curator told him were taken directly from the Mausoleum's ruins in the fifteenth century.

As he descended another set of stairs, he looked out over a lush garden, and further back he saw a minaret atop a Moslem shrine. He had a moment of stillness, of clarity. He thought of Phoebe and Orlando and could almost see out to the section of Bodrum a half mile away where they must be exploring the ancient foundations of the Mausoleum, looking for visions. And clues.

He touched the walls, hoping to get a glimpse into the past, anything to part the veil and burst through the blockage erected by his consuming guilt.

But nothing came, nothing but the empty silence of the dead.

Phoebe and Orlando were at the site, an open hillside, with flowering shrubs and wild grass peeking out from under the fragments of rounded columns and rows of misshapen blocks layered out over the land as they might have been positioned eight hundred years ago, before the devastating earthquakes. All around the site, apartment buildings scaled the hills like ungainly climbers tethered together by a haphazard network of telephone poles and wires. The blaring of horns and creaking of buses sounded sporadically, and the scent of juniper mixed with exhaust fumes.

Phoebe let her hand linger on the stones in passing, watching Orlando do the same. "Well," she said, taking a seat cross-legged in the middle of a set of broken columns. Pulling out a pad of paper, she smiled as Orlando took out his iPad and powered it up. "Let's see what we can see."

Two minutes later she dropped into a trance, back through the centuries, and opened her eyes to a similar hillside ...

... except for the half-finished monolithic construction, the hundreds of workers—carpenters, sculptors, draftsmen and artisans—all laboring on the Mausoleum.

Surveying the work from her porch on a raised platform stands a regal woman with olive skin and melancholy eyes. "How long?" she asks the two men working at a table, studying unrolled scrolls depicting the graphical representations and measurements for the construction, including the statues, the columns and the roof. She points to one robed man, the closest. "Satyros?"

"Another year, My Queen. The structure may be finished by the Saturnalia, but the sculptors will still be finishing their work. So many statues, the reliefs of the Amazon frieze alone will take years. But rest assured, Leochares will get the job done. And the bas-reliefs presenting the battle of the Centaurs—"

"There will be no deviation from my husband's wishes. Especially regarding the depiction of the centaurs. Or its construction."

The other man turns around. His eyes look her over. "How is your health, Lady Artemesia?"

"Not your concern," she responds with a wave, leaning over suddenly and suppressing a cough. "I was strong enough to repel the Rhodians in their attempt to capture Halicarnassus. I will be well enough to see this project finished." She let her gaze linger on the massive columns, the second tier

poised and prepared for the lifting of the roof and the immense golden chariot that would in time house their statues.

"Soon, My King. Soon, we'll be together again."

Phoebe blinked and slowly let her consciousness return to the shining sunlit present where mundane elements pricked at her senses. The barking of a dog, the blast of a cab's horn, the ticking of Orlando's fingers on his iPad. She opened her mouth to call out to him, but saw his eyes, white, the pupils lolling back in his head. His fingers moving rapidly while his lips moved, whispering something unheard.

"Orlando?"

Overcome by need and immediacy, the fullness of the experience nearly knocked him over. No matter how many times Orlando had experienced this, it always took his breath away with its suddenness. Its raw power, colliding with his psyche, at the same instance gently gliding over his perceptions... .

In light chain mail, colorful heraldic symbols blazing on their chests, the knights rise up in a victorious cheer. Under the English tower named the Lion, the men roar and taunt the fleeing soldiers of Sultan Mehmed II.

Cannons smoke and men lean against the walls, dropping their crossbows. Flags wave from the other towers, each one constructed in its own style, and the knights from Italy, Spain, France and Germany cheer each other in repelling this latest offensive. Below, the passages twisting through narrow turns and successfully defended gates bear witness to the strength of this castle's design. The bodies of the invaders litter courtyards and lie in arrow-pierced piles on the steps.

The captain surveys the fortifications, then eyes the wounded forces retreating into the descending twilight. "They will return," he says to his men, then points ahead to the smoking holes blown through sections of the walls by the enemy cannon.

"We must thicken the walls facing the mainland. Take a team in the morning. Gather more stones from the Mausoleum."

Another flash, and Orlando reeled, reaching out and scraping the flesh of his palm against a greenish-hued stone... .

A different commander, with a Fleur-de-lis on his tunic, stands atop the tallest tower. He speaks in French, but the words are understood through some other means. "Suleiman will try again, and the walls are weakening. Gather more blocks from the ancient site and put them to use."

"There are not many stones left, Grand Master," says a wide-eyed youth, a knight with blood spatters on his face. "But what of the statues and the reliefs? There are still more that have not been smashed or crushed for lime."

The Grand Master considers the sprawling layout of the Castle's interior, the blank walls, empty alcoves. "Take them as well. They deserve a place of honor."

Orlando half-emerged from the vision, clinging to it just barely, straddling this world and the other, as he reached for the iPad.

Phoebe moved closer, crawling on her good leg, moving around his side to watch. She put a finger to her lips, stifled a gasp, and stared as he drew a chaotic battle scene—what looked like half-men, half-horse creatures savagely attacking townspeople, and getting more than a little amorous with the women.

Just then, her cell phone rang. She flipped it open.

Caleb's voice. "Phoebe. I'm no good up here. Nothing. I'm not seeing anything."

"Don't worry, we've got it covered." She studied the rendition. "Hey, is there some kind of wall carving there? Mythological? With centaurs?"

"Yeah, on a wall in the French section. Hang on, just walked by it."

"I saw something, and it looks like Orlando's drawing the same thing right now. He's still in a trance."

"Okay, I'm looking at it now, but I don't see anything obvious. Tried touching it, hoped for a vision, but got nothing. Not even a daydream."

"What I don't know is what it means. Why the centaur?"

Caleb took a moment to respond. "The battle symbolized nature versus civilization. Lapithe and Centaures were twin sons of the god Apollo. Centaures was born deformed and later mated with mares, creating half-human, half-horse hybrids. This scene shows a legendary battle between the brothers' descendents, all started over some alcohol abuse at a wedding."

"Why would that have anything to do with the Books of Thoth, and those keys?"

"I don't know, but it might fit—in the sense of reconciling man's nature, both sides of what we're seeking here: the raw physicality of what we've become versus our psychic potential. This scene represents the conflict and the overthrow of one by the other."

"Whatever, but we still need to know where the key is. Maybe Orlando can figure it out."

"He'd better draw fast."

"Why?"

"I don't think I'm alone in here."

Caleb had been kneeling in front of the marble carving of the classic Greek scene, the battle of the Centaurs and the Lapiths, when he heard something. Two heavy scansions and a thick rope set off the ancient artwork from the walkway, but Caleb had stepped over it to scrutinize the carvings more intently. Pulling his fingers away from the most prominent centaur, he snapped the phone shut and backed away toward the northeast corner of the room.

He had heard a step, a scuff, someone trying to be stealthy. He ducked around a corner, into another room with a red coat of arms hanging on the wall and a glass case full of spearheads, axes and maces discovered in a Phoenician wreck. There was one exit straight ahead, which he kept an eye on as he opened the phone and called Agent Wagner.

"Renée here," she answered. "What did you find?"

Whispering, he said, "Not sure yet, but—are any of your people inside?"

"No, why?"

A shadow flitted across the light in the doorway. "Have them look in on my location. I think I'm being tracked. Someone's here."

Caleb backed further into the shadows while keeping a clear view of the corridor.

"Nothing, Caleb. My snipers aren't seeing a thing, and I'm tracking you with the GPS signal on your phone. We can see you in that room through the western window.

"There's someone in the hallway behind me."

"Impossible."

"Maybe someone hid during the evacuation, or there's a secret passage or something. Someone waiting for me. Maybe it's him." *Or worse,* Caleb thought. *It's Nina, and I'm as good as dead.*

"Okay, listen Caleb. If you think you can chance it, run through the other door and keep running. It's a long hallway, but with a lot of windows, and—"

Another sound, and a silhouette filled the doorway.

Caleb hoped Renée knew what she was doing. He snapped the phone shut, ducked his head and started to run for the door—just as a dark figure eased into the room before him.

Caleb froze, raising his hands, still holding the cell phone. Completely covered in black like a ninja, the intruder glided toward him. It said something incomprehensible from under a black facemask and then did a strange thing. It stopped, and bowed.

Caleb didn't know how to react. Should he run, laugh or return his bow? Instead, he shifted a foot to his right, concealing the scansion behind his back.

When the stranger's head raised, his gloved hands rose, and were now holding long curved daggers.

Caleb reached behind him, gripping the cool metal. "Wait, let's talk a sec."

The attacker leapt. Caleb ducked and spun around, hauling the heavy scansion up with him and taking his unaware foe in the chest.

A dagger dropped as he grunted, fell, but then sprang right back up. Only two feet away, the dagger beckoned within Caleb's reach as he let go of the scansion, but he had already made his move toward the door and the long passage.

He ducked and lunged forward, just as something clanged off the granite wall where his head had just been. Then he was sprinting, weaving slightly side to side. Panting, passing each window and getting a glimpse of the towers and walls, the trees, the hills.

Come on, somebody take a shot.

The footsteps behind him were gaining. Maybe preparing another knife for the back of his head. Caleb crossed in front of another window, the last one before the next doorway and a steep winding staircase inside the German tower.

He lunged like an Olympic sprinter at the finish line just as he heard the distant *pop* and, as he skidded into the tower, angling for the stairs, he heard a grunt and a flopping sound.

Behind him, his pursuer was down, his mask half-blown off, brains and bits of skull obscuring what was left of his face.

Caleb turned, biting his hand and wheezing for breath. He reached for the cell phone, flicked it open. "Good shot," he said when he finally found his breath. "Thanks."

"That's it. We're getting you out of there. Sit tight, there may be more."

He glanced out the windows where he half-expected to see the Sultan and half the Moslem army massed at the front gate. "I'll be back in the Centaur room. Give me cover and another ten minutes."

"It's not safe, we have to—"

He hung up, then was about to redial Phoebe when he saw something on the assassin's neck, above the collar and the torn mask: a gold tattoo that looked like a trident, except with nine flowing things attached to the staff. Frowning, Caleb stared at the configuration for a moment before positioning his phone, pressing the camera function, lining up the shot and taking a picture.

He stood up, then called Phoebe as he stepped over the body and headed back down the hallway. "Sis?"

"Yeah, you okay? Feared we lost you there."

"I'll be better if you tell me you've got something."

"About the centaurs? Hang on."

He kept walking, past the windows where now he saw agents converging, running over the ramparts, seeking out hiding places, working their way toward him.

"Big brother?"

"Yeah?" He entered the room and stepped back to the bas-relief of the Centauromachy.

"Orlando's just coming out of it, and—what? Ah, all right, here."

"Hey, boss. You there?"

"Yeah, Orlando, but as I said before, I'm not your boss."

"You pay me for this gig, so that makes you a boss in my book."

"Then I'm going to fire you if you don't tell me what you saw."

"Okay, do you see the main centaur, the big one raising his arms?"

"Yep."

"Is the head still intact?"

"Yes, but not all of the body. Rear legs are broken off."

"Not a problem. I think you're good to go. See his right horn?"

"Yes." Caleb moved in closer and stared. It was slightly larger than the left, about the width of two fingers, and maybe six inches in length. But it was a little darker, greener than its mate, as if the sculptor had used a different material, something only noticeable up close. "Wait, this frieze was originally on the second tier, rather high up if I recall. Even if visitors came to admire it, they'd need a ladder to see the discoloration."

Orlando coughed. "You need to trust me here."

"Go on."

"Twist the horn clockwise; it should release."

Footsteps approached, agents with submachine guns drawn, coming from both entrances. Caleb moved quickly, turning the horn, which at first refused to budge. But then it gave, turned and screwed off. Caleb turned it upside down, looked into the hollow space inside. He held the phone between his ear and his shoulder, then tapped the horn against his palm.

"Is the key in there?" Orlando asked.

Agent Wagner came to a skidding halt, leading two agents from the eastern passage. She held a gun with both hands and wore a bullet-proof vest. "You find it?"

Caleb showed her his palm, which held only a single rolled up piece of paper. He tugged at the edge and flattened it out. Then his heart sunk, along with his hopes to save Alexander, as he saw the words written there in fresh red ink.

No prize for second place.

11.

"They were here," Caleb told her. "We missed them."

Renée holstered her gun, a black Walther .45 with a walnut grip, a weapon Caleb had noticed earlier and thought was a little flashy for an FBI agent. "So," she said, "Montross managed to do in minutes what Alexander the Great failed to do all his life?"

Caleb offered a weak smile. "The Great Conqueror didn't have our gifts." *Well, at least Phoebe and Orlando still have access to those gifts.*

Renée led Caleb back to the dead body. Her men had removed the assassin's mask. "Recognize him?"

"You mean by what's left of him."

She shrugged. "Sorry. He's Asian. We can tell that much, but he's got no ID."

"Nothing but that tattoo," another agent pointed out.

"Wait," Caleb said. He took out his phone, brought up the photo and sent it as a picture message to Phoebe's phone. Then he called her.

Renée frowned. "What are you doing?"

Caleb held up a hand. "Following a hunch."

"Another one?"

"Yeah. This thing looks familiar, and I've got a weird feeling that it's important. Phoebe?"

The phone crackled. "Yeah, we're packing up here. Did you get it?"

"We got screwed. Again. Montross and Nina beat us to it. But listen, I just sent a picture to your phone. Load it into Orlando's tablet and have him do his magic on it. Find a match."

"We're on it," she said. "Call you right back."

"What are you thinking?" Renée asked as they walked back to the room with the weaponry and the ancient ship reproductions. "Isn't this guy just another one of Montross's thugs, like those he used back at Sodus?"

"I don't think so," Caleb replied. "There was just something about the killer's demeanor. He actually *bowed* to me before he attacked."

"He what?"

"It was reminiscent of how someone else treated me when I was trying to uncover the secret of the Pharos. Someone who had been sworn to protect it. It was the same. Like he admired my efforts, but couldn't let me get any closer."

"Okay, but why would he have been protecting something that Montross had already taken?"

Caleb thought for a moment. "Maybe he didn't know it was gone. Montross might have done it quickly, using diversion or just blending in earlier with the other tourists, and this guy—its protector—would have been on the alert only for a direct attempt."

Renée rubbed her forehead. "Like what we did just now."

Caleb's phone rang and he answered at once, putting the call on the speaker. "Orlando, what do you have?"

"An itching for a raise, boss."

"Just tell me."

"All right, but are you sure you don't want to guess first?"

Caleb groaned. "Okay, it's an ancient symbol. Something Chinese, or ..." He blinked, suddenly the emblem on a flag, a waving flag on a pole, or a spear, one spear among hundreds, thousands, massed on a battlefield.

"... Mongolian."

"Bingo!" Orlando cried with impatience, bridling in his voice. "It's the banner of the nine ox tails, the standard symbol of the one and only ..."

Caleb mouthed it just as Orlando said the name.

"... *Genghis Khan.*"

"So if I was confused before, now I'm certifiable," Renée said. "What does Genghis Khan have to do with any of this?"

Keeping the speakerphone connection on, Caleb started pacing, aware that he was treading on the same stones the knights had walked on during the Crusades. "It could have a lot to do with all this. Genghis Khan, whose real name was Temujin, surpassed even Alexander the Great's conquests by ruling a territory four times as large, creating a vast empire across Asia, sweeping through the Middle East, marching even to the doorstep of Europe. But what many don't know was that he wasn't just a savage tyrant; he was a seeker of truth, much like Alexander. And also like both Alexander and Cyrus, he was tolerant of all religions, respecting that in their hearts all faiths were driven by the quest to understand the will of heaven." He thought for a moment. "And there are myths, legends that Temujin even sought out relics of Alexander's legacy, artifacts that would solidify his hold on power and on life itself."

The phone crackled with Orlando's voice. "But he didn't get too far in that respect. In his old age he fell off a horse or something and never recovered from his injuries. Died like all rulers and tyrants—just like the rest of us."

"Knock it off," came Phoebe's voice. "We don't need your anarchy speech here."

"I'm just saying, in the end we're all the same: dead meat."

"It's a good point," Caleb said, "and where I was going next. He died on a way to another battle, a campaign to put down a revolt at Xi-Xia in 1227 CE. But his passing left behind one of the greatest archaeological mysteries of all time."

Renée blinked at him, waiting. "Which is ..."

Caleb gave her a weak smile. "Where is he buried?"

Noting her impatience, he continued. "His body was taken somewhere in secret, as was the custom with all Mongolian rulers. Different theories about the whereabouts of his tomb have circulated ever since. There was a cryptic anecdote from Marco Polo, then some observations from visiting dignitaries decades later. And then some subtle clues surfaced, based on the Mongolian epic work written shortly after his death: *The Secret History of the Mongol People.*"

"Well, does any of it help us here?" Phoebe asked.

"I honestly can't say how much we can rely on. The more colorful legends state that all those who labored on his crypt were massacred, and any unfortunate souls who had come across the funeral procession were put to the sword. And when his procession finally arrived, returning back across the Gobi Desert to his ancestral home in northeastern Mongolia, another force of soldiers were waiting to kill those who had escorted the Khan's body. Some estimates put this burial-related death toll at over twenty thousand, all to ensure Temujin would have an undisturbed afterlife. Archaeologists and treasure-hunters have sought his resting place for centuries, certain there would be tremendous wealth buried inside his crypt with him."

On the other end of the line, Orlando made a choking sound. "How tremendous are we talking?"

Caleb shrugged. "The spoils of all the conquests he had made, all the treasure acquired from the kingdoms he conquered. None of it has ever been found, so the speculation is that it's all still there somewhere, with him or his descendents, whose graves are also unaccounted for, but rumored to be in the same area."

"Like the Valley of the Kings in Egypt," Phoebe said, and then giggled. "Only it's the Valley of the *Khans*."

"Okay," Renée snapped. "But if no one knows where this place is ..."

"Well, there *is* a mausoleum for him."

Her eyes narrowed, and she sighed. "Another mausoleum?"

Caleb's voice pitched excitedly. "Ceremonial only, built in 1954 in Erdos City, now part of China, as a place for Chinese and Mongolians alike to honor their national hero." He lowered his head. "And now I'm thinking when Montross said we'd meet again at the mausoleum, he might not have meant this, Mausolus's ancient Wonder of the World. He may have been referring to another tomb—the tomb of Genghis Khan."

"Or," Renée said sarcastically, "maybe some other mausoleum? One of the Roman emperors? Or hell, Grant's tomb?"

Caleb gave her a look. "I thought you were a believer."

Renée blinked at him, then looked away. "This is too much. We've got nothing to go on, and meanwhile your son's in danger. Let's do this my way."

"Hang on," Orlando chimed in, excitement in his voice. "That symbol, I traced some more references and found that somebody's still using it. One group of people, actually."

"Using it how?"

"As body art."

Renée frowned. "Who?"

"They're called the *Darkhad*. And their function, get this, is to conduct the ceremonies and rites around honoring the great Khan, and also to protect his mausoleum."

"I remember now," Caleb said. "That force of loyal soldiers who waited for the Khan's body to return? They were from the clan known as the Darkhads."

"Yeah," Orlando continued tersely, taking back the spotlight. It sounded like he was reading again. "Originally there were eight mausoleums, then more, set up in portable white tents that moved around the Mongolian steppes. Some actually held relics like his saddle or his sword, but they were chiefly designed to inspire the continued worship and adoration of old Genghis. The Darkhad families, descendents of his two favorite generals, were given special privileges by Temujin—freedom from any other civil duties, freedom from taxes, the right to raise money on their lands—all so they could care for the mausoleums. Originally there were over five hundred Darkhad, and that number swelled to the thousands in later centuries. But during the 1950s the Communist government abolished the roving mausoleums and allowed just one, which housed all the relics. And the Darkhad dropped in number to only eight. And then during the Cultural Revolution, the Commies cracked down even more on any worship of their non-Communist past. All the cherished cultural elements were destroyed, the mausoleum sacked by angry punks, and the Khan's relics were broken or burned. Only recently did the Darkhad rebuild the mausoleum and create replicas of the more significant artifacts."

"Thanks for the history lesson," Caleb said. "But that only strengthens my theory that this assassin, if he was one of these Darkhad, was guarding the key. Mausolus's key. A key that could open one of the locks guarding the Books of Thoth. Why would he be guarding that unless—"

"—unless," came Phoebe's voice, "he knows where there's another one, because he's been sworn to protect it. Genghis must have found one, or both. Maybe he was the one who looted Alexander's grave?"

"And maybe," said Orlando, "he wanted to leave this one here as bait, to see who came looking."

Caleb nodded. "I think we can safely guess that if Montross has this key, then he's off to find the others."

"But," said Renée, "if all the Khan's relics were destroyed and his body isn't even at that mausoleum in Erdos City, then what?"

"Then," Caleb said solemnly, "it looks like we've found our next RV target. One that will provide our greatest test since the Pharos." He took a breath. "If we succeed, it'll make us the envy of archaeologists everywhere, and quite possibly the enemy of billions of people who might not want to have their demigod dug up."

He sighed and met Renée's stare before giving a nervous smile.

"We need to find the tomb of Genghis Khan."

BOOK TWO
THE SEARCH FOR GENGHIS KHAN

1.

Alexander sat alone in the center of the middle row seat of their rented black Jeep Commander. In the large cargo space behind him they had stuffed most of their gear, including tents and tarps, chests of food and water, blankets and sleeping bags. Three plastic chests were tethered to the roof rack. It looked like they were going on a long camping trip, the kind he wished he could have taken with his dad and Aunt Phoebe sometime, maybe in the Adirondacks.

In the front seat, Xavier Montross sat next to their guide, a man they had met outside the airport. Alexander thought he looked like one of those actors in kung-fu movies, a man with a strong build, long braided hair, weather-worn face and penetrating eyes. The capital city itself was congested and noisy, the sights and sounds overwhelming. As they left the airport, Montross had left his window open, and the reek of diesel fumes from the hundreds of buses and taxis mingled with the smell of street vendors roasting some kind of meat, likely marmot, which Alexander had learned from their guide was a kind of dog. The thought of actually eating a dog almost made him sick.

He didn't want anything to do with this place or this search, this quest of Montross's. He just wanted to wake up back home in his room surrounded by all his books, even those comics and graphic novels his mom frowned on despite Dad's insistence that they contained some basic literary merit. A boy needed his heroes.

Alexander even wished he could be back in Egypt, in Alexandria at the huge library where he got such a thrill every day being able to sneak into that private elevator with his mother and go all the way down to the secret bottom level. It had all been so exciting, the most perfect life a little boy with a curious mind could ask for. To be loved by two equally interesting and mysterious parents, spending time with each at their exotic homes, and sometimes, most happily, at holidays or on his birthday, together. But, in just one day, it had all been stolen from him.

The reality hadn't yet sunk in. Instead, he felt that at thousands of miles away he was suddenly too far removed to feel anything. To grieve for his mom, for the life he had. To do anything but try to cling to memories he already felt were fading away. The touch of her, the way she smelled, her giggling laughter when she let him tickle her feet.

Something settled in the cargo area behind him under all their gear, and Alexander sat up and was about to look when Montross barked at him to turn around and buckle up. They were leaving the city, heading off-road into the steppes.

Alexander looked out in awe of the vastness of this terrain, the open grasslands, the few lakes and rivers and the rolling hills stretching far to the north, where the white-capped peaks bordering Siberia glittered pristinely under a fiercely blue sky. It wasn't hard to imagine what he'd been told by the guide, that in another two months this would all be covered with snow and ice and they'd have no chance to make this trip.

They made a slight turn and there was a hill, steeper than the others, with an enormous likeness of a man's face upon it.

"There he is," Montross said, pointing. "Genghis Khan."

"His portrait," said the guide, "laid out in white stones for all of Ulaan Baatar, and Mongolia's visitors, such as yourselves, to see."

Alexander blinked, keeping an eye on the image of Mongolia's national hero as long as it was visible, until they left the main road and started on the bumpy trail northeast.

Toward Burkhan Khaldun, the Sacred Mountain.

Lulled by the jarring, bumpy ride, and exhausted from fitful naps on the plane, Alexander thought briefly about the mysterious woman who had come with them. Nina. He hadn't seen her since the airport, but knew she was up to something, doing her own recon maybe with those military men who had left the sub with them.

At first, Alexander had hoped the stern-faced customs officials would identify Montross from law enforcement alerts or something, or would see that Alexander wasn't along willingly, and someone would rescue him, but Montross apparently knew what he was doing. A lot of money changed hands, and the right officials nodded and let them go on their way, no questions asked.

So here he was, alone with his mother's murderer. He was halfway around the world, so far from his home and his father. Hoping, believing that his dad and Phoebe, and the rest of the Morpheus Initiative, with all their psychic abilities, would be able to find him. Hopefully they'd succeed in no time at all. In fact, Alexander thought, they were probably on their way right now.

That gave him a little comfort, and with the Khan's face still in his mind, Alexander yielded to the embrace of sleep, hoping for a dreamless slumber—anything except what came, gingerly at first, then surging on full-tilt.

Visions.

The nine ox-tail standard, carried high and charging into battle ahead of fifty thousand men on horseback, thundering over the snow-covered plains. A second contingent swarms along the eastern ridge and rains arrows down upon the hapless army caught in the valley, surrounded on all sides.

High above it all, wrapped in a blue cloak as the snow turns to a freezing rain, Temujin sits on a muscled black steed. The Khan's hooded eyes follow the battle with rote interest, as if this was but another annoyance, an obstacle to overcome on the way to a far greater destiny ... towers, domes and minarets covered with colorful mosaic tiles, glimmering in the desert sun, crumbling under the Mongol assault as monstrous catapults launch huge misshapen blocks into the air and over the walls of Koneurgenc, the capital of the Kwarizhm Empire. A hailstorm of epic proportions, the sky darkens as the rain of stones pummel into the stalwart edifices of this ancient city, reaching all the way to the Imperial Palace, where Mohammad huddles in prayer even as his soldiers race out to defend their lord, only to be cut down in a fusillade of arrows and an avalanche of boulders. Walls topple, towers crumble like cardboard game pieces, and soon the city burns.

Miles away, on a dune surrounded by his standard bearers, the ox-tails blowing in the hot wind, Temujin lowers his head and lets his smile form. "Now is the time," he tells his chief. "In the terms of surrender, offer to spare the women and children only if the Sultan delivers me the contents of the tomb of ancient Cyrus, and only once I have obtained the key."

"Surely," says the chief, "Mohammad will deny its existence."

"Then I will deny him his," Temujin replies. "And after we have massacred everyone inside those walls, I will still find it. The agents of Blue Heaven have decreed that I should become the world's savior. But first, I must be its conqueror." His eyes cloud over with visions distant and epic. "And I must have that key."

"What then, master? You spoke of the other two keys. Do we go to Bodrum?"

Temujin blinks. "Not yet. We know that one is safe at the remains of the great Mausoleum. It will be there when we need it. No, first, we must go to ..."

... A crystal blue sea, a harbor filled with multi-colored sails and vessels of all types, and a sprawling city.

Alexandria.

Temujin rides hard, at the vanguard of a hundred men, thundering through the city, out through the Gate of the Moon and charging into the red-sand desert toward a distant outpost.

He glances back ruefully at the tower on the distant harbor, the once-proud Lighthouse. The Pharos. Two-thirds of its former size only, already wracked by earthquakes, it still stands proud and resolute, mocking him. Mocking his earlier attempt to plumb its secrets.

"Failure," he mutters ...

... as men holding torches and descend a dark stairway, passing two huge statues and stand before a wall etched with seven symbols.

He climbs back up the stairs, having commanded his men to turn the symbols, hoping what the old Chinese philosopher told him about the alchemical combinations will work.

But while the door opens, it isn't enough. Only a trick, a ruse. A test—one that has found him wanting. Forty men die. Some burned to death, others drowned. Forty is enough. The Pharos is too strong, and Temujin is not worthy—not yet. But he will be. When the world is his, when the keys are his. Then, maybe then, he will try again. He will truly earn the Way into the Pharos, the path to the ultimate treasure.

So now he rides, his horse kicking up sand and creating dervishes that his followers burst through and scattered. Finally, he arrives at a small collection of huts, altars, stones and markers.

He dismounts before his horse even stops, running ahead, outpacing his men who finally catch up with him at an unassuming hillock under a mass of large stones no different from dozens of others.

Temujin reaches into his burka and pulls out a scroll, which he promptly unrolls, revealing a crudely drawn map. "Here!" he shouts. "It is just as I drew in my vision. Here, beside six other markers, between two blank obelisks.

"Here," he says again, turning to his men, "is Alexander's tomb. Dig! Keep anything of value you find, except for the stone, the one that looks like this." He reaches for the cord around his neck and lifts the charm he took from Koneurgenc, the one from Cyrus's tomb, a tiny piece of green stone shaped like a pyramid. "It will be on the body, around his neck maybe, or set in a ring. Bring it to me."

Temujin steps away.

He kneels on the hot sand, and while his men work he meditates on his life, his future. His destiny.

Alexander Crowe awoke in the back of the jeep just as it came to a grinding halt.

Xavier Montross looked back, smiling broadly. "We're here!"

KHENTI PROVINCE, INNER MONGOLIA, 7:30 P.M.

As their guide drove them over the rough terrain, Montross stared with feigned interest at the scenery, the lush grasslands, the forests of pine, the flocks of sheep and cows, the lone camel. All the while, he had his thoughts primed for just one thing.

And while he waited, he occasionally reached inside the buttons of his shirt to feel the small triangular stone set as a charm on a silver necklace. He felt its power, sensed it tremble at his touch, the same as the Emerald Tablet. One and the same material, he had realized with excitement right away, after Nina had delivered it from the Petroneum. One of three just like it.

The other two were calling, reaching out for their brother.

After sixty miles in the jeep, cutting through rough grasslands, crossing meandering streams and navigating boggy marshes, they stepped out under a darkening sky and stretched, gazing up on the rising hill-ocks and toward the mountain range, and then back the way they had come over the vast steppes leading back to the Mongolian capital.

They had arrived at Burkhan Khaldun.

Their driver and guide, Nilak Borogol, led them to an encampment of a half-dozen felt tents—*yurts*as they were called. "This was all part of the Ikh Khorig, the Great Taboo," he explained. "For centuries, this one hundred-square-mile area was defended ruthlessly. Trespassers were turned away—or killed." He made a smug face. "Now, the government permits pilgrimages, and even allows tourists and foreigners entrance."

"Foreigners like us?" Alexander said in a low voice.

Montross cut off Nilak's response with a question. "Forbidden because the tombs of the great Khans are supposed to be here?" He spoke in a rushed voice, trying to sound like a naïve tourist. "Genghis, his sons Jin and Odai, and grandson, Kublai Khan?"

Nilak smiled, and in the dying light over the cooling winds, Montross could see the tattoo just peeking out over the guide's sweater. "Yes," Nilak said. "But it is sacred for many reasons. Its closeness to the great Blue Heaven, for one. Its majestic scenery, the life-giving rivers: the Kherlen and the Odon. But also it was here that Temujin, Chinggis Khan himself, while still a boy, evaded the vengeance of his father's killers. The mountain sheltered him among its forests and hills, preserving him for his destiny."

"So it was a place he never forgot," Montross said.

"His father was killed," Alexander said, repeating what he had heard. "And he survived? Now I see what made him so cruel to every-body." He shivered in his hooded red sweatshirt.

"Not cruel," said Nilak defensively, "merely just. He was no sadist. While other conquerors delighted in the torture and debasement of their defeated enemies, Temujin only doled out justice to those who had defied him. He once said to the sultan of the Kharmezhm Empire, 'You have greatly sinned upon the world and your own people. Why else would God have sent someone like me to destroy you?'"

Alexander smiled, then gave Montross a cold look. "I like that. A lot."

"Yes, it's all very Homeric." Montross pulled back strands of his red hair into a neat ponytail. "But still a little paranoid, right? He made sure no one could ever find his grave, venerate his body."

"Oh, we venerate him," Nilak said, fingers balling into fists. "Through his relics, his statues. His mausoleums. There are specific holy days of worship. Incense and songs, rituals."

"And what of his body?" Montross glanced at the hills and the steep ascent of the sacred mountain before them, rising to a flattened peak about seven thousand feet high. "Where is it?"

Nilak regarded him coolly as the breezes let up. "No one knows."

"But there are many theories, right?" Montross's voice had lost its naiveté. "And these other camps here—Americans? Come looking for the same thing?"

"They have gone," Nilak said with a dose of satisfaction. "Last month, and left their tents, some of their supplies. Gone the way of the Japanese archaeologists in the 1990s, who brought their ground-penetrating radar, their satellite survey maps and their tools, and found nothing. Some graves, but only of those more recent burials."

Xavier turned his face to the mountain, listening to the wind sizzling through the firs. "They were looking in the wrong spot."

He gazed at the deceptively difficult ascent, to be undertaken only with practiced horses who could navigate the steep rocky hillsides. "The Wall, right? Almsgivers Wall. Discovered by that Japanese team and dating to a much older era. It was the only area the government permitted them to search. They weren't allowed on the peak or at the southern area called the Threshold, where hundreds of stone piles remain and lingering traces of a temple can be seen. And, what of other requests by similar, well-funded projects? Teams hoping to use satellite magnetometry to search for subsurface disturbances in the soil, a technique that would indicate areas that might have ditches—or tombs carved out of the ground? What about those? Why are the permissions not coming? What are they hiding?"

Nilak's eyes turned cold, the blue leeching out into black, mirroring the great expanse of cloudless sky overhead. "Who are you, sir?"

Montross spread out his arms, smiling innocently. "Just a man and his son, out for a grand hike into history."

Nilak stared at Alexander, considered the boy for a moment, then raised a hand, clenching his fingers into fists. At once, two Mongolian men emerged from the nearest tent.

Both had AK-47s slung over their shoulders, weapons which they promptly unhooked and turned toward Montross as they approached.

Montross noted the tattoos on their necks. "Ah," he said, "the Darkhad come to greet us."

Nilak held out a restraining hand and his men paused. A dog whined from inside the nearest tent, sounding more like a wolf, and Montross wondered if there were more men inside.

"You've come for the Great Khanite, the valley of the Khans," said Nilak. "It was obvious the moment you landed in Ulaan Baatar. And your son here is no son. Although, he bears some resemblance."

Alexander frowned. "What?"

"But it does not matter. The grave of my lord will never be found. He will remain undisturbed for all time."

Montross blinked at him. "Why?"

"It was his wish."

Shrugging, Montross said, "Wishes usually go unfulfilled. Now tell me, where is it?"

"You think we know?"

"Of course, you do," Montross said. "You—I also knew you from the moment you volunteered to be our guide. You are of the line of Mubuqoi and Boroochi, Temujin's favorite generals. The leaders of five hundred families who tended the lands in this area. Your master gave your ancestors special privileges in return for your promise to guard his remains, his relics, and to continue his worship." Montross lowered his head, his eyes drilling into Nilak's. "You *know*."

"That was eight hundred years ago. So many generations. Memories fade."

"Not *this*memory," Montross said. "You've succeeded in a great game of deception, clouding the minds of your leaders and your people, the people of China and Mongolia alike, as well as the world. From the beginning, the Darkhad created false rumors, inciting historians and explorers, such as Marco Polo himself, into quoting prefabricated fan tasy and outright misdirection. Throwing out names of fake mountains and imaginary rivers, providing fodder for future treasure seekers to chase their proverbial tails. Classic misdirection."

Nilak's gaze never wavered. "Who are you? How do come by such beliefs?"

Montross merely smiled.

"Very well," said Nilak, glancing around at the wide expanse of the hills, the steppes where once the Golden Horde, the greatest army in the world, had launched their campaigns, conquering kingdom after kingdom and ruling the largest collection of people that had ever fallen under one leader. Nilak looked over the vast grasslands, hills and bogs; the empty, skeletal forest of pines burned in a great fire decades ago. Desolate but for a few packs of roving sheep and cows.

Nilak sighed and spoke two words.

"Kill them."

Alexander cried out as the men raised the machine guns, looking to Montross for help, for some sort of saving word or plea, but Xavier just stood with his arms outstretched, still smiling.

He's insane, completely whacko! Alexander thought, believing it was to be the last thought of his too-short life, before joining his mother, hopefully in Heaven.

Two gunshots snapped the night air. Crisp, loud, echoing off the hills of the Burkhan Khaldun. Alexander clenched his eyes shut, but not before first seeing something out of the corner of his eye: a dark form slipping out from the back of the jeep, from under the tarps and equipment they had packed in the cargo hold at Ulaan Baatar.

His eyes popped back open just as Nilak's head whipped around to see his companions drop silently, guns unfired.

"Thank you, Nina," said Montross, lowering his arms. His gaze never left Nilak's. And his smile never wavered, not until Nina walked right up to their guide and placed the muzzle of her still-warm Beretta against the back of his head.

"Now," Montross said, "where were we?"

"Check the tents," he said after he had disarmed Nilak, taking away the guide's sleek stainless steel Ruger SR9c. "Make sure we're alone."

Nina's head cocked, eyes narrowing. She nodded and approached the first yurt, one with an orange glow inside.

"I will never betray the Khan," said Nilak, still locked in a stare with Montross. "Never."

Montross shrugged. He kept the Ruger pointed at the Darkhad while he reached into the pack slung over his shoulder. "It doesn't matter. We could torture you. Nina is an expert at such things. And out here, no one will hear your pitiful cries. But such tactics are uncomfortable for me, and unnecessary. Especially when I have this."

He pulled out the object, glowing with a shimmering emerald aura, and for the first time, Nilak gave a reaction, as if a jolt ripped through his body. "Impossible."

Montross cocked his head. "I see you know what this is. Why do you say impossible?"

"No one could penetrate the seal."

"Why not? Because your Temujin failed?"

The Darkhad seethed. "Only because he had other demands on his time."

Montross nodded. "Provinces to keep in line, adversaries to crush, I understand. So much to do, and all of it so much more important than the Truth."

Nina came out of the first tent, then headed to the next.

Nilak said, "Nothing was more important than the truth, not to Temujin. It was why he called for the great philosopher-mage Chi-Chan from China to study the seven symbols his men discovered under the tower in Alexandria."

"Lot of good that did," Montross said, hefting the tablet. "Let me guess, you lost a few battalions there, eh? Before giving up? But regardless, we've got it. We did what your great leader could not."

Nilak stared, then slowly nodded. But after a moment, he let his lips curl back into a smile. "But it is not enough, yes? You cannot read what you hold, cannot gain its secrets. Not without—"

"Without the keys." Montross sighed. "Keys your master spent a lifetime trying to find. A search which your sacred book, the *Secret History of the Mongols*, fails to mention."

"Then how do you know of it?"

"I"—he pulled Alexander closer to him—"*we* have our ways."

Nina came out of a tent and headed for the next.

"I have seen," Montross continued, "how your master subjugated the peoples of Persia, the world of Babylon, and took from there some of the greatest artifacts. Pieces he used to bargain for the lives of their princes. I've seen how the great Khan learned of the keys, and once the truth took hold, he would not let it rest. Having found one key, he sought the others. One of which was located in Bodrum, Turkey."

"The Mausoleum," Nilak whispered. "You killed him, my cousin." It wasn't a question.

Montross fingered the charm around his neck. "Not personally, but I had a feeling he might not make it."

"Nevertheless, you will pay."

"Oh? I didn't think vengeance was your thing. Single-minded and all."

Nilak glared at him. "Vengeance is most assuredly permitted, as long as it doesn't interfere with our mission."

Montross held up the tablet. "Oh yes it will. I am close. I have seen many burials, many elaborately staged ceremonies with white tents, rituals and the Khan's standard. But thanks to your infernal exercises, where I know you've spread out his relics, buried some here, some there, and the true treasure only in one place, I don't know exactly where it is, where the two keys have been kept. Except that they are on his body. That much I'm certain of. But I want you to know this one thing whether or not it helps in making your decision. I don't want or care for the rest of your hero's treasure. I just want those keys."

Nilak said nothing.

"Tell me," Montross said, "and you live. You can continue to preserve the secret. Go on playing your little mind-trick games with a billion people. I want the keys, and you're going to—"

Nina screamed.

Something punched through the last tent, a small hole made by an arrow launched from a composite bow, taking her in the shoulder. She dropped her weapon, grunting, the arrow lodged in her flesh. And as Montross swung his gun around, the tent flaps burst open and a bright white stallion erupted from inside, bearing a cloaked rider, a dark-haired woman slinging a bow over her shoulder as she gripped the reins and galloped ahead.

Nina dodged, then picked up her gun with her other hand, turned and aimed. But the horse leapt, darting in front of Montross, then around so the rider could reach down and scoop up Nilak before turning and racing in a white flash to the woods.

Shots rang out, both Nina and Montross emptying their magazines after the fleeing horse. Bullets exploded into tree trunks and branches, kicked up sparks on the rocks as the horse wove in and out of the trees. With her last shot, Nina gave a smile of satisfaction.

A cry followed the dying echoes of gunfire as Nilak tumbled off the back of the horse, hit the ground and rolled. The horse turned and Montross had a glimpse of a face below the hood—a feminine, chiseled jaw line with sharp cheekbones and haunting eyes. Then, as Nina reloaded, the horse turned and fled into the safety of the trees.

For a moment, she had a clear shot at the rider's retreating figure, and was about to fire when Alexander threw himself at her knees, bringing her down and then avoiding a backward slap at his face.

"Damn it!" Nina pushed him away, sprang up, holstered her gun, and then reached for the arrow in her shoulder. She grimaced, and then yanked it out with a muffled scream.

Barely showing a reaction, she scowled as she applied pressure to the wound. "Xavier, I'm sorry. I missed her."

"Forget it," Montross said, listening to the sounds of clawing hooves, the horse racing up the hill, where the jeep couldn't follow. "Check on Nilak. And get on the sat-phone and call in the others." In addition to Colonel Hiltmeyer and his squad of five soldiers, they had secured ten hand-picked mercenaries, ex-Chinese soldiers, dissidents whose loyalty to the highest bidder far outweighed their loyalty to an eight hundred-year-old dead man.

"They're waiting beyond the ridge, as ordered," Nina said, after making the call. "And should be able to get here in twenty minutes."

They approached the fallen Darkhad, Montross dragging Alexander along with him. Nilak groaned and squirmed, his legs twitching. The bullet had caught him between the shoulder blades.

"I'm looking forward to this," Nina said, standing over the man, who looked up at them now, biting back his pain.

"I die as my Lord," he said. "Fallen from a horse."

"Nonsense," said Nina. "You'll die when I say you die. When you beg."

Something whistled through the air and Montross lunged, caught Nina and drove her to the ground just as an arrow *thunked*into the hard grassland at Alexander's feet. He stood there alone, unprotected, and saw up the mountainside the flash of a white horse and the cloaked rider fitting another arrow.

"She's aiming again," Alexander said, still unafraid. For a moment, he thought their eyes met, his and the Darkhad's, but then she looked away, a little to his right. And she let loose another arrow—one that struck home.

Nilak grunted and wheezed a satisfying gasp of air. Smiling, his hand settled on the shaft of the arrow stuck in his heart, and he met Alexander's horrified stare. "Please, leave the dead to their rest."

Another flash of white, and the horse was bounding away, even as Nina let loose with her Beretta.

"Damn," she hissed. "Gone. And this one dead." She nudged Nilak's body with her foot. "So much for the easy way."

Montross sighed, thinking for a moment. "It doesn't matter. Our visions were clear. I saw the coffin buried inside this mountain. The funeral procession was led up these very hills. We're on the right track. It's at one of two probable locations up near the southern side of the summit. Once the rest of the team joins us with all our gear, we'll proceed and narrow down the search."

Nina kept her eyes on the hill, on the shadows within the forest. "I'll go on ahead with the night-vision goggles." She tapped her gun, caressing the newly installed LaserMax sighting device attached to the barrel. "I'll find her."

"Ah yes, your precious Beretta. Sometimes I think you love that weapon more than me."

"It's never let me down. And besides," she said with a cold stare, "I know your heart belongs to another."

Montross was silent for a moment and his eyes lost focus before snapping back to her. "Yes, well then. You take care of our Darkhad antagonist up there, but capture her if possible. And while you're busy, Alexander and I will try again to remote view our long-buried friend."

Qara Lan-Naatun watched from behind an ancient pine tree, gnarled and drooping with age. Watched as the intruders stood over the body of her brother, Nilak.

Her brother. She closed her eyes, praying that his soul now journeyed to the Blue Heaven, and would soon be at peace, rewarded for his lifetime of faithful service to the Master. But her heart ached for him, overwhelmed by the immensity of what she had done. What she had to do.

They would have tortured him, and Nilak was not as strong as some. She couldn't risk that pair tearing him open for the secret. It was up to her now. Especially after the news from Bodrum. Alexia Nomantu had been killed defending the Third Key. Whoever they were they were strong, prepared and ruthless. And yet, this man and his "son" seemed different.Not archaeologists, nor scholars. Not warriors either, although the woman displayed enough skill. Yet the man she had overheard talking to Nilak. He possessed certain knowledge. Dangerous knowledge.

And that artifact ... could it really be the sacred stone, the tablet itself? The one Chinggis sought all his life?

Still, it didn't matter. The traditions were clear. No one was to disturb the Khan. No one. It wasn't a matter of gold, of treasure and plunder. The rules, passed on for more than sixty generations now, were clear. Temujin must be protected so that he might continue his service to heaven. Even in the afterlife, Temujin was still protecting what he had rightfully earned.

And all Qara knew was that given the timing of this team's arrival here, coming just hours after the news of Alexia's death and the likely theft of Mausolus's Key, Temujin's secret was in jeopardy as never before. And if these invaders should succeed, she had no doubt the keys would be used to open something her Lord and Master— and sixty previous generations—had deemed too dreadful to allow anyone else to possess.

But as she watched the team below, and even as she saw the distant trio of jeeps heading her way, likely bringing men as well as heavy equipment, she couldn't help but smile.

After all, despite the presence of the Emerald Tablet, despite what these invaders had said and believed they knew, the secret was still safe. The ruse still held.

They were looking in the wrong place.

2.

Caleb and Phoebe ascended the steps and, after catching their breaths, took a moment to gaze over the three grand halls of the Mausoleum, three structures shaped like Mongolian yurts. White walls with red doors and domed roofs painted with blue and yellow designs. Caleb looked back the way they had come, down the stairs and across the concrete pathway to the well-trodden parking area where their minibus and two jeeps idled. Orlando and Renée were inside the minibus, working on the route for the next leg of their journey. And behind them: the vast expanse of the Ordos Desert.

They were 180 miles southwest of Beijing.

And a hundred miles away from the Mongolian border.

"So why are we here?" Phoebe asked, tugging Caleb's shoulder. "It wasn't really on the way."

"No, it wasn't," he said, contemplating the Main Hall, the largest of the yurts.

"And we don't really have the time. Montross has Alexander, and the longer we take ..."

Caleb started walking, heading inside, behind two older women, heads bowed, carrying beaded necklaces and small bottles of something that looked like milk. "Montross needs Alexander. Needs us, I think. Agent Wagner confirmed that someone matching his description was seen leaving the airport at Ulaan Baatar in Mongolia. So he's got to be heading for the most likely location—Burkhan Khaldun, the Sacred Mountain in the northeast. Poor Xavier. He must have let the literature and history lead his thoughts, control his visions. He asked himself the wrong questions."

"But how sure are you that you've asked the right ones?"

"I'm not. You had the visions, not me. That ability is still inaccessible."

Phoebe gave him a sympathetic look. "Well, you knew enough to pose the question to us. To ask to be shown what was inside funeral procession's great white tent that marched across the Gobi in 1227."

"And you saw it."

"Well, Orlando mostly. We complemented each other, built on each other's visions." She blushed. "Sometimes we do that."

He opened his mouth, about to ask an awkward question, but then thought better of it. "In that huge funeral procession back into Mongolia, to the Sacred Mountain, you saw through the fabric of that tent, through the wooden box itself, the knock-off golden coffin, with *nothing inside.* confirmed that they wanted it to look like he was going back there and did everything to ensure the myth, including the massacre of eyewitnesses and those who made the long march."

Still listening, half-seeing it again for herself, Phoebe bowed her head as she entered the faux mausoleum, mimicking what the other visitors had done. She stepped inside first, ahead of Caleb. "But we also know it's not *here.* This is just ceremonial."

Ahead of them, in the center of the hall, stood a thirteen-foot-tall white marble statue of Genghis Khan in all his triumph. On the wall behind this statue was a map of the Yuan Dynasty and the vast territory he and his sons had conquered.

"Yes," Caleb agreed. "Ceremonial, but also spiritual. I believe it's vital to honor the memory of Temujin." He pointed past the statue, past the corridors leading in either direction, covered with frescoes of the Khan's life, one passage leading to a hall filled with relics from his life, the other containing the coffins commemorating his three sons and his first wife.

"Come on," he said, moving forward. "His coffin's down here. We're going to pay our respects. Honor tradition. And maybe, just maybe, we'll get some hints about where his actual resting place is."

Phoebe nodded and then, afraid that the group of milling tourists and worshippers might overhear, she whispered, "And then apologize for what we're going to do next?"

He gave his sister a reproachful look at first, one that soon gave way to a smile when he saw the excitement bubbling in her eyes. "Most definitely. And pray his spirit forgives us."

Back in the minibus, Orlando leaned forward in his seat from the second row and looked over Agent Wagner's shoulder. Renée was in the driver's seat, ticking away at her laptop, scrolling over field reports, maps and other intel.

"How ya doin'?" he asked, causing her to jump.

She turned, her eyes flashing. "Don't you have something to do?"

Orlando shrugged, sat back and took a swig from his water bottle—water, mixed with Red Bull. He glanced out the windows. "Not really. Just enjoying my first time in a damned desert. Could you turn up the AC?"

"It's fifty degrees outside."

"Really?" Orlando rolled the window down halfway and stuck his hand out. "How about that? Some desert. Hey, so I'm sorry you got stuck with us misfits. I bet you wish this was just a typical domestic abduction thing, something where you could just bring in the SWAT team and take out the perps."

"Seventy-five percent of all kidnappings end in the murder of the abducted person." Renée looked back to her laptop screen. "And one hundred percent of the ten cases I've worked on."

"Oh."

"So no, I don't wish I was back there. But I can't say this one is making me feel any better. In fact—"

"You feel like you're out of control."

She blinked, stared at his reflection in her screen. "Again, don't you have anything to do? Shouldn't you be trying to remote view something?"

"Oh, I already did. While you were driving." He smiled. "I was in the zone. Saw some interesting things."

Renée shrugged. "So do another one. Or go in the mausoleum yourself, or out back and get some of that Mongolian beef I smell. I think they're cooking it up in the field for some kind of re-enactment."

"Mmmm, sounds good, but no. I want to stay and bother you."

Renée turned. "I'm still wearing my gun, you realize. Annoy me again and I won't be responsible if it happens to go off."

Orlando crossed his arms, considering her. He looked back toward the mausoleum, then to their right, to the jeeps which held the second team of three local agents, a guide and a field officer. *Should I risk it?*

"Why not?" he said under his breath. "So, Agent Wagner, I'd like to ask you something."

"Make it quick, I'm busy."

"Okay, well, here it is. How did you get this case?"

She stopped typing. Turned around. "What?"

"I know a little something about FBI procedure. Studied up on it quite a bit before we left the States."

"You studied procedure?" Her eyes were dark, flat stones.

"Seems all this was a little rushed. You guys coming onto the scene so fast." Not backing down from her stare, Orlando continued. "A little unorthodox. And it also seems that your selection as lead agent came from much higher up."

Silence. Then, "How could you know that?"

Orlando gave her a loopy grin. "You know how."

Her eyes darkened. "I see."

He took a deep breath, suddenly aware of the jeep beside them, the three faces pressed against the windows. He swallowed, noticing that the light on Renée's cell phone, on the passenger seat, was on. *Speaker-phone? Walkie-talkie connection?*It didn't matter, he had already taken this past the point of no return and had to continue. "Does this—your interest in this case—have anything to do with that necklace you wear under your shirt?"

The doors on the other vehicle popped opened all at once and the black-suited agents leapt out just as Renée shook her head and reached for her gun.

"You should have gone out for the beef."

Before leaving, Caleb decided to take Phoebe into the West Hall to see the relics.

"These are all replicas, right?" she asked, pushing past the visitors, some of them kneeling before the glass-encased pieces. A curved sword, a milk-pot, headgear.

Caleb walked up to the only item not protected by glass—a weathered-looking leather saddle. "Yes, except for possibly this one. There's an account I read on the way up here, an interview with one of the Darkhad several years ago. Asked about the destruction of the relics during the Cultural Revolution, he inferred that the saddle alone might have escaped the zealots' wrath."

He approached it, glanced around at everyone else involved with the other pieces, reading the descriptions or leaving offerings.

"Want me to cop a feel?" Phoebe asked with a lopsided grin.

"Well, since I still think I'm kind of ..."

"Impotent?"

He looked down as she whispered, "Don't worry, I've got it." She reached for the saddle, brushed her fingers against it, closed her eyes and stepped back.

And as Caleb watched with pained jealousy, her visions took her away.

3.

BURKHAN KHALDUN, MONGOLIA

Nina Osseni darted around trees, dove through brush, ducked and ran from cover to cover as she ascended the mountain, following the trail of the white stallion and the fleeing Darkhad woman.

But after about thirty minutes, the trail had gone cold. Too many rocks, boulders and paths overrun with horse prints for her to determine which were new. And the light was fading, the bright blue of the sky leeched out by hungry violets and grays.

"Damn," she whispered, stopping with her foot it mid-step. Catching her breath, she looked down. In the hazy twilight she had just seen the barest outline of a wire.

She stepped back, following the wire with her eyes, seeing where it ended up a tree on a mechanism controlling a raft of sharp stakes, all pointed down at her. "Diabolically impressive."

Nina scanned the shadows on the mountainside, seeing all the nooks and crevasses. She put on her night-vision goggles and let the world jump into green and white, but it was still no use. *No wonder the Darkhad have been so successful.*She backed up slowly, expecting to hear the *thwang*of an arrow zipping toward her.

She would wait for Colonel Hiltmeyer's team, his men and his supplies. Flak jackets and automatic weapons. Floodlights and flares. Grenades. But they'd have to be careful, and even then ... She glanced at the trap again and imagined what else lay in store on the way up.

Best to send up the grunts first, one at a time. It was the only way they might make it to the top.

Frustrated and growing angrier by the minute, she made her way back down toward the camp.

On the descent, her thoughts turned to Caleb, imagining where he might be right now. Was he remote viewing her this very instant? For a moment she paused, feeling naked, exposed even more than being on this mountain at the mercy of an expert marksman. She narrowed her eyes, then quickened her pace.

Best to get back to Montross, and to the tablet. It had some kind of psychic deterrent built up around it, a kind of cloud that made its presence, and those around it, invisible to scrying eyes. Part of the reason it had gone undetected for so many centuries. And of course, Montross had something else, something like it—a sphere he had stolen from the Smithsonian archives years ago. It had shielded him from any prying eyes while he prepared for this mission. Now, they were doubly protected.

But as she got close to the camp and saw the men suiting up, preparing for the ascent, she found herself wishing their situations were reversed, that she was the one remote viewing Caleb. Seeing his every move, voyeuristically laughing, or cheering at his progress.

"We can make the Threshold before dark, if we move now," Colonel Eric Hiltmeyer said. He was fitting on his vest over his camouflage threads and supervising his team of fifteen soldiers, all loaded with gear and weapons.

Montross was eyeing the mountain in the distance, with its twenty or more square miles of available hiding space just begging him to try. He narrowed his eyes, then turned and headed for the first tent. "Hold on, we need a little more precision before we go blindly tramping up there."

"I agree," said Nina, skidding and sliding down the last few yards to their camp. "And I think our friends up there have devised some rather nasty traps for the unwary. This might not be such a good idea in the dark."

Hiltmeyer coughed in his hand. "Bullshit. We can handle it."

Nina scoffed. "Doubtful, but you're welcome to try. I'll just hang back and watch the carnage from down here. I say we wait until morning."

"No waiting," Montross said. "Get ready to move on my return." And with that, he stormed into the first tent, tossed back the flap, and stepped inside where just a lone candle bathed the white felt material in a pale glow, mixing with the emerald haze from the tablet beside Alexander.

Alexander emerged from his trance slowly, grudgingly. He had been sitting cross-legged on a mat on the hard ground with the Emerald Tablet right in front of him. Its aura had tugged at his consciousness once he was left alone with it, and he had spent several minutes just staring deeply into its oddly angled surfaces, trying to force the images into some sort of cohesive shape. But the edges wouldn't line up, and the letters appeared to vibrate with a frequency all its own. Pulsing into his mind, tweaking parts of his brain, nudging him down paths of sight that were alien, powerful and terrifying.

But at last he gave in. He had to be brave, had to do this for his dad. For Aunt Phoebe. For Mom. It was up to him. He had to see. Maybe if he found what Xavier Montross was looking for, then all this could end. He could go home, be with Dad and forget all this.

But his home was gone. Burnt. All his toys, his books. His treasured books.

Anger swirled in his thoughts, but he pushed the emotion aside and trusted the waves of green, throbbing behind his eyelids, prying open his inner sight. And then he saw ...

... *a camel. One hump, no saddle, but a muzzle and its harness. Led across the snow-covered desert by a lone man wrapped tight in a llama-skin coat and a fur hat. The sun, distant and weak, follows the pair across the wilderness as the moon lights their way at night, enticing them to continue without rest.*

Until finally they arrive at a frozen river, its surface like glass, reflecting the cold, distant constellations.

"Here?" the man asks the camel.

And the beast lowers its head. A female, she makes a whining sound, then half-trots, half-stumbles to the edge of the riverbank. Sniffing deeply.

"Here?" he asks again, setting down his pack, which he opens. He pulls out an ax. And a shovel.

The camel paws at the ground, then lifts its head in alarm.

Two dark shapes sprint across the landscape, converging from the north and the east.

With bows drawn.

The camel's owner takes a step back, and is about to cry out when two arrows simultaneously pierce his chest. He slumps to his knees, eyes wide in disbelief. The ax drops. Arms at his side, he remains kneeling as if frozen, while the two forms approach, slower now.

One of them clicks his tongue, calming the beast. The other circles around it, draws a knife, then holds the camel's head while he slits its throat, spilling hot blood upon the snow and ice.

After the beast stops thrashing on the ground, lying on its side beside her dying master, the two men turn to consider the man.

"He's dead," one says to the other.

"Too bad. We could have asked him."

"But I think we know. This is the camel. The mother of the calf we buried last year."

"Then it's true. Camels have memories like elephants."

One nodded, looking back at the beast. "A mother's love is not easily swayed. We should have killed its whole family after burying the child with our master."

"No matter. The site is safe. Now, even more so." He looks out over the frozen expanse of the river, winding around in a huge, silver-coated "S" back to the distant black hills. "Our Khan is safe."

A flash like a thunderbolt lights up the world …

… and the same river bends in the summer sun. Black flies swarm over a field of men slaving at the land, carving up trenches near the river, carving a path that will give it its S-shape.

"It is almost time," one man on horseback says to his uniformed companions. "Ogadai is coming tomorrow to supervise and to formally close the tomb."

"And then we will punch through the final barrier and divert the river over the entrance, there." The general points to a large, dark aperture carved into the bedrock twenty feet below the earth. Men were still down there, moving up and down a wooden ramp, carrying items of great value—food, gold, urns full of jewels. Next, a single young camel is led by its harness into the depths. And in a nearby tent, twenty maidens are being prepared.

"*Tomorrow,*" *the general says again, swatting a fly from his neck,* "*we fin-ish this, make the sacrifices, and lead his caravan back to the Sacred Mountain. The secret of Temujin's tomb shall be safe.*"

"*What about these laborers? They know—*"

"*I said, the secret shall be safe.*"

Alexander's vision fluttered, wind blew through the tent, the green aura around the edges flickered, and a voice whispered through the sands and the buzzing of flies.

"What have you seen?"

Alexander shook his head, whipping his hair across his face, and finally he pulled himself free. He looked up into the eyes of Xavier Montross, eyes that eerily reflected the color of the Emerald Tablet. Eyes that threatened to send him back into an ancient, inescapable world of dreams and visions, of blood and secrets.

"I—" he started, and then glanced again at the tablet.

And another vision suddenly exploded in a kaleidoscopic rush of intensity, more real than anything he'd ever experienced, except for the burst of fire in the lighthouse vault. It grabbed hold and shook him to his core as if to say: *Not yet. You still need to see something more... .*

The same river weaves through manicured gardens and past cobblestone walkways and under marble bridges scintillating with jewels while fountains spray diamond-like drops high into the air, where flocks of doves fly around golden-tipped minarets, in and out of rose- and hyacinth-covered terraces. The river flows on, right through the center of a palace so breathtakingly beautiful, so bright with its polished white marble walls, its seven golden domes, its pillars of sparkling blue, it makes the rest of the dazzling city pale in comparison.

Thousands of people wander around the city, talking, reading, dancing. Wearing loose and colorful robes, they sit in the gardens and drink from golden cups while strings and flutes play on the breeze.

"*Was this wise?*" *says a man on an arched bridge, dressed all in black robes, with a dark hat shading his face. He speaks to an older man, dressed the same.*

Shaking his head, the elder says, "*Kublai believes in the old philosophy, the adage: Whatever you wish to hide, keep it in plain sight and none will think to look there.*"

"*Nowhere plainer, or more obvious,*" *the younger man notes, pointing to the sparkling water in the river's bend below their feet. He can almost discern the outline of a slight mound, just off-color, distinct from its surroundings.*

"It will be safe," the elder assures his son. "We will see to that. And when Shang-du falls, as all great cities must, and when Kublai goes to join his grandfather in the Blue Heaven, we will make sure this place, and all its towers and golden domes, its wealth and power, are demolished and then spread across the empire, until the ruin of this city is thought of no more."

"A palace!"

Montross dropped to a knee, studying the boy's face. "You saw a palace? What was it like? How big?"

Alexander blinked, willing his eyes to focus. Suddenly Montross had his hands on the boy's shoulders, hauling him up and away from the direct sight of the Emerald Tablet. "Where is it?"

"It was huge," Alexander said, squirming. "Seven domes. Lots of pillars. And a river."

Montross dropped the boy and took a step back. *Remain calm. Work with him, let him speak.* "Okay, what else? What did you ask to be shown?"

Alexander shrugged. "Nothing. I just knelt down, stared at that the tablet, and I started seeing stuff."

"Okay, think carefully, kid. Tell me everything you saw."

Frowning, Alexander raised a finger. Took a deep breath. "What's in it for me?"

Montross smiled. "Your life, for starts."

"And my dad's? Aunt Phoebe's? The Morpheus Initiative? I really like that Orlando guy, he's cool. I don't want any of them hurt."

"Help me and I'll do what I can."

"Same goes for that Nina lady. Keep her away. She doesn't play nice."

Montross laughed. "She most certainly does not. But come on, scratch my back, I'll scratch yours."

Alexander made a face.

"Just an expression. Get me to Genghis Khan's tomb, and I'm done with you, with all the Crowes. And the Morpheus Initiative too."

Alexander raised an eyebrow like he saw Spock do all the time in the old *Trek* . "What do you want?"

"The location. You know that."

"No, what do you want from the grave? How much treasure do you need? And why can't you see it on your own?"

"I don't know why I can't see it. I'm close. I did see them lower a coffin into the mountainside, but I can't tell where. In eight hundred years the scenery has changed. I saw them trample the area with horses, then plant it over with trees. It's probably in the forest, covered with roots, and we don't have the time or the resources to get out the sonar and all the technology. There has to be an easier way."

Alexander crossed his arms and gave a stern look. "I asked you what's in the grave."

Montross sighed, then reached down the front of his shirt. "Fine, I'll tell you. See this?"

"Nice necklace."

"Yeah, well our friend Genghis has two just like it, buried with him. I want to complete this set of three. Is that enough for you?"

"They kind of look like the Emerald Tablet."

Very observant. "How about that?"

"What do those necklace pieces do?" Alexander asked. "Let me guess—make you live forever?"

"Apparently not. Didn't work for Genghis, or the other guy who left me this one."

"Well, you said he didn't have all three, right?"

Definitely observant. Montross smiled. "Enough chit-chat. I told you I'd let you go if you help me. What I didn't tell you was that if you don't, I'll find it anyway, and then I will let Nina and her friends out there finish making you an orphan. Now, *what did you see?*"

Alexander lowered his eyes. His shoulders sagged. "Okay, I'll tell you. But you won't like it."

"Why not?"

"Because what I saw ... it wasn't on this mountain."

4.

Phoebe backed away, holding her head. The room spun, faces melding with artifacts. Tourists and worshippers blending with the walls and displays.

"Oh no," she whispered, reaching for Caleb to steady herself. But he was indistinguishable from the blur all around her, the blur that now took shape, even as she was begging, *Just show me what's happening, show me what I need to see.*

A blast of frigid air blew into her face ...

... as she stands on a plain of ice under a picture-perfect sky. A fire roars, consuming logs and twigs, and roasting a large something that might have been a wild dog. A palatial tent ahead, the folds parting and a wizened old man, bald with a thin white braid of hair descending like a rope from his chin, inviting her inside.

"Come, Master Temujin. We are ready with the designs."

Inside, candles and incense burn, a great llama-fur rug covers the ground, a table is set up with scrolls, maps and designs. "Right here," the old man says, pointing at the map.

Temujin looks at it, recognizes the eastern coast of China and Mongolia, the island of Japan. The man points inland, to part of China. "Here is the burial site you asked to see. The concealed tomb of Qin Shi Huangdi, the first emperor of a unified China, who lived a hundred years after the Great Alexander. The designs for his mausoleum I have here." He patted another scroll and started to unravel it, giving a glimpse of a pyramidal shape, and below it, a vast network of passageways, staircases and arches leading to an impossibly detailed cityscape. "Qin Shi began its construction as soon as he ascended to the throne, and it took thirty-six years to complete, at the cost of"—he waves his hand dismissively—"sources say somewhere around seven hundred thousand lives."

"What of the city where he now dwells?" Temujin asks, and the old man smiles.

"Built in the immense hollowed-out cavern under the mound, his city is complete with everything a ruler would need for the next life: four temples, erected at the cardinal points, a central palace holding his concubines and his own tomb, storehouses of gold and silver, ornamental weapons and artwork. And surrounding the palace stand inner and outer walls, courtyards and gardens, rivers originally designed to run with Mercury."

"Mercury?"

"A substance the emperor believed could bestow eternal life."

Temujin chuckles. "Fool."

"Yes," says the old man. "The old man poisoned himself."

Taking the scroll, unrolling it completely, Temujin studies the designs, unable to read the descriptive words. "Still, mercury has other advantages. What of the city's defenses?"

"Eight thousand terra cotta warriors facing east, guarding against the Japanese threat; several hundred horses; chariots and archers—"

"I want more," Temujin says decisively. "Guarding against every threat. What I protect is much more valuable than what this charlatan believed. He merely wanted to continue his rule, to live forever. But I know better. I know what the others seek, and only I can deny them."

"Very well, master. We shall start construction today."

"When will it be ready?"

"You are young," the old man says, rubbing his thin white beard. "And I have seen ahead. We will have time. All we need now is the place of your choosing. You will let me know soon?"

Temujin nods. He turns and strides out of the yurt, then looks north, following the outline of the winding, frozen Odon River. He blinks and he imagines sparkling lights far to the north, at the head of the snake, which has now become a dragon, and its tail twitching right before him. A tail that will move, one that will be forcibly moved to cover his entrance.

Turning on his heels, he heads back into the tent, slapping aside the entrance and boldly stepping in to where the old man still pores over the designs, calculating how to mimic such a grand and nearly impossible undertaking.

"I have decided," Temujin announces, pointing outside the tent. "It will be done here, right here. I have seen the way. There will be no burial mound, no obvious markers or pyramids. No sign that I am here, and as the last act, your men will divert the river and cover the entrance for all time."

The old man blinks at him, expressionless. Then he smiles, acknowledging and respecting the humility and the single-mindedness of his master.

"As you wish."

When Phoebe's consciousness slammed back to reality, she saw Caleb and reached for him, touched him, but then suddenly she was away again, down in the trenches, years later ...

... digging with thousands of others, climbing scaffolding, chiseling walls, dragging huge blocks down a makeshift ramp into a cavern the size of a small valley. Massive fires burn day and night, providing meager illumination to supplement each contingent's battalion of torches. Smoke, dust, heat and poor ventilation take a tremendous toll, and men drop every hour, only to be carted out along with the next haul of dirt and rocks.

All while the great Khan's mausoleum takes shape, a veritable subterranean city of shining marble and alabaster materializes as if carved from the bowels of the earth itself, as if born from its primordial core.

Here she works on the city's outer walls, carving the massive blocks and sharpening the crenulated towers, thickening the defenses. And here she digs trenches for the underground rivers that will flow—one for a moat, the other bisecting the Khan's great city. And there, she hangs below the domed ceiling in the palace, painting Temujin's visage on the dome's interior, surrounded by his wife Borto and his three sons, all smiling down to the immense marble-form sculpture of a white tent, his crypt, inside which even now others are carving his resting space.

At the entrance, looking down the ramp and into the massive cavern, she sees the first regiment of the twenty thousand terra cotta warriors tethered together and lying four on a side on a wooden sled, dragged down by horses, pulled into the depths to take up their eternal positions.

Forever vigilant.

And she smiles, confident in the mechanical defenses designed inside each one.

She retreats, seeing flashes now of great crossbows, loaded and poised at angles unseen by future trespassers. She sees pits dug into the floor and covered with false doors, trip wires and gear-actioned spikes, false passageways with even deadlier contents.

And she smiles, then retreats all the way, making room for the final procession—the coffin, the twenty silk-covered maidens, the young camel—and then when all is silent and all heads are bowed in mourning, she orders the great slab door shut. The dirt is piled over the entrance, and at last the river is diverted to its new course, concealing everything for all time.

"He's in trouble!"

Phoebe gasped, blinking back to the present and still tasting the smoke in her lungs, the scent of decay and death from so many thousands toiling and expiring underground. "What? Who?"

"Orlando." Caleb clasped her arm, drew her to the side of the door, then pointed across the mausoleum grounds, the mausoleum that now, after Phoebe had seen the real thing first-hand, seemed like such a tawdry shadow.

Two agents were hauling Orlando into the back seat.

"What do you think he did this time?" Phoebe asked.

"I have a bad feeling about this. Should we call Agent Wagner?"

"Don't bother," said another voice. Right behind them.

Caleb turned just as Phoebe said, "Oh shit."

Renée was in the doorway, the tip of her Walther .45 pressed Phoebe's side, just as two of her Chinese colleagues quickly ushered the other visitors out. Then they turned and drew their weapons.

"Sorry about this," Renée said. "But we don't have any more time. Your friend out there went snooping, glimpsing things he had no business seeing. I knew it was a risk, allying myself with psychics, but there was no alternative, not if there's a chance you might recover those keys."

"Damn," Caleb hissed. "I knew you were too good to be true."

Renée leveled her eyes at him, and her lips drew back into a wolfish sneer. "I believe you know where they are, so let's stop wasting time. Neither of us wants Montross to get those keys first."

5.

Back in the jeep, Orlando sat uncomfortably with his wrists cuffed behind him. On the seat next to him, one of the FBI agents aimed a gun at his face while he spoke into a receiver. The other man got behind the wheel.

"We've got him," said the closer one into the receiver. "Want us to hold here, or meet you at the site?"

"Just wait," came the response.

Orlando leaned forward and wriggled his wrists behind him. "Uh, guys? What's the charge here?"

"Shut up," the driver said.

"Okey-dokey then." Orlando offered a grin, seeing himself in the rearview mirror, surprised he didn't have the look of a terrified rabbit cornered by wolves. "You know," he said, "people tried to kill me yesterday and it didn't take, so you might want to rethink this setup. I have a feeling it's not my time."

The driver turned, lowered his sunglasses and stared at him. "Don't worry, when we get the order to terminate you, there's no chance you'll come out alive. Fate or not."

"We're professionals," the other agreed.

Orlando nodded. "Great. So do you want to let me in on the big secret? Who the hell are you guys, really?"

They turned around, ignoring him again. The walkie-talkie crackled and now Orlando heard Renée's voice. She must be inside the mausoleum, with Caleb and Phoebe. *"Tell me what you've seen. And be quick, or we start with your friend out there."*

The agent next to him pulled out a set of sharp-edged pliers, the kind used for cutting off stubborn construction nails. "That's our cue." He grabbed Orlando's left wrist.

Orlando struggled as the man tried to secure his pinky finger. "What the hell! Shit, no—I don't do torture."

"Tell me," Renée's voice again, *"or he loses a finger every ten seconds. You can watch from the window if you like."*

Orlando squirmed, but the agent held him against the side of the car with his knee in his side and his elbow against his neck as he trapped the little finger between the plier blades.

Orlando groaned. "Oh shit, I really didn't volunteer for this!"

Caleb held up a hand. "Please, we'll tell you. Just wait."

Renée held the phone to her mouth, lips parting, ready to give the word. Finally, she lowered it, took her finger off the button. "Speak."

Phoebe tugged Caleb's arm. "I don't know about your visions, but I don't think I got enough. I'm not sure—"

"Talk," Renée interrupted.

Caleb turned to her. "Tell us what you want. Who are you?"

"You're in no position to ask questions."

Caleb clenched his teeth. "Listen, I know you've done your homework on me, just like you gathered intel on Montross. So you know what I've done to protect the Emerald Tablet, what I've sacrificed. You must know that I'm not going to let those keys fall into the wrong hands, and as much as I like that crazy kid out there, if it's a choice between his fingers and the fate of the world, then I'll live with the guilt."

"Will you?"

Caleb never even blinked. "And if you kill him, I'll apologize to his mom and leave flowers on his grave on his birthday. But that will be after I kill you."

Renée smiled. "Now I know you're bluffing. You're not a killer. Prefer to let other people—or better yet, ancient booby traps—do that kind of thing for you."

Phoebe stepped forward. "Why the game, bitch?" One more foot, then she froze as the two agents pointed their AK-47s at her. She held up her hands and backed up. "Okay, okay. Why all this ruse, posing as an agent?"

"I *am* an FBI agent," Renée said. "It's just not my main job."

"A cover," Caleb said. "For what?"

Renée ignored him and stared at Phoebe. "You may not care enough about Orlando Natch, but I'm guessing you might want your sister around a little longer." She spoke over her shoulder. "Shoot her."

The guards cocked the weapons, stepped forward, aimed—

And then Caleb stepped in front of Phoebe. "All right! All right. You want to know what we saw?"

Renée motioned with her hands and the armed agents stepped back. "Every detail."

The cold fire of the pliers withdrew and Orlando wiggled his little pinky. *Still there, whew!* The pressure let up on his neck, and for a second he had his chance and as if on cue, feeling his limbs move as if on their own, he struck.

He leaned back, then swung sideways, threw his elbow around, taking the closer agent squarely in the jaw. He heard a crunch, then drew up his knees and kicked forward, just as the driver's face appeared around the front seat and slammed his boots into his nose, cracking the sunglasses at the same time.

Swinging his legs around again, he hoped for one more bit of luck and a chance to drop kick the first agent, but instead a fist rocked his temple, then the butt of a gun struck the back of his skull, and the world went dim—

—but not dark. Instead, there was a spark, a fizzling brilliance ...

... a lighter struck and a flame brought to a cigarette.

I've seen this before, he thought. Only hours before and now seeing it again, from a new angle, as if the first one wasn't clear enough... .

... Renée, younger—a teen perhaps—kneeling below a man who lights a cigarette. A grey-haired, bespectacled man with similar eyes of cold slate. And a ring, which Renée kisses as she bows her head. A golden ring with an inset gem of black onyx, with a symbol of a lance cleaving a dragon.

Renée stands, pushes back her hair and unbuttons her shirt, halfway down, revealing the orbs of her breasts straining against a tight black bra, between which a necklace settles, placed there by the old man.

On the necklace's charm, the same image of a lance and the dragon.

"You are one of us now," he whispers, and cheers rise up from the room. Others step out from the shadows. Robed, hooded. Not clear if they're men or women. Wine is passed, shared. Music springs from somewhere. Haunting, wild. Primal.

Hands reach out for Renée, nudging her forward. They peel off her shirt. Her bra slips away. She steps out of her skirt, kicks off her shoes and follows where her brothers and sisters lead her.

Toward an altar. A ram's head seemingly floats in the darkness above the marble slab, then moves forward, revealing a golden mask worn by another robed man, one who sheds his robe. He is naked, aroused. He pulls Renée to him, lays her on the altar, dutifully kisses her necklace, and then falls upon her as the congregation moves in to observe.

In the back, the well-dressed man lowers his head. He speaks to another member, the only other robed figure not at the altar.

"This one will serve us well."

The older man nods, his eyes sparkling.

"Underground," **Phoebe said** after Caleb nodded for her to speak. "His tomb is underground somewhere. I saw them building a huge mausoleum under the earth, and then concealing the entrance. But I couldn't tell where."

Renée switched her aim on her weapon, pointing it now at her left eye. "If that's all you saw, let's hope your brother's the better psychic."

Caleb considered lunging, then thought better of it, seeing both men, nearly the size of sumo wrestlers, with automatic weapons trained on him. How did he not think this through, cover the bases, and insist they check Renée out when he'd had time?

It was the same mistake he had made with George Waxman, trusting someone without doing the proper background checks, the kind only someone like Caleb was suited to perform. If only he hadn't lost his *sight*.

And now this snake in their midst had used them to get this far, and for all he knew, despite what she'd said, she might be working with Montross, keeping tabs on Caleb, having him work the Khan's tomb from another angle.

"Warriors!" Phoebe blurted out, and her eyes made contact, just briefly with Caleb's, but it was enough—a steadying of her fright, the widening of her lids just enough as he saw her. A look that said *trust me.*

"What warriors?" Renée asked.

"Lots of them. I saw an army under the ground, Asian soldiers. They were made of plaster, or—"

"Terra cotta?" Renée whispered. "Impossible. You must have had your vision mixed up with something else."

"I don't know what you mean," Phoebe said. "I just saw Genghis—Temujin—giving the command to hide his body, his tomb, inside of this other mausoleum that was already there."

"Where?"

"Somewhere in China. Um ... where one of the first emperors was buried or something. And he had this huge layout underground, with lots of traps and things." Phoebe rolled her eyes. "Of course there's got to be traps. But anyway, Genghis told them to bury him inside with this other dead ruler, since it was conveniently already there, and no one would think to look in someone else's place."

Caleb knew she was bluffing. He didn't need a vision to understand that. Temujin would never defile another ruler's rest, or share his own. But maybe what Phoebe had seen was close enough to make her lie convincing.

Renée took a step back, stroking her chin. She turned to the nearest agent, spoke something in Mandarin, nothing that Caleb could make out. "Emperor Qin Shi Huang. In Xian. An archaeological team is currently excavating the site. They found the terra cotta army back in 1998."

Caleb met his sister's look, and dared flash her a blink of a hope. But then two gunshots tore through the moment and Phoebe screamed.

Orlando's eyes lost focus and then tracked back to something that didn't make sense. A strange red splatter formation down the front of his *World of Warcraft* shirt.

I've been shot, he thought. Those bastards did it, shot a handcuffed prisoner. He blinked, astounded at the lack of pain, sure they'd hit his spine. *Paralyzed. Well, at least that's the way to go.*

His eyes blurred, then focused again when he heard a scream and a loud *pop!* Again something warm splashed on him, on his neck, the right side of his face, with what felt like tiny pebbles. *Why can I feel that?*

He shook his head and wiped his face on his shoulder.

"... are you?" asked a voice.

"Huh?" He still couldn't see. Just a dark, slender shape outside his window, pointing something shiny at him.

"I asked who you are." A woman's voice. Heavily accented, confident and powerful.

"Orlando Natch, at your service." He rubbed his eyes clean with his shoulder, then turned, trying to show off his shiny wrist bracelets. "Whoever you are, please help. I've got friends in there, and—"

"And they're as good as dead," said the woman, "unless you convince me in the next five seconds that you're not after the same thing as these agents. Or the people I left earlier today on a mountaintop in Mongolia."

"Outside!" Renée yelled to her agents. "Shots came from outside!"

She turned but kept the gun trained on Phoebe. "What else? Tell me now!"

"If you've hurt Orlando ..."

"Shut up!" she shouted, then repeated to Caleb, "Tell me now, or she dies too."

"You can't rush remote viewing," Caleb said, quickly getting in step with Phoebe's con. "It's given us one hit, but now we should all sit together and focus our visions on this Xian and the emperor there, see what we can come up with."

"So you can collude together and hone your lies? Send me in the wrong direction? I don't think so."

Another gunshot, then automatic fire. Renée cursed as she turned toward the door. Two dark shapes had rushed in, guns drawn. Renée dropped to a crouch and fired, knocking one back and wounding the other, who returned fire, missing. Caleb and Phoebe dropped to the floor, covering their heads. Caleb rolled, saw Renée get up and aim again. And then saw a shape at the window. But Renée fired down the hallway first, and a red spray burst from the other black-clad intruder's head. She stood, turned, and took two bullets in her chest. She stumbled back, staring down without growing comprehension, then another shot threw her into the wall below a replica shield.

She slumped to her knees, then fell face-forward.

"Go!" Caleb shouted, as Phoebe lay there, too shocked to move. He got to her, pulled her up by the arm, even as the steady footfalls ran toward him. A shadow fell over Phoebe, and Caleb lowered his head. Raised his arms.

He looked up and saw a startlingly serene face, crowned with straight midnight-black hair, tanned skin and warm eyes the mirror of a broad turquoise sky. She was dressed in a black ski jacket and black jeans with knee-high boots.

"Your friend is outside, and he's convinced me not to kill you if you come along with me right now."

Caleb helped Phoebe to her feet, keeping a wary eye on their rescuer. "I guess we're going. And thanks."

"You keep dangerous acquaintances," the woman said, leading them through the hallway, stepping over other black-clothed bodies.

"You," Caleb said, "are you Darkhad?"

She froze, then turned her head, considering him. "My name is Qara, and yes, I am. As you've guessed. But now, I'm taking you to Beijing, and then seeing you on a plane home."

"Can't," Caleb said. "Not until I save my son."

She studied his face. "Your boy?"

"Abducted by a man named Xavier Montross."

"And," said Phoebe, "a nasty bitch named Nina Osseni."

Qara's eyes turned dark. "Montross. He has red hair?"

Caleb nodded eagerly. "You've seen him? Is Alexander—"

"The boy was fine when I left his group in the Khenti Mountains. But they killed my friends."

"I'm so sorry," Caleb said, taking a deep breath, but inwardly nodding to himself, releasing a cry of relief. *Alexander's okay. Kid's probably driving Montross nuts.* "So they're looking on the Sacred Mountain, following the wrong visions."

Qara tightened her grip on the gun. "Why do you say they're in the wrong place?"

"Because," Phoebe said, "we've seen—"

"Because you're here," Caleb inserted, realizing his error. "Just a guess. If Montross's team was on the right track, you never would have left them."

Qara eyed him for a long moment, analyzing his face. Finally, she said, "True."

Over her shoulder, Caleb saw a jet-black Hummer idling with Orlando inside, his face pressed against the window. The other visitors were leaving the parking lot, some running, others driving or biking. In the distance, he heard sirens.

Caleb blinked and looked away from her penetrating gaze. "But I'm sorry, we can't leave yet. We need to find the tomb. It may be the only way to get my son back."

Qara shook her head. "You won't use my Lord's secret as a bargaining chip."

"I don't want to, but I don't believe there's any other choice. Montross will come, and he will find it."

"You said his visions were wrong."

"And he'll figure that out, soon enough." *Or Alexander will.*

She narrowed her eyes at them. "And where do you think it is?"

Back in the western hall, Renée could still hear them. She lay flat on her stomach, wincing. The Kevlar vest had stopped the bullets, but the pain had drilled into her ribs, her breastbone. It felt like her lungs were on fire. But she had to lie still. Couldn't give herself away, even though every cell screamed at her to get up, pick up her gun and blow that bitch to hell, and then start in on Phoebe and Caleb.

But that had to wait.

She had to listen.

This wasn't over yet. She had played her part perfectly on this mission. Played up the dedicated FBI agent, sympathetic to Caleb's plight, and his talents. Got them to lower their guard, but then that damn kid had too much time on his hands and went snooping where he didn't belong. Well, her master and colleagues feared this might happen, and she knew the risks. Which was why Plan B was always ready. Her security force, listening in at all times for any sign the Morpheus team had got wind of who she really was. At that stage, the operation turned from one of stealth to one of brazen force.

More than one way to skin this cat. Besides, she never believed she was in any danger. Not with these people. She was protected, chosen.

She was fated to find those keys and fulfill her destiny.

"Tell her," Caleb said, looking at Phoebe, "what you saw." They were in the hallway, just past two dead Darkhad and before the other pair of Renée's men, cut down at the entrance.

"What do you mean, *saw*?" Qara asked. "When?"

"We're kind of psychic," Phoebe admitted, looking to Caleb first for approval to elaborate. "Remote viewers. We find things, and can sometimes see into the past."

Qara stared at her, then at Caleb. Her face gave away nothing. "And what did you see?"

"He's in a city, a huge city, inside a domed palace." Phoebe bit her lip, eyes losing focus, remembering. *"Underground."*

Qara remained frozen, just listening.

"I saw a river, and terra cotta warriors."

"But," said Caleb, "we told that agent in there it was Qin Shi Huang's mausoleum, and that Genghis Khan just borrowed a pre-existing site."

Phoebe cleared her throat. "But I saw the truth. Saw them merely model a new mausoleum after Huang's older one. Saw them hollowing out great caverns underground, building an entire walled city, complete with a river and a small sea, gardens and monasteries, all for the dead. But it's somewhere else."

"Where?" Qara asked breathlessly.

"Why don't you just tell us?" Caleb snapped. "We're close. An hour or so with Orlando digitally mapping the exterior of the entranceway, designed from what Phoebe saw, and then matching the images to—" He looked at Phoebe, who had slumped forward, rocking. She slid sideways, supported against the wall.

"What?"

"Never mind Orlando," Phoebe whispered. "I'm seeing ... something."

Caleb held her hand and she gripped him back, tighter.

"Paper," she said sharply. "Give me paper, a pencil."

He dug into her pack, pulled out the ever-handy sketchpad. And then Phoebe was down on her knees, eyes gone almost completely white, oblivious to the gun Qara still trained on them, oblivious to her look of confusion.

Caleb set the pencil in her right hand, the pad in her left. And she immediately bent down and started to sketch ...

... a lonely farmhouse on the English moors, not far from a small cobbled church ...

Tear off the page. Next ...

... a single room, a candle and a chair. A man asleep in the chair, an open book on his chest, an empty glass on a nearby table, with a medicine stopper beside it... .

Next ...

... letters at the top, spelling the name "COLERIDGE" underlined twice ...

"Coleridge?" Caleb said, reading it aloud. "Coleridge ... Oh my—"

"I don't believe this," Qara said, barely above a whisper.

Phoebe's eyes focused. She dropped the pencil and stood up. She glanced at Qara, then to Caleb, her face lost in confusion. "What?"

"Phoebe," Caleb said, "you're magnificent."

"I know, but what did I see?"

"A clue. Now I know," Caleb exclaimed triumphantly, "where he's buried."

Qara groaned, raised the gun. "And now I'm sorry, but I think I have to kill you."

A shot rang out, Caleb and Phoebe winced, but only the statue of Genghis Khan was struck—a wild shot, blasting off one of his hands. They turned and saw Renée, hobbling against a wall, leaning out from cover to shoot. She held her ribs with one hand and aimed with the other.

She fired again, but this time Caleb grabbed Qara and pulled her back toward the door and out of the line of fire. Phoebe was already in full sprint, pushing through the door, stumbling outside. Qara followed, but Caleb stopped over the body of one of the fallen agents and scooped up the AK-47. He hefted it, then throwing caution to the wind, turned the corner and squeezed off a burst of deafening fire at Renée. Never holding such a powerful weapon, it nearly rattled free from his grip. The bullets went wild, spraying the walls and the ceiling, missing Renée by a mile.

Then her hand swung around, finding Caleb in her sights.

Caleb turned and bolted as more shots rang out.

Through the door he ran, just as the Hummer launched forward and the back door opened, Phoebe waving him in. Four large strides and he was there, jumping inside, slamming the door behind him.

Renée appeared in the mausoleum's doorway, still firing at them, when four white and blue jeeps roared into the parking lot—Chinese military—sirens blaring. Caleb looked back and saw Renée confidently running toward them.

Did she have connections with this crowd as well?

"Just who the hell is that FBI chick?" Phoebe asked from the back seat.

"I don't know," Caleb responded, then abruptly swung his weapon around, aiming at the back of Qara's head. "But one thing at a time. Orlando, get her gun, and Qara, please just drive."

He saw her eyes flash in the rearview mirror.

"I'm sorry," he said. "I know you're sworn to protect his secret, but believe me in addition to us psychics, you've got another team of highly resourceful treasure-hunters on the trail of your master's whereabouts. And unless you've got an army of Darkhad left to help, you might need our help."

"I thought," said Qara, "you were planning to break into the tomb."

"We are," Caleb admitted, "but not to steal. Temujin can remain, along with all his treasure and his secrets. We just need to protect what Xavier Montross is looking for. If he finds it—"

"We're all screwed," Orlando said as he snatched away Qara's gun.

Qara accelerated, keeping an eye on the dirt road behind them as they roared into the desert, bounding over the sparse grasslands toward a dusty horizon.

"I'm guessing," Caleb said, "that you don't have any Darkhad at the actual site."

"There are not many of us left," Qara whispered.

"How many?" asked Phoebe.

"I left four on Burkhan Khaldun, but Montross brought in rein-forcements—soldiers. They will try to pick off those men there, but—"

"But that's it?" Phoebe asked. "Your people didn't stay close to the real site?"

"Why would we? That would only draw attention."

"What real site?" Orlando asked. "Did we find it? Where are we going?"

"Yeah," Phoebe said. "Where? I'm still lost underground somewhere. What's with this farmhouse I saw and someone named Coleridge?"

"Samuel Coleridge," Caleb said, sitting back, still keeping his grip on the AK-47. "The English poet. The story goes that in 1797 he was in ill-health and stopped for a rest at a secluded farmhouse somewhere near Devonshire. It's believed that he took some opium, and while reading a travel book, fell asleep"—

"Been there, done that," Orlando said. "But maybe not opium."

—"and had a dream. I'm wondering now if it might not have been more of a vision, a *remote vision*. He woke and wrote down part of his dream, but then a guest showed up, and when he sat back to finish it he could only capture fleeting bits of it."

Qara's expression fell. She shook her head. "I don't understand how this is possible, how you know."

"We don't understand how it works either," Caleb admitted. "Sometimes we're just shown what we ask to see, other times we see what we need. It's as if some unseen hand controls the projection booth in our minds, and we're just in the audience, watching."

"I'm still lost," Phoebe said. "I was a science geek. English lit I kind of slept through."

"Ditto," said Orlando, "but that's why God invented Google." He flipped open his notebook tablet and accessed the web.

"I don't remember all of the poem," Caleb said. "Just a few lines: *Where Alph, the sacred river, ran / Through caverns measureless to man / Down to a sunless sea ...*"

Orlando clapped his hands together. "Aha, you skipped Coleridge's first line: *In Xanadu did Kublai Khan / a stately pleasure-dome decree.*"

"Xanadu," Phoebe whispered, and Qara made a soft moan.

"Kublai Khan was Temujin's grandson," Caleb told her, "and built his marvelous summer palace and imperial center, the likes of which dazzled visitors including Marco Polo, here in Mongol-controlled China. At Shang-du or Tei-bing—also known as Xanadu."

"And he built this place," Phoebe asked, "over the spot of his grandfather's tomb?"

Caleb saw Qara's reaction, the brief closing of her eyes, and knew he was right.

"As above, so below."

6.

Alexander felt like a farm animal, herded into the lead jeep—more of a tank-like thing with seriously thick metal plating, tinted windows and leather seats—and forced to sit right between Xavier Montross and Nina Osseni, on the hump.

The military guy, Hiltmeyer, drove, while someone named Harris, a soldier with a crew cut and a square jaw, sat in the front passenger seat. He had a machine gun in his lap. Alexander squirmed in his seat, looking over his shoulder, past the containers, portable generators, body armor, weapons and digging equipment, to look out the back window at the other four vehicles revving up behind them.

"On our way," Hiltmeyer said, turning from the base camp and away from the Sacred Mountain, leaving the Khenti Mountain range in their wake. "Program the route, sergeant."

"Already done," said the soldier up front, after finishing up with the GPS assistant, and lighting up the map on the small built-in screen.

"Xanadu." Montross shook his head, his eyes blinking quickly. "All this time, everyone who looked for the Khan's grave ... right under their noses."

"They tricked you good," Alexander said quietly.

"Tricked everybody good." He glanced past Alexander, to Nina. "Now that we have time, let's be sure about this—and see exactly where it is we need to excavate. I don't want to waste any time when we get there. Go ahead, Nina. Touch him."

"What—?" Alexander bolted upright, but Nina had already reached down, grasped his right wrist and took it in an iron-fisted grip.

"One of her special talents," Montross said, his words drowning in the gunning of the motor, lost in the moans coming from Alexander's own throat. Unbidden sounds released from the primal source of his most recent visions, rising up again.

Replayed, this time for the sole enjoyment of the woman clenching his wrist. Nina, her eyes gone white, head back, in almost ecstatic pose.

Taking.

Seeing.

She released him, flexed and rubbed her fingers as if singed, and took a deep breath. "Got it." She rubbed her hands together, then gently touched Alexander's head. "I saw the spot over the river, the entrance. There were early Darkhad members staring down at it from a gilded bridge in Xanadu."

"It'll look a lot different now," Montross said. "I considered visiting Shangdu years ago on a trip to Beijing to see the Wall." He grinned. "To *see* the Wall actually defended and rebuilt, first-hand. But I thought better of wasting the time to go all that way, since there's nothing at old Xanadu anymore, and no other sites of interest in the vicinity. Just some perimeter stones and an archway. Almost no tourism."

Alexander perked up, trying to get over what had just been ripped from him. "The whole city's gone?"

Montross nodded. "After Kublai Khan's death in 1294, later generations couldn't sustain the Mongol empire. Xanadu fell out of use, despite its splendor, and the Chinese emperors chose the more strategically located Beijing as their capital."

"So," Colonel Hiltmeyer said, glancing in the rearview mirror, "we're going to a field of old rocks?"

"Exactly. The perfect hiding spot. They sent us scurrying up distant mountainsides, even sacrificed themselves to make it look like we were close, and all the while, they knew it was far away, in the middle of nowhere." He leaned forward and started talking to Hiltmeyer, discussing strategy and deployment of the men once they got there.

Nina took that as her chance to go back—back to the well for more.

"Alexander," she whispered, leaning in close even as the boy shrank away. She again took his wrist, hissing, "Play along. This will be over in a moment."

"What are you doing?" he whispered back.

"You've been keeping secrets," she said. "I saw a glimpse. Something else, something you've been seeing. A lot."

"No."

"Oh yes, boy. The Sphinx. And the door. Show it to me."

"No, please, it scares me. I don't like to—"

"*Now!*"

A rush of something like electricity tingled through Nina's fingertips and up her arm, jolting the synapses in her brain, firing the spaces between them, lighting up a holographic screen in her vision.

Maybe, she thought, it was the proximity of the Emerald Tablet, in a sturdy plastic case at Xavier's feet. Or maybe it was just being so close to the boy and to Montross, their power seeping into her, augmenting what talents she had.

Dimly, she heard Montross and Hiltmeyer talking, someone asking about the whereabouts of Caleb Crowe, and the fact that they had lost him after Turkey, assuming he was on his way either to Mongolia, or else he was already ahead of them, nearing Xanadu.

"Wouldn't surprise me," Montross said, "which is why I took his son. Had a feeling it would charge Caleb up, get him to the church on time, as the old song goes."

Nina tuned him out and tuned in to the presentation she had tapped into: the boy's vision, his suppressed dream. Just as Caleb's childhood had been plagued by recurring dreams of his father in an Iraqi torture cell, and images of an eagle and a star—implicit answers to his life's most desperate questions provided by his hyper-aware subconscious—so too did Alexander's psyche conjure visions that he might someday need to see ...

... the Giza plateau, on a torch-lit walkway leading to the forepaws of the Great Sphinx. Only, its head is different, that of a lion instead of the ill-proportioned pharaoh countenance that sits on its body today. Behind the

Sphinx looms a triangular leviathan, an enormous pyramid blotting out the stars, its shape only visible by the absence of light.

Approaching the stairwell between the paws, descending the marble stairs. Down a flight of large steps, into a room of solid gold walls bereft of writing, and two emerald pillars flanking a great door—a huge imposing slab of onyx, black as the blackest starless night.

Before that doorway stands a man dressed in regal attire, a pharaoh's headdress, a gilded snake crown on his head, the flail and staff held in his hands.

"Welcome, Djeda. Thank you for obeying my summons."

"I had little choice, Lord Khufu." The voice was sad and resigned.

"You are a magician."

"Some call me that."

"And you have certain access to knowledge, lost wisdom concerning what may lie behind this door." He motions over his shoulder. "This door that cannot be forced, bent, dislodged or even scratched. My workers uncovered it while excavating this area, but have found no record of its purpose, much less how to proceed beyond it. But I believe you may know."

"I do, My Lord."

"You can open it?"

"I did not say that."

"Do not try my patience."

"I said I know how it can be opened, but I do not have the power to do so."

"Who does?"

"There is a tale, recorded on building texts at the Temple of the Great Horus in Edfu, that refers to sacred books and objects of power that our Lord Thoth deemed too dangerous for mankind. And so he gathered them all and hid them away in a great underground temple, protected by power staffs and pillars, and he then sealed the entrance, leaving only its guardians to know of its whereabouts."

"Until I discovered it," Khufu says. "Perhaps I am destined to collect those objects, those sacred writings, and become like the gods themselves. Who are these guardians? Are you one?"

"I am not worthy. But I gained some knowledge, scraps of the truth, so that I know what this is. I know this is the place, the door to the sacred temple which lies below this plain, through passages remote and twisting, further guarded by magic and cruel invention. I know this only, but no more."

The Pharaoh makes an impatient, wolfish snarl. "Who can open this door?"

"A prophecy tells of three keys."

"Keys?" The Pharaoh turns. "I see no place for keys."

"Three keys," Djeda continues. "For three brothers."

"What brothers?"

"I do not know. It is said they were, or will be, born on the fifteenth day of Tybi, to the wife of the high priest of Ra."

"And you do not know if they have already been born? If they walk among us?"

"No."

"Then I will send for this priest. And every priest of Ra."

"You may have a long wait."

Pharaoh Khufu turns and faces the door. He bows his head. Places a hand on the smooth door. "I found this for a reason. I will not be denied."

"It is not for me to say, Lord, if your destiny lies behind that door."

"I heard you, magician."

Nina blasted out of the vision, rocked with a jarring bump on the rocky terrain as the jeep banked around a bend in the Kherlen River, speeding toward the Chinese border.

She released Alexander, who was sweating, eyes heavy, barely open.

"What happened to him?" Montross asked, turning around. Alexander slumped to the side, breathing slowly, exhausted.

Nina shook her head, lowered her eyes. "Nothing. Car sick, maybe."

"Tough it out, kid. Going to be a long ride."

Nina took a deep breath, then leaned back, trying to appear relaxed. "Xavier? I never asked you about your childhood. Did you have sisters? Brothers?"

Frowning at her, he shook his head. "Remember? Parents killed when I was six? And no other rugrats before or after me, far as I know."

"You never *looked*?"

His expression darkened despite the waning sun blasting through his window. "Okay, my father? He wasn't my real father."

"You were adopted?"

"No, I only said my dad wasn't my dad. He married my mother after she had me." He sighed, and his eyes dulled with anger. "I only tried to find my real father once. Saw my mother with someone. An oily haired college-type." He waved his hand. "Some quick tryst, and she never saw him again. I got that much."

"What else?"

"What else? That's it. That's all I wanted to know. He was a prick, and I had more important things to chase after than someone who only wanted to chase after coeds."

"Oh. Okay, then. So, when was your birthday?"

"What the hell is this, twenty questions?"

She gave a weak smile. "Maybe I want to send you a card, and a tie."

"It's October fifteenth, okay? My favorite color is red, I love pistachio ice cream, long walks through ancient ruins, treasure hunting and seeking magical objects of immense power. And I'm not afraid who gets hurt—or killed—in the process. Anything else, dear Nina? Are we a good fit?"

She laughed. "No one's a match for me, you know that."

"Black widow?"

"The blackest." She closed her eyes, thinking. *The Emerald Tablet, so close.* could enhance her visions, but she was never good at initiating them, only in bringing such powers out of other people, and then sharing in the sights. She could try it with Xavier, try to view his father again, but she wasn't sure if this was something she wanted to share with him just yet.

Three brothers.

Three keys.

Alexander had been seeing this vision for years, but never anything more. No further details, but whatever this was, it was vitally important, crucial that he understand it. But he was still too young, and couldn't rationalize it out.

But maybe she could, given more time with the boy.

On the drive, as Montross closed his eyes, meditating or dreaming, she wasn't sure which, Alexander fell completely asleep. He rested his head on Nina's shoulder, perhaps drawing comfort there in a longing for his lost mother. She shifted in her seat to prevent it from lolling forward.

Who were the three brothers? she thought. Surely they hadn't been born in Khufu's time, around 2600 BCE, or any time in the following forty-five hundred years, or else the door would have been opened, and the keys would not still have been hidden away, protected.

Guarded.

Some prophet and seer had glimpsed the future, seen enough to reveal a prophecy. It was possible the three could be here, right now. *Who were they?*

She had an idea now, based on what Montross had told her and Alexander's vision of his parents' car crash. His true father.

A college-type.

She thought back to her time in Alexandria, one night with Caleb, sharing his visions, his dreams. And of course, she had read George Waxman's extensive file on the Crowe family. Especially the details on Phillip, Caleb's father. The college professor.

A smile formed on her lips.

Things were certainly getting a lot more interesting.

7.

Renée Wagner put away her badge and her credentials. The lead sergeant, Chang Xiaolong, returned her satellite phone after his supervisor in Beijing had sternly ordered him to provide Renée with anything she wished.

She spoke in Mandarin, with authority, as she removed her Kevlar vest, trying not to wince. "He told you what we have here?"

"Yes, Agent Wagner."

"A threat to your national security. And an opportunity. Your men, are they trustworthy? Loyal?"

"Of course, every one."

"Good, then not a word of this gets out. And they are now under *my* control, is that clear?"

He bowed his head quickly, and Renée smiled. *Must've gotten his ear chewed off.* "I want all these vehicles on the road now. But first, load them with halogen floodlights, generators, dynamite, shovels and flashlights, extra ammo. And call in a helicopter. I want you and three of your best shooters there ASAP. And find me a new vest. Please." She dropped the one that had just saved her life. She touched the chain around her neck, pulled out the charm and stared at it—at the lance spearing the dragon, the ancient symbol.

Soon, they would have the keys. Caleb and his new friend couldn't stop her. And if Montross was on his way, she would deal with him, too.

"Agent? The jeeps—once they have the supplies, where should I send these men?"

She turned her face to the cool wind and the bright blue sky. "To Xanadu."

WASHINGTON, DC 1:13 A.M., THE PENTAGON

Senator Mason Calderon followed his armed escort through the sub-basement halls, around a corner and through a door requiring a palm-print verification and retina scan. He moved slowly, deliberately, walking with a cane although he didn't need it. Smooth mahogany shaft, the cane had a golden handle in the shape of a coiled dragon with a spearpoint through its skull. Calderon's fingers gently held the solid gold tip, carrying it more than using it to lean on as he glided down the silent polished floors.

Various black-ops projects were given space down here in these well-protected and anonymous bunkers, and this one's budget was modest compared to some. Not concerned with regime change, terrorist tracking or domestic surveillance, this one had simply existed for the purpose of monitoring certain sites of archaeological and cultural significance.

But eight years ago, after the incident at the Pharos site, its mandate had changed from passive observation to direct participation, and preparation for an event more than five thousand years in the waiting.

A new leader had assumed control, a man that was particularly motivated, a high initiate in the true organization behind this project.

As soon as the door whisked shut behind him, Senator Calderon set his briefcase on the table and ignored, for the moment, the man sitting at the far end, in the shadows, visible only by the dim glow of his cigarette.

Something smelled foul, not entirely masked by the smoke.

Calderon stared at the eight flat screens mounted on the side walls. Four screens displayed only text and numerical data, coordinates of various teams in the field. The other four showed satellite images of several sites: a familiar blue-domed structure; a downward-facing view of the desert plain, three pyramids and a reclining stone sphinx; and then moving views of two sets of vehicles speeding across barren terrain.

"How close are they?" Calderon asked.

A throat cleared in a raspy, agonized cough. "Which team? The Morpheus Initiative or Agent Wagner's?" Calderon could barely make out the words. The voice, ravaged, grating as though speaking through a mouthful of hot ash. He could only imagine the pain the man must be enduring, and to have refused drugs and treatment. True, it was a miracle he survived, and clearly he was favored, but maybe this was his punishment for failure.

Calderon looked at the screens. "Where's Renée?"

"On her way. She'll catch them soon." His voice tapered and faded in a shrill hiss. "But, you should be more concerned about our third party." A scarred and bandaged hand emerged into the cone of light, a hand with two fingers free of wrappings, revealing a single large black ring on the ring finger. A ring with a familiar design. The hand pressed a button on the table-top remote and the scene with the mausoleum switched to another view, zooming down in increments until focusing on a gap in a pine forest where four jeeps were parked, the occupants outside.

"Rest stop for Montross?" Calderon asked.

"Probably the boy," said the voice. "They'll be on the move again soon. Intel from Agent Wagner seems reliable. Confirmed by the Montross team as well, after their initial mistake."

"Xanadu," said Calderon. "Amazing. So, now we take them out?"

"No." The shadows deepened as the cigarette went out. "Finding Genghis's mausoleum was the easy part. Getting inside, through the surprises he's got waiting for us, will be hell. So no, we need them. Caleb and Phoebe, and their talents. See that Agent Wagner doesn't start shooting right away."

Calderon's hands clenched into fists. "It was too risky putting her in the middle of their group when they were still so paranoid after Waxman. Just one probe and that kid got pretty close to us. Lucky he was too preoccupied and distracted to focus his abilities. But we don't know. What if they've figured out who we are?"

"Doesn't matter what they know. Caleb's preoccupied with saving his son. He'll get those keys."

"Or Montross will. And who knows what he'll do with them?"

"He'll do exactly what we fear he'll do," said the voice. A raspy sigh. "So he dies first. Tell Renée. Remove him as soon as he's no longer of use."

"What about Hiltmeyer? Do they suspect him?"

The bandaged hand waved in the air, scattering the lingering smoke. "I would think Nina suspects everyone, but Hiltmeyer's ready. He'll keep up his guard."

"This is a dangerous game, playing with people who can see your best-kept secrets as if you've stapled them to your forehead. I don't like it."

"We have no choice."

Calderon stared at his feet. "Don't we? The tablet is there, with Montross and our man. We can get it any time. We could work at our own method of translation."

"The thought has crossed my mind. But no, I don't think even the NSA computers would succeed with this. We need the sacred box."

"And your scrolls, the ones you Keepers recovered from the Pharos? They can't tell us anything?"

A spark and another cigarette was lit, briefly highlighting a gruesome face burnt and blackened, oozing with pus, one eye scarred shut, the other fiercely blue.

"I have learned all I can from them. Found further verification, focusing the time now, here at the end of the Age of Pisces. One of Three Brothers will open the great sealed box of Thoth."

"Yes. We know two, but who is the third?"

The man stood, easing himself out of the shadows. His scorched face and bandaged neck emerged into the dim light.

Robert Gregory offered a lipless smile. "If we depend on a loose reading of the prophecy, I believe it's me."

8.

"Fifty miles to go," Orlando said, noting the mileage on the GPS.

Caleb relaxed his hold on the gun. Qara seemed to be playing along, at least for now, following the route and keeping quiet. He could only imagine what she was thinking.

"Plenty of time to do a little recon."

"What are you thinking, big brother?" Phoebe asked, stretching in the seat beside him.

"Thinking about our brush with death, about how I hate surprises and have had enough double-crosses for my life. I want to know about Renée."

"Like who the hell she really is?"

"I can tell you what I saw," Orlando said, glancing back. "What set her off."

"Oh," Phoebe said, "now I see. This was all your fault?"

He grinned. "Yep. I think she would have just been content to have us lead her to it, until I blew it by asking her about a necklace I saw in my vision."

"Start from the beginning, please," Caleb said. He might not be able to help with first-hand psychic visions, but his knowledge of history and the arcane facets of myth might just provide the help they needed.

"Okay, so I saw Renée. A bit younger, at an initiation-kind of ceremony. One of those things where there's lots of people in black robes, and she, well ..." He blushed and looked away from Phoebe. "Well, she wasn't really wearing much. Some old dude gave her a necklace with a charm that looked like the one on his ring, and then some other guy took her on an altar while the others watched."

"Sure this wasn't just one of your sick fantasies?" Phoebe asked.

"Close, but no. I saw it, and when I asked her about the necklace, she unleashed hell on me and went after you guys."

"Cover blown," Caleb thought out loud. "Okay, so what was the image on the charm?"

"A dragon, run through with a spear."

"Not a sword?"

"No, not really St. George-like. I looked at some images of him online, but it wasn't a match. It's different, it's—"

"More ancient," Caleb said, catching Qara's eyes darting to his in the mirror. "It could be a number of symbols, but I have a theory."

"Of course you do," Phoebe said with a smile. "Let's hear it."

"Tiamat," he said. "An ancient Sumerian goddess. She took the shape of a dragon or sea serpent. She represented the primeval chaos before creation, and she and her consort Apsu were credited with creating all the deities. In the Babylonian epic of creation, the *Enuma Elish*, the world, including humanity, is created around her remains after she is destroyed by the storm god, Marduk, whose symbol is the lance."

"Ah," said Orlando, searching for it on the Internet, "got it! Found a symbol, and it looks pretty much spot-on. And wait! It says Tiamat possessed something called the *Tablet of Destiny*! With it, she was given the power over the universe. Wow, that sounds familiar."

"What else does it say?" Phoebe asked.

"Well, her offspring rose up against her to fight in some great primordial battle, and Marduk was chosen to be their hero. He bested Tiamat with arrows of the winds, a net and a powerful magic lance. But first, knowing they were coming, she had given the tablet to her son, Kingu, who somehow merged it with his armor, hoping to become invincible. But it didn't help. Marduk went after him. With the power of his lance he overthrew Kingu, then took the tablet for himself."

Caleb nodded. "But later, if I recall, he was forced to give it back to the eldest god, Anu, the lord of heaven."

Phoebe leaned forward. "And what, dare I ask, did Anu do with it?"

"Well, he was part of a triad of gods, with Enki, lord of the waters, and Enlil/Marduk, lord of the sky. Anu was sometimes called their father, because he was the oldest. In any case, it was Enki who got the tablet. Anu must have trusted him more. And Enki, as he was known in Babylon, had another name in Egypt."

"Oooh," said Phoebe, raising her hand. She promptly put it down after a scowl from Caleb. "Of course, it's got to be Thoth."

"Bingo."

"Here we go," said Orlando. "So where does that leave us? What is Renée a part of? Some Marduk-lovers cult, jilted after doing all the work of beating Tiamat, wresting the tablet from her, only to have his daddy take it away and give it to his no-good brother?"

"Seems that way," Caleb said. "And now they want it back."

"Wait," said Orlando. "Was Marduk ram-headed by any chance?"

Caleb nodded. "As Amun-Ra in Egypt, he was ram-headed during the Zodiacal age of the Ram. Why?"

"Oh, just because Renée's boyfriend-lover in my dream wore a ram's mask."

Caleb scratched his chin. "Qara? You've been rather silent. Does any of this make sense?"

She was silent for a long time, merely staring ahead at the dusty road and the glimmering, hazy horizon. "It seems," she said, turning her eyes on Caleb in the mirror, "there are two ancient forces contending for that tablet and the keys to unlock its power. Which side are you on?"

One hundred fifty miles to the northeast, Montross stretched his legs and stared at the road ahead. He sucked in a deep breath of air so pure and crisp it was as though his lungs were bared to the outside, directly absorbing every molecule.

While Colonel Hiltmeyer called in their location on his secure satellite phone, Nina stood by the back of their jeep, cleaning her guns and checking their equipment. Montross noticed she still kept a motherly eye on Alexander, off in the nearest set of bushes, busy relieving himself.

It was time. He opened his pack, reached down and touched the tablet. Caressed its impossibly smooth angles, felt its power as his index finger lingered over symbols that seemed to react to his touch. His heart rate increased, his eyes grew heavy, his legs weak. He reluctantly closed the flap, stumbled back to the jeep, then slid into the back seat.

"What's wrong with you?" Nina asked, gliding over at once and ducking her head inside.

Montross held up a hand. "Nothing I didn't ask for."

"What, are you trying for a vision? Now?"

"Need to snoop on our friends. See how far they've gotten."

"Okay fine. But do you"—she reached over, touched his face seductively, turned his chin toward her as she leaned in, placing her lips inches from his—"need any help?"

"Ordinarily, I might say yes. But now that I've got the tablet, I have what I need. And you, my dear, ought to keep an eye on our guest."

"The boy's not going anywhere. He's just ... Oh shit!" She stared out the window, incredulous. "The little brat's actually making a break for it."

"For what? We're in the middle of nowhere. Just go get him."

Montross knew she was still speaking, but there was no sound in the jeep. It was as if the world had fallen away, dissolving around him into an absence of color, pure white like a blank canvas, one that he longed to fill. He moaned, then opened his eyes and pushed his face forward, through what felt like a thick, gelatinous curtain, to pry this vision free—except it did more than that. Just as once before, down in Caleb's lighthouse vault, it plucked his very psyche from his body and hurtled it across time and space, until ...

... in a field of stones, weeds and grass. Broken pillars, moss-eaten stones that once ran in some kind of pattern.

Ruins.

Xanadu.

Shimmering, the landscape, the dying sun, the sickly grouping of nearby oak trees, oddly translucent, the bark glistening in the twilight, reflecting the dim glow of approaching headlights.

Headlights brighten, the engine coughs and the lights go out. A Hummer stops near the main archway, the only significant standing feature left of Xanadu. Without making any physical effort, Montross is closer, with just a directed thought.

Doors open. Two women get out. Two men.

One of them ... Caleb!

In that instant, Caleb looks around, and Montross pulls back, trying to disappear, to reel himself back. The sudden fear of discovery leads to the panic of being non-corporeal, of being unable to make it back. Could he be trapped like this? Far from his body, so distant, slumped in the back seat of a jeep? Vulnerable.

Caleb turns toward him, mouth open.

He knows! He can see!

Frowning, Caleb takes a step toward him, then another, reaching out. Now he is running.

Montross tries to get away as Caleb's image flutters, breaks into pieces and scatters like a million multicolored leaves blowing all around him, spinning, circling, then reforming into the interior of a jeep.

Nina's face …

… over his, Alexander thrust into the seat beside him, Nina's hand still clutching his hair. "You, sit still!" Then to Montross, "You okay? I thought we'd lost you."

Montross, taking deep gulps of air, wiped the sweat from under his tangled red hair, turned to Nina and smiled at Alexander.

"Just saw your dad. He's waiting for us at Xanadu."

Hiltmeyer let Private Harris drive while he sat in the front passenger seat and reviewed the site. "Remote, no tourist centers, guards or anything. Sounds like the annual visitors are pretty much nil, a bunch of backpackers maybe, but that's it."

"So much for their national treasure," Nina said.

"Just the way the Darkhad wants it," Montross added. "They couldn't have been too happy with Kublai Khan's decision to build his summer palace right over the secret mausoleum."

Alexander stirred, squeezing his shoulders free. "But I get why he did it, don't you?"

"What?" Nina asked.

"A palace and a city, right over the underground caverns. And then another city." Alexander beamed. "As Above, so Below!"

Montross shrugged, then let a smile form. "Still, the Darkhad didn't like it and were happy to let the place go to hell after Kublai died. They probably helped to scatter the remnants and encourage the focus to shift to Beijing."

"So," said Hiltmeyer, "the top, the 'Above' as the kid puts it, is a piece of cake. Assuming Crowe and his team find the entrance for us, what can we expect in the 'Below'?"

Montross sighed. "To answer that question, I'll need some peace and quiet." He looked back to Alexander. "And maybe a little help from our guest."

He lifted up the satchel with the tablet, feeling it hum, vibrate through the leather. Waiting, impatient. "We're going to check it out. I can only imagine, though, what old Genghis has in store. But I bet," he said to Alexander, "it'll make your dad's defenses down in your old lighthouse look like a walk in the park."

"Oh great," said Alexander, trying to sound confident, but Montross could feel the boy tremble.

Good, he thought. *Fear will sharpen his senses, attune his visions.*

"Help us, kid. And you help your father too. Because this time he doesn't have years to ponder and study and prepare for this descent, not like the Pharos. This time, he's only got a few hours. Aunless he's asking the right questions, and seeing the right visions, he and your aunt won't last a minute down there."

9.

"I saw him!" Caleb yelled, spinning around, waving his arms through the dimming light. "Montross. He was here."

Twenty yards from the main archway and the jeep, he had run chasing the phantom. Around him the stones and broken pillars of once-mighty Xanadu lay in their eight hundred-year-old positions, fodder for weeds and moss, dismissed by the centuries.

"I might have seen something," Orlando said, his voice uncertain. He still trained the gun on Qara, who seemed to be edging a little too close. He waved it at her. "Back away, I'm watching you."

Phoebe scanned the area, looking into the distance, over the hills, the wide spaces. The only cover being a few trees in the distance. "I don't know, I don't see anything. It's been a long drive. A long trip, no sleep."

"I saw him," Caleb countered. "But it was different. It was like when I saw Dad."

"What?"

"Years ago, in Alexandria, and back in Sodus at Mom's deathbed. Like he was there, but he wasn't."

"I wonder," Orlando said, moving closer to Caleb, who still carried the AK-47.

"What?" he asked.

"Being in possession of that tablet now, if it really can grant the owner the secrets of the universe. Well, Montross may have picked up an ability or two."

"Like what?" Phoebe asked.

"I was thinking," Orlando said, "of *Star Wars*. The whole Obi-Wan 'Strike me down and I'll only become stronger' deal. He was able to send out his spirit, separate it from his body so it could appear all ghost-like and stuff."

"Astral Projection? But that was after Obi-Wan died," Caleb argued. "Like what I believe my father managed to do. He could appear, but only for a brief moments, to convey something, to lead me to the truth."

"Maybe," Phoebe said, "Montross figured out how to do it while still alive."

"Or maybe he *is* dead," said Qara hopefully. "There were other Darkhad I left behind, guarding the Sacred Mountain. They would not have hesitated taking his life."

Caleb thought for a moment, then shook his head. "No, he's alive. I feel it. In fact, I think he was searching for us, and I fear we may have given ourselves—and this position—away."

"Damn," Qara said, then flashed an annoyed look to Orlando. "Please, take that gun off me and let me use my phone. I need to fortify this site."

"No time," Caleb told her. "We have the edge here, for a few hours anyway. We can uncover the entrance, get inside and secure the keys before he even arrives."

"And then what?" Qara asked. "Use them to barter for your son? I won't let that happen."

Caleb stared at her, and his fingers holding the gun began to sweat. Phoebe and Orlando were in a triangular position around Qara, silently waiting for Caleb.

"Please," Qara said. "Do not go any farther with this. Leave my Khan alone. Nothing good will come of his discovery."

"We could wait," Phoebe said. "Maybe hide out. We know Montross is coming. We can surprise him."

"Unless he looks for us again," Orlando said. "And then he'd be able to get the jump on us. And he's got Nina. Nope, I say we go in. Wait for him down there."

"No," Qara pleaded.

Caleb let out a sigh. "I'm sorry, but all I can do is promise you I will do everything I can to ensure Montross never gets those keys, that Temujin is not disturbed. We will never speak of this location, never betray his secret."

"Not good enough," Qara said, dropping her arms to her side. Her legs tensed, fingers unclenched and clenched into fists. "No one gets inside."

"Wait," Orlando said, looking around, turning in a big circle. "Where is it anyway?" "What?" asked Phoebe.

"The river. I don't see any damn river."

Qara's face relaxed. She opened her fists, then folded her fingers together, bowing her head. "You don't know."

Caleb came closer, raising the tip of his weapon. "We'll find out. Orlando, what did we use two years ago in Cambodia to locate the lost temple of Anuk-Beng?"

"Satellite radar imaging from NASA combined with public databases provided by National Geographic Atlases. Thermal imaging. Hang on, I'll start it." He took off his backpack and pulled out the iPad.

"The maps are very detailed," Phoebe said, "highlighting things we'd never see from this vantage point. Like ruins in the middle of a jungle or old dried-up riverbeds."

Qara hung her head. She glanced back to the arch.

"Come on," said Caleb. "We can do it the hard way, or you can help us."

She turned to him slowly. "And if I show you the door, what's to stop you from killing me?"

"Hey!" said Phoebe. "We're not the thugs here, honey. But if we don't get in there and find those keys first, we're all as good as dead. Come on. Please help us."

"And betray my sacred duty?"

Caleb lowered his gun, switched it to his left hand, and approached. "All right, I'll leave it up to you. Here's my gun. Orlando, put yours away. Now it's your choice, Qara. But if you really mean to protect your Khan, you had better think about letting us in."

He held out the gun, and Qara's dark eyes flickered with uncertainty. They flashed to Phoebe, and then Orlando.

"From what my sister saw," Caleb continued, "there's still a lot of ground to cover beneath here, in 'caverns measureless to man.' So showing us the door isn't the end of this. We may still stop Montross and Renée before they can get to Temujin's crypt, but we can't do it from up here. Not out in the open, not like this. And even if we run, Montross, with my son's help, will find the way in if he doesn't already know."

Qara reached for the gun, touched it. And for a moment both Caleb and Qara held it, then he let go, bowed his head and took a step back.

Qara shouldered the weapon and took aim.

She wavered, then lowered the tip, pointing it at the ground. She sighed. "Dig under the arch, directly in the center. About five feet down you'll find the door."

Caleb nodded. "Thank you."

"I'll help you dig," she said, "until we reach the door. But then you go in alone."

"No way!" said Orlando. "You'll seal us in."

"No. I'll stay out here," she said, hefting the gun, "and wait for your friends. Kill as many of them as I can. And if I fail, I must trust you to finish them off and leave my Lord intact. Can you promise me that?"

"We can," Caleb said.

"And re-bury the door? And tell no one?"

"Cross our hearts," said Phoebe.

Suddenly the wind picked up, swirling, kicking up leaves and twigs. And a rumbling sound rattled the earth. Qara turned, switched her aim, and fired into the sky—

—just as the sleek black helicopter descended, pinning them in a spotlight. A helmeted woman, perched in the open door, fired back.

Qara felt the sting of the bullet in her side, then screamed as another ripped past her head. She dropped the gun and watched helplessly as the helicopter landed and the shooter jumped out, followed by six commandos in camouflage.

"Don't raise your gun," Caleb yelled to Orlando. "Just drop it."

"Listen to him," said Renée Wagner, as she ripped off her helmet and let her hair whip in the winds of the dying helicopter blades. "I've also got six jeeps on their way, another forty men." She advanced on Qara, who had fallen to her knees, her good hand trying to stop the flow of blood from her side.

Qara grimaced as a tsunami of pain swept through her side. glared at Renée, now lording over her. In the corner of her eye, she saw Orlando, surrounded by three commandos, guns pointed at his face. He raised his hands.

"All right," Renée said. "Nice try, luring me to Qin Shi's mausoleum instead, but you failed. You killed four of my best men, bitch." She pressed the barrel of her Walther to Qara's forehead.

"No!" Caleb yelled, trying to push free of two other commandos who had him restrained. "If you kill her, we'll never find him."

Renée paused, tilting her head. "Really? Doubting your abilities now, are we?"

"I'm just being practical," Caleb said. "Remote viewing is just a tool. We may know where the entrance is, but beyond that there's a lot of real estate to cover before Temujin's body."

Renée smiled, a smile meant for Caleb, but delivered right to Qara. "And you honestly think this Darkhad will help us? I'd rather pull the trigger and trust in you and your friends."

"I promise you," Caleb insisted, "we won't be enough."

Qara tensed for one last lunge, more than confident she could take Agent Wagner, but what then? Dimly, as the blood oozed from her arm and flowed through her fingers, she heard Caleb lobbying Renée to spare her life, and for a moment she regretted doubting him. Because of her blind adherence to tradition and loyalty to a man dead for eight centuries, she had placed them all in danger, and may have unleashed something far worse upon the world. If Wagner or Montross succeeded ...

She had to make up for it. Had to give Caleb and his team a chance. But not like this, she needed time.

"Please," Caleb urged. "Don't be stupid."

Renée sighed, lifted the weapon and stepped back. She pointed to one of the commandos. "Cuff her. Bandage her up, but no drugs. And keep her awake." She glared at Qara. "And for your sake, I hope Caleb's impression of your usefulness is not overrated. The moment I believe you're no longer helping, you're dead."

Qara looked at them all, in turn. "The Khan's armies are down there, waiting for you, with deadly surprises that no one, Darkhad and psychics alike, can possibly foresee. We will all soon be entombed along with my master."

BOOK THREE
UNDER XANADU

1.

Robert Gregory hung suspended in a tank. Naked, supported by straps around his back, neck and legs, with a mouthpiece between his charred lips supplying oxygen, he drifted in and out of consciousness while electrodes attached to his index finger and his temples relayed his vitals.

His bath consisted of ninety percent water, ten percent "other"—a collection of esoteric herbs and rare compounds detailed in the *Bogratus Manuscript*, a three thousand-year-old scroll, once part of the Library of Alexandria, recovered from the Pharos vault. This particular item detailed the treatment of burn victims, a way to heal the scars and speed the patient's recovery without the use of skin grafts.

The Keepers were going to release this secret surreptitiously to the medical community next fall, allowing a promising researcher to "discover" the treatment by accident. But now, because of the disaster at Caleb's place, Robert had to use it personally. The first such patient in millennia.

He scowled, and he could only imagine the doctor out there suddenly getting edgy because of his spiking blood pressure.

Montross. Xavier had promised he'd foreseen everything, and there would be no chance of failure. Now Robert cursed his gullibility.

Lydia. Poor Lydia had been right. Montross couldn't be trusted. Most likely Montross *had*seen this outcome and hadn't cared. He survived, and he gained the tablet. That's all that mattered to him. He had turned the tables on Robert, left him to burn.

Fortunately, the shock of being shot had worn off. His lungs had begun filling with blood, which may have saved him, as he coughed his way out of unconsciousness long enough to drag himself out the open front door, but not far enough. He'd heard the explosion, seen the lighthouse in flames, the billowing smoke and the fire spreading to the house, roaring through the rooms and leaping across the roof, seeking him out. He had tried crawling further, coughing up blood, too weak to stand, but then the roof collapsed, pouring burning material on top of him. From that point on, he had maintained consciousness only long enough to direct the medics to call in his special agents to save him and cover up his survival.

Now he took deep, slow breaths, trying to get his vitals under control. *Stop thinking about Montross.*

Never mind that Robert was going to do the same thing to Xavier, as soon as he could get his hands on the tablet. He was reasonably sure Montross wouldn't have thought of the right questions to ask in order to poke around in Robert's past or to discern his current motivations. He would have thought only about the Keepers, a bunch of dusty old librarians who had gotten their wish, and now had a new responsibility: protecting and disseminating the ancient documents.

All except for Robert. Montross would have accepted the obvious—that he still craved the Emerald Tablet, the lone lost object from the library's catalog. *No need to remote view anything further to probe my motivations. Nothing about my true master. Or the other artifact I seek.*

Still, Robert let a little anger back in. He did not take kindly to liars, or thieves. And Caleb Crowe was both. But as bad as that was, to be lied to again by Montross was unforgivable.

Robert tried to stifle a laugh, coughing up bubbles into the tank. His skin tingled and felt cold, brittle, but surprisingly good. Then, he gave into a little laugh, thinking about how alike his two great enemies were.

He had long known of *The Westcar Papyrus*. His father, Nolan Gregory, had prepared him for his destiny by often retelling one of its stories, sometimes by firelight while he and Lydia lay in their beds. *The Westcar Papyrus*, written in the eighteenth century BCE, had been discovered in Egypt by Henry Westcar in 1824. It contained a collection of tales, in the vein of *The Arabian Nights*, told to Pharaoh Khufu by his sons about the deeds of magicians in those days.

But the fourth story dealt with something else altogether, something of great interest to the Keepers. The Hall of Records, the sanctuary of Thoth himself, and the prophecy that only one of three brothers could open the door and reach the books inside. Never mind, his father had said, that the fifth story, fragmented, only details the birth of triplets to a woman years later, one of whom was fated to open the door. There was no mention of the brothers' success, or what would come of the prophecy. The fifth story might have been nothing more than literary denouement, or nothing less than an outright deception. Nothing had happened. Nothing yet.

But in time, and with research and study into the most mystical texts to survive the Dark Ages, the Keepers learned that Thoth's great book, although unreadable, had been moved to an even more secure location under the Pharos Lighthouse. And as further protection, it had been separated from its translation. But to work, to gain its true power, both elements were needed.

And, Nolan Gregory came to believe, both pieces might only be found by individuals with extraordinary powers. Psychics gifted above all others. Psychics that might even be related.

Enter Caleb. With a little research, the Keepers had found that his father had another son, unknown even to him. Brother number two.

And so they had kept an eye on both of them, encouraged when both wound up in Alexandria, part of the Morpheus Initiative. Caleb had found the tablet, but Xavier was by no means out of the hunt.

While his father continued to search for brother number three and to hope, Robert began to believe in his own destiny, in the stretching of the words of prophecy, which often ruled by vagaries of language.

Robert was, after all, a brother through marriage. And while he lacked his brothers' abilities, he excelled in what they lacked.

Power.

He had consolidated his position, used the other influential members among his fellow Keepers to win key appointments. And then, of course, he was chosen from an early age by the senior leaders of another organization. Chosen, just as Renée had been chosen to play her part.

He smiled, thinking of her initiation ceremony, of the mask he had worn to welcome her to her new identity. And now she was his, body and soul.

He clenched his fists, feeling the newly healed skin prickle, threaten to burst, but then hold.

He was close.

Death couldn't claim him, not when prophecy had set his fate. Soon he would be well enough to stand. To dress. To hold a gun.

And fly to Cairo. Then to Giza. To be ready when Renée returned with the keys and the tablet, and with confirmation that Caleb and Xavier were dead, leaving only Robert with the chance to enter and claim his legacy.

To fulfill Marduk's plan.

And of course, to be justly rewarded.

2.

Caleb made his way through the deepening shadows to where Phoebe was tending to Qara. Her side had been bandaged and a Chinese medic had removed the bullet without finesse and without anesthesia.

"She seems to be doing okay," Phoebe said. "But she needs a hospital."

Caleb risked a glance toward Renée, where she stood close to the arch, arms folded, as her team of commandos dug a nine-by-twelve square out of the earth. They were at knee-depth, and Orlando was in their midst, looking miserable with his face caked with dirt, his eyes alone shining in the four floodlights they had set up. Caleb could tell he was complaining every minute about his "talents being wasted."

"Uh oh," Phoebe said, her voice barely audible over the pitch of the portable generators. "Here comes the bitch. Gonna make us get back to work."

Renée strode up to them, tapping her gun. "Shouldn't you be in a trance or something by now?"

Caleb didn't look up, but just kept his eyes on Qara's peaceful face, wondering what she might be dreaming right now, if maybe she were receiving some final words of instruction from the great Genghis just as he often prepared his generals before battle.

Phoebe cleared her throat. "Shouldn't you be off torturing small animals?"

Renée glared at her. "Once we're behind that door, we'll need your *sight*. And I plan on marching Phoebe here right up front. I know you, Caleb. I know how you agonized, believing you caused her paralysis years ago. So unless you now want to be responsible for whatever those barbaric traps might do to her, you'd best find us a way past them."

Caleb nodded slowly, swallowing. He debated telling Renée the truth—that he couldn't. His powers had abandoned him, but he knew she wouldn't believe him. *Best to stall.* "I know what we need to do; it's just not that simple. I have no idea what's down there. I've tried looking, but—"

"Try harder!"

"It doesn't work that way. Sometimes we have to be right there, actually in the presence of the dangers we're facing. And right now, to be honest, I'm a little preoccupied. My son's in terrible jeopardy, and then I have you to worry about. Some kind of connection to an ancient Babylonian deity that I believe disappeared or died along with Thoth millennia ago."

Renée opened her mouth, her face a mask of dismay.

"And all I know is that the god of wisdom, who did everything he could to teach humanity and raise early man out of the darkness of ignorance and spiritual bondage, was determined to hide this tablet from the likes of your "master." Caleb took a step toward her, but was stopped by Phoebe's hand on his arm.

"Not now," she whispered. But then a shout from Orlando broke her concentration.

"Found it! I freakin' found it!" Orlando raised a fist, grinning around at the blank faces of the Chinese soldiers. "Well," he said, looking over to Caleb and pointing down, "I did. Here's your door."

They cleared away the slab of dark granite. It had six deep indentations, with bars across it, sealed into the stone.

"Handles," said Commander Chang, pointing. "In Temujin's day, they use ropes and horses to open door." He smiled at his men, his brown teeth flashing in the spotlights. "But now, we have four-wheel drives."

He turned to his men and ordered the setup to begin. They moved the halogen floodlights around the southern edge of the door, attached the six triple-braided nylon ropes to the back axle, and cleared everyone out of the way.

Orlando walked over to Caleb and Phoebe, rubbing the dirt off his face with his sleeve. "Why do I get a real bad feeling about this?"

"Because," said a weak voice, as Qara struggled to sit up, "opening that door inflicts the curse upon you all."

A moment later, the engine revved, the tires spun, the granite screamed, and something popped. The door launched from its ancient resting place, just as the jeep flew forward, lost its traction and spun sideways, then stalled as the floodlights highlighted the terrified face of the driver a second before the slab crashed through the cab, flattening it and crushing the man inside.

"Dear God," Phoebe uttered, turning away.

Qara stood up, smirking at Renée, who returned her stare with pure hatred.

Orlando whistled. "Good thing I didn't call shotgun."

"Enough," Renée hissed. "Chang, get your men to pack up these lights and the generators. Bring the weapons and everything else we need. And leave a team here to take care of Montross when he arrives. I'll try to reach Hiltmeyer, but just in case, have our team stand by. Make sure we get the tablet and the other key from Montross's dead body."

"And the boy?"

Caleb snapped his attention to Renée.

Renée waved her hand. "Bring him, alive, and meet up with us. I'm sure we'll find a use for him."

She turned away from them, pulled out a satellite phone and walked to the edge of the hole, looking down the stairs descending into the waiting dark.

She dialed, and when a choked, gravelly voice answered, she said, "We're in."

3.

They stopped a mile from Shang-du, at a small ridge before the descent. The jeeps came to a halt, with their vehicle in the lead. Night had fallen and the stars were out, burning fiercely, dominating the sky before the full moon's ascent.

Nina leaned forward. "I say we kill the headlights, come in slow. We don't know what's down there."

"Yes," Montross said, "we do." His eyes popped open, having been closed for the past ten minutes. "Colonel, do as the lady says. Kill the lights."

Nina smiled, and between the two adults Alexander squirmed. "I have to go to the bathroom."

Nina frowned. "Again?"

He lowered his chin. "Too much water."

"Hurry," said Montross. "Colonel, go with him."

"What?" Hiltmeyer turned in his seat. "I'm no babysitter. Private Harris here can—"

"You both go."

Alexander looked from one to the other man. "I can go by myself, really."

"No way. Flight risk," said Hiltmeyer. "We'll go. I need to talk to my men in the other jeeps anyway. What's our plan?"

"I'll tell you," said Montross, "when you get back."

Hiltmeyer shot him a concerned glance, then opened his door.

Alexander slid out, helped along as Nina pushed him out the door. "Be quick." When the doors had closed and they were alone, Nina asked, "What's up? What did you see?"

"It seems," said Montross, "that our colonel has other loyalties."

Alexander found a cropping of small bushes. He unzipped and turned away from the man who had lit up a cigarette, watching him. He glanced over his other shoulder, toward his jeep, where two shadows in the back seat bent in close to each other.

"Wonder what they're talking about," Alexander said, loud enough for Private Harris to hear.

"Shut up and pee, kid."

"I bet they're talking about you." Alexander zipped up, folded his arms over his chest and turned around, shivering. He could see his breath. He looked up and saw Orion, low and sideways, with Sirius poised above the tree line.

"What?"

"I see things too, you know."

"Yeah?" Harris had a buzz cut, heavier and black at the top of his head, which Alexander thought made him look like a rooster after getting his head stuck under a lawnmower.

"Well, I saw—"

Harris leaned in. The ash dangled on his cigarette.

"—you." Alexander, trembling even more, his eyes wide so as not to blink and see the vision again, added, "With a rusty spike through your chest."

The soldier's face went pale, the cigarette dropped from his mouth. "What?"

"Harris!" Colonel Hiltmeyer yelled. "Back in the jeep. We're moving."

"But—"

"Now! You too, Alexander."

Head down, he followed, staring at the colonel's boots as they crunched into the hard ground. Suddenly Hiltmeyer spun, pressed a hand against Alexander's chest and leaned in.

"Quick. Tell me what you saw."

They rode in slowly around the south side of the site while the other two jeeps approached from the east and west. Hiltmeyer was on the walkie-talkie, coordinating with his men as their jeeps descended into the valley. He glanced back at Montross. This was going to be tricky.

They stopped on the ridge and Nina stepped out, going to the trunk for the sniper rifle. "We'll provide teams A and B cover from up here," she said.

Hiltmeyer nodded, then flashed Harris a look. They stepped out of the jeep. Montross and Alexander got out last. "Now we watch," said Nina, setting up a tripod, then passing around night-vision goggles. "Pick out our targets, and then—"

Suddenly she spun, kicked away the tripod, and aimed the rifle at Hiltmeyer, even as he was going for his gun. Montross pulled out Nilak's gun and pointed it at Harris's forehead.

"Now," said Montross, disarming Hiltmeyer and Harris, "Colonel, kindly get on your walkie-talkie there and tell your teams this is for real. We've already given them information on where Renée's commandos are hiding out, and with any luck, your men might live through this."

"But—"

"Yes, we know. Renée's men are your men too." Montross gave him a slanted look. "I guess you need to make a choice here."

Nina stepped in, reversed the rifle and slammed Hiltmeyer in the ribs. He swore, then lunged for her, but she had the business end back on him in a flash. "Talk to them. Now!"

Groaning, holding his side, Hiltmeyer reached for the walkie-talkie and stopped, catching Alexander's eye. He saw pity there, maybe even sympathy.

Damned psychics.

Colonel Hiltmeyer brought the phone to his lips and closed his eyes. *I'm sorry,* he thought, and pushed the button. "Do it," Hiltmeyer ordered. "Turn on your lights, go in strong!"

Nina turned and set up her rifle as Montross kept his gun trained on Hiltmeyer and Harris. She sighted with her scope, and as soon as the headlights pierced the blackness from two directions, she chose her targets and began shooting.

Alexander shrank back as far as he could, all the way against the side of the jeep. He put his hands over his ears, but couldn't help but watch the firefight on the field ahead. Cringing with each of Nina's shots, he imagined bodies plucked from the shadows, heads exploding, men dropping without knowing what hit them.

He heard automatic gunfire, shouting and screaming in a foreign language. More gunshots. He watched Harris and Hiltmeyer, standing impotently, fists clenched. Then he saw Nina reload, sight, track a target and fire. And in the flashes after each shot, he saw the rush of excitement on her face. And finally, as the blasts subsided, a contented smile.

"Done," she said at last, after scanning the field with her binoculars. She stood, disconnected the tripod and returned the rifle to the trunk. Business-like and efficient. Then she pulled out her Beretta and jabbed it against the Colonel's ribs.

"My men?" he asked.

Nina led him to the back seat, pushed him in. "Colonel, I'm sorry to report that nobody from either side survived."

They stood around the pit before the archway and the first six stairs descending into the earth.

And a lot of dead bodies.

Montross stood on the edge, looking down while holding up the Emerald Tablet like a lantern. It glowed faintly, pulsing along with the charm on his necklace, lying against his chest.

"It's time," he said. "Alexander, you're with me. Nina, escort our guests. They'll be going first."

"No way," insisted Colonel Hiltmeyer. "I'm not going down there. I heard what the boy said."

"That's right," Private Harris agreed. "No way."

Nina slammed the back of her Beretta against his forehead, turned him around and then shoved him ahead, sending him tumbling down into the darkness.

"I'll kill you—!"

"Enough!" Montross yelled. "Colonel, it's up to you. You go first, or Nina puts a bullet in your head so you can stay up here with your men."

"You'll kill me anyway."

"No," said Nina, "we're pretty sure what's down there will do that for us. But at least you'll have a chance."

"And," Montross said, "look at it this way. Now you get to see history in the making. People have been searching for the tomb of Genghis Khan for eight hundred years, and you're about to find it."

Hiltmeyer grit his teeth. "All right, but if I get hit with something down there, I'm going to do my damndest to make sure I take all of you with me."

"Or maybe," Montross said, hefting the tablet, "along the way you'll realize you and your boss are on the wrong side. You can't fight us."

Hiltmeyer shook his head. "You don't know anything. All your abilities, and that thing you carry, you don't even know who or what you're fighting."

Nina jabbed him in his side, then pushed him ahead. "Lead the way, Colonel. Genghis awaits."

4.

Forty minutes before the shooting started, before all the ensuing carnage, Caleb and Phoebe had descended into the mausoleum.

They went ahead of Orlando, Qara and Renée, with two other Chinese soldiers following at the rear making sure they didn't turn and flee. Ahead, sixteen soldiers led the way. Chang's team entered with four rows of four men each, equally spaced in the passageway. The air was thin, stale and brittle. Every soldier carried Type 81 assault rifles—the Chinese version of the AK-47, but with enhanced designs and better accuracy. They all had Maglites fitted onto the barrels, and when Caleb looked down the ramp he saw only the dozen-plus flashlight beams stabbing out wildly, tracing the sloping ceiling, the wide, descending steps and the pockmarked granite walls.

Remarkably free of dust, the beams were pure white energy striking here and there, illuminating faces and betraying fear in the men whose trembling hands wielded the rifles. "Shouldn't we be worried?" Phoebe whispered, glancing right and left, trying to see in the sporadic light, looking for telltale signs of traps. Immediately she felt like she was back in that Mayan temple in Belize. Out of her element, blind.

"Not yet," Caleb answered. "I believe we're safe until—"

Some commotion ahead, shouting.

"A wall!" Chang yelled back.

The four flashlight beams at the front position converged into one thick laser-like spear that thrust up against a solid wall.

"Don't touch it!" Renée yelled. "Wait for me."

They all reached the bottom, fanning out into a larger rectangular chamber with a low ceiling. The beams darted around, highlighting cracks, a root sticking through one side.

"We must be what, a hundred feet down?" Orlando wondered.

Caleb looked back the way they had come, past the two commandos with their guns pointed down, their faces and emotions lost in shadow. Already the way behind them was gone, as if the blackness had swallowed up their trail, stealthily consuming their one route of escape. "I've counted seventy-two steps."

"A little too familiar," Phoebe said. Did Sostratus have a hand in this, too?" She saw his look. "I'm kidding. Of course I know this was built fifteen hundred years after the Pharos."

Renée pushed between Caleb and Phoebe and approached the wall. All the beams reflecting off the pale white surface made it hard at first to see the mural painted there. Well-preserved in the darkness, the vibrant face of Genghis Khan sternly gazed at them, superimposed upon his banner of nine ox tails. In a series of four vertical columns, Mongolian script covered the right side of the wall.

"My master," whispered Qara, from just ahead. She tried to lower herself to one knee, but a soldier hauled her back up.

"Everyone back," Renée barked, moving ahead. "But not you, Caleb. You come up here. I believe this sort of thing is your specialty."

Phoebe held her brother's arm. "Be careful. We haven't had time to study this." Then, whispering, said, "Fake it if you have to. I'll do the heavy work back here."

Chang played his flashlight beam over the letters. "This is difficult. I recognize not many symbols."

Renée grabbed Qara by the back of her neck and shoved her forward. "Read it, Darkhad. And no tricks."

Qara stumbled weakly, hair over her face, hands tied behind her back. She squinted. As she read, a smile formed. "It says, *If you have come seeking death, continue. If you have come seeking agony beyond measure, enter. If you have come seeking madness, proceed. But if you have come seeking treasure, turn back, for there is nothing here for you. Turn back, and live with the one treasure alone that never lasts.*"

Chang frowned and turned around. "What treasure never lasts?"

"Life," Phoebe said at once. "He's talking about your life."

Renée snorted. "Caleb? Shouldn't you be drawing something?"

"I'll do it," Phoebe said, "since I saw the vision the clearest." She stepped forward. "Orlando, can I have your iPad? I'll show you what I've seen, the design of this door, and the chambers immediately beyond it."

Orlando his backpack and fished it out, turned it around and handed it to her. "All yours."

The light from the screen stung at her eyes, but Phoebe concentrated, then moved closer to the door and sat, crossing her legs.

"Hurry," Renée said.

"If you want us all dead, I will."

Renée played her light along the edges of the slab, dancing over Temujin's face and banner, looking for seals or handles. "No stalling. Get this door open or I'll have my men blast it apart."

Orlando cleared his throat. "You can't rush this kind of thing."

Caleb fidgeted, feeling useless. "Not unless you like pain and agony and madness. And all the other stuff he talks about on that wall."

"Yes," urged Qara. "By all means, blast it open."

"Shut up." Renée glanced back up at the darkness behind them, as if expecting it to release a surge of armored warriors.

She headed into the shadows and spoke into the transceiver attached to her shoulder, attempting to communicate with the team outside. When no response came, her face fell and she gave up the effort.

Phoebe called up the images she had seen, flashes of workers toiling with the creation of diabolical traps, of masons crafting elaborate sliding walls and interlocking shafts, holes bored through the earth and fitted with gears, levers, pulleys and springs. Finally, she withdrew from those sights and instead focused on the structure of the passageways, viewing a general layout.

And then she started sketching. The men milled about quietly, breathing shallowly, some of them extinguishing their lights to save the batteries.

"Here," Phoebe said, standing again. Chang moved in first to get a look while Orlando and Caleb tried to peek around them. She showed them the design.

"It's a little crude, since I wasn't allowed much time, but here's the door, and beyond it you've got a double T-shaped area, with a small chamber almost immediately to the left and right beyond this door. And then a short distance ahead, the passage ends in a wall where you can go right or left. Long passageways extend both ways, with a sizeable chamber at the end of each hall."

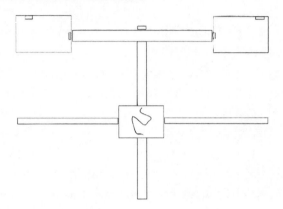

She pointed to the first intersection, then glanced at Qara to see her reaction, but her face was cloaked in shadow. "Here, there's something nasty waiting for us."

"What?"

"Huge metal spikes. As far as I could tell, they blast out from either side."

"How do we avoid them?" Orlando asked.

"There's a trail I saw, highlighted in green, something about the stones which make up that section. I think we'll see it when we get past this door."

"And how," Renée said, flashing her light back to the Temujin's haughty face, "do we do that?"

Phoebe sighed, then turned to Qara. "On this part, I'm sorry to say, I'm blind. I saw them build it, set it in place. It's seriously thick, but I couldn't see how it opens."

"That's unacceptable," Renée said.

Caleb turned to Qara. "You want to help?"

The Darkhad grinned through her pain. Shook her head.

Renée raised her .45, pointed it at Qara's leg. "Oh, she'll help."

"Wait!" Orlando shouted. "Hold on, I'm not bad at these things, either. After all, I did see you."

Renée lowered the gun. "Very well. Go on."

Orlando studied the door, narrowed his eyes and took a deep breath. He took a few steps forward, palms out. Phoebe experienced a moment of dread, fearing that to touch the door would release some kind of horrific trap to bury them all. She really hadn't seen anything about this door, and that alone surprised her. *Had no one been through here since they set the door in place?* She had concentrated on seeing the door open, had asked that question, but nothing came of it, just a humming and the consistent view of the mural-covered wall.

"Try remote viewing the unlocking mechanism," Caleb suggested. "They must have built one, although my guess is that no one has ever used it."

"That's exactly what I'm trying, boss."

"Wait," Renée said. "I thought Kublai and his other sons were buried here too. Wouldn't they have had to open the door?"

Phoebe shrugged. "That's what I thought too, but I'm not getting anything."

Qara had overheard and when Caleb glanced in her direction, she gave a grudging nod. "Temujin alone lies here. His descendents, like the rest of Mongolia, feared to trespass upon his necropolis."

"But Kublai had no problem building his own city above it?"

"That was part of Temujin's will," she said. "We never knew why. It made the sacred mission of the early Darkhad difficult, since it brought undue attention to the very area we wished to conceal."

"I can think of two reasons," Caleb said, raising his hand with two fingers out. "One is that Kublai would have subscribed to the same tenets as his grandfather. He knew the value in hiding secrets in plain view. And the second reason has to deal with symmetry and the mystical precept of 'as Above, so Below.'"

"That never gets old," Orlando says. "Kind of like Twinkies."

"So where are they? His sons?" Caleb asked. "Back on the Sacred Mountain?"

Qara's expression never wavered. "Perhaps."

"Hang on," Orlando said, brushing off more dirt from his face. He lurched toward the door, shook his head to clear a vision, then headed right. Three soldiers moved out of his way, keeping their lights on him as he moved along the wall, past the script and to the corner. He pointed. "Up there."

The lights followed his outstretched hand and index finger indicating the broken section Caleb had noticed before, the area he thought had crumbled through, pierced by a tree root.

"That would have to be some seriously deep root."

"Not a root," Orlando replied. "Although designed to look the part. Get two of your men, Agent Wagner. One boost the other. Grab hold and pull."

Renée snapped her fingers, then brought her flashlight to the scene as two commandos rushed around Orlando. One knelt and made a step out of his hands to lift the other, then pushed him up on his shoulders. The top man gripped the root-like thing.

"It is tough rope," he shouted back in accented English. "I—"

"Wait!" Orlando shouted. "I didn't finish. You have to pull it, hand over hand, like you're opening a set of curtains. And you pull from left to right. If you go the other way ..."

Phoebe gasped, holding her head. A flash revealed ...

... a scene where dozens of men with helmets and torches stand back on the stairs, bows drawn, arrows aimed at a man on a ladder in the same corner. With a sheepish look, the prisoner grasps the rope and pulls right to left as he was told. And something shiny, flickering with all the torchlight, rips across the room, at about neck-height. It is secured by three iron bars from the ceiling, running on embedded tracks. The ladder is severed at the eighth rung, just below the man's feet, as the room-width blade whisks past. He falls, rolls and is about to get up when he sees it coming back, hauling across again to its starting position. So he ducks, hugging his knees—

—which leaves him in the perfect position to be sliced in half by the second blade, which rips from the right to left, two feet off the ground.

Phoebe staggered back, fighting the bile rising in her throat, still blinking away the sight of the prisoner's two halves flopping and unraveling on this very floor, while the Khan's men admired the effectiveness of their trap.

She grabbed a flashlight from one of the men and directed it to the side wall. "There. See the three vertical tracks? And it's probably imperceptible, but there should be two horizontal ones too, for the blades. The first one decapitates a normal-sized man, the second, coming from the other side, ensures that at the least, they aren't walking forward."

"Jeez," Orlando said to Qara. "You guys aren't very hospitable to visitors."

Renée started backing up, heading to the stairs. "Okay, left to right then, but just to be sure ..." She took a few steps up, then nodded to

Chang, who remained in the middle of the room, his face cloaked in fear. "Now, do it."

The man took a deep breath, closed his eyes, then pulled. Once, twice. Something made a grinding noise, the room shook, and the great stone door trembled. He kept pulling, and then a crack released from the left-most edge. He pulled, as the man holding him strained to keep his balance. The crack grew. Two feet. Four. Five. Six.

"Enough," said Renée.

The man released his hold on the rope. But then the door started to close. He grabbed it and kept pulling. "Get it open all the way!" Orlando shouted. "Otherwise it slams shut, and I think that just might set off that trap."

"Pull!" Chang ordered, and eight flashlight beams, including Caleb's, stabbed at the blackness through the gap as the door continued sliding open.

Qara inched closer to Caleb, watching as the portal that hadn't been opened in almost eight hundred years moved to one side. She held her ribs, wheezing. "That," she said, "was the easy part. I hope you've got a lot more in your bag of tricks, because once we walk through there, I'm not going to be much help."

"Don't let Renée hear that," Caleb whispered.

"I don't care. I've failed my master. Brought you right to his doorstep."

Caleb touched her elbow, leading her ahead. "I thought that only death released a Darkhad from her sacred obligation."

She nodded grimly. "Then my release, which will come at the same time as yours, is imminent."

Just past the door, Chang set up the generator and hooked up the portable floodlights. Soon, all the soldiers had gathered inside the first area before the intersection, and the passageway was bathed in light. What stopped them, piled high in a heap against the left wall, were skeletons. The laborers, killed and left here to ensure their silence.

"Hey there," Orlando said reverently, meeting the hollow stares of bleak eye sockets set in a dozen cracked skulls. "Should've unionized."

"Shh," Phoebe scolded. "And don't move any closer."

The walls were bare, white and sturdy. But the floor, revealed in the brilliant light, was smooth up until the "T" twenty yards ahead, where they could see the large square about forty feet to a side set in the floor between the east and west passages. It was set with a mosaic-tiled surface. Beyond this square and the intersection, the passage continued on into the regrouping darkness.

"A map," Renée said, pushing past the others and gingerly walking close to the edge and gazing at the mosaic picture on the floor. "Looks like China and Mongolia, Arabia, and part of Russia."

"The Mongol Empire under Genghis Khan," Caleb said.

Orlando whistled. "And let me guess: step on the wrong one and you wind up on a rotisserie?"

"You got it," Phoebe said. "I saw at least a dozen spikes from each side, spring-loaded and launched across on some kind of harness."

Renée pointed and Chang's men complied. A few of the soldiers shined their lights east and west, glancing their beams off the far wall, highlighting a slab that looked like Swiss cheese, full of various-sized holes.

"Okay, so where's the path?"

Caleb passed the iPad back to Orlando, then stood beside Renée, hands on his hips. He scanned the map, the beautiful mural with its vibrant colors, mini-tiles making up each of the four hundred or so larger tiles.

"Need me to RV it again?" Phoebe asked.

Caleb shook his head. "No, I've got it. Even without your vision, I think we could have figured it out."

"Maybe after a few of us got spiked first?"

Caleb turned to Chang. "Do you have a piece of chalk, or I don't know, a paint gun?"

"No."

"Bread crumbs?"

Chang thought for a moment, then called one of his men over, who carried a cooler. "We have raw Marmat meat." He smiled at Caleb. "Very raw."

"Ewww," Phoebe said, covering her mouth when the lid was opened.

"That'll do," said Caleb. "Give it here. I'll use the blood to mark each tile as I cross over, and you can follow after."

"What's the trick?" Renée asked.

"His last siege," Caleb answered, heading for the fifth square from the left and setting foot on it. "Lucky I'm a history professor with a good memory. Here, at Xi-Xia, he died, most believe after a fall from his horse weeks earlier. He had been boar hunting, despite warnings from the philosopher Chi-Chang that he should give up hunting. Internal injuries perhaps. But while laying siege to the rebellious Xi-Xia, he passed on. Although there are some who claim the besieged kingdom had sent him a princess who delivered him a mortal wound while in bed together, but that's—"

"Vicious lies," Qara said under her breath.

"Probably. In any case, the path to take would be the reverse of his last mission, back from here, through Ghazni and Balkh, here." After marking the first tile with the dripping Marmat meat, he took another step, diagonally to the left. When nothing happened, he smiled and smeared another X with the bloody chunk of flesh. He closed his eyes for a moment, remembering the history. "Around Samarkand, through Bukhara ..." He took two steps ahead, covering two more squares, marking each.

Then he paused, thinking again.

"To your right." Phoebe pointed. "I can see it again, from my vision. I'll guide you if you get lost."

"Ok," he said, taking a step. "Then northeast through Otrar, and continuing at this angle ..." Slowly, carefully watching every footstep, he took ten more large strides, marking each as he picked up speed, seeing it all now, just as Phoebe must have seen it. "Back to Lake Baikhal where his armies launched their missions."

He was one foot away from the edge of the mosaic floor. Marking this last tile, he stepped off onto the clear granite on the other side. He turned around, breathing a sigh and only then realizing how tense his muscles had been. He set down the cooler and wiped his hands on his pants, a little disgusted.

Then, one by one, the others came across, following the trail of blood across the tiles. Phoebe and Orlando went next, followed by Qara, who almost slipped at one tile, having some trouble walking while handcuffed and still weak. Finally, Renée and Chang made it over.

They had to leave the heavy lights on the other side and reverted to using flashlights going forward.

"Keep moving," Renée ordered. Then all the Maglites aimed ahead, piercing the darkness. "Any more surprises we need to know about?"

Phoebe waited for her to catch up. "Yes, and a choice to be made." She pointed about fifty feet ahead, where the passage came to a dead end. A corridor led to the east and another to the west.

They stood at the crossroads, lights shining in either direction. Two scouts went ahead, one left, one right. Moving cautiously, assault rifles at the ready, their lights darted around. Orlando turned on his iPad again, displaying the image Phoebe had drawn.

"You've got a long passageway in each direction, both ending in large rooms. Any other impressions?"

Phoebe held her forehead, her eyes closed. The air was growing tighter, thicker. The taste of fear and dread became almost palpable. "No. I can't see. But I do sense something." She stepped forward and rubbed some dust off the wall ahead.

"What are you doing?" Caleb asked.

"Saw something here." She brushed away another section and revealed a single line of script. More characters like before, this time in a single horizontal line.

"Darkhad." Renée aimed her light on Qara, then the wall. "Translate."

Stepping forward, giving Renée a dull glare, Qara bent down and analyzed the symbols. "It says, *Sometimes the best choice is not to choose.*"

"What the hell does that mean?" Renée snipped.

Just then, twin screams cut through the passage. Then a merciless thudding sound came from the left. Men bolted in each direction, flashlight beams shaking. Chang barked orders amidst the shouts and frantic screams.

"What's happened?" Renée yelled into her transceiver. Garbled answers returned, men screaming all at once.

"So it begins," Qara said, ominously.

"What?" Phoebe asked.

"The curse. Turn back now and you will live."

Fuming, Renée ran to the right, grabbed hold of Chang and spun him around. "What happened?"

His face paled. The commander pointed to where the beams revealed something rising slowly. The floor itself was ascending, but there was something thick dripping from the center.

"The ceiling," Chang said. "It fell!"

"And the other?" Renée turned, looking in the other direction.

"False floor," Chang said, relaying what his men were screaming back to him. "And a pit of spikes."

"So there's our choice," Orlando said. "Go right and get crushed, go left and be skewered."

Renée took a moment, thinking it through. "We can, it seems, set off the trap in this direction, wait for the ceiling to drop, and then run across it, assuming there's a door or some other exit on the far side."

"True," said Caleb. "And this direction"—he pointed to the left—"might work the same way. Trigger the collapsing floor, prevent it from rising somehow, lower ourselves down, avoid the spikes, then walk to the other side. So we still have to choose."

"Do we even know there are exits?" Renée asked.

"Yes," said Orlando, pointing to the iPad screen. "I think Phoebe's got them drawn here."

"I saw that much," Phoebe recalled. "And I just had the impression that beyond each of those rooms there were under-ground streams in the darkness. Both leading to a magnificent city set in a cavern."

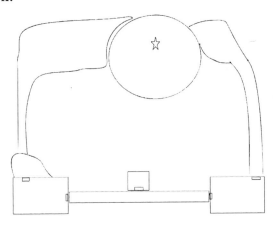

"So which door?" Renée asked.

"How about neither?" Caleb offered. He pointed to the wall ahead. "Remember the riddle? Sometimes the best choice is no choice. I would say that means—"

"To stay here," Orlando said, eying the wall ahead of them. "And what then?"

"Shine your lights here," Renée ordered. "All around this wall. And use your gloves, sleeves, to clear the dust so we can look for outlines."

Caleb noticed Qara in his peripheral vision. Her head down, breathing excitedly. He moved closer to her and in the noise of scuffling and rubbing, he whispered, "What is it? You know this too, don't you? Is it a trick?"

She shrugged, poker-faced. "Use your mind powers if you want the answer, and make sure you see the right thing. I will say nothing else."

"Please help us. My son is going to be coming this way soon, and I can't let him get caught in one of these deadly traps."

"Then I hope he's better at this than you are."

Caleb glared at her, then turned his attention back to the soldiers brushing away at the wall under Renée's supervision. He wasn't sure which woman he was angrier at right now—Renée or Qara. But then, of course, he couldn't forget Nina. It seemed, all in the course of this single day, his wife was snatched from him and cruelly the gods put in her place three heartless substitutes.

"Found it!" Chang yelled, pointing. "Outline here, a small door. Do we push? I see no other mechanism."

They all looked at Qara, who merely shrugged. Caleb walked over to Phoebe and Orlando. And silently, as if communicating telepathically, they each lowered their heads, closed their eyes and willed themselves forward in space and backward in time, searching, seeing.

"I've got it!" Orlando yelled, clapping his hands for the want of a game-show buzzer. "Just push anywhere along the right edge and it'll swing inward."

"And beyond the door?"

"A staircase," Phoebe said, rubbing her temples, feeling like a sudden migraine just bored through her skull. "Leading down to what looked like a fancy golden crypt."

Renée's face brightened. "We've found it!" And she quickly ordered her men to open the door and light the way.

"But—" Caleb started to ask, then kept his mouth shut.

Phoebe also didn't share the others' enthusiasm. She looked at Qara and then Caleb. "I didn't see this the first time. I saw a journey along an underground river of silvery water, then to the gates of a palatial city basking in the dark and protected by soldiers."

Qara's eyes softened, and she gave an almost-imperceptible nod.

Renée snorted. "It seems you can be fooled just as easily as everyone who's read the *Sacred History*. It's all a big game of misdirection. Sometimes," she said, confidently, "the easiest path is the best. Occam's Razor. And sometimes, the best choice is not to choose. We go in."

The soldiers smiled, their steps lighter. They believed they were close, and the prospect of not having to pass over or around their mutilated comrades in either direction was a popular one. Chang ordered four men ahead through the door and down the stairs, into a slanting passage that was so dark no one could see the bottom.

"I suggest you to wait here," Chang said to Renée. "Maybe more traps."

"Doubtful," she said, "given that we needed psychics to get this far and find this door, but just to be safe, we stay here and see what they find."

"Agreed."

Renée turned and pointed her gun at Qara's face. "And if we lose these men too ..."

Qara shrugged. "You're acting rashly. If those men die, it will be your fault. I warned you."

Renée took a breath, trying to calm herself. "Do you, in fact, know anything about what's down here, or should I just put an end to your suffering?"

"Please," Caleb said, "can we just focus? Qara can help. And I have seen that she will. But right now, you should have your men come back. We can try to remote view what's down there again, try to visualize—"

"A coffin!" someone shouted, the voice amplified by Renée's transceiver.

"Describe it," she said back into the device.

In broken English, almost too choppy to comprehend, she heard, "We at bottom. In room, eight wall. Box in middle. Gold. Three meter long."

"Carefully," said Renée, "approach the casket." She took a very deep breath, glancing from Caleb to Qara, seeing their expressions of resigned fear. "Touch it."

"*Hao.*"

Seconds passed without sound or commotion.

"Report?"

Crackling. Shuffling.

"Fine. Okay. We move top. Look inside. We see ..."

"What? What do you see?"

Nothing.

"What's going on?" Renée barked. Chang took a few steps down and Caleb moved close behind him, peering down. Maybe only forty steps and the stairwell widened, revealing the four beams of light playing around a room bare of any artwork, furniture or treasure; nothing save for a gilded coffin.

And the four men on their knees around it, holding their throats. Coughing, wheezing.

Chang started down, but Caleb caught his arm, even as he stepped back. "Gas. Poison." Chang aimed his light past the contorting men, and for an instant Caleb caught a glimpse of a man's face: a foaming mouth, blood trickling from his nose, his eyes crimson. The light stabbed through the triangular opening into the coffin, to reveal—

—nothing but a few strips of rags.

"They treated the cloth with something that would ferment, turn and release a gas that would be trapped in that air-tight coffin," Caleb said, backing up and hanging his head, "until opened."

Qara smiled. "By intruders who wouldn't heed the warnings."

Renée swung her fist, slamming it into Qara's cheek and knocking her down. Then she pointed to Chang, whose horrified face had turned to bitter resolve. "Shut that door."

Caleb couldn't help but let out a snicker. "You're running out of men, Agent Wagner. At this rate, pretty soon we'll outnumber you."

"Oh, I'll make sure the odds stay in my favor. As I see it, Orlando and Qara here are nearly useless. They'll go first. Now talk. Tell us which way."

"I don't think it matters." He scratched his chin, staring again at the inscription. "*The best choice is not to choose.* Maybe it means that our choice doesn't matter."

"So, what then?" Phoebe asked.

Caleb looked at each of them, including the ten remaining soldiers. "Who's got a coin to flip?"

"Tails," Orlando said, flipping and catching a gold dollar. "Looks like we're headed left, for the old spike pit."

"Damn," Phoebe said. "I would've preferred the pancake room."

Renée stared at the coin in Orlando's open palm, two flashlight beams dancing across the eagle's wings. "So, that's it? All your vaulted abilities and we're reduced to a coin toss?"

"That's about right," Caleb said. "Like I told you, our process takes months. Weeks at least. Even then, if we do see something, it's hard to separate truth from imagination. In this case, the flip of a coin is as good as anything else."

"I think," Phoebe added, "that whichever way we choose, it won't be easy."

Qara cleared her throat as the soldiers prepared to move on Chang's orders. Her eyes were haggard, and blood from the fresh cut on her cheek trickled down her bruised face. "Death walks with us."

5.

Nina led Colonel Hiltmeyer and Private Harris down the stairs first. Alexander followed after taking what he feared might be his last gulp of fresh air. Montross descended last, still holding aloft the Emerald Tablet in his left hand, his gun in his right. At the bottom, they followed the glow, approaching the threshold with caution.

"Left their floodlights behind," Nina noted when they had passed the first door and saw the large halogen bulbs resting amidst the pile of skeletal remains.

"Good thing too," Montross said, pointing at the mosaic floor. "Now we can follow Hansel and Gretel's grisly trail."

Alexander shuffled his feet, hands in his pocket, the chill reaching deeper as they proceeded. The air was dank and oppressive, stifling. The corridors on either side loomed dark and full of menace, and the stairs behind them only reminded him of the field of corpses above.

Death up there, death down here, he thought. As Above, so Below.

Private Harris went first, looking miserable and terrified all at once, rubbing his elbow which had been banged up during the fall down the stairs. Then Hiltmeyer went, glaring back at Nina with every step. Harris's foot slid on one spot, almost connecting with another square tile. "Still wet," he said with a shaky voice.

"We're not far behind them," Montross said.

Harris suddenly froze, unable to take another step, glancing in both directions, expecting a hail of spears to rip through him at any moment. He glanced back at Alexander. "Is this it?"

Alexander thought for a moment, then shook his head. "I don't think so. I can't tell."

"A premonition?" Montross asked. "About Harris here? Ah, well if that was the case, the danger may now be passed."

"You can change fate?" Harris asked hopefully.

"We all can," Montross said. "We do it every day, every minute. But you're only conscious of it when you can see the tracks ahead and you know what's coming. Then, your choices seem to make you all powerful, make you feel almost godlike."

That seemed to be confusing enough to mollify Harris, and he continued for now, following Hiltmeyer along the red-smeared tiles. Montross waited at the edge of the mosaic floor, staying back with Nina and Alexander.

"What's up?" Nina asked.

He hugged the Emerald Tablet to his chest. "I just saw a flash of something. A glimpse ahead. Your friend Hiltmeyer ... near the last tile, if we were still behind him, he was going to drop to his knees and roll over the wrong tiles, releasing the spikes from both passages—"

"Running us through while he rolled to safety." Nina's eyes burned. The Beretta felt lighter in her hand.

"You saw the future again?" Alexander asked Montross, overhearing. "You keep seeing your death, don't you?"

Montross glanced down. "Observant boy. Yes. Seeing it—and avoiding it."

"Wow. How many times?"

Montross shrugged. "I've racked up more wins against the Reaper than I can count."

Alexander gave a little laugh. "Yeah, but he only has to win once."

"So true. Now, let's get going. Nina, keep your gun on Hiltmeyer until I'm across."

"With pleasure."

Alexander followed Montross, matching his steps, finding comfort in the fact that he was also following in his father's footsteps. Finally, they crossed the map and were past the border of the mosaic, joining Hiltmeyer and Harris, where the colonel refused to make eye contact. Instead, he gazed ahead, into the shadows.

Montross held the tablet in one hand as he waved Nina forward and pulled out Nilak's Ruger with the other. The tablet's glow provided enough illumination to see by, but not much more.

When Nina was across, she threw one of her backpacks at the colonel. "Flashlights inside. Also water and food." She patted the goggles hanging around her neck. "I'm keeping the night-vision goggles."

"What's up ahead?" Hiltmeyer asked, finding a flashlight and turning it on. He and Harris advanced, probing the shadows.

Alexander took a light from Nina and shined it straight ahead as he walked, following them. Then left, then right, down the newly revealed passageways.

"I smell something," he said.

Montross wrinkled his nose. "Something toxic." He pointed left. "From that direction."

"I saw water," Alexander said, closing his eyes and focusing again. "Water, or something like it. Shiny, like silver. And a boat filled with people. And my Dad!"

He took off running in that direction, but didn't get far. Nina was on him in a flash, collaring him and holding him still. "Don't do that again. Apart from not wanting you to escape, running into shadows is the best way to get yourself killed down here."

"I know," Alexander said. "But they went this way."

"If they went that way," Montross said, quietly, as he turned and faced right, ignoring the partially open false door ahead of them, "then I believe we'll to go this way."

"What?" Hiltmeyer asked, shining his light back and forth. "Why?"

"Because we need to make up time, and because that"—he shined his light on an inscription on the wall ahead of them—"says our choice doesn't matter."

Nina came back, pulling Alexander with her, even as he dragged his feet, looking back over his shoulder, fighting the tears in his eyes.

"This way may even be faster," Montross said, urging Hiltmeyer and Harris toward the room with the ceiling-press trap. "I have seen the river too. It's beautiful. And fortunately there's a vessel there as well, waiting."

"For what?" Harris asked.

"I don't know. For Temujin's use in the afterlife, should he desire a scenic boat ride?" Montross tightened his grip on the tablet. "Or just for someone who might come knocking with the right key."

Alexander moaned, still looking the other direction. "But Dad and Aunt Phoebe! They don't have the key, any key! And that way, the one they picked ..." He closed his eyes and shook his head, trying to dislodge the horrific visions.

"That way is worse. *Much* worse. They're not going to make it!"

6.

The river Caleb had seen in his vision wasn't fresh water at all, but a highly contaminated mercury-enriched stream. An oily, silvery river of perfect calmness, shimmering deceptively, hiding its toxicity beyond a lustrous sheen.

Back before the shore of silt, small rocks and dry earth, their footsteps mapped their progress through the arched doorway from the room of spikes, where Caleb had carefully led the team around seven-foot long metal lances, spaced only feet apart. They had crossed diagonally, and uneventfully, to the northern side of the room to the open archway and the waiting beach. Chang's men had found a grooved ladder on the western wall, just under the place where the floor had given way after they had tripped the weight sensor by tossing a heavy pack in the center of the floor. Once the floor had dropped, simply jamming a rifle into the visible gears at the lower corner prevented the floor from resetting and allowed them to descend.

They carried four flare guns and twenty-eight flares, hoping that would be enough. Caleb took a flashlight and played it over the river, the light skipping over its metallic appearance. Then he shined the light higher, the beam darting across the arched ceiling twenty feet above. Mostly earthy, their rooftop sported occasional stalactites hanging like swords.

More lights fanned out from the soldiers, finding the two gondola-like boats tethered with chains to iron posts thrust into the shore. Gazing at the river besieged by flashlight beams, Orlando whistled. "It looks like that cybernetic liquid alloy stuff in *Terminator 2*. nothing pops out of there and slices us in half." He turned to Caleb and Phoebe. "I think we should take this fine opportunity to psychically Mapquest the next leg of our journey."

"Definitely," Phoebe whispered, holding her hand over her mouth, coughing.

The tunnel ahead beckoned, shimmering in the flashlight beams before disappearing around a bend into darkness. It gave Caleb the impression of the start of a watery amusement park ride, like one he had taken Alexander on just last year at Busch Gardens. "Hold up," he said. "Anyone think to bring gas masks?"

Sniffing the air, Chang motioned one of his guards who wriggled out of a backpack, opened it and began passing out masks.

Good old Chinese efficiency and preparedness, Caleb thought.

"This will be a very toxic stretch," he said, pointing ahead, down the tunnel into the darkness. "Especially as we begin paddling, as the oars will stir up the mercury. It'll combine with the air and get in our lungs, and depending on the levels, which I imagine are quite high, we'll soon be suffering a host of nasty symptoms. Burning lungs, stinging eyes, coughing. It gets into the bloodstream quickly, impacting the central nervous system, and could cause paralysis and even death, given enough exposure."

"Twenty masks," Renée said, counting them.

I only hope Montross and Nina are likewise prepared, Caleb thought.

"We have extra," he said. "Can we leave some for Montross and my son? If they come this way?"

Renée narrowed her eyes at him.

"Please."

"Fine, drop three. Only because I think you may be right, and we may need your son."

Orlando took a mask, making sure he got his before they were all accounted for, then moved closer to the edge to examine the boats. "Sturdy bastards. Looks like iron plating and reinforced wood. Very little decay. Maybe the mercury helped."

"How did this water get so contaminated?" Phoebe asked.

"On purpose, I believe," Caleb said. "He may have just been copying, but like Emperor Qin Shi Huang, Genghis Khan may have also come to believe in mercury's alchemical powers. For centuries, mystics used mercury—also known as quicksilver—as a combining reagent to induce elemental changes, attempting to turn lead into gold for example, but it was also believed to be a source of a great many cures. And possibly, if mixed just right, an elixir for immortality."

"No thanks," Orlando said, fitting on his mask after coughing into his hand. "That's the crap they used to put in dental fillings."

Phoebe groaned through her mask. "Here we go. Conspiracy time. Let me guess, dentists are all part of some master plan to monitor our thoughts, weaken our resistance, make us sick—"

"Scoff if you like." Orlando shined his light into his open mouth. "But I'm a brushing fanatic, not one cavity."

"That's because you've never been to the dentist."

He smirked. "At least I'm confident that my mind is my own."

"Trust me, no one else would want it."

"Please shut up," Renée snapped. "And let's get moving."

Afraid to move, Phoebe stared at the water. "So emperors actually tried drinking this stuff?"

Caleb nodded. "It was what killed Qin Shi, if the legends are true."

"Enough talk," Renée said with her mask on. "Get in the boats. Eight in each. Chang, you're with us. And two of your men will row. You keep an eye on Qara. Caleb, Phoebe and Orlando, remote view the path ahead. I want no surprises."

"Best to do it here, on the shore," Caleb said, tightening his mask. Phoebe did the same.

"No, in the boat," Renée replied. "I believe you will perform better in the thick of things. Urgency sharpens your need."

"Aren't you suddenly the expert?" Phoebe quipped.

"Get in, and get to work."

They settled into the two boats. Caleb's team left second, after the boat full of soldiers pushed off. Phoebe and Orlando sat on one side, at the stern, with Caleb and Qara facing them while Renée stood at the prow, her .45 still in her hand, scanning the shadows ahead.

It all looked surreal and mythical: two gondolas carrying men and women wearing gas masks along a silvery river into a dark tunnel. Caleb thought it would have made a great Salvador Dali painting, an interpretation of Charon ferrying the dead into the waiting embrace of the Underworld.

"iPad," Phoebe said after a minute of intense focus. She held her hand out to Orlando, who quickly passed it over. "I think I've got the next leg of this map."

She leaned in to Caleb and whispered, "Just keep faking it, big brother. I've got you covered."

"You're the best," he replied. "I'm trying but ..."

"Nothing?"

"I keep seeing her. Lydia. But it's not like our visions. They're just memories."

"Ah. Worse, then."

Caleb nodded. *But maybe just as important.*A catharsis, perhaps. A flood of images played against the back of his eyelids every time they closed. Meeting her for the first time at the book signing in SoHo; their growing connection on the book tour, working together on research trips to exotic ancient locations, the steamy nights under the stars, or under the cool sheets in five-star hotels; the reunion after he had thought her dead, the moment her emotions cracked through and she revealed he had a son.

All these memories swam in his thoughts, clouding the psychic pathways like arterial blocks, suffocating the power he kept trying to access.

He couldn't fight it any longer, and didn't want to. She was there, in his mind, living in the only place left for her. Part of him hoped that he was seeing all this because she was trying to show him one more thing, to force him to understand some vital aspect of himself he needed to learn.

Or else, it was only his guilt.

He had killed her. As surely as if he'd pushed her off a cliff. By his silence and distrust. By his arrogance in thinking he alone could own and protect the Emerald Tablet. It was a guilt he needed to accept and overcome if he was to move on.

It's up to you now. Her last thought, he was sure of it, was about their son.But how could he save Alexander when his hands were tied? He could only stand by, watching and hoping the others could do what he couldn't.

Someone coughed. He heard the soldiers' raspy breathing over his own. Every sound was amplified in the cavern, the slightest movement roaring in his ears, explosions rattling in his head. The splashing of the oars echoed off the walls, and it was easy to imagine the flashlight beams scraping the ceiling or the sides, and eliciting sounds like nails on a chalkboard.

Phoebe sighed, the sound grinding in her ears as well. She took a deep breath of hot air and began drawing, expanding the previous sketch, filling in the right side of the diagram. Renée moved closer, stepping around the men rowing so she could watch.

"What's that?" She pointed to the bottom of the screen where Phoebe had drawn the terminus of this river passageway that ended at the boundary opening up into a larger section: broad at the far end, but peppered with dots. Phoebe kept jabbing at the screen, creating the dots in a haphazard pattern until it began to look like an actual formation.

"Don't know," Phoebe replied. "I saw faces. White faces. Hundreds of eyes. Thousands, maybe."

Qara made a snickering noise.

"What?" asked Renée, turning in the boat, then peering ahead. The flashlight's glow had bounced off her mask, amplifying a mix of fear and excitement beyond the plastic. "What's up ahead?"

"Death," Qara said. "And I don't need to be psychic to see that. We're all—"

"Shut her up," Renée snapped. "Phoebe, elaborate on what you saw."

A gasp, and Phoebe dropped the stylus pen, causing Orlando to jump for it, and scramble at the bottom of the boat before they lost it. She shook her head, blinked and stood up. Ahead, the flashlight beams speared around, barely penetrating the thick gloom hanging over the silvery river.

She squinted, rubbed her faceplate, and tried to peer through the unresolved shadows. "Wait! There's something before we reach the shore, something—"

But that's when an iron sphere as large as a refrigerator came swinging down from the cavern's roof on a steel chain, crashing into the first boat.

Soldiers scattered like bowling pins, two of them taking direct hits, bones shattering, bodies crumpling. The hull cracked and the boat capsized, spinning to the left and upturning the whole team.

"Duck!" Chang yelled as the sphere swung all the way back up, just missing the prow of the second boat. Everyone ducked low and his men paddled sideways, moving the boat out of the reach of the sphere's downswing.

One member of the first craft wasn't so lucky. A soldier had scrambled back into the boat after flipping it, and just stood, dripping and coughing, when the ball swung back and caught him in the chest, bringing him along for the ascending trip. A hideous crunching sound echoed off the ceiling, and his body splashed down in the darkness.

Men were screaming, splashing, scrambling. Flashlights spun around and dimmed as they went underwater. Chang and the two soldiers in Caleb's boat kept their lights trained on the first boat, keeping it illuminated for the capsized men to get back on.

The sphere came back for another swing, but this time both boats were out of its range, off to the side.

"Shit!" Renée grumbled. "What else do we have to contend with?"

"You have no idea," Qara said.

"I do," said Phoebe. "I'm sorry, I wasn't looking close enough. But that's it. Just that iron ball, a little pre-welcoming gift from Genghis."

"You'd better be right," Renée said, ruefully counting the soldiers ahead as they climbed back into the battered boat.

"We lost three," Chang said, shining his light on the three floating, battered bodies.

Renée nodded. "Acceptable. Keep going. And you"—she glared at Phoebe—"had better be right about this."

Phoebe nodded, but Orlando stepped up between them. "Listen, you want our help, you better start asking nicely."

"Orlando," Caleb cautioned.

"Fine," Renée said, raising her gun in front of Orlando's face. "Please just do what I tell you, or I'll shoot your girlfriend and toss her over the side."

"Hey," Phoebe said. "I'm nobody's—"

"Save it. Kid, help her out. And Caleb, maybe you should actually start contributing. I don't recall your being of any use so far, except for prattling your academic bullshit."

"Which," Caleb said, "if I recall, helped to get us this far."

Renée looked around the gloom, past the dead bodies. "Which is where, exactly?"

Caleb glared at her through his fogging facemask. Then he peered over her shoulder, to where the lights of the first boat were striking something a hundred feet ahead. A rough shoreline. "Here," he said, moving to the head of the boat.

Chang barked a command to the lead boat, and a soldier pulled out a gun, aimed ahead as the boat approached the sandy shore, and fired.

The crimson flare left a sparkling smoke trail on its ascent. It rose at a slight angle, and kept ascending, illuminating odd shadows, glinting off impossibly white structures.

Caleb's boat pulled up alongside the other, and all eyes were on the still-ascending flare. Chang whispered something, and three more flares fired out into the darkness. The first one dipped over a tall minaret and was lost over a skyline of domes, walls and turrets. The other, rising at a steeper angle, hit the roof of the immense cavern and stuck, sparking and smoking.

"More," Renée said.

The flare guns fired again, four of them lighting up the darkness, dispelling shadows that had ruled undisturbed for eight centuries.

"Holy crap," Orlando whispered, as they all gazed at the flickering red outlines of the city visible over the walls: palaces of polished white marble, temples of golden tiles and blue mosaic domes; winding walkways and soaring bridges, fountains and ponds; pillared temples and massive halls.

"The real Xanadu," Caleb said.

Qara bowed her head, whispering something in Mongolian.

"Wait," Renée said, pointing ahead, to the quarter-mile field stretching before the immense wall. Hard to see with the flares so high up, but it looked like the ground was composed of ridges, bumps and pockets. "Flares. Fire them straight ahead, now."

As the men prepared to shoot, Phoebe cautioned, "I don't think you want to see this."

Three flares streaked out from the first boat, heading off at slightly different angles. The first struck something only fifty feet out, fizzled and then dropped. The other two went farther; one hundred, two hundred, three hundred feet.

Then each struck something and held, smoking, casting the surrounding area in a ghastly glow.

"Double crap," Orlando said.

Twenty-thousand strong, they stood organized by their regiments, infantry on the right, cavalry in the center; archers on the higher ground to the left; and chariots, catapults, siege machines and banners on immense poles interspersed throughout. Grayish-white terra cotta statues, each one carved perfectly, detailed down to the grooves in their armor, the notches on the saddles, the hardened eyes brimming with loyalty, ferocity and menace.

"The welcoming party," Caleb said. "Genghis's army."

7.

Montross covered his face with his sleeve while Hiltmeyer and Harris coughed, backing away from the boat. "No way," the colonel said, pointing to the cavern and the river with the silvery sheen that bent around a quick curve and headed into the blackest reaches beyond their flashlights' beams.

"Hang on," Montross said. He backed up, closed his eyes and hugged the Emerald Tablet close. "Alexander, let's see how your father handled this from his side."

"Masks," the boy said at once. He was rubbing his eyes, also breathing through his shirt. "I saw them. All the soldiers had them, and they left three behind. For us."

"Three?" Harris said, choking on the word. "Come on!"

"Easy," said Montross. "Nina, go fetch them, and—"

"Be careful, I know." She smiled wolfishly. "Your concern for me is touching."

"I just want my mask."

As she left, Montross pulled Alexander back to the tunnel leading from the room with the trap ceiling. "We'll wait for her here where the air's clearer."

"What about us?" Harris asked.

Montross shrugged. "Tear your shirts, or jackets. Make yourselves something to cover your faces."

Hiltmeyer grumbled, "You'll poison us."

"Either that, or I'll shoot you." Montross waved the Ruger. "Your choice." He cleared his throat, then turned to the boy. "And you, Alexander, I need you to use this time to scout out the area ahead while I keep an eye on these clowns."

Alexander shook his head. "But I don't want to. Anytime I try, I know I'll just see Dad, and I can't, don't want to see ..."

"See what?"

"Can't bear it." He shook his head, covering his eyes. "What if I see him die, too?"

Montross knelt down and switched his gun to his other hand, still keeping an eye on their prisoners. "Just focus your mind, ask yourself a question, and only think about that question when you let your visions come."

"What question?"

"Jeez, didn't your father teach you anything? Never mind. I already know: 'Learn by doing, learn from experience.' Still, you must have sat in and listened to the Morpheus Initiative sessions."

"A few times," Alexander admitted.

"Well then, you know how it is. The question frames your visionary experience. You remote view what you've asked your mind to show you. In this case,"—he waved beyond, to the darkness along the river—"we need to know what's waiting for us. Ask to be shown any traps on this river, anything that could stop us from reaching the great underground cavern and the city of Genghis Khan."

"Too vague," Alexander said.

"What?"

"The question. I know enough about it, as you said. I sat in on a lot of sessions with my dad, with Aunt Phoebe. I know you can't have those multiple-part questions. Or you get crappy visions, something that just might get us killed."

Montross grinned. "All right, smarty-pants. Just remote view the next section of this river. Period."

Alexander nodded. "I'll try. And I'll try not to see my dad."

"Try hard," Montross said. "I know it's not easy to pull away from your feelings, or your fears, but it's the only way. If you want to see him again, trust that he knows what he's doing, and trust that for this part, we need your skills. Go to it."

"Can I touch the tablet first?"

Montross held it out, balancing it in the palm of his right hand, watching as it reflected in the boy's deep brown eyes, mixing with his irises, turning them a swirling shade of green.

Alexander reached for it slowly, his fingers trembling.

Nina found the masks, as predicted, on the shore beside the two posts and empty chains that had tethered two boats. She waved her flashlight ahead, scoping out the area, but couldn't see a thing. She held her breath, sucking in a whiff of the foul, toxic air and holding it just to listen.

From somewhere, far, far off, something loud, a report followed by another muffled thump echoing along the stretch of the dark underground waterway, reached her ear. A tiny ripple stirred along the shore.

She didn't need to be psychic to know that the other team faced something deadly at the end of the waterway. But all the same, she felt a twinge, a sudden connection with someone.

And it wasn't Montross.

Caleb.

She felt him, saw through his eyes just for a brief instant ...

... *a flickering field of immobile warriors, thousands-strong, weapons ready, facing them, barring their advance.*

Why? Nina thought. *Why did I glimpse that? Why Caleb? Why now?*

She took the masks and slowly backed away, shaking her head, clearing that nagging sight, when something else, something that suddenly blossomed like an exploding fireworks display in her mind... .

Two sets of small hands, gripped by larger ones, held in a grandfatherly grasp.

Two hands ... belonging to two boys.

Two scared boys, looking out over a harbor from a great height, gazing out at hundreds of boats while a raspy voice whispered of destiny.

Nina trembled.

She coughed, fell to her knees, heaving. Gasping.

What ... the hell ... was that?

She closed her eyes, but the visions were gone, leaving behind nothing but wispy shadows.

She gathered up the masks and stumbled back to Montross.

They pushed off as Nina stood behind the rowers, Hiltmeyer and Harris. She had a gun in each hand, the Beretta in her left, the muzzles at the back of their heads, and she couldn't help but feel like a slave master on the old Roman galleons, ready to execute whoever dropped out of pace first.

Harris complained through his makeshift face mask of his torn sleeve tied around his neck and across his mouth. Colonel Hiltmeyer only rowed in silence, his eyes burning as each stroke released fumes that stung at his eyes.

"What next?" Montross asked.

Alexander sat in the front, gas mask wrapped extra tight around his head. He held up a hand. Then pointed. "Hug the right wall."

Nina nudged the gun against Harris's head, prodding him to row harder, pushing the boat in that direction.

"Farther," Alexander said, scanning the rooftop as nervousness crept into his voice. "Otherwise we're bowling pins."

Montross directed his flashlight along the ceiling, locating a huge round ball tucked into a niche in the center, to their left now as they steered around it. "Good catch, kid. What else?"

Alexander closed his eyes and focused his breathing. *Don't do it, don't view Dad, or Phoebe.*

Instead, he saw his ...

... mom, engulfed in the flames.

Except she wasn't hurting. Wasn't even singed. She walked through the fire calmly, arms out to him, a sweet smile on her face.

"You're not alone," she whispered, smoke puffing from her mouth.

"Not ... alone ..."

He snapped out of it, blinked and then saw—

"Spikes!" he shouted. "At both sides. *Stop!*"

Harris pulled back, oaring fast the other way, and Hiltmeyer slipped, a second later, turning and jamming the oar. He coughed, hacking into his mask and cursing. Something black and shiny roared straight up from the river a yard from where Alexander had been sitting in the prow. It pierced the tunnel's roof, dislodging stones and dirt, and then withdrew with a silent splash.

"What the hell!" Harris said. His oar was out of the water now, and he was bent over, almost hugging his knees. "What do we do?"

"Remain calm," Montross said. "Alexander's got it."

"Cutting it a little close, don't you think?" Hiltmeyer said.

"Turn now," Alexander said with a shaking voice. "Straighten it out. And stay straight if you can. There's just a narrow channel where we'll be okay."

"Yeah," said Nina, jabbing the soldiers with her guns. "We get it.

You heard the kid. Straighten out and row."

They moved ahead, cutting through the luminescent water. Moving slower, carefully.

"What else?" Montross asked.

Alexander shook his head. "I don't know. I didn't see anything else, except ..."

"What?"

He slumped forward, then straightened his back. He turned his head and Montross could see the pained eyes filling with tears.

"I saw you again," he said. "Your mom and dad—"

"What?"

"Alexander!" Nina started.

"—dying. The car crash. Except, he wasn't your dad."

"I know that," Montross snapped. "But why? Why are you seeing this? What question are you asking?"

"Nothing. I didn't ask a thing. I just keep seeing it."

Montross stared, open-mouthed, and Nina glanced at him, taking her attention away from the soldiers. "Xavier, it's nothing."

"Don't tell me it's nothing. He's young, and his power is being augmented by the tablet in ways we can't imagine. It must be showing him something important. Or at least something his mind feels he needs to know. So, I need to know it too."

Damn, Nina thought. *It's too early for this.*

"Not your father," Alexander said again. "But I think ... I think your dad might be ..." He held his head, rubbing the back. He coughed. A little sob escaped.

"What?" Montross asked, almost a shriek. "What? Who?"

"I don't know, I don't know." Alexander shook his head. "I see it, but I don't know what it means."

The oars continued paddling, the boat skimming faster and faster ahead. All flashlights were pointed inside at Alexander, almost blinding him.

"Well," said Montross gripping the tablet even tighter, "now that I know that something about my heritage is important, I'll just have my own look-see."

"No," Nina whispered.

"What?"

"Don't. Not yet."

Montross faced her as the tablet's aura sprinkled them both in a sheen of fairy dust. "What aren't you telling me?"

"I—"

"Uh oh," Harris said, dropping his oar. He stood, just as the nose of the boat struck something and they all lurched forward.

We hit the shore," Hiltmeyer yelled. He collected himself, leapt to his feet and spun around, hoping Nina had dropped her guns, but in an instant she was there, tripping up his legs and pushing him back down into the belly of the boat.

"Don't even think about it."

Montross grunted, fumbled for the tablet and retrieved it, then held it up to illuminate the boat. "Alexander?"

He was outside, picking himself up on the shore, right behind Harris who was scrambling to his knees. Suddenly both were caught in flashlight beams probing wildly ahead. They were on a small inlet, a pathway sparkling with gold bending in a thirty-foot S-shaped pattern to the gate.

Alexander took out his flashlight. "Wow." His beam stretched out and searched, then struck a wall of immense marble blocks around a huge sealed archway. Above the arch, between two turrets, stood four immense statues.

Giant terra cotta warriors, each manning huge crossbows.

"Oh no," Harris whispered.

Just as something whistled through the air.

He grunted, making a surprised choking sound as he clutched at the end of a six-foot iron bolt protruding from his chest. And with the point erupting out his back he looked like game piece on a foosball table. He stumbled backwards, past Alexander. His mouth opened as he fell, arching backwards until the silver point stabbed into the soft earth and his head flopped backwards.

Alexander opened his mouth, tried to cry out, tried to insist that he hadn't seen this, knowing that the reason was because he hadn't asked the right questions. *I only asked about the river!*

Desperately, he looked back to the ramparts, to the silent, impassive guardians, three of which had yet to fire.

8.

Caleb hadn't even stepped off the boat before the first scream ripped through the cavern, and suddenly there were gunshots, flashlight beams probing desperately. Men yelling.

More gunshots, and Phoebe, Orlando and Qara ducked low on the boat just as a sudden volley of arrows whistled past, sailing behind them and plunking into the water.

"Back!" Chang shouted. "Stop firing!"

The soldiers formed a semi-circle around Renée, Chang and the boats. Their flashlights swept back and forth, revealing the first rows of terra cotta warriors, many of them now shredded with 7.62mm rounds. No more arrows flew, and the army rested in silence and apparent innocence.

"What happened?" Renée asked.

"Someone went scouting ahead."

"Who told him to do that?"

"Procedure." Chang said. "Sorry."

Renée shoved aside two soldiers and looked at what their lights had settled on. One of the soldiers lay face-down about five feet beyond the first row of warriors. His left leg was severed above the knee, lying by itself a short distance away. His back was punctured by three arrows.

Another soldier came limping back, shrieking for a medic, an arrow in his hip and a gouge cut through his left arm.

Renée shined her light in the direction he had come from, and saw a statue with a sword held up before his face. The blade was wet. The statue wobbled slightly as it returned to its dormant position.

"Ballistic vests," Chang said, pointing to the fallen man. "Help little against arrows. Or swords."

Renée lowered her gun. She scanned the shot-up faces of the nearest terra cotta soldiers. "Okay, lesson learned. No one's going in there until we know what this is. Apparently Temujin has this field rigged as well, with pressure-sensitive plates that trigger the statues into attacking."

After testing the air and believing themselves safe for the moment, the soldiers removed their gas masks and started checking their gear. They tightened their flak jackets, still hoping they'd provide some protection, donned their helmets and prepared their weapons, reloading and checking their lights.

Caleb walked carefully out of the boat, then helped Qara disembark as Phoebe and Orlando got out on the other side.

Renée scouted ahead with night-vision binoculars. "I see something. Looks to be about four hundred yards, past this field and the army. There's a gate. That's the entrance into the city, and where we need to go."

Chang nodded, surveying the field. "But direct path is most fortified. See? Largest concentration of soldiers appear to guard way."

"So what do we do?" asked one of the men.

"No one moves ahead," Renée ordered, "until our seers show us the way." She glanced back at Caleb, waved her .45 at him. "Come on, Kreskin. What's the trick this time? A certain path to take, or maybe some tune we all need to sing to let us waltz on by?"

Caleb shrugged. He took his flashlight and swept it around the shore, along the walls on either side, walls that widened from their river approach, encompassing and enclosing the massive underground field, the army and, eventually, the distant walled city. He blinked, focusing out there, wondering if Alexander had gone around, taking the other passageway with Montross, and if he might even now be up ahead now, looking this way for him.

"Wait," said Orlando suddenly. "There! Above us."

Phoebe brought her light up as she stepped closer to him, brushing against him and noticing that he trembled, but still leaned in toward her. She gave him a smile, then looked up at the letters hammered into a marble crossbeam overhead. "Nice work. You keep bailing us out like this and my brother will have to give you a bigger bonus this year."

Orlando's voice cracked after the compliment. "So here's more of those funky letters. Qara, can you do your thing?"

She stumbled forward, her wrists still tied behind her, the bandages on her side soaked through with fresh blood. She looked pale and weak, but she lifted her eyes and with dried lips, read the inscription: *"The Secret of the Way Past is the Secret of the Way In."*

Renée glared at Qara, then looked at the script, and then to Chang, raising an eyebrow.

He shrugged. "Pretty close."

"The secret of the way in?" Renée asked.

"What was the secret of the way past?" Phoebe asked, shining her light on Caleb, who blocked it with his hand. It reminded her, for just a moment, of the descent into that tomb in Belize when as kids they joked at blinding each other to ease their fears. *What we can't see can't hurt us, right?*

Caleb stopped the smile and looked back past Renée and over the field of warriors, the guardians. Thinking. Imagining a course through them, past them. But they covered every square foot, in no particular pattern. *The secret of the way past is the secret of the way in.* Very symmetrical. Perfect. But no help.

"I have no idea," he said.

"RV it, then," Renée barked. "All of you. Do it now, before I risk any more of my men."

Caleb glanced at Phoebe and Orlando and nodded. The three of them sat cross-legged together on the hard ground away from the mercury-laden water.

"Shouldn't we hold hands or something?" Orlando asked, reaching for Phoebe.

"Keep dreaming, Romeo." She gave him a look, then relented. "All right, but only because I know that sometimes psychics can chain their powers if they're touching." She noticed Caleb and stopped talking.

"Don't worry," he said. "I don't think I'll kill your mojo if we link up, but if it's all the same to you—"

"Just hold our hands," she snapped.

Caleb sighed and held up his hands. Orlando took his left, Phoebe his right.

"No caressing," Phoebe hissed, a smile breaking free. Then lower, "At least make this look good for prying eyes."

Renée glowered at them. "Hurry."

Phoebe closed her eyes, squeezing both hands, just as Orlando gasped. But it was Caleb who jerked as if electrocuted, snatching his hands away.

"Holy crap," Orlando said, still holding onto Phoebe. "What was that?"

Caleb frowned, staring at his hands as if expecting them to be covered with second-degree burns. "I don't know. I saw something, though."

"What?" Phoebe asked, leaning over.

"Lydia. It was like she was here. In our circle, holding both my hands. Like she had taken your places."

"How the hell does that help us?" Renée asked.

"It doesn't," Caleb said. "But it might help me."

"I don't understand."

Orlando coughed. "Wait! I saw something. Honestly I did. A trail. Glowing, weaving through the soldiers."

Renée cocked her head. Chang moved in, listening intently.

Phoebe gave Orlando a subtle look to ask if this was just a ploy, but he didn't even look at her. He stood, releasing her hand, and headed through the Chinese soldiers to the front of the shore. Nodding, he pointed ahead. "I saw it in my vision, a glowing pathway, highlighting the trail we need to take."

"How wide?" Chang asked.

"Four or five feet."

"Can you still see it?"

Orlando rubbed his temples, stuck his neck out and stared. Nodded. "I can lead you, just like Caleb led us before on the mosaic floor. I see it."

"Okay," Renée said. "Let's go."

"I don't know," said Caleb. "Why would there be something such as a trail? The clue was that the way past these soldiers must in some way mirror what we did to find the entrance above."

"I'm not into riddles," Renée said. "Let's just test it out. Your boy here thinks he's seen the way. Let him go a few steps. See how far he can get. If he makes it, then who cares what the clue means? You're psychics. You don't need logic."

Orlando stopped. His gaze swept over the first five rows of warriors lurking in the shadows. He turned and met Phoebe's eyes. "Um, maybe not. Maybe we should think this through a little more."

"Did you see it, or didn't you?" Renée waved him on with her gun.

"No, Orlando!" Phoebe reached out, but two soldiers blocked her way.

"Go," said Chang, more than happy he wasn't risking his own men.

Orlando swallowed hard, his raw throat burning with the effort. A dozen flashlights led the way. He tried to look back and catch Phoebe's eyes, but could only see a swarm of bright lights, blinding him. "Can I get one of those bullet proof jacket things?"

Renée laughed and her voice came back. "Didn't you say that they won't help?"

It took a minute for the blind spots to wear off, and then he started to move forward. Lifted his foot and set it ahead, between two infantry men, the hilts of their swords gripped in both hands, the points directed up and inwards, making an inverted V that Orlando had to walk beneath.

His foot touched the ground and he closed his eyes, praying before he put weight on it. He could see it again—the aurora-like trail misting under the feet of the warriors, starting here and then twisting left, then extending forward, around a great bend and then circling up again around the chariots, through the horsemen and in between two largest catapults.

Please work.

"Orlando," Phoebe called out. "Please be careful."

A deep, clear breath filled his lungs. And with renewed confidence and trust, he bent under the swords and took one step, then another, following the trail, approaching another warrior, this one with a curved sword over its shoulder, poised as if preparing for a decapitating swing.

His right foot touched down, he put all his weight on it, moved his left foot ahead. But before he picked up his right foot again, the statue moved. head swiveled, blank white eyes fixing him with a deadly stare.

"No," Caleb whispered. Then, "NO! Orlando, don't move!"

All the flashlights converged on Orlando, dancing around, then hitting the statue, the one that had twisted, the sword rising, trembling.

"Don't lift your feet!"

Orlando turned his head, trying to balance on the bridge of this foot. His hands were outstretched, reflexively reaching for something to hold until he managed to pull himself back without grabbing another statue, one holding two daggers at the ready. "I think I'm on a pressure plate."

The lights danced on his face, bringing out tears in his eyes as he refused to close them, hoping to get one last look at Phoebe.

"Sorry," he said glumly. "I screwed up. I don't know how, but I must have. I know this is right, I see the trail, but—"

"You didn't screw up," Caleb said. "I did."

"What?" Phoebe was at his side, clutching his arm.

Renée turned toward him. "How is this your fault? Other than not seeing it for yourself and trusting this crucial task to a junior member."

"Nothing junior about him," Caleb said. "And he's seeing the right trail."

"I am?" Orlando asked, his voice cracking. He looked down at his feet, even as his knees started wobbling.

"It's the right trail," Caleb continued, "just at the wrong altitude."

"Huh?"

"The riddle," he said. "I figured it out. Unfortunately, a little late."

"The way past," Renée intoned. "Same as the way in?"

"Yeah. The secret of the entrance. Remember?"

Phoebe slapped her hand against her forehead. "They moved the river!"

"Exactly." Caleb pointed down. "I'm guessing there's an entrance or a tunnel back here somewhere, where the river we just came down continues under this section in another subterranean tunnel. Weaving its way *under* the warriors."

"Damn it!" Orlando hissed. "I should've figured that out. I even saw what looked like water, glowing water, but I thought it was just part of the vision."

"Don't worry, you did good." Caleb sighed. "Now we've got to get you out of there."

"Impossible," Renée said. "He takes his chances. Just duck, roll and run back. With any luck, he'll make it."

The other soldiers had taken wary steps back, and were spreading out, ducking their heads.

"Get some cover if you can," Renée barked. "I suspect the arrows might be flying any second." She turned to Phoebe. "Sorry about your boyfriend, but at least we don't have to worry about his untrustworthy visions anymore."

Caleb had to hold Phoebe back as she squirmed. "You bitch!"

"Stop," he said. "Just wait. We need to think."

"No time. Chang, find that entrance. Check the walls and the ground back by the water."

As Chang busied himself with that task, Caleb moved ahead, scanning around. He put his hands down, then slipped off his backpack. Turned around. "Get supplies off that dead man. The heaviest things he's carrying." He dropped to his knees and began digging, prying out rocks and chunks of earth and stuffing them in the pack.

Phoebe knelt beside him and started helping. "Good idea." Her eyes were red and heavy.

"We'll save him," Caleb whispered.

Phoebe tried to smile. "I'm not so sure."

As they filled the pack as much as possible, then zipped it up, Qara, who had been standing mutely near the shore, came closer. "Maybe," she said quietly, so only Caleb and Phoebe could hear, "this is an opportunity."

"What do you mean?"

"To free yourselves."

"If you've got any secrets, spill 'em now," Phoebe said.

"I believe," she said, "your friend has a chance. Not only to save himself, with the help of your counterweight here, but also perhaps to set off an attack by these warriors. A volley of arrows that would surely injure most, if not all, of Agent Wagner's men."

"And not us?" Caleb asked.

"Not if we're lying flat at the right moment."

"What are you talking about?" Renée spun away from Chang and came in close.

"Do you want to survive this or not?" Qara said, holding her head up.

Renée studied her. "I don't trust you. But for now, you live. Just move back, away from Caleb."

"I have it!" Chang yelled. Two men were on their knees, brushing away the earth in a section just a few yards ahead of the prow of the second boat. Lights converged on the area, illuminating a rounded outline cut into a marble-like surface.

While they went about clearing out the handle and prying it open like a manhole cover, Caleb dragged the backpack toward the field of warriors, where Orlando stood teetering on the balls of his feet, ten yards out. Surrounded by warriors poised to strike both high and low, he looked terrified and miserable.

"Please hurry, boss. Don't want to get all cliché on you, but I don't want to die just yet. So much left to do and all."

"Hang in there, Orlando. I'm coming."

"I could tell you, but you probably won't believe me. I've never even—"

"I don't need to hear this, really."

"—kissed a girl." He smiled back. "What did you think I was going to say?"

Caleb shook his head. "Never would have guessed. A suave guy like you."

Then lower, "I love your sister, you know."

Caleb ducked under the first two warriors. He held his breath, trying to step exactly in Orlando's footsteps as he lugged the eighty-pound pack. "You can tell her that yourself, when we get out of this."

Orlando shook his head. "Nope. I think I'm shish kebob. Or hibachi. Whichever."

"For hibachi you need fire. Kebab is skewering."

"Ah. Well then." His body gave a tremor and his back foot almost slipped before he caught himself and regained balance. "These hungry fellows here have waited a long time for their dinner."

"They can wait longer." Caleb crouched, dragging the pack right up to the back of Orlando's legs. "Keep the light on us!" he yelled back, then winced against the blaze.

"Tell me when," Orlando said.

Caleb could see his feet shaking. His boots, dirt-caked and torn at the sides, wobbled on a plate tilting out of the earth. He could see the levers underneath leading to the closest statues, somehow triggering them into movement.

He dragged the pack onto the back of the plate, inching it forward little by little. "Lift your foot, Orlando. Just slightly. Lean forward. Keep your toes on it. There ..."

Something grated and Orlando flinched. It took all his effort not to move off the plate. "Boss? They're gearing up, and their blades look freakin' sharp. Vorpal sharp, even. At least I know I won't feel it when—"

"Stop. Now, just ease forward. All your weight on your left foot." Caleb slid the pack two more inches, covering now the space where his right foot had been.

Balancing, back foot in the air, Orlando slowly set it down, next to his front foot.

Caleb took his hands off the pack, gently, with his eyes closed. Then opened them and looked up, breathing a sigh. "Okay?"

"Still in one piece," Orlando said. "It's holding. Can I run for it?"

"Not yet." Caleb glanced back and saw Qara behind the others, pulling Phoebe with her. Saw their eyes. Saw Qara's expression, and her lips moving: *Do it.*

Caleb put his hand back on the pack while getting up into a kneel, and with his other hand took Orlando's arm. He could pull him down easily, down and away from the statue's reach, just as he pulled the pack off the plate. Both of them would be ducking, and after the two statues swung horizontally, the arrows would fly at perfectly coordinated angles, missing the other statues and striking with a maximum spread at anyone standing on the shore.

Take them all out. Do it.

He tightened his grip on the backpack, glancing around at all the lights dancing off the taut visages of the warriors standing in their eternal positions, poised and waiting for this chance to defend their master.

Caleb blinked away a bead of sweat. Shook his head. *No. Not like this.*

He eased Orlando back, around the plate, even as he stood up from a crouch, and led him slowly, carefully back along their footsteps.

Back to the party on the shore, away from the frozen warriors, who watched them with resigned indifference.

Qara stood up, fury in her eyes. But Phoebe pushed past Renée and Chang and threw her arms around Orlando's neck. She pulled back, looked into his eyes and gave him a big kiss before pulling away and slapping his cheek. "Don't ever do that again!"

"What?"

"Risk your life on an unsupported vision. You want to be part of the Morpheus Initiative, you'd better wise up."

Orlando's grin was unwavering. "It was worth it. For that kiss."

"I'd rather drink that mercury water," said Renée, "than listen to any more of this crap. Let's get moving." She moved behind them and pointed her gun at their backs. "Let's go. Down into the tunnel."

9.

"Don't move, kid!"

Montross tightened his hold on the Emerald Tablet. The giant warriors on the wall were bent over, crossbows aimed to take out anyone on the shore. "Not a muscle. Do ... not ... move." He glanced back. "Nina? Options?"

She thought quickly, looking to the large duffel bag at her feet. "RPG?"

Thinking for a moment, Montross nodded. "I'm sure, given enough time, we could RV this moment, try to figure out what the builders had in mind, how to bypass this trap and get that gate open."

"But time is something we don't have," Nina said, unzipping the bag. She put her Beretta away and reached inside the bag for the rocket launcher and one of three missiles. She screwed it in and stood, raising the rifle butt to her shoulder, flipping over the reticule and peering through it.

"Aim for the ledge between the second and third warrior," Montross said. "Right, Colonel? Would that be your advice?"

Hiltmeyer, his face ashen, his flashlight trembling, only murmured his assent. He kept staring at the body of his last soldier, staked into the ground, back arched at an awkward angle, head swiveled with dead eyes locked on him.

Nina aimed. "Duck, Alexander. *Now!*"

She fired. Just as Alexander's movement triggered something and the second archer swiveled four degrees, lining up a shot with the boy's location.

The missile struck, exploding the entire rampart under the statue warriors, blowing two of them into chunks and sending debris in all directions. Alexander tucked himself into a ball, wincing as a few smaller pieces struck his back and a powdery dust swirled in the flashlight beams. He rubbed his ears, amazed that anything could produce such a tremendous sound, then waved away the smoke and stood, not sure which direction was which.

"Wait," Montross cautioned.

He and Nina led Colonel Hiltmeyer out as the smoke cleared and they looked up. The statues were gone, all but the lower torso and crouched legs of the left-most warrior, standing on a cracked edge over the gap. "Nice work," Montross said. He pointed to the gate and said to Nina, "Now kindly open that door."

"Wait!" Alexander said, shaking his head. "I see something." He closed his eyes, after ripping off his gas mask and taking in deep breaths. The air was clearer now, smelling of something fresh and pure blowing over the walls. "Water," he said. "A lot of it, just past the gate."

"A 'sunless sea,'" Montross whispered. "Coleridge." He glanced back. "It couldn't have been the river he was talking about, and it surely wasn't anything topside. But beyond these walls ..."

"A sea," Alexander repeated. "And I think it's fresh, not like that river."

Montross nodded. "You're right. Genghis created an underground Venice. His city, his mausoleum. It's half-submerged. Instead of a moat on the outside of his castle-city, he built the moat on the inside, an enormous lake, enclosed by forty-foot-high walls."

Nina scanned the area above the wall where now she could just make out a series of glowing lights, and as her eyes adjusted, shapes appeared: towers and domes, long spires and lonely minarets. She pointed. "I think Caleb's team made it to the other side at least. Look. Flares."

"So what happens," Hiltmeyer asked, "if you blow open the gate?"

Montross scratched his chin thoughtfully. "Out comes the sea?" He glanced left and right, shining his flashlight. High walls in either direction beyond the tunnel from which they'd just arrived. Walls that met other walls of Genghis's city.

"We drown," Alexander guessed. "That's what happens."

"Back in the boat," Montross said. "We'll latch ourselves down."

"Wait, I've got a better idea," Nina said. She dug into the supplies and pulled out a coil of rope and a grappling hook. "Why not just go over the wall?"

They chose a section of the wall unguarded at the top and Montross climbed up first, followed by Hiltmeyer. Alexander went next, hauled up by Hiltmeyer as Montross supervised.

When he got to the top and clambered over, standing on the five-foot-wide precipice, he felt like he was standing on China's Great Wall, gazing out into the gloom over an ancient city. His eyes followed a pathway below, bathed in a flickering radiance, a bridge over the sea, winding in a serpentine fashion and branching out into smaller avenues, connecting the various palaces and halls, reaching distant temples and monasteries, which in turn had tributaries joining other domed buildings and structures whose purpose eluded any guesses he could come up with. All around these silent buildings lay the darkness of the subterranean sea. Placid, motionless. Reflecting the towers and domes in the faint light of the scarlet flares burning high above.

In the flickering light, Alexander could only shake his head in wonder. And then he let his roaming eyes focus and follow the length of the wall as it stretched into the shadows and circled around the great city. Across the dismal sea, he could picture his father somewhere on the opposite wall, staring out over the vast gulf of crimson-tinted shadows, over the final resting place of the great Khan, and across to Alexander.

Just hold on, Dad. We're coming. I'll find you.

"There," said Nina, pointing down over the wall. "We can lower ourselves to the walkway."

"I don't like the looks of that," Hiltmeyer said, squinting. Extending from about half-way up on the gate's interior below, the walkway-thoroughfare was made up of a series of great blocks, connected to each other by short arched bridges. "I'm not psychic like you guys, but I suspect those blocks might fall into the sea when we step on them."

"And," voiced Alexander meekly, "maybe there are piranhas in there. Or sharks. I hate sharks."

Montross shone his light down on the first section, then over the bridge. "If it's a trap, I don't see what can be done to avoid it."

"Unless," said Nina, "we're meant to swim."

Alexander shuddered. "With the piranhas?"

"Or," she continued, "we bring up the boat, then drop it on this side and just row over to his mausoleum."

"And just where is this mausoleum supposed to be?" asked Hiltmeyer.

Montross unzipped his pack and reached in for the Emerald Tablet. Took it out and held it up. "Turn off the lights for a second. I want to try something."

They did, and the bridge went dark while Nina shifted her aim, watching the colonel stiffen in the green radiance.

Alexander's eyes adjusted, and then he saw something strange. Like a reflection of the tablet itself, something flickering in the distance. It came from a large rounded structure surrounded by immense pillars and defended on all sides by water, except for a lone pathway from the center avenue.

The light—actually a pair of lights—came from a window in the upper reaches of the dome.

"There," said Montross. "That's where we're going. There's his mausoleum."

Alexander whispered, "I'm guessing those lights are your keys."

"It would seem so." Montross lowered the artifact. "They're responding to the tablet, I imagine, and to the one around my neck. Now, Alexander. A quick glimpse, and let's see if old Genghis has any more diabolical tricks up his sleeve."

At that moment, with Nina's attention fixed on the distant lights of the mausoleum, Colonel Hiltmeyer took his chance. All his anger, fear and drive for revenge exploded at once. He lunged, striking Nina, roaring into her, gripping her under the shoulders and flipping her over the wall.

Before Alexander even heard the splash, the big colonel had raced past him, leaping for Montross.

A second before it happened, Montross had gotten a flash, a glimpse of Hiltmeyer charging him, bowling him over, grabbing him by the neck.

So late! Usually the visions came long before any such threat of death. But recently, with so many crisscrossing events and track-jumping, the future was being constantly rewritten, and his sight took a hit.

Better late than never, he thought, grunting as Hiltmeyer struck him. He had managed to lift the arm holding the tablet and to grip it tighter. He absorbed the impact, letting Hiltmeyer bash him against the rampart, and then, with one big effort, he brought the tablet down on the colonel's head.

Not enough force to kill him, but enough to daze him, and with that slight loosening of his grip, Montross slipped around, raising the tablet again for another strike.

Hiltmeyer rolled onto his back, bent his knees and kicked out, catching Montross in the gut and knocking him to the floor. The Ruger had fallen and was kicked across the stones in the melee to where Alexander stood, too shocked to move.

In a flash, Hiltmeyer was on Montross, this time slamming a knee into his stomach and bringing a fist down, hard, against his cheek. Then another to the mouth. Hiltmeyer was an enraged bear, striking again and again and—

—until the shot bellowed through the cavern, echoing across the walls, domes and among pillars.

Hiltmeyer staggered to his feet, then shuffled backward. It looked like he was choking himself, except for the dark liquid streaming from between his fingers. His eyes were open in wide shock, staring into the gloom, to the area above the shaking light held in Alexander's hand— opposite the hand holding the smoking Ruger.

Which promptly fell, released from trembling fingers.

Montross craned his neck and looked past the swelling on his face. He spit out blood and grinned. "Thanks, kid."

Hiltmeyer dropped to a seated position, his back thudding against the wall, his head falling forward, hands at his side as the blood continued to pump down the front of his shirt.

"I killed him." Alexander stared at his open hand as if it belonged to someone else.

Montross stood, wobbling. He picked up the tablet, then snatched up the Ruger, sliding it under his belt. Then, with a glance at Hiltmeyer and a look of newfound respect for Alexander, he went to the wall and scanned the darkness below.

"Flashlight."

Alexander remained motionless.

"Now, kid! Snap out of it or we're going to lose her."

The light bobbled, came over and aimed below. Alexander held it in both hands, still shaking. Montross focused, looking left and right.

"Here!" shouted a voice.

The light sought her out, then found her, clinging to the side of the first block. She looked ragged. Her sleeves were torn. The beam fell on her battered face, illuminating streaks of blood and a patch of her hair ripped away.

She squinted, then with great effort pulled herself up and rolled onto the platform, chest heaving. She held up a hand to ward off the light, and said, "You definitely do *not* want to fall in."

She stood, testing her balance, and Alexander and Montross tensed, expecting the block to fall into the waters or to break apart and drag her under. But nothing happened.

"I guess we're safe on the walkway," Alexander said.

"Appears so. At least that one," Montross agreed.

"And," called Nina, "at least the water's fine. Drank a gallon of it under there while I fought with something. I don't know exactly what, but they were slimy, long and had lots of teeth.

Montross eyed the bubbles below. "I think we still want to RV this area, to be sure. And now, thanks to Alexander, we don't have to worry about getting backstabbed by Mr. Liability over there."

Alexander hung his head. "Why did I shoot him?" Alexander asked. "When I could've shot *you?*"

Taking his hand away, Montross looked down, meeting Alexander's grave stare. "I'm sorry kid. I really am. About your mom. About all this. But someday, soon I hope, you'll see what I'm doing—what I've done—and you'll understand."

"Never."

Montross shrugged, and his face darkened before the tablet's glow lit it up again. "Come on, I'll lower you down to Nina, and we'll make our way to the Mausoleum."

"Where we'll see my dad?"

"I'm positive of it."

"What about all these other buildings. These temples, those palaces? All that treasure ?" Alexander's eyes lit up and he licked his lips. The enormity of what he had just done was fading under a renewed boyhood enthusiasm for adventure, overwhelming the onslaught of witnessing so much death. "All that gold must be piled up somewhere in here."

"If you want to explore and sightsee," Montross said, "then you come back here with your own annoying kids someday. We're only here for the keys."

10.

The underground river below the terra cotta army was more like a sewer tunnel system than a river. The water was about knee-deep, and fortunately it was fresh, without a hint of the toxicity of the outside stream.

Cupping some in his palm, Caleb took a tentative drink. A sip, then a hearty swallow. Then he washed off his face as the others saw him and gratefully did the same.

"Keep moving," Renée ordered. "Unless you want to RV this portion of the tunnel as well. But it seems odd that they would trap the very route just rewarded to us for solving that riddle up there."

"They'll booby trap everything," Phoebe said. "It's what they do. Sadists."

Qara made a clicking sound.

"Or," Caleb said, "they just want to make sure we're worthy."

"You're not," Qara said quietly. "No one is."

Renée turned to her, splashing in the cool water. "Then why is this tunnel here?" The radiance from the flashlights reflected off the water, and danced like sunbursts in her eyes. "Why have we gotten this far, if your great Khan didn't want someone to find him?"

Behind her back, Qara's wrists worked the straps. Blood dripped into the water, the flesh cut through almost to the bone. Her face bore no expression.

"No," Renée continued, "our presence here is proof. It was meant to be found. Found, and taken."

"By you?" Phoebe asked. "I don't think so. This is just like the Pharos Lighthouse. It was designed to keep out everyone except those with our kinds of abilities. And despite your minor glimpse at our RV session, I don't think you qualify."

"We'll see," Renée said. "I'm blessed in other ways. Chosen."

Qara worked her shoulders, pulling, tugging, twisting her fingers back at a nearly impossible angle, getting under the plastic.

Caleb stood by his sister and addressed Renée. "You want these keys, the translation and the tablet. Want it returned to your master. But Marduk's long gone. And your cult, it's nothing anymore, is it? So what is this really about?"

Renée smirked. "You have no idea. Once we have those keys, and once we find the—" She stopped herself suddenly, smiled and turned away.

Find the what? Caleb thought. *Something else of Marduk's?*

Renée looked back and smirked. "Thoth's failure will be complete, and all this secrecy and protection will be all for nothing."

"You're wrong," Qara whispered. She separated her hands, snapping through the frayed bonds, then raised her arms over her head in an angelic stance.

She bent her knees, and charged.

Renée felt the Darkhad's talon-like fingers around her throat before she could free her gun. She fell back into the water, with the Mongolian witch on top of her, choking her, trying to gouge her eyes out. She got a mouthful of icy water and her head struck the bottom, sending up starbursts in her vision. But then, mercifully, the pressure withdrew.

She sat up, shaking her head and coughing. Chang and another soldier had Qara pinned against a wall. Renée pulled out her gun, shook off the water, and aimed. But something hit her hard on the side, spinning her around.

Orlando grabbed the gun. "No!" Then he grunted as a soldier bashed his side with the butt of his rifle. Renée shoved him off and turned back to see that Qara had broken free. She kicked one soldier in the groin and then elbowed Chang in the face, ripped herself free, and ran back for the ladder.

Guns trained on her, but Caleb and Phoebe blocked the way.

"Damn!" Renée hissed, then leapt ahead, pushed between the brother and sister, and fired, just as Qara jumped up the ladder, scaling it like an energized spider monkey. She fired twice, one round hitting the ladder, the other causing a sharp cry from Qara. But the Darkhad still pulled herself up and out.

Renée chased her. *You are not getting away.* had a flash of a vision, maybe something psychic—or just her imagination. A brief clip of Qara hiding up above, somewhere in the tunnels, and firing on her as she returned with the keys.

Not going to happen.

Renée hauled herself up, dove and rolled, bringing out the flashlight in her left hand, the .45 in her right, sweeping the beam around in a tight circle around the opening.

A legion of blank-faced white-eyed warriors glared at her in the light, swords and shields glinting, horse's rearing.

Then, a glimpse, legs scuttling back by the water's edge.

Renée settled the flashlight, sighted, and fired.

Qara stood up, back arched. Knee-deep in the mercury-river, she staggered ahead. Turned, her mouth open in a silent curse.

Renée shot her again.

Qara jerked back. Fell, and was swallowed up by the water.

The flashlight beam played over the rippling silver surface until the bubbles stopped, then pulled away. *Good riddance.*

Renée turned back to the tunnel entrance, and with twenty thousand eyes watching her in the darkness, she descended. She re-entered the tunnel, and amidst the silent stares of her men, and the desperate eyes of her prisoners, she marched ahead.

She thought about calling Robert Gregory, informing him that she was close, but was doubtful certain communications would even work this far down. And besides, he had unwavering faith in her. She wouldn't fail. He was surely headed for the Sphinx even now, trusting she'd be there as soon as her mission had been accomplished.

Soon, the ancient box would open and the books would be theirs. And once the senator had found the other artifact, they, with the Emerald Tablet, would be unstoppable.

They would hold the power to fulfill their long-awaited destiny.

11.

Alexander dropped to the platform first, lowered by Montross who jumped next, letting go of the rope. Brushing himself off, Alexander looked out over the Khan's necropolis. Bathed in sickly light from the half-dozen flares, the minarets appeared to sway and bend in the mix of shadows and crimson haze while the domed temples swelled to enormous size.

Alexander peered over the side, took a flashlight and aimed it down. He could see flashes of wickedly sharp protrusions like narrow teeth, and suddenly, as if drawn to the light, four eel-like creatures, sinewy and sleek with eyes on stalks and razor-sharp teeth, drew close to the surface, snapping at the light.

"What's down there?" Montross asked.

Nina gripped Alexander's arm and pulled him back. "Something nasty. Stay away from the edge." She took Montross's pack and pulled out a roll of gauze tape, and set about bandaging the wounds on her arm.

Alexander watched in fascination as she then replaced the wet dressings on the arrow hole in her shoulder, all without wincing. "That looks gross."

She shook her wet hair as she finished, then stood up and went to work on her Beretta. She ejected the magazine, resupplied the bullets and fit it back in place. "So, what happened to the colonel?"

Alexander shrank back, lowering his eyes as Montross said, "Our boy here bagged his first kill."

"Seriously?" Nina stared at him, nonplussed. "Impressive. Now, can we go?"

"Not just yet," Montross said. He surveyed the city, sweeping his light over the nearest bridges, the sparkling water, the marble pathways leading through arches and tunnels. After finding the route to the mausoleum, he said, "I think we might have more to fear."

"These walkways," Alexander whispered. "They can drop. I've seen it."

"Me too." Montross approached Nina. "And I've seen something else. Something I would not have survived. *We* would not have survived."

"When? Where?" Nina glanced around, gun ready.

"Later. This whole area is a trap, but it won't be sprung until we take the keys."

"So we're fine until the mausoleum?"

"Yes, but this is good. Perfect in fact." He leaned in close to Nina, and Alexander strained to hear what he said.

"I need you to do something for me," Montross whispered. "Something crucial."

She turned her eyes to his; their lips were an inch apart. "Anything."

"When the time comes, I need you to die."

Alexander wasn't sure if he heard that right, but in any case they were soon walking ahead of him, making plans, and leaving him to himself. It wasn't like he could run anywhere, so he followed dutifully, occasionally looking back over his shoulder, half-expecting Colonel Hiltmeyer to come loping along out of the shadows, zombie-like, to grab him and haul him over the side into those submerged spikes and make him food for the eels.

Shuddering, he rubbed his hands together, staring at his right hand. The one that had pulled the trigger. He almost stumbled on the rise of an arched bridge just as something broke the surface underneath, snapping at the air. He passed by other branching pathways and bridges covered in sloping oriental-style rooftops. Here and there statues of warriors atop great steeds stood as the centerpieces of fountains, where the only movement came from swarming things under the water.

He swept the light across each statue's face that they passed and saw the same visage in each: it was him. Temujin. Genghis Khan. He was watching their approach, watching from every angle, every building and every column. Watching with the haughty scorn of one who knew he'd still have the last laugh.

Alexander passed a magnificent temple, with open doors beckoning beyond a façade of marble columns. Was there something glinting inside, catching the glow from his flashlight? Was that part of the treasure inside there? He shone the light to his left side now, spearing it into the open base of a tower whose tip graced the cavern's ceiling high above, right beside a sputtering flare. Inside the minaret, another statue, and eyes reflecting back a look of hatred and recrimination.

Murderer, they said, and Alexander shuddered again.

It was his fault. Not just Hiltmeyer, but worse. His mother. She was gone because of him. He never told her, never hinted about what he was doing in their basement. So loyal to his father, he had made promises. And then she had come down, totally unprepared. It should have been Montross and him burnt to a crisp.

But instead, his mother was gone. The guilt was crushing, weighing him down.

When he turned, he discovered he had lost track of Montross and Nina. They were somewhere up ahead, lost in the deepening shadows.

But which path? He saw their lights, bobbing there to the side, approaching the mausoleum, which seemed larger now, more immense than he could have guessed. But he couldn't find the path they had taken.

He was about to call out when something trembled again from the interior archway of the nearest tower. A glowing shape flickered, and for a moment it took on a familiar form. He turned, stepped onto a cobbled walkway, different from the others, then proceeded over a bridge. His flashlight cut through the shadows ahead, spearing through the arched corridor. His footsteps quickened, along with his pulse.

And then he was through the tunnel, approaching the tower's base and heading for a white-robed figure standing there. Her dress caught in the flashlight's beam, scattered it like a swarm of fireflies. Her face was lost in a blur of blinding light, but her arms, formerly at her side, stretched out for him.

He skidded to a stop, only ten feet away. Shielded his eyes and flicked off the flashlight. "Mom?"

He blinked over and over and rubbed his eyes. Took a step forward and in a moment of clarity he saw her face, saw her shining green eyes and playful smile. The smile she always had ready for him after a summer away with his father, a smile that released all the heartache and fear she had endured in his absence, letting it all out before a huge bear-hugging embrace.

You're not alone, she whispered, and the words echoed in his mind.

But then, as he reached for her—

"Alexander!"

An iron hand clasped upon his shoulder and drew him back. He cried out, reaching, only to have the image of his mother burst into flames, swirl into a maelstrom of light, and then vanish.

"No!"

He was spun around, tucked into a chest and hugged. "Easy, kid. There's nothing there. You're safe."

"Mom ..."

Montross pulled away, but still clasped him about the shoulders, searching his eyes. "You saw your mother?"

Tears rambling down his cheeks, Alexander nodded and glanced back to the shadows in the empty doorway. Montross aimed his light there and Nina, just arriving, did the same. She walked ahead and scoped out the interior, shining a light above and around. She turned, shook her head.

"She was there," Alexander said.

"I believe you. At least that you saw her." Montross pulled him back. "Don't fight it. Visions of our lost loved ones come with the psychic membership card."

Alexander wiped his eyes.

"Come on, kid. Sorry we lost you back there. Stick close this time." Montross stared into his eyes. "We're almost done. Just help us out a little longer, okay?"

Alexander hung his head. Then raised his eyes and looked around the city basking in the dying light. "Are you sure we'll make it out of here alive? With my dad?"

"Not sure of anything, kid. Except what happens to me. But I'll tell you this, stick close to me and you'll be all right, because I've seen every permutation of what's coming my way. You remember asking how many times I've beaten Death?"

"Yeah."

"Well, remember that. I can outsmart it over and over, all these petty attempts upon my life. These little ones I'm not worried about."

Alexander frowned. "Then what *are* you worried about? If you can see everything that might kill you, what do you need the Emerald Tablet for? What—?" His eyes widened knowingly. "Oh, is it something else, like cancer? Is that it?"

Montross held up his hand as he started back the way they had come, with Nina moving Alexander along. "It's not cancer."

"You told me I wouldn't understand."

"That's right."

"I bet I would. I want to know." Alexander fiddled with his flashlight as he dragged his feet behind Montross. "I saved your life, by the way. Did you see *that* before it happened?"

"Nope," he said. "Most likely because you were already on the path to save me, so I didn't need to change anything."

"Still, I saved you. The least you can do is tell me why. What it is you're trying to do, why—" He stopped moving, and Nina walked right into him, almost knocking him down. "Why is my mother dead? Tell me that much."

Montross turned and gave him a look of tired sympathy.

"I can't tell you because if I did, you couldn't handle it. I need you sharp. And if I tell you, you won't be able to function. Fear would crush your confidence, and your abilities would wither away to uselessness."

Alexander shook his head. "Fine, then. I'll guess."

"I wouldn't do that."

"All right, I won't guess. I'll view it. For real." He stopped and closed his eyes, furrowed his brow.

But then Nina slapped his face, hard. "No! Stay with us. No more trances until we get to the mausoleum."

She shoved him along, grumbling, but he knew he'd hit a nerve, and he knew they were afraid. Afraid he could see their plans.

And that filled him with just enough confidence to try.

They approached the centerpiece of the city, the grand blue-tinted dome situated over an octagonal building the size of a football field. So immense, Nina could scarcely imagine what it contained, or how it had been fashioned down here, so far from the light. Such a feat of marvelous engineering. Like everything in this city. But already she knew one thing for sure would be inside, besides the body of Genghis Khan.

If Montross's plan didn't work, her body would soon be joining his.

Still, she was grateful his attention had been diverted from questioning his past, but she knew he'd come back to it soon. It was a secret she couldn't keep from him much longer.

As if he had read her mind, Montross slowed before the entranceway, then turned. He held up the Emerald Tablet so the eight-foot-tall arched door glowed in the aquamarine radiance. An ancient script appeared, scrawled over the top like a rainbow. But he ignored it. Instead, he sat, pulled out his pad of paper from his pack, set the tablet down and picked up a pencil.

"Sketch time. Alexander, you may want to join me. Nina, pick one of us to tag along with. We've got some targets to view and a little time before my *brother* his face."

Nina gasped, and Alexander just frowned. "Your brother?"

Montross smiled at him. "I'm just going in to confirm it now, but given Nina's reaction and my sudden affinity for you, kid, I'm fairly certain I'm your uncle. Half-uncle at least."

Nina lowered her head. "I—I wanted to wait till I was sure."

Alexander froze wide-eyed. "I've been dreaming about brothers. Before a door under that Sphinx thing. And one of them—"

Montross's face lit up. "Yes ...?"

"One brother," Alexander said, "can open the door with the right keys."

"Now I know," Montross said with a wide grin. "My father ... I was so blind, not realizing I had a higher connection to all this."

"So that's why you're psychic," Alexander said excitedly. "Like my father and me."

"And one more," said Nina. "A third brother. My guess is he's the one pulling the FBI's strings in this venture."

Montross nodded. "I'll check it out, now that I know the right questions to ask. Meanwhile, you and Alexander need to figure out this door." He closed his eyes, lowered his head, and grabbed his pencil.

And Nina sat beside Alexander. She took his hand, which he offered now with little resistance, his mind still processing Montross's revelation. She closed her eyes and tapped into Alexander's thoughts, opening to his visions, guiding him to the door, but not quite yet.

There were other things that she needed to see first.

12.

Caleb and Phoebe helped Orlando up, pulling him away from Commander Chang and the other soldiers. They were just recovering when they heard the two gunshots echoing through the access tunnel.

Phoebe stopped what she was doing. "Uh oh."

Holding his side, Orlando coughed and spit up blood. "I think I just got my ass kicked for nothing. I'm sorry."

Caleb waited, and then his heart sank when he saw Renée climb back down the ladder.

"I think," Phoebe whispered, "you should have taken that chance up there."

"What chance?" Orlando asked.

Caleb was holding his head. "Qara wanted me to set off the warriors when I reached you. If I had acted, she might still be alive."

"Ah." Orlando combed back his hair. "Well, I'm inclined to thank you for your restraint. Not sure if I was up for dodging arrows."

"Move," Renée ordered, motioning with her gun. "I'm not wasting any more time with fanatics. Or psychics."

Caleb started splashing ahead. "You seem to be forgetting who got you this far."

"And you're forgetting who has the weapons."

"Oh, you won't let us forget that." Leading his sister and Orlando, Caleb waded cautiously ahead, with small steps. "Phoebe," he whispered. "Can you see anything? Orlando? How about you? Are we good here?"

"Far as I could tell," Orlando said, "the path was the only thing I saw. Just follow along and we should be copasetic until the end."

"Phoebe?" He looked back and saw, with some surprise, that his sister and Orlando were holding hands.

"Hang on," she said and closed her eyes. Cocked her head, then peered out. "All clear. But at the end, like Orlando said, there's something. We go up, and there's a portal. And beyond that I see something bad. Blood, a lot of it. Death."

"Ours?" Orlando asked.

"I'm not sure."

"Traps?" Renée asked, right beside them now.

"No. Not that I can see. Although, I'm not sure how the portal opens."

"Maybe we need Qara," Orlando suggested.

"Well," said Renée, "that option's no longer available to us. You'll get us in, or we blow it open."

"Not too smart," Caleb said. "Unless you want a cave-in."

"I'm confident you'll figure it out. Now move."

After nearly thirty minutes of trudging through water that gradually numbed their feet, the cold traveling up their legs, they rounded a bend and came to a complete dead end. Just a blank wall.

One soldier approached cautiously, then abruptly disappeared. Lights blasted at his last location and they highlighted his escaping air and submerged body, thrashing as he sank into the murky depths.

"Gone," Chang whispered, standing at the end of a rounded pit in the floor, shining the light down into the pool. "I see no bottom."

All the flashlight beams then turned up, converging on a rounded, twenty-foot-wide barrier, a circular door above the pit. The center was a pure black onyx material that absorbed the light. The outside frame was an exotic marble structure etched with more script all the way around.

Orlando whispered. "Anyone watch *Stargate?*"

"Huh?" Renée asked.

"Never mind. But since you killed our translator, what do we do?"

"Stand back." Renée said. "Chang, set the C-4."

"But we cannot reach door. Nothing to stand on."

"Then position it carefully as far in as you can. We'll blow the area around it."

Caleb shook his head. "Wait, give us a chance." He was shining his light about the corridor, checking the ceiling, the walls, even stabbing it into the water, looking for switches or levers.

"Hurry," Renée said. "You've got until the charges are set." She glanced at Chang, who was busy with their packs, assembling the explosives.

"Ten minutes."

Renée crossed her arms and nodded to Caleb and Phoebe. "You heard the man. Do your stuff in ten minutes, or I do it my way."

Phoebe pulled Orlando closer to her, took both his hands and got up on her tippy-toes to whisper in his ear. "We've got to cover for Caleb, so let's do this."

"A little hard to concentrate," he said, "with you so close. My thoughts are kind of running amok."

"They can run amok later. The door. Now. How do we open it? Think about nothing else." She withdrew her lips from his ear.

"Easier said than done."

She closed her eyes as Caleb splashed over to them. "Give it a try, big brother. Whatever comes."

"All right."

But that was all she heard, as the surroundings melted away and the water around her feet dried up... .

"It is ready, my lord Ogadai."

A man stands in the shadows behind the smoking torches.

"The markings around the door ..."

"As you instructed, master. The scribes have written the curses your father chose. The usual horrors to be visited on any who choose to violate the mausoleum beyond."

"And the door, once set?"

"Can be opened only from the other side."

"And only when Temujin rises."

The man nods. "For he will need a way out, should life be restored."

"Pray," said Ogadai, "that his spirit prefers the next world to this one. But if not, at least his city awaits. He may rule here as he wishes." He lowers his head. "Seal the door, and let us depart."

Phoebe's eyes bolted open, and she stared at Orlando.

"Crap," Orlando said. "I didn't see anything about the way in from this side." He nodded grudgingly to Renée. "You're going to need to blow it open."

"Unless," said Phoebe, "Montross is already up there."

13.

Nina was pulled out of the vision too soon, hearing a rumbling, grinding sound that made the very floor shake and dust fall on her from overhead.

But she had been there, in that other vision again ...

... somewhere so very high up, an impression of being inside the eyes of a giant, a colossus wading into the sea. Looking down over churning waves and boats of all sizes traveling below.

Her arm hurts, as if struggling to keep something raised high.

And then she senses two children, as if perched on her head, clinging to her hair, staring down in awe and excitement.

And then she was ripped out of it and saw Alexander standing a little wobbly as he pulled his hand away.

"The door," he whispered. "It's already open."

Nina stood before the mausoleum entrance. She held her head, dizzy, and glanced around. "Where's Montross?"

Set in the walls, across each of the eight sides of the chamber, hooded brass lamps came on, their lights dim in the glare of the flashlights.

"Turn off your lights," came Montross's voice.

Behind him, Nina and Alexander switched off their flashlights. Oil lamps, set in horizontal runners, sparked to life, flickering and then illuminating a cathedral-like interior with a high apex at the crest of the dome overhead.

"Wow," Alexander said. "Freakin' wow."

The glow extended and the chamber began to breathe a sound like an exhalation, as if a giant had been holding his breath for centuries and only now let it escape. Everything scintillated with gold; it was plated onto the floor, pounded into the walls, ringing the base of the dome. In marvelous artistic design, beautiful tiles created the shapes of zoological creatures, familiar species and some far more fanciful beasts, all composed of gold, with gems for eyes. They crawled across the floor, scaled the walls, bridged the gap and stretched onto the dome above. Sapphires and rubies blinked in the spreading dawn, and night-black mouths yawned. Oxen frolicked with elephants, reindeer with tigers. Polar bears swam in the night sky over giant scorpions while centaurs rode the backs of sea turtles and gryphons carried immense spiders in their talons.

"Look at that," Alexander said, pointing here, then there, walking around open-mouthed. "I guess some of the treasure's right here." He hadn't gotten his fill of the designs and the artwork yet when the centerpiece of the otherwise barren chamber caught his eye and held it fast. An interior tower, a minaret without doors, windows or stairs of any kind, stood in the center of the room like a rocket in a silo. It was plated with gold, ringed in silver highlights like stars in a golden night sky. But at its top, just below the domed roof and level with the sole open window, was a flat surface. A plateau instead of a point, supporting what looked like a coffin made of dazzling gold and surrounded by nine banners. But from this angle, it wasn't possible to see if the lid was open or closed.

"We've found it," Montross said. He still held his sketchpad in one hand, the Emerald Tablet in the other.

Nina caught her breath. "How did you get in?"

Montross's gaze remained fixed on the pedestal. "I just opened the door."

"What?"

"It wasn't locked."

"Then why did you—?"

"Have you focused on it? Frankly, I wanted you thinking about something else. Clearly Alexander's mind is still elsewhere. With you assisting, I figured you might learn something that could help us later on." He turned now, lowered his head and fixed her with his steely blue eyes. "So, did you?"

"I saw something." Nina shook her head, but pulled her eyes away and looked at Alexander. "I don't understand it yet."

Montross pointed to Alexander. "What about you, nephew?"

Alexander shrugged, still blinking at all the gold. "I don't know. I just got this weird feeling of *height*. Like I'm floating or flying. And there are these two kids."

Montross tilted his head. "Interesting." He gave Nina a long look, uncertainty and distrust flashing in his eyes. Then he continued to the base of the narrow tower and looked up.

"Wait." Alexander pointed to Montross's sketch pad. "What did you draw?"

Montross tore off a sheet of paper, folded it four times and then, after putting his pad back in this pack over his shoulder, gave it to Alexander. "Look at that later."

Alexander reluctantly put it in his pocket. "When?"

"You'll know when." He sighed and returned his attention to the tower and the crypt at the top. "Why don't you two figure out how we get up *there*?"

Nina glanced around, scouting out the walls and the floor, looking for anything out of place. "There's got to be something that would lift us up there."

"Or," said Alexander thoughtfully, "bring *it* down here."

Montross clapped his hands. "Now that sounds more like it." He considered the walls, the dome, thinking. But Alexander was ahead of him.

"The animals," he said, pointing to the base around the minaret. He turned on his flashlight again to get a better look. "The creatures nearest the tower? In the first row, they're all set up inside circles, see? And I noticed when I stepped on this dragon-creature here, the floor dropped slightly, and I heard a click."

He stepped away, and it slowly rose back up with his weight off it. "See?"

"We see," Nina said, turning on her light and shining it around the other animals, then to the walls. "You look for those stepping stones, I'll look for the traps that waste you when you step on them in the wrong order."

Montross stepped back, watching his footing. He thought for a moment, and then set down the Emerald Tablet, pulled out his necklace, so it dangled down his chest. It seemed to be vibrating, tugging alternately between the floor and its brothers, higher above. "We're almost there. Hurry."

He closed his eyes and winced. Held his head as he shook it. "Still there, damn it. Still there."

"What?" Alexander asked, distracted as he moved around the tower.

Montross trembled, then waved a dismissive hand. "Something in the future."

Alexander poked his head around the tower, then disappeared again. "Is it where you're killed?"

"Of course. But this one in particular, this death ..." Montross was still shaking his head. "It's not cleared yet. I had hoped it would be, just by getting this far, but now it seems there's more to do. It won't be enough to find all the keys. We have to use them somehow."

"I got it!" Alexander yelled. In a few seconds he appeared again. "At least, I think I do."

"Do you or don't you?" Nina snipped. "Did you RV it? Because if not, I'd rather you didn't guess."

"I didn't, but I don't think I need to. Look," he insisted, "I might not have seen all the clues back at our lighthouse, but it's like it was made for a young boy. A kid like me."

"How so?"

"The animals, there are nine "normal" ones. You know, a monkey, a giraffe, a horse and a rhino."

"Yes, normal," Nina said, "if you're in the zoo."

"Well, normal compared to three creatures that I'd say don't belong."

"Three?" Montross perked up.

"Yup." Alexander rubbed his hands. "See, it's also almost as if he knew we'd be coming, and that there would be three of us. Just like the three keys."

"Or," said Montross, "he knew it would take a different form of three to do what has to be done after gaining these keys."

"The three brothers," Nina whispered. "So where are these three special creatures?"

Alexander shrugged. "Well, there's the dragon, which I already found. And then there's a gryphon and a centaur." He looked up sharply. "Hm. So, if they're supposed to represent the brothers, I wonder which one you are? And which one's my dad?"

Montross smiled. "Well, since I'm the only one here, I'm picking the one I like." He circled around until he found the centaur and stood on it. "Nina, be so kind as to set your feet upon the gryphon. And Alexander?"

"The dragon, I know."

"So we're sure about this?" Nina asked, standing outside the boundary of the gryphon, its forepaws raised up in attack, its jaws wide.

"Sure about nothing," Montross said, "except that I don't die in the next few hours. If this doesn't bring down Genghis Khan, then we'll need to think of something else."

"But what about me?" Alexander asked, suddenly shivering. "Will I die?"

Montross shrugged. "No, only one of us will, and very soon." He shot a glance to Nina.

"Yeah, I'm ready. Ready for this too." She took a step, then brought both feet onto the gryphon's body. It dropped, then all three circular stones turned.

Suddenly, they were all facing outward, and there was a wind, a rush of air—and all the lights went out except their two flashlights.

The main door slammed shut and something slid across it with a grating sound.

The tower rumbled and shook. Then it began to lower into the floor.

They ducked and winced, afraid of being hit by some kind of protrusion as the tower descended. It fell with incredible speed, grinding through the hole.

Shielding his eyes, Montross looked up, keeping his attention on the golden centerpiece as it roared down to their level.

I hope it stops, he thought, just as the entire structure jarred to a thundering halt. About six feet of structure remained, six feet of the tower structure until the apex upon which lay the glorious funeral barge under an open tent of white cloth. The coffin itself was more like a curved boat, carved with circles and sun-wheels and crescent moons, but no text.

As for the body that lay regally upon it, all Montross could see from this angle was an array of extravagant silk coverings and the shadowy silhouette of armor made of leather and fur, a helmet containing a grizzled face gazing skyward.

On the side he was facing, he saw three vertical indentations. Footholds.

"Nina. Now's the time. Take your position."

"Can we step off the circles?"

"I believe so."

"Let's try," Alexander said, moving off it. In a moment, he and Nina were together with Montross.

"It's not rising," Nina said.

Montross set one foot in the lowest groove. "It doesn't appear so. Maybe it was only designed to descend once. But one thing is for certain. Come with me, Alexander." He pulled himself up to the second rung, then reached out a hand to the boy.

"I'm not going up there."

"Yes you are. And I'll tell you the one thing I have *seen* for certain."

Alexander took his hand, and Montross pulled him up. "When I take these keys, when I lift the body of the great Genghis Khan to retrieve them, a door will open and we'll see your father again. Along with a lot of trigger-happy soldiers."

Nina walked away, into the deeper shadows against the farthest wall, taking from her pack the sniper rifle and night-vision scope.

And a lot of ammo.

14.

"Look out!" Phoebe yelled, pulling Orlando back as Caleb leapt out of the way, amazed. The door suddenly burst apart in a blur as something immense dropped into the chasm. And kept dropping. The noise was deafening. Some of the soldiers turned and fled, believing at last the curse of Genghis Khan had caught up with them.

"What the hell?" Renée yelled, her voice barely audible over the cacophonic sound. She splashed backwards through water that was swiftly rising .

"Oh no!" Caleb shouted. "The cylinder. It's displacing the water from the tunnel."

Phoebe fought a wave that had risen almost to her shoulders." Displacing it onto us!"

Orlando reached out and caught her hand, just as Caleb grabbed his collar. They stood fast against the swirling waters rising up to their chins, and Caleb immediately had a flashback to the room under the Pharos.

Stop!

As if on cue, the corridor rocked and jarred with a thud as the cylinder seemed to have hit bottom. Pebbles and dirt dropped from the edges on the ceiling, and the rounded portion of the block in front of them trembled. And as the lights above the water aimed at it, something appeared. An outline.

"A door!" Renée said, pointing.

It shook, trembled again, and then the rectangular section opened, sliding upward and letting in the water.

"It's draining," Caleb said, dropping after trying to stand on his toes. He directed his light into the opening. There was a ladder of sorts, but the rest of the wide cylinder looked like the interior of a hollow tunnel, sucking in the water down into its base.

Renée splashed forward first and shone a light inside and then up. "Stairs rising in a spiral. Only one direction, so at least we don't have to make any more choices."

"What's up there?" Chang asked, getting closer, shaking the water out of his gun.

"Would you believe," said Renée, "another door?"

Alexander climbed up after Montross and he stood in the only spot left, right between the body's feet. "What are you doing?" he whispered, shining his light up to where Montross was fumbling with something around the corpse's head.

The corpse ...

Alexander shuddered, squeezing his legs together and trying not to touch anything, not even to brush against any part of the body.

"Just wait," Montross said. Then as Alexander's light reached him he snapped, "And shut that off!"

Alexander flicked off the light. But not before it had flashed onto the face under the helmet. Alexander had seen mummy movies before and read his share of archeological articles with photos showing unearthed Incan kings and Egyptian burials, where they'd peeled off the funeral masks and revealed the leathery, grizzled faces, the sunken eye-sockets, the browning flesh, the long teeth and hair that had continued to grow. This face was similar, and yet more regal, more peaceful. *He's held up pretty good down here,* Alexander thought as he shut off the light.

And then the eye sockets began to glow with a green aura. Temujin's entire face seemed to pulse with light flickering from within the eyes and seeping out from between his mummified lips, from the cracked teeth still set in the dried gums retreating in a wide smile.

"Damn," said Montross, whose necklace with its pyramidal stone glowed and pulsed to an unheard heartbeat. "Looks like the keys are in his head."

Alexander bent forward and tried to look into the mouth, but couldn't see anything down in the throat. It seemed more like the light pulsed from higher, behind the eyes. "They may have drilled into the back of his skull. Saw that in a *National Geographic* special once."

Montross held the tablet in his left hand, then set it on Genghis Khan's chest, over the folded arms. "Here, hold this a sec, Genghis. Sorry, but I've got to lift you up."

"Wait," said Alexander. "I think there might be another trap."

Montross pulled up the body by its shoulders. "I know," he said as a lever, previously kept down by the weight of the Khan's body, now rose, making a grinding sound as if gears somewhere were turning, spinning.

Opening a door beneath them.

"Nina!" Montross yelled to her out in the darkness, beyond the emerald glow. "It's time."

"Go!"

Caleb heard Renée shout, and then the men were rushing up the spiral steps and bursting out of the newly opened doorway. The interior section had suddenly shaken and made a shrill scraping sound before it separated and descended, hauled below by inner gear works triggered by something above.

All the soldiers ran through, their flashlights secured to their weapons, their heads down. Then Renée went up—after first hesitating. *Probably waiting for the screams*, Caleb thought. He couldn't believe she had them just rush in. *Getting desperate?*

Only Chang had stayed behind, and he promptly jabbed Caleb in the back. "Move. You three. Now—"

But that's when the automatic gunfire started, and the echoes of screaming men tore through the entrance and into the empty tower.

Alexander cringed and tucked himself into a ball, right on the edge of the funeral platform next to the great Khan's legs, and right in front of those glowing eyes. Eyes in a head lolling forward with Montross's less-than-ceremonial treatment. A head shaking side to side in violent denial as Montross rooted around within the hollowed-out hole in the back of the corpse's skull and dug out his prizes.

Gunshots. Men crying out. Swift, precise death zipped across at the soldiers. Nine men stumbled about with crisscrossing flashlight beams and automatic gunfire erupting chaotically. Everyone trying to find out who was shooting at them. Alexander ducked lower and toppled sideways as a shot zipped past and took out a chunk out of the Khan's shoulder, exploding powdery flesh into his eyes. He crunched into an embrace with the body, screamed and then felt Montross's arm around his back, his body in front of him protectively.

He shouted something lost in the gun blasts.

Alexander glanced over the side and saw another flashlight beam spin around, then crash onto the floor as its wielder fell. Another scream and a soldier was thrown back against the stairs Alexander had just climbed, blood spraying from a punctured skull. Alexander had a sudden moment's fear that all Genghis needed to be reawakened was human blood.

But nothing moved, no life stirred in his bones, no heartbeat throbbed in the chest pressed against Alexander's ear.

Another scream, then more gunshots, this time concentrated toward one section. "There!" Someone yelled. A woman's voice. Followed by a single-fire weapon, blasting off round after round.

Another scream. Alexander cringed. That sounded like Nina.

She's been hit!

"Stay low," Montross said as he pulled free, stood and withdrew the Ruger from his waist. He aimed and fired at the one soldier in view, taking him down. Then he turned and froze in the beams of light immediately brought to his location.

"Drop it!" someone yelled with a thick Chinese accent.

And Alexander could see the lights blasting into Montross's eyes, blinding him. He lifted his gun and his other hand to ward off the light.

And then someone was climbing, rustling up the steps behind him, standing over him and snatching the gun from Montross in one quick movement. Then Montross was grabbed and hurled to the mausoleum floor.

A woman wearing a thick black vest and a shiny gold badge turned to Alexander, where he was still locked in a death-embrace with the great Mongolian conqueror.

"Oh, Caleb!" she called over her shoulder. "We've found your boy."

Caleb ran out into the mausoleum, stepping around the soldiers lying in bloody piles, their skulls expertly perforated. He turned to the sound of Renée's voice and ran to Alexander, scooping him up before the boy even took the last step down from the crypt.

"Dad!" Alexander leapt into his father's embrace and clutched him tight.

Caleb hugged him tighter and made room for Phoebe, who had run behind him and added her arms to their reunion hug.

"And this," said Renée, standing over a kneeling man, "must be Xavier Montross." She pointed the .45 at the center of his forehead. "Now, give me what you took from him."

Montross ignored her, instead smiling over to Caleb. His white teeth glittered in the light from Chang's flashlight. His red hair had fallen, sweaty, over his left eye.

"Hello, brother."

Nina heard them talking, barely, over the pulse thundering in her ears. She lay perfectly still, her limbs splayed, her neck and shoulders supported by the wall. She had done her part the best she could. Leaving a lone flashlight against the wall ten feet away, then firing from a distance using the night-vision scope, she had taken out seven of them. All but two, and the woman who had emerged last. The FBI agent had seen the light finally, after all the chaos, and fired at it repeatedly. Nina let out a shrill scream, and let herself tumble that way. Hoping it would fool them.

She was aware of two lights falling on her, dancing across her face, her body. *If they don't see enough blood, I may draw some more fire.* But then Montross, God bless him, had drawn their attention away, shooting one of them. Nina hoped it was that bitch, but soon enough she heard the woman's voice.

They had captured Montross and Alexander.

But in another moment, still playing dead, she had to stifle a smile when she heard another voice. Caleb Crowe. Still alive.

Good, she thought. *We still have a score to settle.*

Brother? **Caleb gaped** at him. Then turned to Alexander, pulled away and looked at him, then Phoebe.

"It's true," Alexander said. "I saw it. Grandpa and another woman. Before grandma."

"One big happy reunion," Montross said, grinning. "I told you, didn't I? That we'd see each other again, at the Mausoleum?"

Phoebe choked on a breath. "Then you're also my—"

Montross nodded. "Hi, sis."

Caleb turned to him. "A brother you might be,"—he clenched his fists, approaching—"but you're still a killer."

"Back off," said Renée. "As interesting as all this is, let's first relieve Mr. Montross of this." She snatched the necklace from his neck, then struck him across the face with the butt of her gun. He moaned and opened his right hand.

"And these," Renée continued, grabbing the two glowing triangular pieces from his palm. Chang emerged behind her, stepping down from the crypt. He held the Emerald Tablet in his hands like it was a piece of expensive glass.

"Put it in its case," she whispered, hungrily eying the artifact.

Chang nodded and opened the pack over his shoulder, retrieving a stainless steel briefcase. He popped open the lid, revealing a black foam interior with one large rectangular indentation and custom slots for three smaller objects.

"So that's it?" Orlando asked. "We come all this way. You cause all these deaths. We find *him*, and that's it? You take the keys?" He looked over his shoulder, shining the light on the armor-clad, silk-covered Mongol corpse. "What now?"

Chang offered Renée the open case, where the Emerald Tablet pulsed intently as if aware of its impending confinement and uncertain use. Keeping the gun pointed at Montross, Renée set the stones inside the case and then had him close it and set it by her side.

"What now?" she said, repeating Orlando's question. "What now, is I—"

Something creaked, and a gasping sound echoed in the room.

Genghis Khan shifted. Phoebe screamed and Alexander jumped back, clutching at her. The corpse turned to them and Chang's flashlight, which he had desperately snatched back up, caught the mummified face—the hollow eyes, the grinning mouth—as it descended, slowly. Reclining again. *Depressing the lever.*

"Uh oh," Montross said through a mouthful of blood, grinning. "Here comes trouble."

Caleb turned to the new sound of moving blocks grinding against the floor. And then a rushing, bubbling noise. He aimed his light and saw the source. About a foot off the ground, the gap left by a single missing block, too small for anyone to squeeze through, had opened in the wall. Eight other holes also appeared, one in each wall, simultaneously and were now letting in the water.

Letting it in, and filling up the mausoleum.

"No problem," Orlando said, heading for the door in the tower. "Just back into here before it might happen to close again."

"Wait!" Renée backed away from Montross, heading for the door.

Caleb looked between them, seeing something out of place: a body crumpled against the far wall. In the shadows, he couldn't tell, but it looked familiar.

Nina?

He closed his eyes for a moment, not sure why he felt what he did. After all, she had tried to kill them. He wasn't sure, but he felt remorse. And a little curiosity. But Montross didn't seem worried. He checked him out, his new brother, and saw the red-haired man still kneeling there, apparently at ease.

He knows something.

"Nobody moves," Renée ordered as she scooped up the briefcase. "And now, Commander, the detonator for the C4, if you please."

Chang handed the small remote to her, somewhat reluctantly, searching her eyes. "It's all set below, activated by that trigger. What are you doing?"

She motioned to Montross. "Tying up loose ends. No need for further bloodshed when the water can cleanse this situation for us."

Chang nodded, seeing the wisdom in that.

"But maybe," said Renée, "we should pay Mr. Montross back for his attack on your men. Go ahead, Commander."

"With much pleasure." Chang approached the kneeling man and lifted his gun.

"No," Alexander cried, and Caleb stepped forward as Chang aimed. As much as he'd dreamt of revenge, his visions—his only visions in the last two days—had been of Lydia. Of her calling out to him, not for retribution, but for understanding.

He was about to call out to Renée to stop when he noticed that Montross still seemed unconcerned, a smile even tugging at his lips as Chang leveled the weapon at him. A slight movement caught his eye, and Caleb realized Renée had just shifted her aim.

A gunshot.

Caleb lurched backward, out of the way of the Chinese commander Renée had just shot in the back of the head. Chang fell face-first into three inches of rising water and lay still.

Orlando put his hand to his mouth. "Holy crap!"

Renée pointed the gun at each of them as she backed up into the doorway, which for reasons Caleb couldn't fathom, hadn't closed. He had already surmised that what had opened the door was Montross's lifting Genghis up. So it only stood to reason that the corpse's descent should close the door, yet instead it released the water, apparently to drown them inside.

Or to force them back through the open door.

Is that it? Caleb glanced at Montross and saw the left eye give him a wink.

"Good-bye," Renée called. She hefted the briefcase. "Thoth has failed, and the vengeance of Ra-Marduk is at hand, although you won't live to see it."

She descended the stairs, and as soon as she was out of sight, Orlando ran for it. Halfway to the door, Phoebe caught him about the waist and pulled him back.

"No!" he shouted. "We've got to stop her!"

An explosion rocked the mausoleum. Rock and debris hurtled up and out through the doorway. The remaining portion of the tower, including the reclining body of Temujin, trembled, but held.

The smoke cleared. Flashlight beams found the doorway and delved inside.

"No chance," Orlando said, watching the water spill over the doorway and splash onto the rocks and slabs that had blown out sideways.

Below them, the stairs ended in an avalanche of exploded debris blocking the way. They all turned, Caleb first, and shined their lights on Xavier Montross.

He got up, brushing himself off, wringing the water from his pants legs. "Now," he said, "let's get to work on finding the real way out of here."

15.

Robert Gregory took his keycard from the slot and strode through the elevator doors as soon as they parted. Down in the library's sub-level, a level unavailable to the public and absent from any maps or designs apart from the one a select few Keepers had drawn up, he headed down a corridor that was dimly lit from edge lights that sensed his presence, glowed, and then turned off after his passing. There was a time when he had been thrilled with the effect, feeling as if his appearance symbolically illuminated the darkness and banished ignorance. There was a time when he had thought like his sister. Like Lydia. And even to some extent, like Caleb.

But that was before he had learned his true purpose. Before he had discovered certain scrolls and ancient cuneiform texts retrieved from the storehouse under the Pharos. Babylonian in origin, drawing from even more ancient sources, long lost, these scrolls spoke of the true nature of the universe, and how to become its master. Robert had his own opinions as to whether the ancient ones had been truly "gods" or only appeared as such to those whom they controlled, but the scrolls were clear that the knowledge was sacred and bound up in a single tablet, legible only to one with the keys to decipher it.

He continued walking, feeling the lights alternately bathe and then shade his face, soothing the raw skin which had begun to heal. And as he approached the end of the long hallway and the glimmering golden door at its terminus, he replayed the tales in his mind. The battle for supremacy between chaos and order, between Tiamat and Marduk. And with every step he felt he was becoming like the god of storms himself, ready to don his armor and claim the tablet—and its power— for himself. The power to restore balance.

What he had discovered, through the translation of five thousand-year-old Babylonian epics never before seen by historians, was that the cult of Marduk had been established in those olden days, much as the Keepers themselves had been initiated, for the purpose of reacquiring those ancient artifacts and ultimately to bring about the return of the ancient god of war. And when he learned that the cult still existed today, he began his search. Subtly at first, putting out feelers, describing himself as a collector, then a believer. And soon, he had discovered how power-ful the cult still was, even though it had been relegated to a secretive ceremonial membership involving the usual initiation rites and sexual domination. As such, Robert had soon ingratiated himself into their upper echelons, discovering at the top of the cult's membership powerful members that included United States political and military leaders.

Senator Mason Calderon had especially latched onto Robert's revela-tion that he was close to fulfilling the prophecy, to acquiring the very artifact that had once been their master's rightful possession, until it had been rudely snatched away and given to an inferior for safekeeping. Calderon and his colleagues had chomped at the bit, mobilizing their members, providing Robert everything he needed to fuel his search, including the dangerous gambit of seeking out and working with Xavier Montross. But Robert knew more than enough about the workings of remote viewers like Montross and the Crowes. Knew them to be easily affected with tunnel vision, unable to see the big picture, much less the manipulative strings over their heads.

Montross had served his purpose, and according to the latest text from Agent Wagner, she had succeeded. The tablet, and now the keys—whose location the agents of Thoth had tried so desperately to hide—would soon be in his possession.

He smiled, the motion cracking open fresh skin along his cheeks. But he didn't flinch. His muscles, exhausted from the healing process yet fueled with newfound energy at being so close to the prize, moved faster, and soon, after a retina scan and a fingerprint match, he was inside the vault. The Keepers' Sanctum.

Two other Keepers, at their stations inside, worked at translating bits of scanned parchments, line by line, decoding the most esoteric texts, while behind them in hermetically sealed alcoves, thousands of manuscripts, scrolls and tomes remained unread, catalogued but waiting in the queue for attention.

"Sir." One of the Keepers, an older woman with sandy hair and a large racoonish face, looked up from her screen. "We received your message. I've transferred the translation program to your station. It's ready, and loaded with First Dynasty and early Egyptian variations. You need only feed the scanned portions of the texts showing both hiero-glyphic and the unknown script, and once it has enough of a sample, a cipher will be created."

"Perfect," Robert said. "Keep your channels open. Within the hour, I'll be leaving for Cairo." He closed his eyes, took a breath, and then sat at the head of the table and lowered his head. "Soon after that, I will have the Books of Thoth. I'll scan the side-by-side scripts and upload the data to you here."

"Then, the program will produce the translation, but then what?" The woman leaned forward expectedly. "This is it, isn't it? What you've been searching for?"

He smiled again and wiped the seeping splits on his skin with a red handkerchief. But he wasn't about to answer her. Being a Keeper was nothing, preparation only for his true mission. He had been in the right place at the right time. But really, if he hadn't been the one to discover the Babylonian documents, someone else would have. And someone would have made the connection to the Emerald Tablet.

Someone would have seen that Caleb was the enemy. The thief who sought to deprive humanity of its just rewards.

Some, like Renée, might call what he was about to do vengeance.

Robert called it destiny.

And as the other Keepers returned to their menial but crucial work, Robert used his terminal to set up a live conference call with the station in Gacona, Alaska.

The screen flickered and the view of a laboratory-like interior filled three quarters of his screen. Out the window behind an empty desk could be seen a snowy expanse, broken up by a series of giant antennae-like structures.

A face suddenly appeared: bald, paunchy, with pale grey eyes that Robert imagined hadn't seen the light of day for months.

"Is it ready?" he asked.

The scientist nodded, and as he did so he rubbed the ring on his index finger—a black gem inscribed with a familiar dragon impaled on a lance. "I have everything in hand, just awaiting your specifications."

Robert smiled. "You won't have long to wait."

16.

"Everyone!" yelled Caleb. "On top of the crypt."

"Why the rush?" Phoebe asked. "The water's not rising that fast, let's think this through. There's got to be another way out."

"There is," Xavier Montross said quietly. "But the rising water isn't our only problem."

"Eels," Alexander said, already climbing. "With sharp teeth. Come on."

Phoebe looked back, and shined her flashlight down, then at the nearest opening in the wall, where something even now wriggled through. Something with slick skin and golden eyes on stalks. "Ok, I'm convinced."

"I'm not," Caleb said, picking up an AK-47 from one of the fallen soldiers. He shook it, then leveled it at Montross. "You obviously know more than you're saying. And it's clear you've seen it all along. Now spill it!"

Montross smiled, his gaze lowering to the red dot darting across Caleb's chest.

"Oh shit," Orlando said, and flashed his light to the origin of the red beam. A shot rang out and the flashlight was torn out of his hand.

"Drop the gun," came a familiar voice from the shadows.

"Better do as she says," Montross told him, grinning. "You know how she likes it. With you at her mercy."

Caleb dropped the gun into the water.

"Hello, Nina."

She strode through the water, discarding the sniper rifle and pulling out her Beretta. Stopping abruptly, she kicked at something under the water, then aimed and fired. She booted free a dead eel, then aimed at Caleb again. "So, you really did miss me, didn't you?"

Caleb said nothing, just trying to process everything at once.

"Dad, get up here now!"

"Sorry," he said, "but I've kind of got a gun pointed at me."

"Listen to the boy," Montross said. "Get up to the higher ground."

Phoebe climbed the rest of the way up and stepped around the body. "Are you sure about this? We can't all fit."

"Toss the corpse," Montross said, following Caleb up just as something nicked his leg.

"No," Caleb snapped. "We're not desecrating the body. I promised that much."

Dead soldiers floated past, bumping against each other, their blood drawing the eels.

"Well, I'm not touching him," Orlando said. "Apart from the disturbing aspects of moving an eight hundred-year-old Mongol warlord off his funeral perch, who knows what traps are still waiting if we try something that stupid?"

"He's right," Phoebe said.

Montross climbed up last, after the others had pulled themselves up and arranged themselves around the body. "Well, isn't this cozy?" He hung onto one side while Nina clambered up and perched by the corpse's feet, arms resting on her knees, keeping her Beretta visible.

Caleb fixed her with a stare as he tiptoed over to Alexander and put his arm around his shoulder. "You all right?"

He nodded. "I'm sorry Dad. I blew it down in the lighthouse. Couldn't protect the tablet. Couldn't save mom."

"Don't blame yourself," he whispered, finding difficulty forming the words. "It's my fault she's gone."

"Ours," said Phoebe, glaring at Nina. "We didn't ask the right questions, ones that could have made sure we had it protected from the likes of this one. And whoever's pulling Renée's strings."

Montross chuckled. "Won't you be surprised."

"What's that supposed to mean?" Caleb asked.

"It means he already knows," Nina said. "But hasn't told us."

"Later," Montross said, eying the rising water level. "No distractions. All of you should quickly put your considerable talents to use to find us a way out of here."

Caleb gave him a dark look. "And you, brother, what is it you're going to do?"

Montross grinned. "I am going to get my stuff back."

He found some room away from the others, kneeling beside Nina. "I just hope I can still do this without the tablet."

"Do what?" Phoebe asked.

Caleb's eyes widened.

Montross folded his arms and closed his eyes. "Just don't disturb me."

Renée Wagner ascended the ladder, climbing with her left hand while hefting the suitcase in her right. After jogging back through the long access tunnel, now mostly empty of water, she made it to the ladder. But partway up, she paused. From her training, and from the paranoia of the past hours, she paused. Something was wrong. Different now.

She took out her light, shined it up. She ascended another rung so she could get a better look, then aimed the beam around.

Her eyes widened, mouth opened in a gasp. Only an hour ago, this entrance point had been isolated, not far from the shore, with nothing around it. But now, from what she could tell, there were at least four terra cotta warriors remaining.

Guarding the exit were two archers, one swordsman, and one brandishing a spear. The weapons were all pointed at the entrance. Renée inclined her neck, stretching to get a look at the ground. She wasn't sure what would set off the statue's attack mechanisms, but was fairly certain these didn't possess motion sensors. More likely there was a trigger on the top rung of the ladder that would unleash a barrage of death upon hapless exiting tomb raiders.

She directed her light at the feet of the warriors and saw disturbed earth: straight lines back into the general army's ranks. They were on a track system of sorts, likely shifted into their new positions by the mausoleum's desecration.

Fine, then. Let's play. No lifeless hunks of rock are going to beat me.

She wedged the suitcase between two rungs, then stepped down. Holding the light with one hand, she sighted down the barrel of the Walther held in the other. With eight shots, fired with precision, she was able to blast apart the archers' bows and shatter the third warrior's spear.

Reload.

Then, moving around to the other side of the ladder, she knelt and sighted through the rungs to blast off the swordsman's right hand, letting the sword clang to the ground. Satisfied, she lowered her weapon and put it back in its holster.

She retrieved the suitcase and climbed. Near the top, just to be sure, she yanked down on the top rung, while standing on one foot on the edge of the ladder, leaning out into space away from the direct path into the hole.

All the statues moved. The archers merely jolted in their positions, but only the fingers opened, launching non-existent arrows. The one that had held the spear moved its right arm forward and down, tossing nothing, and the swordsman cleaved forward, then sideways with an empty stub of a wrist.

Smiling, she ascended and pulled herself out the hole. Staying in a crouch, she aimed her light back, sweeping over the motionless army. No others had come forward. Carefully, she stood.

The swordsman wobbled. Swung again with no weapon. Missed.

She smiled and patted the briefcase. "Sorry boys. You failed your master."

"What's he doing?" Phoebe whispered to Alexander. The boy opened his mouth, but it was Nina who responded.

"He said he's going to get back our artifacts, so I'd imagine he's doing that."

Caleb said, "He's done it? Astral projection?"

Nina nodded. "Guess your father learned it too. Lot of good it did him."

Alexander tugged on Caleb's sleeve. "I think Mom's done it too. I saw her."

Caleb looked away from Nina, met his son's eyes. "Me too, Alexander. But I don't know if it's really her, or if you and I are just projecting her image, calling her back. What does she show you?"

"I think it's important, but I don't understand. She said I'm not alone." He shrugged. "And there's something else I keep dreaming about. A door. And behind it, a box."

"Enough," Nina snapped. "The water's rising, or this mausoleum is sinking. Either way, theorize about the departed another time. If you don't focus on getting us out of here, we'll be joining the Genghis in his watery afterlife."

"I'm on it," Phoebe said, making a face as she looked into the corpse's eyes. Orlando was at the other side, holding on to the edges and wobbling, trying not to look down.

"You too," Nina said to Caleb, waving the gun at him.

He slowly shook his head. Raised his arms. "Can't. I've lost it."

Nina narrowed her eyes. "Again?"

"Since Lydia died, I can't see anything but her ... accusing me."

"Bullshit. Get past it. Do it for your son."

"I'm trying."

Nina sighed. "You really need to unmoor yourself from this bottom-less pit of guilt. Last time you punished yourself for little Phoebe's carelessness, and now it's for your wife's bad luck? Well, this time I'm not bailing you out." She gave a smirking grin. "Besides, there's not enough room up here for me to help you out. And the dead guy's got the only bed."

"Shut up," Caleb said through clenched teeth.

Nina aimed at his face, then shifted her sights lower, to Alexander. "How about this? A little immediacy to get you over your inner road-blocks? Get past your guilt, access your visions, or I shoot your kid."

Caleb pulled Alexander closer, trying to get in front of him. The water rose and things splashed and snapped below his feet. "I'll try," he said through clenched teeth.

"Good boy," Nina said, still keeping her finger on the trigger. "I'd say we've got about five minutes before we're lunch, so make them count."

Renée headed for the closest boat. She played her light over it, then its neighbor. Seeing nothing unusual, she nudged it ahead into the silvery water, then placed the briefcase in the boat. After another bout of coughing, she picked up a gas mask, fitted it over her head. But before she could slide it down, she heard something.

A splash? Minor, but just out of place enough to notice. Her senses tuned to the absolute silence down here, she listened again.

She felt a ripple against her shins. Then she heard it: *a breath.*

She froze. Shined her light back in the boat, seeking every corner. Nothing.

Another breath, weak and pained. Raspy. Like the sound her grand-mother had made on her deathbed.

She swung the light back around to the shore, suddenly certain that someone had followed her, crept up behind her, ready to strike. But the beach was empty.

Another low breath, its very weakness defying placement.

She swept the light back. Over the water on the left, then to the walls. Even onto the ceiling.

Another wheezing breath, and Renée swung the beam down to the right, where an almost imperceptible ripple was spreading out back-wards. Heart jack-hammering in her chest, she moved the light in. Closer. Left and right, methodically sweeping the river's width.

Closer.

Stop. Back. *What was that?*

She lost it, then went past it, then came back and found it. What looked at first like a pale rock, flat. Except—

—in a rush of mercury-tinted water, gleaming in silver, a body roared up from below as if spring-loaded and launched like a catapult.

Qara!

She stormed ahead like a demon possessed. In the jarring flashlight radiance, Renée noticed two bullet holes: one through her sternum and another in her stomach, wounds that barely slowed her down. But worse was her face and the skin on her neck and her hands—blistered, oozing pus, cracked open like a plaster-of-paris mold hit with a tennis racquet. Her eyes were blood-red, seeping crimson tears. Her hair all but gone, slid out in patches, the skin underneath almost black with toxic scarring.

Renée's training kicked in, overcoming the sudden shock and disbe-lief. She reached for her gun as she stepped back, lined it up. But Qara was faster, lunging the final distance and connecting under Renée's aim, catching her around the throat with both hands.

Renée had a second to see the flesh hanging in strips from the fingers, the blood clotted in the mercury water, gleaming silver, and in a few places where the bones had protruded, white. And then the pressure around her throat was like nothing she had ever imagined. All at once, the air was gone and her head felt like it had swelled to the size of a basketball.

Her spine was bent back and she fell to her knees in the water, arms waving. Reflexively she pulled the trigger and fired into the ceiling. But finally, she had the presence of mind to pull her aim back, slide the .45 under Qara's arms and press it against the woman's heart—and fire.

Qara lurched backward but held fast to Renée's throat. Fetid water and blood gushed out of her mouth, spitting onto Renée's mask. Another shot weakened her grip. Qara shook her head, tried to speak but only made a gurgled sound, and slid back into the water.

Renée gasped, massaging her throat, shaking her head. She couldn't see. *Where was the flashlight?* There, by her feet, the light dimming.

No!

More splashing. The impression of movement, then wood creaking.

The briefcase! She raised the .45 again, reaching down for the light at the same time. Pulled it up, even as it dimmed to just a dull orange glow, just enough to see Qara turning back again, this time with something silver in her hand.

Impossible ...

Qara had enough strength to do one last thing for her master. She hefted the case, turned sideways and then—

"NO!" Renée aimed and fired two more rounds that ripped into Qara, taking her in the neck and then the skull.

But it was too late. Qara's motion completed and the case was flung in a high arc over Renée's head. She turned the fading light on it, and had only the barest glimpse as the silver case turned end over end, sailed over the first ranks of the terra cotta warriors, then dropped in the midst of the second row.

Renée turned to watch Qara fall, bullet-riddled and lifeless, as the river welcomed her body in a silvery embrace. She cursed and headed back to the shore

And then the light went out altogether, leaving her in complete darkness at the threshold of Genghis Khan's army.

She stood motionless, taking deep calming breaths. The light from the flares was fading, and too distant to help.

Think, think. This isn't the end.

There were others here: the bodies of her men. Surely she could recover the weapons and flashlights of the dead, then retrieve the case.

It all depended on planning. Precision and memory. She was careful not to move from her last position. She remembered exactly her location relative to the first line of warriors, the walls on either side, and the water at her back. Now it was only a matter of a careful sweep, side to side, inching forward until finding what she needed.

She had time, there was no need to panic.

She began. Working in utter darkness, her own breathing echoed across the chasm of darkness, past the lifeless army standing just ahead. *Let them mock me*, she thought. *I still have destiny on my side. I am the chosen of Marduk. And this is but a test.*

She moved ahead, sweeping the earth now with both hands, crawling on her knees. After a minute she paused. Had she been this way before? Was she sure she had moved parallel to the water, or had she veered off at an angle, and the next sweep would only take her farther away? It was like the open-water scuba test the first time she had taken it, where the final portion involved going deep and getting from point A to B only by using a compass. While assuming she was on track the whole time, she had failed; the slightest deviation from the compass heading had led, over time, to a major variance.

She froze, and her pulse quickened. Paralysis was creeping in. Too afraid to move in any direction, she decided to go back to the water and get her bearings again.

But just before moving back, she saw something appearing out in the darkness.

A glowing shape. Not far. She squinted, shook her head and tried to focus. Yes, there it was. Someone was there. Someone with a light.

She pulled out her gun. Stood up and aimed. "Freeze!"

But it didn't stop. She could tell it was a man now, emitting a radiance, which must be from a flashlight directed on himself. Saw his clothes, his stooping shoulders. His red hair.

Montross.

"I said freeze!"

Damned psychics. There must have been another way out, or else the explosives hadn't done a good enough job. Oh well, this was actually good news. Proof that she was chosen. Marduk had sent her a gift.

"Montross! Get over here and give me that light."

He stopped, turned toward her. Didn't speak.

The light was odd. It only seemed to glow around his body, without providing any illumination beyond. She couldn't tell if he was back at the shore, heading for the boat, or maybe just past the portal. The only thing she was sure of was that he couldn't be in the army's midst. Or else the arrows would be flying and swords would be hacking him to pieces.

That was good news for her. And it was his fatal mistake.

Screw this. She aimed and fired.

But he was still standing, maybe a little to the left of where he had been. She aimed again. *Wait.* This was Xavier Montross. She remembered. He could see his own death. That meant her attempts at taking him down would have been foreseen. He was toying with her. But she could get around that.

Look at him. So arrogant.

Fine. If you can only see your death, then I won't kill you. Just hurt you real bad.

He'd never expect it. She lowered her shoulder and flexed her legs, judging the distance. He had to be only about twenty yards ahead. Just like Quantico's qualifying tests. She'd be on him before he knew it.

She took off. Bursting with speed, running headlong, preparing take him down and beat his face in with her gun.

Six strides in, she realized she'd been played. The first giveaway was that Montross—or whatever it was that looked like him—broke into a huge smile. The second was that she brushed against something hard that jarred her sideways into something else, something man-sized.

Another stride and she realized her left arm had been cut to the bone, blood spurting and flailing uselessly.

I'm in the army.

She tried to stop but her momentum carried her forward, almost ten feet away from him now, where he had folded his arms, and his smile had vanished, replaced by a look of grim satisfaction.

At his feet lay the briefcase.

Mine! She thought, and lunged for it.

She heard a click, and the ground beneath her feet settled.

There was movement. Lots of it. Grating sounds as warriors swiveled to her location, limbs flexed, swung and drove. She felt her rib cage snap as it was penetrated from left to right as a cold implement burst through her spine and out her stomach. She looked down to see the glint of steel. Looked back up and Montross's glow was fading, his image disappearing even as that smile returned.

She had only time left for one brief thought.

I'm not ... the Chosen.

17.

Montross opened his eyes. His fingers unclenched from each other. Disoriented, he teetered on the edge of the crypt, almost falling backward into water before Nina caught him.

He blinked, took a moment to catch his breath, then glanced around before nodding to Nina. "I've taken care of securing our items for later retrieval. Now, what's up with this crew?"

Nina shrugged, aimed the light at the feet of the four psychics, with their eyes closed, lost in their own trances. "They've been like this for three minutes. We don't have much time left."

Montross pulled himself up. He bent down at the head of Genghis Khan's coffin. "Grab his feet," he told Nina. "Let's make us some room." They lifted him, gracefully, carefully. Then, following Montross's lead, Nina gently set the body down, lowering it onto the surface of the rising water. Then Montross gave the leather shoulder pad a reverential push, sending the body floating away.

"Farewell, Lord Temujin." He stood on the center of the crypt dais next to the lever that had brought down the tower and studied it. "Give them another minute, then we'll try something. It has to involve this lever somehow."

"Or not," said Phoebe, blinking and standing up fully. "It might be something much worse."

Orlando woke himself up, then Alexander looked their way. "I couldn't see anything."

"Me neither," said Orlando.

"And my dear brother Caleb?" Montross shined his light on Caleb's face, which remained placid, motionless except for his eyes, which seemed to be fluttering in the full stages of a dream-vision.

"Don't need him," Phoebe said with a slight smile.

"So, what did you see?" Nina asked.

"I saw that somebody's going to need to brave the eels." She took a deep breath. "Those three step-stones down there that you used to activate the tower's descent? They've got to be unstuck, pressed down again. Dragon, gryphon, centaur."

Orlando took off his boots and got ready to jump in.

"What?" he said when everyone turned to look at him. "I've just done the math. I'm the expendable one here, the only one with a shot at this. And since gnarly girl here has still got the gun, I'm not going to wait to be asked."

Phoebe smiled at him. "You're my hero."

He dropped over the side where Alexander was pointing. "That should be the dragon."

"I hope," said Orlando as he jumped in. With a splash, his feet struck the bottom and the water rose to his neck. The stone beneath his feet shifted, then rose up. "Okay, one down. And then up, I guess." He watched the lights stabbing into the dark water around him. "Uh, Nina? I hope you're as good a shot with these eels as you were with those soldiers."

From above, a light darted around his body, scanning for movement. "Only because we need you," she said. "Otherwise, you're not worth the price of ammo."

He was about to move clockwise toward the gryphon at the twelve o'clock position, when Nina fired. He flinched with the splash right in front of him. A gout of purplish blood erupted, and an eel thrashed and spun, contorting itself into knots. Orlando saw a flash of yellow eyes and needle-sharp teeth, then it was gone.

"Great," he said. "Now you've made it bleed. It's going to lure its friends. Hope they're cannibals."

"Maybe not," said Montross, pointing to the soldiers' bodies, "but you may luck out. There are a lot of other lunch options floating around."

Orlando moved, treading water and swimming to where the lights led him. In his peripheral vision he saw a floating body, waterlogged. A head turned his way and a single eye, half-eaten, blinked at him from a partially devoured face. As he watched, a grayish-blue eel slithered around the corpse's neck, then attached its jaws to the man's neck.

"Eyes ahead, Orlando," Phoebe called.

"Easy for you to say."

"Almost there."

Another gunshot, another eel popped and splashed spastically behind him. He cringed, floated to the narrow portion at the head of the crypt, then waited.

"There," said Alexander. "Hit it."

Using his arms, Orlando pushed up like the start of doing a jumping jack but with his palms open, and sent himself down. He stomped with both feet and felt the stone give way, release and push up. "Got it."

"Okay, one more. Hurry. Three o'clock position."

Treading water again, he swam a half-hearted breast stroke, reaching out and helping himself by pulling along the crypt wall.

Another shot, and an eel's head exploded right in front of him.

"*Judas Priest!* Do you think you could—*Ow!*" he screamed, as he jerked his hand out of the water and shook it, trying to dislodge the eel sawing its teeth into his flesh.

"Stop moving!" Nina yelled. "I can't get a shot!"

Still screaming, Orlando spun around, then slammed his arm sideways, pounding the eel's body against the crypt's side. There was a satisfying *crunch*, and the jaws loosened. In the dazzling white light, those glowing eyes were locked on his, even as the jaws loosened.

"Get off me!" he yelled as his blood rushed down his wrist. Another swing, hard, vertically up and then down and then it snapped free. "Those things are evil." He rubbed his hand, then washed it under the water, not caring at this point about attracting more critters.

"You're almost there," Alexander shouted. "Another few feet." His flashlight beam pointed the way, and under the water, Orlando could just make out the outline of a centaur. He moved to it and was about to step ahead when something nipped his leg, just above the calf. Then, a pain as great as anything he could imagine as something chomped into his back, just above the tailbone. It felt like it was trying to burrow inside, gnawing and thrashing into tendons.

He barely heard the gunshots over his own screams, and he certainly didn't notice that he had staggered forward, depressing the centaur stone and then he slipped under water, struggling against a sudden onslaught of eels. A veritable horde, jumping and wriggling like spawning salmon, converging on live prey.

"Orlando!" Phoebe's shout was the last thing he heard before they dragged him under.

"No way I'm losing him!" Phoebe jumped to the edge, leaned over and yelled back. "Someone grab my hand."

"Ah shit," Nina said, putting away her now-empty Beretta, and gripped Phoebe's wrist with one hand, then hung on to Montross with the other. She lowered Phoebe down, just above the thrashing pile of slithering eels, and then a hand, thrust up in wild desperation.

Phoebe lunged and caught it, gripped it tight. His head emerged, bloody, an eel snapping at his ear. And then Montross yanked backwards, reeling in Nina, who slipped, but caught herself and got her footing just as Phoebe fell halfway in. Nina found some leverage and heaved her catch out of the water.

Four eels were still attached to Orlando. Phoebe hauled him up and together they slid him onto the flat mortuary slab, and as he writhed, screaming, bleeding from a dozen wounds, Nina pulled out a military knife, ten-inch standard-issue, serrated.

"Just like Fridays at the fish market," she said with enthusiasm, and hacked down on the first eel, lopping its body free from its head. Again with the next one. "Hold his leg still!" she yelled, as she slashed down again. She turned to the last one on his neck. It must have seen the fate of its friends as it let go, hissed at her, and flopped sideways to escape.

But Orlando's left hand rose up and caught it by the neck. He sat up, still screaming, and turned to the side, whipping its head down hard against the stone. Once, twice, three times until it was a bloody, lifeless mess. He pushed it aside, then looked down at himself. The torn clothes, the blood seeping everywhere.

And he smiled. "Did I do it?"

"Yes, but we've got other problems," Alexander said, and he seemed to be shaking, swaying back and forth. "We'd better hold onto something."

Phoebe pulled herself up, then reached over to grab Caleb, who was still somehow unconscious through all the screaming, still lost in the depths of an unbreakable vision.

"Hang on tight!" she yelled.

The tower shuddered, rocked, then roared upwards. The gears released. Hidden counterweights offset levers and pulleys and shot the tower back up, pulling free of the debris from the explosion with just a bump in its ascent, grinding upwards. Water spilled from its length, eels and bodies tumbled away with the recoiling waves.

Their lights reached out, illuminating the golden walls of the octagonal chamber until they gave way to the aquamarine siding of the dome, the murals now visible in multiple sections. Quiet images of Burkhan Khaldun, of women and children, of proud soldiers on horseback. And then the ascent slowed. The ceiling was only ten yards away as the minaret, scraping and shaking, finally grinding to a halt.

Phoebe's flashlight beam sought everyone out. "All here," she said with relief, still clinging to her unconscious brother. And then she looked below, shining the light all the way down the length of the tower.

"But why are we here?" Alexander asked. "Now we're even farther from the door, and—oh." He pointed over Nina's shoulder. "There's a window."

"And there," said Phoebe proudly, "is the other thing I saw in my vision." She played her light over something that at first wasn't even visible: a walkway, disconnected from their position, but level with the crypt, held up by angled supports cut into the walls. Perfectly blue, just as the dome, the walkway blended in, invisible from any other angle.

Montross clapped his hands. "Nice work, Phoebe." He took off his backpack, so much lighter now without the tablet, and tossed it to her. "First aid in there, maybe even enough bandages for your friend. Make it quick and let's go."

She caught it, then gave him a wary eye. "Thanks. I think. But I still don't trust you."

"Don't trust him later," Orlando snapped, reaching for the bag. "Right now I'm bleeding to death."

"We can trust him," came another voice, and for a moment, Phoebe didn't recognize it, so weak and shaken, like it came from a long distance away.

Caleb was awake.

His face was ashen. His eyes haunted. "I almost wish it wasn't true, but my visions, my powers ... they're back."

He stared at Montross. Stared until the other man lowered his eyes, nodding. "So you know."

"I know," Caleb said. "And I forgive you."

18.

"Well?" said Orlando, while having the deep bites in his cheek disinfected and bandaged up. "What'd you see? What could possibly justify what he did? Trying to kill us in Antarctica, stealing the Emerald Tablet, killing your wife!"

Caleb looked away from Montross. "Not now, Orlando. We don't have time. And I need to understand more before I bring you in. It has to do with the tablet, with the keys. With everything."

"We figured that much," Phoebe said, tending now to Orlando's back, lifting up his shirt and wincing. "You really need stitches. A hospital."

"Or a proper medic," Montross said. "But our dear brother is right. We don't have time. Need to move now."

Phoebe frowned. "But you said—" She flashed her light around. "Wait. Where's Nina?"

Everyone except Montross looked around, even shining their lights down into the gloom.

"Don't worry," Montross said. "She's left on a little personal errand for me."

Caleb eyed him carefully.

Montross turned and headed for the walkway. "Let's go. I'm sure we'll be seeing her again. Very soon. Meanwhile, there's a long trip back to the surface ahead of us."

Nina circled the mausoleum dome twice, walking along a six-inch-wide ledge before finding the most appropriate place from which to drop to a walkway. This was after avoiding the gold-plated boat moored on the side, on a platform with a gear system and a lever-release.

Obviously, Montross and the others would need that. This transport would have been intended for Genghis Khan's use, ceremonial perhaps, but those early Mongolians at least had the foresight to make it practical as well. Their leader could have simply awakened, travelled along the walkway out of the mausoleum, turned right and entered his waiting barge, which had been on the opposite side of the dome, hidden from the walkway entrance. The lever would lower the boat down to the sea.

It was carved beautifully, a masterwork of art and design. Exquisite carvings of mountains and lakes, scenes of warfare and conquest. Two metal-plated oars on the inside, it looked like it could hold eight comfortably. More than sufficient for the old conqueror to travel about his necropolis.

Leaving the boat, Nina instead took the hard way, hanging from the ledge and then dropping almost twenty feet. She bent her knees and rolled back, but still felt a painful jarring up her legs and back. Then she was up, securing her backpack. Inside it she carried a grappling hook, extra flashlights, spare magazines for the AK-47 slung over her shoulder and two fragmentation grenades.

She only hoped it would be enough. Where she was going—over the wall behind the looming monastery ahead—she had no visions to guide her. No roadmap of the future and no intuition of the time or place of her own death.

As she approached the western-most wall of the city, she leapt to the monastery steps, scaled a wall, jumping from alcove to ledge to windowsill back to another ledge. And then she was on the roof.

Close enough to jump, she thought, eyeing the distance between the western point of the rooftop and the thick wall. Foregoing the grappling hook, she got a running start, a huge push-off as she leapt into the open air forty feet above the seawater and the gleaming spikes below.

She caught the edge and the rock wall slammed into her chest on her way down. Wincing, but clinging to the ramparts, she kicked, found a toehold, and pushed up. Taking only a short pause, she retrieved her flashlight and directed it ahead, over the wall and down onto the field. Swept it across the ranks of the terra cotta multitude. All of them were facing the other direction, but Nina had no illusions about their vigilance—or deadliness.

Montross had told her where the case was, not far from the shore, but to reach it she would have to go through the very teeth of Temujin's eternal defenders.

Through, she thought. *Or around.*

She started walking to her left, aiming the light down over the wall, watching for a gap in the warriors. None appeared, not until she nearly reached the edge. The northern barrier, the sheer cavern wall. Up about fifty feet, a flare sputtered, losing its vitality but still flickering enough to cast wicked shadows over the backs of the army's rear guard.

Nina took out her grappling hook, attached it to the rampart section, then without a second thought, rappelled down the side of the wall. At the bottom, cloaked in darkness, she flicked the rope hard, freed the hook and got out of the way as it landed beside her. After rolling it up and putting it back in her pack, she turned on the flashlight, examining the path along the cavern wall. There was a gap of at least ten feet as far as she could see. She hoped that the architects of subterranean Xanadu had expected only a frontal assault to the gate, and so didn't bother to fortify the roundabout approach.

She was wrong.

The boat cut through the water easily as Xavier Montross took the first turn with the oar. Phoebe continued bandaging up Orlando, who shied away from the edge and flinched every time something broke the surface. Caleb sat in the front with Alexander, shining their lights at every building, marveling at the magnificence of the silent marble halls, their first glimpses of massive columns that had endured centuries in darkness. They steered alongside walkways and under majestic bridges, around silent gilded fountains, amphitheaters, and in one case, right through a temple whose center aisle had been submerged. Over their heads, the flashlight beams illuminated a painted daytime sky, complete with clouds and flocks of geese amidst an infinity of blue.

Past all these silent wonders, beyond immense statues of Temujin, some on horseback, others standing in silent repose, some as colossal as the pharaohs at Abu Simbel, they finally approached the western gate.

"Can't we stop?" Alexander urged, looking back the way they had come, seeing the somber monoliths returning to their shrouds, consumed again by the ancient shadows.

"No." Montross paddled harder, gasping for breath now.

Orlando coughed, craning his neck to look around. "But the treasure. We didn't even find one ounce of gold that wasn't nailed down. Come on, we can't go back empty-handed."

Montross grumbled. "I'm no longer in the mood for rusty spikes, poisoned arrows or any other diabolical madness. Not to mention customs agents and military police."

"Just talking about a few trinkets," Orlando muttered. Then he looked at Phoebe and smiled. "Maybe a nice ring?"

Alexander shook his head sadly, watching another golden-tipped minaret sail by. "I am *so* back here."

Caleb opened his mouth, about to discourage any more chatter, when the boat bumped against something under water. "What was that?"

Montross kept paddling. "Just as I figured. We've triggered the main gate." Their lights stabbed ahead, highlighting the forty-foot doors in front of them, doors that pushed outward around the walkway. The seawater streamed out in a rush between the doors, pulling their boat along. It flooded the rocky beach outside, crashing into the mercury-tainted river, diluting it with thousands of gallons of downward-flowing fresh water.

The boat bumped against the bottom, and was then lifted and sent on ahead as if they were in a white water raft ride. Montross set down the paddle, reached into his pack and handed out three gas masks, one each to Alexander, Phoebe and Orlando.

Caleb looked at him with something approaching respect.

Montross smiled back. "I know I'm not fated to die from mercury poisoning, so I can spare the masks for those who might need them most. And besides," he said, breathing into his collar, "the water from the necropolis seems to be taking the bite out of the toxicity out here."

Caleb nodded, coughing a little as he fit the mask over Alexander's head. "When we get out of this, we have to talk about what I saw."

"I know," said Montross. "But don't celebrate yet." He tossed Caleb the paddle. "Your turn for some exercise."

As Caleb took up his position and Montross took a seat at the front, Alexander took something from his back pocket. The folded piece of sketch paper. "What about this?" he asked Montross quietly when his dad's back was turned. "You gave it to me back in the mausoleum."

"Put it away. Show it to the others, but only when the time is right."

Alexander stared at the folded paper, then frowned as he slipped it back into his pocket. "How will I know when the time is right?"

Montross turned away, watching the silver-coated water. "You'll know," he said, "because everyone will have lost hope."

Nina crawled the next twenty feet, inching along the ground, feeling out with her hands and fingertips for any irregularities on the surface ahead. She was bleeding from a multitude of cuts and had narrowly missed being skewered after only three steps along the cavern wall, when a spike had shot out from small hole in the rocks. After that, she scanned the rocky cavern wall and had identified eight more unnatural crevasses from which things could shoot out at her.

The walls had been booby-trapped as well, forcing invaders to go straight through the army. *Damn Montross*, she thought, wriggling along the ground. She aimed her light ahead, through the legs of two warriors, swords held in each hand, knees bent as if they were about to spring forward and attack. She had dropped to her belly about eight yards back, after dodging the worst of a swinging blade, suffering a cut across her back, then spinning away from the thrust from a spear, and again getting caught, her biceps nicked.

The pressure plates were highly sensitive. Sometimes just the touch of her hand, with little weight, set off the statues and she had been forced to make some acrobatic rolls, dodges and ducks just to make it this far. And, by the indication of her flashlight beam probing out an indeterminate distance ahead, over the helmets of countless warriors, she had a long way to go. Their backs were to her, and she believed that fact alone accounted for her continued survival. The attacks were all planned to deal with invaders advancing from the river, not those escaping the mausoleum.

There has to be a better way.

A deep breath, and she smiled as she carefully stood up.

Why didn't I think of this before?

The tricky part would be providing light, but she thought for a moment and came up with an idea. She had one more flashlight in her pack. She cursed herself for neglecting to salvage a flare gun from the dead Chinese soldiers. She fit her flashlight onto the statue in front of her, fixing it in a groove between his armored shoulder-pad and his neck. It lit the way ahead, the bright beam scattering and diffusing around the multitude of soldiers and horses between her position and the river's edge.

Then she chose the statue to its left—a crouching warrior gripping two scimitars crossed before his face—and she climbed onto its back by grabbing his head and pulling herself up until she stood on his shoulders. And then she looked out over the helmets, shoulders, saddles and banners lit up in the narrow trail of weakening light. She had to believe this was the right choice, the way Caleb's group could have crossed this field, if it had occurred to them.

After a breath, deep and cleansing, she willed herself to relax. She bent her knees and stepped out in a long stride, reaching the next warrior's shoulder in a straddle. Then she pushed off with her right foot and brought it up beside the left. She wobbled and nearly fell over as the statue leaned forward beneath her weight, but it held. She nodded, smiling, and gauged the next move.

She'd have to jump onto the back of a horse, which was preferable to leaping over two yards and trying to gain a foothold on the back of an archer in the same direction.

The horse worked. And from its back it was another simple stretching move to the broad shoulders of a swordsman. She caught her breath, and then carefully proceeded to the next one, and the next. In one area, she breezed through, hopping across a catapult, then dancing along the edge of a chariot, then across the backs of a team of horses. In most cases she didn't need to jump, only to be nimble. Staying in the light, or at its edges, she made her way to the army's forefront.

After pausing only to give her straining muscles a rest, she started up again. Near the end of the light's reach she paused on the back of a stallion surrounded by six archers, took off her pack and retrieved the other flashlight. She shined it left, then right, then— *there.* A glint of silver.

The case.

Just where Montross had said it would be.

Nina judged the distance, eyed the best approach accessible from the side. Once there she could easily scoop up the case with the grappling hook, then leapfrog the remaining statues back to the shore. The problem was the darkness. With careful aim, she threw the flashlight in an underhand toss so it rolled between six terra cotta warriors and came to a rest, facing backwards, against something lying on the ground.

Ah, there you are, Agent Wagner.

Nina flexed her legs and leapt to the nearest warrior, hugging him about the neck before climbing to his shoulders.

Five minutes later, she dove, ducked, rolled and then stood up in a crouch, ready to drop flat at the slightest sound. But there was nothing. She looked over her shoulder as she scooped up the light she had thrown this way. The army. Thousands of heads and arms and legs and torsos, all standing motionless in the shadows, glaring at her impassively, perhaps inwardly seething at her escape.

She bent down, grabbed the handle of the silver case she had tossed here, picked it up and walked calmly to the nearest boat.

The way back wasn't as hard as Alexander had figured. But what made it more difficult was that Phoebe and Orlando were dragging behind, and they all had to go at the slowest member's pace. Orlando had lost a lot of blood, and they didn't have much in the way of nourishment or drugs to help him. But they carefully retraced their steps, back through the room with the collapsed ceiling and up the rope, Orlando's condition making it considerably more difficult. They continued down the corridor and headed left, back across the tricky mosaic floor, which they managed to cross without slipping or touching any trapped stones.

When they reached the upward-sloping ramp, Caleb, his arm around Alexander's shoulders said, "Almost out."

"What next?" Phoebe asked, from behind them. "Do we wait for Nina?"

"She'll be here," Montross said.

"Then what?" Orlando asked, his voice weak. "I think I can find us some translation software and we can scan in the text."

"No." Montross had quickened his pace, walking ahead of them. His voice was still strong and forceful, echoing in the hallway.

Alexander pulled ahead of his father, trying to catch up with Montross, always eager to be first. "I wonder what time it is. Will it be light outside?"

But then Montross turned, and there was movement at his back, like darker patches of shadow pulling away from what Alexander now realized to be the night sky. As he froze, more shapes detached, separated, circled around Montross, and then spread out into the descending passage—

—surrounding them.

Caleb's light caught one figure, then another, revealing their black body armor and their face masks. They came equipped with helmets, Kevlar suits, gloves, HK submachine guns, and flashlights attached to their head-gear. Beams that suddenly turned on, ten times more intense than their own flashlights. All those beams, stabbing at once, blinding them.

"I'm sorry," Montross said. "I thought we might have more time, but I knew this was coming."

"What?" Caleb held up his hand, shielding his eyes. Alexander couldn't see a thing, having covered his head with his arms. The light was so painful after being in the gloom for hours, and his eyes began to water and his head throb. But then rough hands grabbed his arms and held him fast, just as he heard Phoebe scream.

"Don't resist." Montross called out. "Do as they say."

"That's right," came another voice, authoritative and brusque. Foot-steps marching down the ramp.

Alexander blinked away the tears, looked up, tried to focus. He saw a large man with his helmet off, short blond hair and a face like an anvil. He spoke into a heavy satellite phone.

"Sir. Yes, we have them." A pause. Then he aimed a gun—some kind of nasty automatic thing—at Alexander's face. "One of you kindly hand over the tablet and the keys."

"We don't have them," Caleb protested.

The hammer pulled back.

"He's right." Montross again, his voice still surprisingly calm. "We left our treasure back inside the tomb."

"Bullshit."

Phoebe cleared her throat. She rose to the occasion quickly, playing along. "Yeah, just go on down there and get it. Take your first left, and then—"

"Shut up." He turned away. "Edgars, what do you have?"

Alexander saw another man running up, with a box with a handle and a TV screen, and stared at it as he waved it around ahead of him.

"Heat signatures of all present here," Edgars said. "And one more. Coming towards our location. About ninety yards away."

The commander nodded. He made a motion with his free hand, and eight commandos slipped away down the ramp. He smiled at Alexander, but kept the gun pointed at his face.

"So, your boss," Montross said, crossing his arms, "it's Mr. Robert Gregory, is it? Made it out after all. And here we were, all mourning his incineration."

"Robert?" Phoebe gasped. "He's alive?"

Montross nodded. "Alive and apparently far more involved than I gave him credit for. Seems I didn't investigate my earlier partner carefully enough."

His shock wearing off, Caleb sighed. "Robert wanted that tablet all his life. He'd stop at nothing to get it. But he fooled me too. I thought he had no more resources than those of a Keeper."

"Enough," the commander said. "Let's all—"

And then gunfire erupted behind them. Three screams in quick succession. Then more. One, two, three.

A soft chuckle escaped Montross's lips. "She's led them across the mosaic floor."

"What?" The commander bristled, then barked into his comm-unit, "Hayes! What's going on down there? Hayes!"

Nothing.

One more scream, agonized and desperate, as if someone not quite dead writhed on a skewer.

A woman's voice over the speaker: *"Hayes and your men are incapacitated. Who is this? And where is Xavier Montross?"*

"Who is *this?*" the commander snapped back. But then he saw Montross smile. "Ah, Nina Osseni. Your reputation is well-deserved, it seems. Those were some of my best men."

"*I had some help. Now, why don't you let Montross go, get back in your choppers or tanks or whatever you brought, and get the hell out of here before I pick you off one by one.*"

"Give me the artifacts," said the commander, "and I'll let your friends live. Best I can offer."

"*No deal.*"

The commander pressed the barrel of his gun against Alexander's head and made him cry out. Caleb tried to lunge but couldn't break free of the strong, restraining arms. Montross calmly held out a hand. "Let me talk to her. I'll get you what you want."

The commander looked him over. Then he shrugged and gave him the walkie-talkie. "Fine. But if you order her back inside the tomb, I'll kill you all, then we'll go in with every resource I have."

"Agent Wagner lost almost twenty men down there," Phoebe pointed out.

"Agent Wagner. Where is she?"

Montross lowered his voice, but couldn't hide the satisfaction in it. "Alas, she didn't make it."

The commander thought for a moment, then shrugged. "You have five seconds."

Montross took the transmitter. He spoke softly into it. "Nina. Now's not the time to be a martyr. Come on out peacefully."

"What?" Caleb pulled at his bonds again. "You can't—"

"Just do it," Montross repeated. "And turn over the artifacts."

Nina's voice. "*But ...*"

"Do it."

He handed the transmitter back to the commander, then turned his back on the others and started up the ramp. The commander pointed to Caleb. "Take that one too. In my chopper along with Montross. The others can go in the transport helicopter. Chain them to the chairs. And I don't want a peep out of them."

"No!" Alexander cried. "I can't leave my dad."

"Shut up, kid. Your Uncle Robert has plans for him. For both of them."

"You know about that?" Alexander whispered. "The prophecy?"

The commander winked at him. "Mr. Gregory knows everything."

"I doubt that," Phoebe said as she walked by, head down. They dragged Orlando next. He seemed to be on the verge of passing out. "Can we get him some medical help?"

"In the chopper," the commander said, waving them on as he stood in the center of a line of commandos waiting near the entrance.

In under a minute, Nina appeared, walking stoically up the center of the ramp.

She stopped in front of the commander. Her eyes were grim, full of resolve. She handed over the case.

He took it from her, then drove his fist into her gut, driving her to her knees. "When we're done," he whispered in her ear, "I'll flay the skin off your bones for what you did to my men."

He left her unable to speak, and as he turned and sprinted to the first chopper to join Montross and Caleb, his men restrained Nina and brought her aboard the other helicopter.

Inside, they had only handcuffed Alexander's left wrist to the seat while the others were cuffed, both wrists and ankles, and belted in. As they rose, and as Alexander glanced at each of the faces beside him, seeing their complete desperation, the overwhelming sense of failure, he thought of something.

Digging into his pocket, he pulled out the sheet of paper Montross had given him. He opened it up, flattened it out.

The pilot and the guards in the front seat never turned around.

"What's that?" Nina whispered. She looked pale, about to collapse from pain and exhaustion.

"Something Xavier gave me earlier," Alexander said. "Told me I'd know the time to show it to you." He studied the drawing, frowned, then held it up so Phoebe and Nina could see.

"It's us," Phoebe said after a glimpse.

"The same scene, at the tomb's entrance. It's what just happened down there," Alexander said. "He saw it. But I don't understand."

"What does it mean?" Orlando asked weakly. His eyes were lolling back in his head, still trying to focus. They had a saline bag hooked to his arm, re-supplying electrolytes and pumping in antibiotics.

Nina's lips broke into a smile. Her whole face suddenly brightened. "It means that he knew we'd be captured. And he still brought us out of the tomb. We could have waited it out down there, or lured them in to pick them off, but he led us out."

"So?" Phoebe asked.

"So, Montross doesn't do anything without thinking it through and seeing the consequences. He saw this, and must have seen something else. Probably that we'd have a better chance of ending this, of winning, if we let ourselves be captured."

"But," said Alexander, "that doesn't make any sense."

Nina leaned back in her chair. She closed her eyes and kept smiling. "I think it does. I think Montross knows where they're taking us. And knows, or at least suspects, what's going to happen. And that we have a good chance of surviving."

Alexander frowned, rubbing at his handcuff. "Where are we going?"

"A place we probably couldn't get into by ourselves. Someplace where we'd need the connections and resources of your other uncle to provide access." She opened her eyes and met their stares.

"We're going to Egypt. We're going under the damn Sphinx."

19.

Robert Gregory faced the smooth onyx door. With the electric torch-light at his back, his huge shadow stretched over the golden floor and was abruptly devoured by the implacable onyx barrier, the unyielding door that had denied Pharaoh Khufu forty-five hundred years earlier.

Taking a deep breath, Robert spread out his arms to embrace his destiny. In minutes, his brothers would be coming down the stairs behind him, coming to join him on this day of victory, joining him in the fulfillment of the great prophecy.

In 2560 BCE, Khufu had discovered this entrance and attempted to proceed beyond, naively believing himself worthy when he was not. And throughout history, many others have sought that right, believing themselves to be something greater than themselves.

The fools. Today they still believed the Great Pyramid was Khufu's, when in fact he simply had the arrogance to claim the ancient monument and storehouse for his own tomb. He had expanded the area, building rough imitations for his sons and stamping his name on the whole complex here. But the more reliable sources such as *Herodotus* maintained that the Great Pyramid was built by "a shepherd named Philitis." And in Robert's studies of all the resources at the new library, as well as those recovered from the old, it was clear that what was meant here was a derogatory term for a prince from the land of shepherds—or wanderers. The land of the biblical Chosen Ones. The land of Palestine. And the man ...

This Philitis, this enigmatic character, could be traced to another whose identity is one of the chief mysteries of the Bible.

The time frame pointed to only one of sufficient fame and wisdom to construct such a complex pyramid, something so grand it was never to be duplicated again. One who was mentioned only twice in the Hebrew Bible, yet held a position of mystical, almost divine reverence. *"Without father, without mother, without descent, having neither begining of days, nor end of life; but made like unto the Son of God."* One who many claimed to have built the Ark of the Covenant himself. The Dead Sea Scrolls and Nag Hammadi texts describe him to be ageless, godlike. Many believed him to be the Christ himself, ageless, and later reborn as the Christian world's savior.

Melchizedek. The King of Righteousness. The Prince of Peace.

Or, as Robert believed, another incarnation of the ancient enemy.

Thoth.

Suddenly he heard noises from above. The motors dying, helicopter blades subsiding.

Almost time. No more waiting. No more wrangling with prophecies or scouring the globe for lost keys.

Thoth's hiding place was about to be plundered.

Robert smiled as his great shadow mustered and solidified, his hands clenching into fists that could seemingly plunge through the door itself.

Soon, the ancient secrets would be his.

Shoved at gunpoint out of the helicopter, Caleb had little time to marvel at the one element of the familiar landscape utterly and magnificently out of place, revealed in the spotlights between huge mounds of excavated sand on either side of the ancient paws of the Sphinx:

A descending marble staircase.

But all around the pyramid complex, a small army of jeeps, soldiers and even tanks patrolled the boundaries of the Giza perimeter. Three more helicopters circled overhead.

"I heard them talking," Montross said, stumbling at Caleb's side, pushed ahead by two commandos. "Apparently Robert Gregory called in his contacts and falsified a terrorist threat."

Caleb nodded. "Smart. Close down the whole area. Create a plausible scenario to keep the tourists and the media away."

"Keep moving," the lead commander hissed, striding ahead of them. Caleb had learned his name was Benito Marco, an Italian officer who fancied himself a Roman general, and apparently had fantasies of epic battles to come, with himself as the supreme commander.

Marco carried the silver case reverently in both hands as he approached the steps. He appeared to bow before the ancient Sphinx. Caleb imagined that the colossal statue might actually shake itself awake and ask him to solve three riddles in order to proceed.

Caleb glanced over his shoulder to see the other chopper descending, landing beside theirs. Pressed against the glass inside, squirming for a view, was Alexander. And behind him Phoebe and Orlando were craning their necks, trying to see. The door opened and two men in camouflage carrying MP5s stood there, making no move to disembark or lead anyone out.

"Move it!" Marco snapped, and Caleb and Montross were herded to the stairs. Caleb got one last glimpse of the Great Pyramid, lit up in greens and reds, glowing with god-like energy under the pale stars. A hot breeze blew across the sands, and mini dust storms swirled around the Sphinx and over the excavated burial grounds.

Caleb followed Marco, descending the ancient, smooth steps down to a golden subterranean chamber devoid of markings, where two huge emerald pillars supported the cavernous roof, flanking a door of polished onyx—a door, he saw at once, without markings, signs, indentations, handles or holes of any kind.

From behind one of the two floodlights set to light up the door, Robert Gregory emerged. He wore a perfectly fitted silk gray suit, with a gray tie and leather shoes that betrayed only a hint of dust. He was bald, and the skin on his hands and his face was pale, translucent. But nothing at all like Caleb expected. No blisters, pus, blackened skin.

"Just like the Phoenix," Robert said, spreading his arms, wing-like. "Back from the ashes. With a little help from the ancient books you helped recover for me, Caleb."

"Helped?" Caleb shifted, feeling the gun at his back. His wrists tugged at their bonds. "If I recall, you guys didn't really do much except mop up after I did all the hard work."

Robert's smile never faltered. "And who was responsible for getting you that far? Would it have anything to do with my sister?"

Caleb paled. "The sister you caused to die."

Gregory waved a hand in anger. "Not me. *Him.*Xavier, you double-crossed me, stole what's mine, and then killed my sister. Inadvertent or not, I won't forget it." His eyes flashed, then softened, shifted to the door. "But now, let's be civil. We have a job to do, the three of us." He motioned for Marco to bring the case.

"Do you even have a clue what you're doing?" Montross asked, his wrists still bound in front of him.

"Don't make another mistake," Caleb said. "You don't have our skills, you haven't glimpsed ahead."

"And you have?" Robert laughed. "Tell me, then. If you think you know what happens next."

Caleb looked at Montross, who merely shook his head.

"Fine. Didn't think so. Your powers were never that good. Or precise for that matter. But I have read everything about this chamber and what it contains. I've studied the *Coffin Texts*, the *Westcar Papyrus*, and I've found so many more references scattered throughout the recovered scrolls. So we're at least on equal footing, except I can tell you I have not been without my own visions. Dreams of such wonderful transition." He reverently opened the case as Marco held it out for him. And as he stared inside, his lips quivered and his body trembled as he at last gazed upon the Emerald Tablet.

"If you're going to drool all over it," said Montross, "maybe you should buy it dinner first."

Finally, Robert broke the spell and picked up the first of the three stone keys. Twirled it in his hand, touching it with each finger, holding it up to capture the light. Then he handled the other two. All set on chains, he placed them one after the other around his neck, then turned away from Marco, toward the door.

"If you have any last-minute visions or warnings, now is the time to speak. As you're going to be right behind me, anything that comes out of that door, or anything in this room which is triggered to kill if I don't do this right, then you go too. And Caleb, my orders for the men outside are to slaughter your family if anything happens to me."

"Then just stop," Caleb hissed. "Let me RV this part. I don't have any idea if this will work. There's nothing, no keyholes? What, are you just going to knock?"

"Don't be obtuse," he replied. "One doesn't knock at the doorway to the universe." He took three strides, right to the edge, so his face was just inches away from the surface. "One demands, one insists." His reflection took on a hideous caricature in the stone.

"One *pushes*."

And with that, he set his palms against the smooth surface and bent his knees.

Caleb noticed the glow at first. Overpowering even the great flood-lights, the Emerald Tablet gave off immense radiance, and the three keys around Robert's neck began pulsing, shining brighter with each throb of the tablet's simulated heartbeat.

Robert arched his back, dug in his feet and pushed harder, groaning like an Olympic weightlifter. Pushing, pushing ...

A scraping sound broke the silence, then a hiss.

Caleb tried to take a step back, but the soldiers had pinned him in. He closed his eyes, willing to *see*.

And then he was struck by ...

... a rush of heat that blows away the bright lights, the emerald glow and the soldiers, and he is standing now before an open space where the door used to be. Except, a man in blue robes and a long, white beard looms in the threshold. Holding a staff and nodding, he gazes beyond the door to approve the placement of the sole object inside the next chamber. The room has one other exit, down a ramp to the left, leading to the start of an immense passageway. But against the back wall sits a huge chest. Nothing special, just an iron box, without a trace of gold, jewels or mark-ings of any kind.

Just a box with three pyramidal indentations near its lid.

The old man smiles, then spins around after tapping his cane twice on the floor—an action which seems to trigger a reaction. The great onyx door ap-pears, descending from a groove above and filling the space, slamming down and sealing the room forever.

The man walks up the stairs and out into the hot sun under the shadow of the Sphinx, and Caleb ...

... snapped back to the present just in time to see Robert fall to his knees, still pushing. Grunting, screaming and finally cursing. He pounded his fist against the door, twice, coming away bruised and bloodied. He lowered his head, then stood up and spun around. The skin on his face was cracking. His suit and shirt were streaked with sweat, his eyes full of fury.

He gripped the necklaces in his bloody fist. "Why isn't it working?"

Montross let out a soft chuckle. "For the simplest of reasons. You're not worthy. You're not the one."

"I am, damn you. *I am!*"

Shaking his head, Montross said, "It was a long shot at best. You knew that. Caleb and I—we're related at least. Half-brothers, an estimable relationship to the ancient people, but you're only a brother-in-law. Did you really think it was enough?"

"It's my birthright. Marduk has chosen me!" He stood fully erect, then composed himself, brushing off his suit and smoothing his head. "Marco, get on the phone. Call in the demolitions team. We're breaking through."

"I wouldn't advise that," Caleb said.

Marco turned away from them, set down the case with the tablet, then dialed on his satellite phone and turned away so they couldn't hear.

Montross spoke up. "Come on, Robert. I knew you were ambitious, but really? You're the chosen one? You, a Keeper? That's all. You're no messiah, no psychic even."

"Shut up, Xavier." He tensed, weighing his decision, and then barked to his commander. "Marco, once you're done with that, kill this man. In fact, kill them both. I thought we might have needed all three brothers present, but if it doesn't help, if only one needs to use the keys, then they're expendable."

"Wait!" Caleb protested. "I saw—"

But he never finished.

Marco put the phone away, pulled out his .45, aimed it square at Montross's unflinching face, and then turned and aimed to his left.

He fired three times. Twice in the heart, then right between Robert Gregory's startled eyes.

Blood coated the black door as Robert Gregory stumbled into it, slumped to his knees and fell forward without a word.

Caleb continued to stare at the blood and bits of brain oozing out the back of Robert's head, and didn't look away until Marco bent down and not-so-gently tugged the three chains off his neck. He placed them back in the case. Then, keeping the gun on Montross and Caleb, put the phone to his ear again.

"Yes sir," he said. "It's done."

Marco was quiet for a moment, listening, then nodded. He pushed a button on his shoulder-equipped transceiver and yelled out to his men. "Bring her down. And the boy."

Caleb shook his head. "Not Alexander. What are you doing?"

"Easy," advised Montross. "Just wait and see."

Caleb stared at him. "What do you know about all this? What have you seen?"

He smiled. "I believe all will soon be revealed."

Down the stairs came Alexander, his hands free, but his face wrapped in a mask of fear—which cracked wide open into a relieved smile when he saw his father. "Dad!"

But Caleb was too surprised to respond, too shocked at who followed Alexander down the stairs. He had assumed Marco meant Phoebe, and had intended to use both his sister and his son for leverage. But then *she* appeared, still moving with her usual catlike grace, her head held high like a priestess marching at last into her temple.

"Here," said Marco, and handed Nina the satellite phone. "He wants to talk to you."

20.

Senator Mason Calderon took a moment to catch his breath after the exhausting climb. His aide and secret service agents were about to come to his side for support when his cell phone rang. He waved them off, then opened his phone as he slowly walked to the edge, catching up to the young boys.

After hearing the news from Commander Marco, he nodded grimly, but without a hint of surprise. "I feared as much, Commander. Then I fully authorize you to go to Plan B."

He sighed, holding the phone a few inches from his ear so the echo of the gunshots didn't make him wince. *Poor Robert,*he thought with a rueful smile. Oh, the man had his aspirations. His resources after all, were quite useful, and his access to the ancient texts, while providing nothing new to the knowledge the elders already had, at least corroborated it. They had voted to let Gregory play at his vaulted role, but at the same time, others were being groomed.

The chamber at the top of the crown was empty, cleared by the secret service just for Calderon and his wards. The two boys giggled, climbing up on the ledge to gaze out the windows.

"Wow!" one of them shrieked as he helped the other up to gape at the view of the harbor far below. "Gosh, we're high up," said the other.

"Boys," Senator Calderon snapped. "Be quiet a moment, I need to take this call." He waited, then heard a shuffling, some static, and then her voice.

"Hello? Who is this?"

"Hi Nina. You don't know me, but you're about to do exactly as I tell you."

"And why in the world would I do that?"

"Because," he said calmly, "I have something here that belongs to you."

He smiled at the two boys, the twins, as they looked back at him with their mother's eyes.

21.

Nina listened as Marco held the phone to her ear. Her hands were still restrained behind her back and despite coming in from the sweltering heat, she trembled.

"I have something here that belongs to you."

"What—?" she started, and then froze as a vision suddenly blasted back at her. A vision of a ...

... gigantic crowned head, with blue-green radiating spikes, and viewing holes in the crown. Two young boys look out with amazement at the view, then glance up, hoping to climb the last part up to the torch.

And a well-dressed man on the phone, a man with gray hair and piercing blue eyes.

"Nina? Are you listening."

"I ... I see you."

Silence, then, "Do you, now?"

"Statue of Liberty."

"My, my. What big eyes you have, my dear."

Nina swallowed hard, her vision locked on the blood-stained onyx door, seeing beyond the splatters into the first layer of smooth darkness, the black portal that trembled in her sight like a vertical pool of water at night in a breeze.

And suddenly, she saw *into it.*

Into its depths that had become the past. She saw herself ...

... lying on a slab-like table inside a white room. A pod. A decompression chamber. Unconscious, in a coma. Almost dead. George Waxman looking in on her with concern, and fear... . Another room. Darker, but more spacious. At the end of a long, shadowy hallway with non-descript

walls and doors. A subterranean facility somewhere. Soldiers standing guard at the only entrance.

Inside. Strapped to a table. Monitors checking her vitals. IVs hooked to her day and night. Machines to keep her alive, extract her wastes, keep her warm, nourish her body, monitor her pulse, blood pressure, heartbeat …

Hers. And the two heartbeats inside of her.

She sees it now, suddenly with abject clarity. Something so undeniable.

Her belly, swollen under the sheet. Nine months from the accident under the Pharos. Nine months from the night with Caleb.

Nine months.

She blasted out of it, almost falling backwards, unable to gain her balance without her hands. Marco and another soldier caught her and held her in place.

"Nina?" asked the voice on the other end of the phone. *"Where did you go just then? Did you see something? Did you finally ask yourself the right question?"*

Her mouth went dry.

Her vision slammed across the room, settling on Caleb. Then on Alexander.

She whispered something to herself, her eyes still wide in amazement. How could she have been so blind? Alexander's visions of standing before the door. He, and two others …

"Caleb," she said, louder. "I'm sorry."

Caleb frowned, his mouth working. Glanced to Montross, whose eyes had widened.

He knows, Nina thought. "You *knew*," she said, to the voice on the phone, to Montross, to Caleb, and lastly to Alexander. "All this time, it was you. You, Alexander." She let a smile free, took a deep breath and willed with it all the memories of their lives, memories she would soon be sharing, recapturing, enjoying as only a mother could.

"You," she repeated, turning from Alexander to stare at Caleb, "and my twins. My boys. *Our* , Caleb. You have *three* sons."

22.

Caleb watched in numb dislocation as Commander Marco handed the three necklaces to Alexander, and his son regally bowed his head, letting the stones settle low on his chest. The keys sparkled, vibrated and hummed.

He looked up at his father first, and immediately Caleb's heart went out to him, but he was still in shock, glancing back at Nina. That one night in the Alexandrian hotel, before the initial descent under Pharos ...

Twins.

They would be two years older than Alexander. Brothers. Psychics too, maybe more so since Nina also carried the trait.

All the time, it was Nina. She was the queen of the prophecy, the mother of legend. The one that ancient remote viewer had glimpsed.

And here was the youngest brother, turning toward the door. Holding out his hands.

"Alexander," Caleb pleaded. He turned to Commander Marco. "We need to make sure this is right, that he can get in."

"I can do it," Alexander said quietly, staring at the door. He placed a hand on it, then cocked his head as if listening to a subtle heartbeat. He nodded, whispering something, then closed his eyes and clenched them tight.

"Alexander ..." Caleb moved, but Nina stepped in his way.

"Don't." She turned to Marco. "Untie us please."

"No way."

She fixed him a deadly look. "Give me back the phone, then. I'll get him to order you to do it. Or don't you think your men can handle three unarmed prisoners?"

He debated the question for a moment, then nodded to one of his guards, who moved behind Nina and cut her bonds, then proceeded to release Caleb and Montross.

Rubbing his sore wrists, Caleb nodded his thanks to Nina. He was about to check on Alexander when his son backed up, hands raised, eyes wide open, a smile on his face.

The door began to rise.

He had seen it clearly. Beyond the wall, into the next chamber. As if he had just projected his mind through the door, just as Xavier Montross had been able to do. Except this time, he knew it was more than that.

In the darkness, Alexander could still see. Everything shimmered in violet hues, outlined in silvery-purple. He saw it clearly: the box-like chest against the far wall, between two pillars supporting the roof. Then, through some effort, he was able to will his mind-self to turn and view the door from the backside. And there, glowing brighter, almost golden-white, was a lever.

Without thinking, he reached for it and felt contact. Thrilled and invigorated, without a thought to logic or understanding, he muscled the lever up. It barely budged at first, as if resisting an unfamiliar hand, but then it clicked into a groove and rose effortlessly.

This is why I had those visions. This is what we—my brothers and I—can do!

The room shook, the colors on the onyx door pulsed and flashed, and as it ascended, he ducked and glided out of the room, slipping under the rising door like a contestant in a limbo contest.

Back in the main chamber, he saw his body and went to it, embracing himself and gasping for a breath.

Montross knew that timing at this point was everything.

He hoped Caleb and Alexander would catch on, and do what was needed. Maybe they already knew, maybe Caleb had seen, or maybe Alexander had, in whatever astral state he had just projected himself.

But quickly, Alexander was brought forward by Commander Marco, dragged into the room beyond the door, where the illumination from the floodlights spilled through and highlighted the plain-looking chest sitting alone between two nondescript pillars.

"That's it?" Marco asked.

"Appearances are deceiving," Nina replied, walking ahead until one of the soldiers, at a look from Marco, stepped in her path just before the open door.

"Not you," he said.

Alexander turned around. He was alone with Marco, standing in the room before the pillars. "I want Dad. And Uncle Xavier. They need to be here."

"No," said Marco. "You do it. There's the box. It's got three keyholes in it. Put them in."

"Uh-uh," Alexander said, shaking his head. "What if all three of us need to do it at the same time?"

"Why should it matter?"

Alexander shook his head. "Are you crazy? Of course it matters. Dad?"

"He's right," Caleb said quietly. "I don't know if it has to be all three brothers, but I'd be surprised if the keys didn't need to be inserted simultaneously."

"Like the keys to activate a missile launch aboard a nuclear sub," Montross added.

Marco thought for a moment. "And if you only do one at a time?"

Alexander shrugged. "Most likely, you and I are toast."

Taking a step back, Marco waved on Caleb and Montross. "All right, you two. Get in here and do it like he said. But no games. First hint of anything funny and I'll cut you down."

"Wouldn't dream of it," Montross said, walking past the soldiers and giving Nina a wink.

Caleb followed, wide-eyed. "I still don't know if this will work."

"It'll work," Alexander said quickly, glancing sideways at his father. He took two of the necklaces off. "Remember our vault back in Sodus?"

Caleb approached the box, standing beside it with Montross. Alexander was in the middle, and Caleb was getting ready to touch the box first, to get some kind of psychic glimpse into its past, and hopefully see something about how to open it, and whether there were punishments for not following the prophecy. But then Alexander's question stopped him.

"Our vault?"

"Yeah, Dad. Remember what would happen inside when the stand was touched?"

Caleb blinked at him, and Montross smiled, a shine in his eyes.

"Give them the keys," Marco ordered, pointing the gun at Alexander. "No more talking. Insert the keys now and open the damn box."

Nina said something from behind the guards, and she tried to push through, but they closed ranks, keeping her at bay.

Alexander knelt in front of the box, the non-descript yet ancient-looking chest. He met his father's eyes, and then looked for Montross, but his uncle was already moving back, taking two steps to position himself closer to Marco.

"Alex—" Caleb started, but his son was already in motion. The keys still in his left hand, he reached out and slapped his palm hard against the box's lid.

And the great onyx door rumbled, released—and then fell.

Nina yelled. The guards turned, then backed away, guns raised. She got a glimpse of Marco, spinning around in confusion, and then as the door descended she saw Montross shoving him hard from behind.

The commander tumbled, fell and slid on his stomach. He screamed, tried to roll once more, but the two-foot-wide door came crashing down on him, crunching through muscle and bone, flattening his pelvis, his ribcage and his skull in an instant. One leg on each side continued twitching as his arms flailed for a couple seconds, then lay still.

Nina ran to the door and pounded at it. Screaming, yelling, trying to send her voice to the other side.

But it was too thick to be heard.

But she did a hear a voice. Distant, questioning.

The satellite phone, still in Marco's lifeless hand. She snatched it up, and before the dumbstruck guards could react, she grabbed the spare gun from Marco's belt. In one quick motion she brought around her arm and fired twice, dropping both men with clean headshots. As they fell, she darted to the side of the entrance. Two more men came running down, guns drawn.

She shot them both.

Sensing there were more at the top of the stairs, she waited with her back to the wall, then put the phone to her ear.

"Hello, Calderon? Nina here again."

"Nina? What's going on? Did Alexander open the box?"

"I don't know that, sir. All I know is the door came down again. Caleb, Montross and the boy are all trapped inside."

"Damn! And Marco?"

"Crushed."

"What was that shooting?"

"Just me. Cleaning up." She peeked around the corner and saw a black helmet duck out of sight at the top of the stairs.

"Nina, be reasonable. Wait there. I need to come to you now."

"I know that."

"With your boys."

"Of course. Someone needs to get that door open again. And fast. I'm surprised you didn't bring them here for the opening." It had been bothering her for the past few minutes. "Why not?"

"Because they were needed here. Because there's something else that they need to find first."

"And have they found it?"

"Not yet. We're having some difficulty. I know it's here, but ... Well, perhaps we can try later with Alexander's help. We're coming now. Give this phone to one of the other soldiers, and then you can stop killing people. I'll tell them you're in charge now. Guard the door until we arrive."

"But Alexander, and his father—"

"They're not going anywhere."

"I'm not so sure. I remember Montross speaking of an underground complex, a labyrinth built ages ago, before the pyramids even."

"I doubt that." He didn't sound sincere. *"But even if you're right, they can't hide from us."*

Nina paused. "What do you plan to do with the contents of the box?" She had never gotten an answer out of Montross, what he would do with it. Only that it was vital to his survival. That, and the fact that she owed him her life was all she required. But now the stakes had changed. She had children. Two boys. Kept from her for more than ten years. So much missed time. Despite her deeds of late, despite who she was, this changed everything. "I want to know."

"When the time is right, I'll tell you. For now, if you want to see your children, do as I say. We'll be there soon."

"Wait! What is at the Statue of Liberty? What are you looking for?"

"See you soon, Nina. Now, give me to one of the men."

She glared at the phone, then yelled up the stairs, "Hold your fire!" She stepped into the hall, hands raised, and let the men rush down to her, weapons drawn. She handed one of them the phone, and then turned and regarded the silent, black and unyielding door.

23.

"So now we're trapped," Alexander said, looking about the room. In the dark, Montross had managed to find a flashlight on Marco's right side, clipped to his utility belt. It was small, but more than sufficient to probe the room's meager dimensions.

"No," said Caleb, taking the light from Montross and aiming it into the far left corner. "I saw something in my last vision. When this room was designed and furnished. The man, almost familiar, in a blue robe, with a staff as he ordered the box sealed. There's another exit."

"It can wait," said Montross.

"What?"

"They're not getting back in here any time soon. So we have time. Time to open this box, time to get the books inside. Time to talk." The light hit his face and he squinted, turning away.

"Yes. Let's talk."

"Talk about what?" Alexander asked. "How we're going to get out of here?"

"No," Caleb replied. "We need to talk about what Montross has seen, and what I saw. Compare our versions. And I need to understand how much is fact, and what's merely imagination playing with myth."

"Can't it all be fact?" Montross asked.

Caleb held his head, then massaged his temples. "I don't know if I can believe what I've seen. It's too much to contemplate."

"Well, let's start with what we know to be true."

Caleb aimed the light down at their feet. He took slow breaths, not knowing if the air down here was circulating somehow. It tasted stale, but yet still pure as if its isolation through the millennia had protected it from outside contamination. "So here's what I know. Robert Gregory believed the Emerald Tablet possessed the power of the universe: a concept similar to the *Enuma Elish*, the Babylonian Epic of Creation. We know he somehow allied himself with the cult of Marduk, whose members seem bent on reacquiring what the god Anu took from Marduk and delivered to Enki, better known as Thoth, for safekeeping, thousands of years ago."

"But why?" Montross guided him. "What was the supreme honcho worried Marduk might do with it?"

Alexander scratched the back of his head. "Make a mess of the universe?"

"Precisely," Montross said, smiling as the flashlight beam drew away from his face and settled on the enigmatic iron chest. "You asked about my dreams? What I've seen to make me plan that assault on your team, on your home? And cause such regrettable loss."

"Yeah," Alexander said, finding himself choking up again. "Why?"

Montross hung his head. He scratched over his shoulder, where the backpack would have been, the one confiscated in the helicopter, the one with his sketchbook.

He closed his eyes, and when he spoke, the descriptions echoed the visions he had suffered. Dreams pervading into his every waking thought, nightmares parading about his nocturnal slumber; images that never relented, despite every attempt to thwart the final assault on his mortality. Visions that never, ever let up.

All his life.

He stands in the shadow of an immense statue, a figure whose crown blots out the sun, and whose upstretched arm has served as a beacon to millions of hopeful voyagers.

He stands with his arms out, ready to embrace what he knows is coming.

What he has failed to prevent. What he can never prevent.

At least, not alone.

His face turns to the heavens, but first settles on the face of the Lady high above, on her sad, impassioned eyes that seem to cry for him.

For the world.

The ground trembles.

In the harbor, the water boils.

Something crashes beside him, shatters into thousands of pieces, none of which hit him.

Her arm.

The torch bounces, rolls, then falls into the seething water where boats are capsizing, tankers exploding. The air sizzles. Beyond the statue, the city's skyline erupts from an invisible wave that crashes through the buildings, exploding glass and concrete as if they're mere castles of sand. But the debris— instead of falling, seems to suck back, vacuumed to the west, along with huge chunks of earth. Central Park's trees are uprooted, skyscrapers topple, then shatter, collapsing and hurtling away.

The shadow is gone.

Lady Liberty is bent backwards, spine broken, head sheared off, crown tumbling.

And trails of phosphorescent light streak across the globe, rending the fabric of the very air, tearing through the world, splitting the earth, the seas, sweeping away the atmosphere itself until only the blackness of space, bedecked with frightened stars, remain.

Montross opened his eyes, then looked deep into Caleb's before shifting to see Alexander.

"I'm sorry," he whispered, and pointed to the box. "But that is all that matters. Preventing it from falling into their hands. Or destroying it utterly. Nothing else. I've done what I could. Stopped every vision of death from coming true, all my life. Countless times, I've cheated mortality. So I know it can be done. But this one ... this vision. I've tried everything, RV'd every strand of my future. I know what causes my death. And I know, this time, it's not just me." He lowered his eyes.

"It's *everyone.*"

24.

Caleb shuddered. Took a step toward Alexander, put his arm around his son. "I didn't see all that exactly, but I did see what could happen. What the tablet contains and how it's been used before."

"Before?" Alexander asked.

Montross nodded. "You saw it? The first war?"

"Tiamat. Marduk. Whoever they were. Whatever they were. Ages ago, something was released. Marduk was reckless, desperate to beat her at all costs. Tiamat and her son had used it for defense only, protection, but when Marduk got it, deciphered it and understood its powers ..."

"He destroyed her. Utterly. And her people."

Caleb closed his eyes and again saw an unbelievable vision, something straight out of Hollywood science fiction disaster epics. He felt the cosmic explosion, felt the seismic rift before the release of such energy, shattering an entire world, spitting debris across the system, remnants floating in space.

Alexander looked from his uncle to his father, not understanding. "What do you mean? What's going to happen if they get the translation?"

"I'm not exactly sure how it works," Montross said, "but it starts in the most unlikely of places."

"Where?"

"Alaska."

Caleb blinked at him. "What's there?"

"That's what I wondered, but a quick search showed only one thing of interest." He sighed and said, "HAARP."

Alexander chuckled. "A harp?"

"HAARP. Short for High Frequency Active Aural Research Project. HAARP is a facility dedicated to the study of the ionosphere for the purpose of improving radio communications and surveillance efforts. Currently, there are all sorts of wild theories and paranoia about tests being done up there in Gacona, Alaska. Rampant fears that such powerful radio transmitter array—capable of outputs nearing billions of kilowatts—could disturb the ionosphere over any part of the earth, manipulating weather, and possibly, using scalar wave technology, even instigating earthquakes. *Powerful* earthquakes."

"That's nuts," Alexander whispered. "But still cool."

Caleb thought quietly, then said, "So this facility, Robert Gregory must have had a connection there? Another cult member? And the information contained on the Emerald Tablet—there must be something, some calculation or set of instructions that could be used to enhance the power of the array."

"To do what?" Alexander asked.

"To do what I saw in my vision," Montross replied.

"Destroy the world? But they'll just kill everyone, even themselves."

"The ultimate sacrifice?" Montross voiced. "Possibly. I don't know if it's a simple matter of revenge, or if it's something more. Maybe they have some way out reserved for themselves."

"I think you're right," Caleb said. "It is something more. Much more." He considered everything he had learned, everything he knew about the tablet, about its connection to alchemy, to psychic powers and spiritual transformation. "I think they believe in a special kind of reward. An immortality to be obtained, at the expense of the rest of humanity."

"Reincarnated off-planet maybe?" Montross suggested.

"I don't know," Caleb said. "But there are other players at work here, other forces. I can't help recall the story of the Tower of Babel."

"Why?" Alexander asked, then thought it through. "Oh wait. All the worlds' people working together. Building that tower to go to heaven."

"Maybe it wasn't a tower," Caleb suggested.

"Then—?"

"A rocket?" Montross said, shrugging. "But in any case, what's important is that the gods, of which Marduk was a chief entity, were greatly alarmed by this challenge humanity was mounting against what they perceived as their realm. Their space."

"So they knocked it down."

"And remember the main part? They confused our tongues, made it impossible for mankind's races to speak one language again, so that we could never again collude in such a way."

"Yeah," Montross said. "I never really understood that story until recently. Its implications, in light of our powers, are a bit staggering."

"I don't get it," Alexander said.

"One language," Caleb said with emphasis. "One language, which I believe wasn't a spoken one."

"Telepathy," Montross offered. "Psychics. Maybe they were all psychics back then, able to share visions, thoughts, impressions. Communicate mentally, instantaneously. Combining their ideas, working through scenarios and calculations at vast speeds. Pooling their resources in ways we can't imagine today."

"The gods didn't like that," Alexander said.

"Maybe because they thought only they should be able to do it, and having a race that multiplied and expanded like ours, with access to that kind of unchecked power was just too much. Who knew what we'd do?"

"So," said Montross, "they knocked us down. Took away the gift, wiped it from our minds somehow."

Caleb nodded, still working it through. "But maybe a few of them didn't agree with this action. Some had mankind's interests at heart, and felt responsible for our protection."

"Thoth," Alexander said.

"He preserved a way for us to reacquire those powers. Codified it, wrote it down on something that would outlast even the gods. And his followers, even if they couldn't read it or discover a way to find it, sought to protect it from the other side, the lingering elements of those like Marduk. Men who now realized they could have it both ways—restore their own powers, advance themselves to immortality, and then close the door on the rest of us. Forever."

Montross nodded again. "So, back to HAARP. I went there, entered with a visitor's pass, and studied the layout, analyzed the guard shifts, the defenses. All with thoughts about blowing it up somehow, or killing everyone who might be involved. But in the end, I couldn't get in where I needed to, couldn't get close to the central control chamber."

"Why not?" Alexander asked. "If it's just a research place?"

"Co-funded by the U. S. Army, the Air Force and the Defense Department." Montross smiled. "Further fuel for the conspiracy nuts who, by the way, have been blocked at every turn, discredited and turned away despite some quite logical questions about the functions and research done at HAARP, and the patents they have on file—patents which demonstrate clear military applications."

"Okay," Caleb said. "So sabotage isn't a likely possibility."

"Every time I embarked on an idea or outlined a mission, I was struck with a vision of pre-emptive death. I would fail. They would kill me before I even got close. The place has defenses no one could have imagined. Nobody gets close without their permission." He sighed again. "No, the only way, the only possibility that offered a glimmer of success, was this one. Getting the tablet myself."

"But that wasn't enough," Caleb said.

"No. But I knew it would buy us time. Robert was going to find it soon himself if I didn't trick him and take it first. He would have used Alexander against you and made you open the vault. So I had to do it my way."

"You could have destroyed it," Alexander said in a shaky voice, as if fearing even by voicing such an option he might be committing the worst sacrilege.

Montross shook his head. "It's nearly indestructible."

"What about going all *Lord of the Rings* on it and tossing it in a volcano? That should do the trick." Alexander beamed at the concept. "Or—like in *The Incredibles*, remember, Dad?"

"What?" He frowned, trying to follow.

"The only thing that could break through the metal skin of the indestructible enemy robot?"

"Oh yeah," Caleb said, remembering. "Itself. Something made of the same material."

"Maybe," Montross said. "But the point is moot now, since we don't have it."

"But," Alexander said, still giddy with the thought of a new quest, "once we get it back, we need to be ready. And can't let it get in their hands again. I say destroy it."

"We could hide it," Caleb offered. "I don't want to lose such a gift, if possible."

Montross shook his head. "No, it gives off radiation. Minimal, but enough to locate it if you've got the right equipment. Satellites   could locate its signature. Can't bury it. Can't drop it in the ocean. No, short of launching it on a rocket to the sun, I had to find another way."

"So you knew there were two components. The tablet alone wasn't enough. No one today could still read it."

"I needed the translation, the cipher." He pointed to the box. "Located here."

"Well," said Caleb. "We've secured it, stopped them."

"For now. But they're coming."

Alexander's face brightened. "Can we destroy these things? The books in the chest? Or the keys themselves?"

"The keys, no. They're made of the same stuff as the tablet. But the books? I would assume we can demolish those."

"Then let's do it!"

"The only problem," said Montross, "is that we might not be able to open the chest."

"But we have the keys."

"Try them."

Alexander glanced at Caleb.

"Trust me," Montross said. "We don't die now. I just think it won't open."

"Why not?"

He shrugged. "Kind of like the door outside, I'd wager. Having the keys gets you to the event, but you still have to ask the right girl before you get to dance."

Alexander frowned. "You mean, I have to ask the right questions? RV something else—maybe inside the box?"

"I don't think so. I believe you were right before. All three of you are needed."

Alexander looked crushed. "Well, so what do we do? The box looks pretty heavy, we can't take it with us. If there even is a way out of here."

"There's a way," Caleb insisted. "I saw it."

"We have to leave the box," Montross said.

"Can we blow it up?" Alexander asked. "Shoot it open, throw a grenade at it?"

"Don't have guns," Montross replied. He shined his light on Marco's body. "And no grenades on our friend here."

"Then we're screwed," Alexander said, glancing at his father. "Sorry. Anyway, they'll just bring the other two here. My brothers. And they'll open the door."

"But they won't have the keys," Caleb said excitedly. "We've got them, and we're going to get out." He pointed the light at the corner again, and this time moved in closer, finding the outline of a door. He closed his eyes as he touched the wall. Furrowed his brow, and let his mind break free, scatter into the infinite and pluck the answer from tangle of his visions.

"Damn it," Caleb said after a moment, holding his head. "This means that Waxman was right after all."

Alexander frowned. "What do you mean?"

"Waxman believed the Emerald Tablet was the greatest threat to the security of humanity, and now I realize he was right after all. He just didn't know the true nature of the threat, didn't know what it would be used for. But another one of his psychics had foreseen this and warned him. Which is why he spared no effort to get into the Pharos Vault." He shook his head. "Maybe I should have let him succeed."

"But he wouldn't have been able to burn it like the other scrolls," Montross said. "You did the right thing. Now it's up to us to finish it."

Alexander pouted. "But, what about Aunt Phoebe and Orlando?"

"They'll be ok," Caleb said. "If I know my sister, she's already figured a way out of there, and they're on the run, somewhere safe."

"And Nina?"

Caleb paused. "She's got other priorities now."

Montross shrugged. "She's inscrutable. She owed me for breaking her out of that facility, but that debt's been repaid many times over. My guess is that she's going to side with her boys. You know how she was always drawn to power, and she's just been elevated to their high queen, the mother of the messiahs. At least in their minds."

Caleb shook his head. "Then let's go. This isn't over."

"But what can we do?" Alexander asked. "Even if we make it through the maze that I know is waiting for us under the pyramids, probably loaded with more traps and things to squash us or impale us, how do we stop the end of the world?"

Glancing from Alexander back to Montross, Caleb smiled hopefully. "I keep coming back to that image the Morpheus Initiative had been seeing every time we asked about the tablet, asked to be shown its origin and its function. There's something else we're missing, some piece that I have to believe we're being drawn to because it might help us." He thought again for a moment. "Remember, Marduk wasn't the only one with followers. Thoth had his believers, scholars and philosophers who, knowing the threat, may have secreted something else away. Something that we can use to counter what the other side is planning."

Montross's eyes sparkled with sudden vigor. "Yes. I hadn't thought back on this. Hadn't considered this aspect. Instead, I just used it as a lure to get you away from guarding the tablet. But you're right."

"What are we talking about?" Alexander asked.

"The head," Montross said. "The crowned head we've been seeing and searching for."

"Nina said something," Montross whispered, "about the Statue of Liberty."

"Yes," Caleb said. "The twins were there. With someone. Why?"

"I don't know," said Montross. "But if something we need is on Liberty Island, we've got to get it before they do."

"Something else to RV when we get the chance," Caleb said, then paused, frowning.

"What, Dad?"

Caleb nodded to himself. "I just thought of something. I may know what it is—what they're looking for."

"What?"

"You jogged my memory just now. *The Incredibles* ...the sharp claw-thing used by Mr. Incredible to tear through the robot's shell."

"Yeah," Alexander said. "So what?"

Montross's eyes went wide. "I think I know, too."

Caleb smiled. "The symbol of Marduk. The slaying of the dragon. He had—"

"*A lance!*" Montross licked his lips and then swooned, holding his head.

Alexander glanced around helplessly as Montross slowly recovered.

"Later," Montross said. "I'll tell you later. Now we need to get out of here. Fast."

Caleb went to the first pillar and turned it clockwise, then went to the second, twisting it in the other direction for three rotations.

The side door opened. Inside, a hallway flickered into view as floor-lamps filled with glowing light, like a runway guiding them in.

"Time to move," Montross said, a spring in his step. "And trust me, we don't die down here in this sprawling, sadistic labyrinth of hell, one that I fear might make Genghis Khan's place look like a kid's playpen." He stopped, glancing back, frowning. "Well, at least I know I don't die."

25.

Despite Caleb's assessment, Phoebe remained restrained in the back of the helicopter, along with Orlando, until the pilot, acting on orders transmitted over his headset, came into the cabin and cut them free. He disconnected the transfusions and saline drip, bandaged Orlando up, then escorted them out onto the desert to a waiting limousine.

Between the Sphinx's paws, Nina stood in the middle of a crowd of soldiers, barking orders and pointing to locations around the site. She glanced over to them once, nodded, then looked away quickly.

"Here," said the pilot, tossing Orlando's pack to him, then pushing both of them inside the limo. "This man will take you to the airport, where you'll have a flight waiting."

"Going where?" Phoebe asked, her mouth dry, her head spinning.

"New York. Your part in this is done."

"But my brother? My nephew—?"

"I won't say it again. You're going home, where you'll be watched. If you try to leave the country, we'll have you detained." He smirked under his visor. "Or killed."

"That seems fair." Orlando leaned on the open car door, trying to be chivalrous and let Phoebe in first. Then he slid in beside her, with his pack on his lap.

On the ride to the airport, as they passed through the perimeter of jeeps and men with guns, Orlando took out his iPad and turned it on. He leaned back, then fell sideways, resting his head against Phoebe's shoulder. Her breathing was quick, raspy.

"Don't," he whispered. "No crying. Not yet. We're not done."

"I heard gunshots down there."

"Hey, we'll find out how they are. Just a moment. Let me get my strength."

"You do that," she said. "I need to *see*."

Behind them, the Great Pyramid glowed brightly, dwindling in their window before they turned, and Cairo's choppy hills, crammed with homes, stores and museums, took its place.

"Okay, but—"

Just then, the iPad beeped. Groaning, Orlando sat up, opened to the screen and blinked at it for a long time before cursing.

"What?" Phoebe said, looking over. Her eyes focused and her brain slowly perceived the image. "What is that?"

Orlando could barely breathe. "It's the program I've been running."

"Jeez, Orlando. Which one? Your Morpheus Initiative work, or something related to finding the perfect World of Warcraft character, some blend of mage, warrior and thief?"

"The head," he whispered. "The crown, *the program!*"

"I thought we gave up on that after Antarctica."

"I never give up." He gave her a lopsided grin. "You know that."

"Okay, so what was this program?"

"The usual. I had it searching all known images and visuals for a match to the drawings our group had done. You know, the pictures of the head buried in sand-like stuff, crown partially revealed. Unknown size and specs."

"Yes, I know. The only match was in Antarctica. The fake Montross planted, knowing we'd find it."

"Not true," Orlando said. "There were actually two other, earlier matches. Both passed over because they didn't fit the location. But the head itself was a match."

"I wasn't aware of that. Why wasn't I told?"

"Only spoke to the boss-man about it in private, and he said we'd come back to these, but they weren't likely to be major hits at the time. Nowhere to spend our energies."

"So, what were they?"

Orlando clicked on the upper left section of the program's read-out. An image appeared, an artist's rendition of a giant head, severed at the neck, on a beach, being worked on by artisans. In the distance was a statue astride a circular harbor, pyramids and obelisks along the shore and a sail boat departing under its legs. It held a torch aloft.

"The Colossus of Rhodes," Orlando said. "Another of our friends, one of the Seven Wonders of the World. Itself a lighthouse, the immense Colossus collapsed in—what else—an earthquake, in 226 BCE. But its remains, so huge and impressive, stayed on the ground for over eight hundred years, a major tourist attraction."

"What happened to the pieces?" Phoebe asked. "Where's the head?"

"No one knows for sure. Lots of rumors about Arabs taking the remnants, melting them down or storing them somewhere. At the time, I didn't think much of this, but I did try to RV the head. But never got anything specific. Thought we should bring it up at the next meeting, but then we got the Antarctica hit."

"Okay, so that's a possibility. What's the other one?"

Orlando smiled and clicked. "This."

"Ah," Phoebe said, and whistled. "Lady Liberty."

"Yep, inspired by the Colossus. Built almost exactly to its specifications in size and possibly posture."

"Except they changed the gender."

"Yeah, well you can't fight progress." He smiled. "At this point, if Caleb were here, he'd go into all sorts of conspiracy stories about Freemasons and symbols, about the significance of the dedication date, the Masonic service, and hidden purposes behind Liberty's delivery to the new world of light and reason, yada, yada."

"Of course," Phoebe groaned. "And we'd all just nod and hope he got to the point. Which is ...?"

Orlando shrugged. "No idea. The head's still on her shoulders, and doesn't fit our images, so we passed on this hit. Although, I think it might still be worth a look. Maybe there's something there."

"Maybe," Phoebe urged, leaning in. She clicked on the back button, returning to the first image that had filled the screen. "So what's this?"

"That," he said slowly, "is new. Hit Number Three."

"It's ..." Phoebe said, squinting, "small. Can you enlarge it?"

"Hang on." He expanded the magnification, and the view increased, the details solidifying. It appeared to be a photograph taken from high above, of a desert with boulders, rocks and mountains, a desolate plain. Except there was something imbedded in the desert floor. Something half in shade, with a mouth, an outline of a crown, and an eye staring back at them.

"I've seen this before somewhere. That's a face?"

Orlando nodded. "If you believe the nutcases out there. The same people who see the Virgin Mary in potato chips and Elvis in some guy's liver spots."

"But—"

"Yeah," said Orlando grimly, now taking the pointer and decreasing magnification. *Ten times. Fifty. A hundred.*

"Jeez."

"Yeah," Orlando said again. "You see, back in China, waiting for you guys at that mausoleum, I had the idea of expanding my search, looking for matches ... elsewhere."

"You expanded it all right," Phoebe said, staring along with him at the reddish globe set against the stars.

"It's—"

"Yeah," he repeated, one more time, incredulous.

"Mars."

END OF BOOK TWO

*For a preview of Book Three of the
Morpheus Initiative, read on.*

And so begins

THE CYDONIA OBJECTIVE

PROLOGUE
NUREMBURG, GERMANY – APRIL 30, 1945

The three American tanks rumbled through the devastation, drove around Panzer tanks decimated from the early morning Allied air strike, and crunched over the wreckage without slowing down. Buildings were still smoldering, entire housing blocks flattened. Locals moved about the wreckage, calling for loved ones and searching for valuables. Dogs barked, children ran fleeing from the invading tanks, and a pall of thick black smoke hung suspended between the jagged rooftops and the steel-gray sky.

The Tanks continued along their determined course, following narrowed streets, heading for the southwestern corner of the city. Speeding there, in fact. Despite the lack of any sort of resistance, they seemed to be on an urgent mission.

The objective soon became clear: a small church. With one needle-like steeple, St. Katherine's was a prime example of gothic architecture with yawning archways and romantic columns. Badly burnt, but otherwise structurally undamaged in the raid, it stood resolute, but defenseless.

The tanks slowed, then split, moved to cover three of the sides, then stopped. Hatches opened and green-clad soldiers rushed out, climbed down the sides and rushed to set up a perimeter. They took up positions, aiming at the doors, the windows, looking for snipers.

From the center tank, two more individuals emerged. One, a large grey-haired soldier with a cigar trapped between his lips, which he promptly lit as soon as he touched the ground. He was helped down by what looked to be his aide, a smaller, bookish man with spectacles and a thick crop of sweaty red hair.

One of the soldiers stood up from his kneeling position and shouted back, "Church secure, General Patton, sir! Do we move in?"

Patton drew in a huge breath of cigar smoke, let it sit in his lungs, then expelled it slowly. He stared at the church without blinking. A long, slow stare. Then he said quietly to his aide, "You're sure it's here?"

The red-haired man thought for a moment before responding. At least, it seemed he was thinking. His eyes closed, his head lowered, and his fist to his forehead. Sweat broke out along his temples and he started to tremble. Patton pulled his attention from the church to study the man with rapt admiration.

Finally, the red-haired man nodded and opened his eyes. "A specially constructed vault below the foundation. Reinforced walls and steel doors that you will need to blow up to get inside. It's inside the vault, in a crate, hidden among the church ornaments and other stolen relics."

Patton smiled. "Guards?"

"Two just outside the door to the vault room. One inside, guarding a golden box near the back. Inside is a false relic. Don't be fooled."

His smile widening, Patton strode forward. He waved to his soldiers and pointed to the front door. As the men raced ahead, Patton slowed, then turned back. The red-haired man still stood in place, hugging his arms, shaking slightly as the wind blew smoke trails around him. A plane roared overhead and he winced with the sound. He met Patton's gaze and his dry lips parted.

"You'll keep it safe?"

Patton drew another breath from the cigar and thought before answering. "Better than Hitler did, the egomaniac. To think, he actually let it out of his grasp. And look what happened."

The red-haired man nodded. "So it's true? They're advancing on his bunker in Berlin?"

Patton shrugged. "I don't need your skills to see that the coward will probably take his own life before we get there. It's over. The Reich is finished, and—"

"And America? Will it take its place?"

Patton's expression formed a look of annoyance at the question. "America will be what it's meant to be." He pointed to the church. "When we reclaim what Hitler stole from that museum in Austria, we'll be unstoppable. But power is just a means to an end. Eisenhower no doubt will order that we return the relic to its rightful owner, like all the other stolen artifacts we reclaim from these Nazi bastards."

"But you won't let him do that, will you?" The red-haired man's lips curled in a tight smile. "And don't bother answering, I've seen it already."

"Ah, then I suppose I must insist you keep that little vision to yourself." Patton grinned back at him, even as gunshots sounded from inside the church—a short, brief exchange, and then quiet resumed as the church's defenders met their quick ends. "So, if I might ask, what else have you seen?"

The red-haired man closed his eyes for a moment as if recapturing a series of fond memories. "You are going to trick your commander. Your artists will create a perfect forgery, and you will let General Eisenhower return *that* to the Austrian government. Meanwhile, you are going to place the true artifact somewhere that makes perfect sense. Not only hidden in plain sight, but keeping it where it can be wielded by the most important symbol of everything America stands for as the preeminent world power."

General Patton blinked at the man for several seconds, chewing on the end of the diminishing cigar until the ashes fell, joining others from Nuremberg's burning skyline. Then, he nodded once more. "You have surpassed all my expectations, Jordan Crowe. I thank you. And your nation thanks you."

The red-haired man closed his eyes. And after Patton turned and at long last strode into the church to claim his prize, Crowe spoke, directing his words into the rising wind. "Hide it well, General."

He sighed and closed his eyes, the lids flickering with a far off vision.

"Hide it well, so that it may still be there when it's truly needed."

ACKNOWLEDGMENTS

You know what they say about sequels: up the stakes, up the body count. In writing this book I felt you could also say, double the research. I think I read every book out there (and there are hundreds) on the life and legacy of Genghis Khan. The one I found invaluable, with vivid first-person descriptions and even interviews with a living Darkhad, was *Genghis Khan: Life, Death, and Resurrection*, John Man. I also followed the exploits of Chicago millionaire and professor Maury Kravitz, who has been visiting Mongolia for years with a research team, narrowing the search for the lost tomb. Good Luck Maury! (But beware those traps if you ever find it.)

I confess to feeling some pressure writing this, as teams from several countries are currently on the hunt to solve this archaeological mystery. If they find him somewhere else, then I may look a little silly. But then again, if he's where I've got him, I expect a share of the treasure.

I'll also acknowledge here the usual bits about historical accuracy. The Westcar Papyrus is real, as is its prophecy related to the secret chamber. So too is the description Herodotus gave of the Great Pyramid's origin—the legend that a shepherd prince, not an Egyptian Pharoah, had been its engineer. And as for HAARP, there are many books on the subject of what's going on up in Alaska. I only scratched the surface here; much more to come in Book 3.

Of course, thanks goes out again to all the fine people who helped make Pharos so successful, and did it again here—Stan Tremblay, Shane Thomson and Tim Schulte from Variance Publishing.

And I'd also like to thank my best Buckeye friend, Kim Klever—world-renowned adventurer in her own right, for the pictures and descriptions of Bodrum, Turkey, after her trip there in 2008. And thanks again, as always, to my faithful first readers (you two know who you are!). And finally, thanks go to everyone who came along for this thrill ride. May the Morpheus Initiative continue to entertain (and enlighten) you!

-DJS, 2011

ABOUT THE AUTHOR

David Sakmyster is an award-winning author and screenwriter who makes his home in upstate NY. He has over two dozen short stories and five novels published. In addition to The Morpheus Initiative psychic archaeologist series (*The Pharos Objective* and *The Mongol Objective*), he has published the horror novel *Crescent Lake* and the historical epic, *Silver and Gold*. His screenplay, *Nightwatchers,* has just been optioned for production, and he's currently at work on several other screenplays and novels. You can find more adventures of The Morpheus Initiative in two short stories: *The Smithsonian Objective* (at Smashwords.com) and *The Shiva Objective* (in the anthology *The Game,* edited by Sean Ellis). Visit www.sakmyster.com for more information.

CPSIA information can be obtained at www.ICGtesting.com
Printed in the USA
BVOW071035150513

320760BV00002B/185/P